Books by Thea Devine

By Desire Bound
Desire Me Only
Sinful Secrets
Secret Pleasures
Desired
Beyond Desire
Tempted By Fire
Angel Eyes
Southern Seduction
Montana Mistress

Published by Zebra Books

ALL I DESIRE

Thea Devine

Zebra Books
Kensington Publishing Corp.

http://www.zebrabooks.com

Prologue

Braidwood Manor
Stonebourne, Lincolnshire, England
June, 1874

She called it *the forbidden room*.

She knew it was forbidden because it was so artfully hidden, a mystery space in a house full of rooms with wide-open doors.

But not this beautiful satin-and-velvet-shrouded room concealed from prying eyes where nobody could ever find it.

She had found it—and nobody knew.

She hadn't told anyone, not even Colm.

"Fran-*ces* . . . ! *Fran* . . . CES!"

Francesca started at the sound of her aunt's shrill call. It was close, too close, as if Aunt Ida were right in the secret room.

But even if she were, Aunt Ida couldn't see her. The curtain of the dust ruffle obscured her from view. Her aunt couldn't know she was *here* instead of her usual hiding places in the library, but she couldn't even be sure of that.

Aunt Ida knew everything.

She heard her aunt's heavy footstep nearby. Too nearby, she thought in a panic, huddling her body even more tightly against the back wall under the bed. If her aunt ever found her . . . !

She knew she would be in the deepest trouble, so deep that no one could save her, not even Colm, and that it was such a heinous thing, her being in the forbidden room, Aunt Ida would probably send her to the orphanage if she ever found out.

Because only Aunt Ida knew about the forbidden room.

"Fra-a-a-an-*ces* . . . !"

She shivered. That name. That god-awful name. She'd been at Braidwood for perhaps six months, but it felt like forever because all she'd done since she'd arrived was defy her aunt.

Her guardian.

But she couldn't help it—she couldn't. It wasn't only *her* fault. Her aunt made everything impossible, just impossible.

And Aunt Ida was relentless in their war over her name.

"Francesca is too frivolous," Aunt Ida had pronounced when Francesca arrived at Braidwood. *"I will not have a Francesca living in my house. You shall be Frances from now on."*

"No, I won't," Francesca had shot back rebelliously. *"I will never EVER answer to that awful name. . . ."*

And here she was again, hiding and hoping Colm would come home soon and defuse the situation.

"Damned girl. Impossible brat," her aunt muttered. "That's what comes from being raised by bohemians. . . . *Frances!*"

Her aunt's sharp tone made Francesca jump. Her heart pounded. She could hear her aunt stomping around the library impatiently. Stopping. Searching. Moving furniture. The thud of her knees as she crawled beneath the desk where Francesca had hidden last time. The squeak of hinges as she opened a door.

Francesca couldn't breathe. The forbidden room was one level below the library, behind an ancient Oriental altarpiece that some obscure relative had imported from the East fifty years before and installed at Braidwood.

And she wasn't certain that she hadn't left something askew when she chose to enter the forbidden room—something she'd never done if she hadn't been so desperate to hide. Aunt Ida had been too close, and she noticed every little detail. It was impossible to outwit Aunt Ida, and yet here she was, risking yet again what little credibility she had with her aunt.

"Honestly, Ida . . ." Aunt Clarissa's voice echoed above.

Oh, dear God. Thank God—Francesca expelled her breath in one explosive puff as she heard Aunt Clarissa come twittering into the room to defend, as always, her darling sister's only child.

She was safe now. Aunt Clarissa would deflect the search and calm Aunt Ida's temper.

Francesca crept out from under the bed and up the long, winding stone steps that led to a thick wooden door, which she closed carefully behind her as she stepped into the tiny square passage that was fronted by the huge carved wooden altar.

It encompassed an entire wall, from floor to ceiling, with a narrow confessional through which there was a second secret door that opened into the hidden passage.

She opened that door and crouched down just outside the confessional to listen.

"Honestly . . . don't you think this battle of wills has gone on too long?" Aunt Clarissa was saying. "Let the child have her own name, for heaven's sake."

Aunt Ida rounded on her. "Well, my dear devoted sister-in-law, who is such a fountain of wisdom—I'll tell you what. *You* take her in hand, and *you* teach her to be a lady, and *you* try to marry off that exotic-looking baggage with that impossible name. . . . Women named Francesca do *not* get married. They become artists and kept women, and that is *not* my responsibility to your sister's child."

"She's only ten years old, Ida."

"It's never too soon," Ida said huffily. "She has to be whipped into shape. Lily would have wanted it that way, in spite of everything."

"You don't know that. And what's so urgent anyway?"

"The tutor is here, and she, of course, is nowhere to be found. It is a waste to spend any money on that one, giving her lessons in language and deportment."

"My dear," Clarissa said conciliatingly, "you know she's on the estate somewhere, probably out sketching, and you're getting all worked up for nothing."

"Exactly right. *Probably sketching,*" Ida mimicked her. "Look at this, and tell me I'm getting all worked up for nothing. The apple doesn't fall far from the tree, does it?"

A rustle of paper. Francesca's heart pounded. Aunt Clarissa murmured, "Oh. *Oh-h-h.* But, Ida, don't you think she got the face just right? She looks almost beatific, a martyr on the brink of sacrifice. . . . Who do you suppose she is?"

Francesca cringed. *Oh God, the sketch. She'd hidden it in her room under a pile of papers. . . . How had Aunt Ida gotten hold of it? How?*

"A milkmaid in all probability, and *not* from Braidwood," Ida said stiffly, "because I would have sacked her already for wasting her time posing for an ungrateful little orphan who won't even answer to her name."

"It's not her name." Clarissa said gently, though boldly for her.

Ida threw up her hands. "I'm doing what is best for the child. I always will. But no one understands me. No one. Not even you. Taking her side on this issue ever since she walked into this house. It's insupportable. And now this . . . this waste of time. . . . Bohemians, Clarissa. Edmund Reay was useless. What did he ever do, except bring her mother down to his level? Bohemians, the lot of them. You cannot trust them, you cannot educate them. And why should I be the one to try? *You* go find her, my dear Clarissa, and bring her back for her lessons. It's the least you can do after almost picking a fight with me."

Aunt Ida stamped out of the room, muttering to herself, and Francesca, in her mind's eye, could just see Clarissa, fluttering,

hesitating a moment as she thought it over, before she followed
in Ida's wake.

Silence ensued.

Francesca didn't move because, if she moved, she would
disturb the silence, and she just wanted to sink into it and make
her aunt and the newest nightmare go away: Aunt Ida was now
going through her things.

Why? She had no secrets. No, she had one. The forbidden
room. And that secret drawing of a girl she had seen there. But
the sketch wasn't part of anything that had to do with her aunts
except that Aunt Ida had found it. She couldn't even begin to
assess what that meant. But Colm would know. Colm knew
everything, and Colm would tell her what to do.

But what if Colm came right now looking for her? And what
if she were just emerging from the confessional? How could
she explain it—she who had kept no secrets from Colm since
the day she'd come to Braidwood . . .?

She had to get away from the confessional before anyone
saw her. Colm could *not* know about this. She didn't stop to
figure out why. Things were too confused as it was.

She listened to the silence, and when she was certain that
no one was in the room, she eased herself into the confined
space, closed the secret entrance, and then, holding her breath,
she slowly, slowly, slowly pushed open the confessional door.

Empty. The room was empty. She closed her eyes. She felt
like a deflated balloon, weightless and boneless. She leaned
against the desk, holding on for dear life.

"*Ssttt . . .*"

She jumped and whirled around, her heart pounding wildly.

"Frannie . . ." Her beloved nickname on the lips of the
person she most loved in the world, who was standing so tall
and handsome in the doorway.

She ran toward him just as he stepped into the room, and
he folded her into his arms.

"Oh, Colm, Colm . . ." she cried brokenly, masking her fear
that he *had* seen her coming out of the confessional. It was all

Aunt Ida's fault, she thought angrily, for forcing her to hide in the first place.

"She's so impossible," she whispered, laying her head against his chest. "She never stops. She's searching my room now. She found a drawing and she showed it to Clarissa."

"Shhh, shhhh—" Colm murmured comfortingly. "Shhh. She's trying to do the right thing." He was just sixteen years old and already he was the conciliator and her protector. She loved him fiercely, intensely, a simmering volcano of adoration on the heels of the explosive deaths of her parents.

And she prayed she wouldn't have to tell him about the forbidden room. Ever.

"Shhh . . . It's not that bad. She's doing her best."

"If she just wouldn't call me Frances—"

"Frannie—" he sighed. "If she must, she must. . . . Can't you just—"

"I can't. I said it, and I won't," Francesca said stubbornly, hopefully.

He hadn't seen her. He hadn't. He wouldn't have let her go on this much about Aunt Ida if he had. He'd have wanted to know why she was in the confessional, and she wasn't sure that her usual excuses would work this time.

She wasn't sure of anything anymore.

Colm went silent for a moment. "Well then, take your lesson, at least."

"I was doing something else," she said, her voice low. She didn't have to define what. He knew. Aunt Ida knew. And it was the thing in her that Aunt Ida most wanted to suppress. "And she found out *what* because she sneaked into my room."

"Then give it up when you have lessons, and she won't go skulking around your room."

"I don't understand why I have to learn that stupid old German anyway. I hate it. I hate everything."

"Shhh, shhh. . . . You have to start getting ready for school, Frannie. You know you can't live the way you did with your parents. Aunt Ida's doing what your mother would have done. Really, she *is*."

"She's *not* my mother. My mother was good and kind and she's mean and spiteful. I *hate* her. *I hate her*."

"She's never been mean or spiteful," Colm said. "She's done her best to take care of you—of us—since your parents died. You can't keep up this way, Frannie. You have to make some peace with her. You have to have lessons. And you *will* have to go to school. What's going to happen when I have to leave?"

She didn't want to think about it. "You're not going yet," she said shakily. "Not for a long time."

"Don't delude yourself, Frannie. You know I'm going up to Fenchurch in September. That's less than three months away."

"That's forever," she cried, wrenching her body away from him. He didn't understand, but it was also impossible that he didn't, because Colm understood *everything*.

"You have to learn to get along with Aunt Ida."

"I can't."

"You won't."

She felt the sting of betrayal. Colm never took Aunt Ida's side. Colm loved *her,* and they'd been allies against her aunt ever since she had come to Braidwood.

"You *must,"* Colm said urgently. "I can't be here . . . maybe on the weekends sometimes . . . but that won't be enough, Frannie, not if you don't make some effort. . . . You've *got* to make the effort."

"But she won't let me do anything," Francesca wailed. "She's mean."

Colm gathered her into a big hug. "It doesn't matter, Frannie. This is what you have to understand. It doesn't matter. She's our guardian and we have no choice. But I promise you, if you try, if you just try to behave, if you just give me some time . . . give me time, Frannie, as long as it takes for me to finish school. I'll study harder, I'll finish sooner. And then, I promise, I swear, I'll find some way for us to be together."

Chapter One

Berlin, Germany
Summer, 1888

Samara Teva was dead.

The most famous exotic dancer in the world—who had performed for kings and potentates all over Europe and the Mediterranean, and who had ultimately given up everything to marry the youngest son of a powerful Earl—was dead.

Francesca leaned over Samara's bed, which was heaped with the glittery silk and satin costumes she had worn, at a loss as to where to begin the hopeless task of sorting through them.

Such flashy things, she thought helplessly. Such a futile death.

No one could have saved her. You tried. You were the only one who tried. There wasn't anyone else.

Only her. She had been nurse, mother, and confessor to Samara after the death of her young husband, and in the end it was all the same.

Samara had died too, her strong curvaceous body wasted

away, diminished by illness to a pitiable skeleton who lived on memories.

But memories didn't pay for medical treatment, and the doctors refused to help after she ran out of money for treatments and sanatoriums. She had no resources, no family. No, there was William's family, who hadn't responded to her summons.

There was nothing else, except those memories.

"All that money," Samara would moan. "All the accolades, the gifts, the diamonds . . . everything—gone."

"Shhhh. Don't use up your strength."

"So kind," Samara would breathe, clutching at Francesca's arm. "So beautiful. You're like a sister to me. . . . Don't leave me. . . ."

"I won't leave you," Francesca had promised. She could do nothing less. But not for Samara. For herself.

She was waiting for Colm. Her beloved Colm, who, all the years he'd been away in Scotland at medical school, had still intervened in her eternal war with Aunt Ida, had made sure that she went to school, that she got her precious drawing lessons, that she followed him to Fenchurch to study art. Colm had done all of that and more for her while he was completing his studies and making his reputation as a doctor of internal medicine.

Colm. He'd been summoned to Berlin that March along with a phalanx of specialists to treat the Kaiser's throat cancer while the nation held its breath and prayed that the newly crowned Emperor would survive.

Colm. He'd sent for her then, perhaps five months ago, over the endless objections of Aunt Ida; he had set her up in this pension and arranged a portrait commission for her with an extremely amorous general, who paid her a generous fee for her generous enhancement of his physical attributes.

But there had been no word from Colm; however, by then, all indications were that Friedrich's condition was grave; otherwise Francesca was certain Colm would have come for her. And what else could she do but wait?

"Someone will come," she kept telling Samara as much to keep up Samara's spirits as her own. "William's family will come."

"There is no family," Samara spat. "There is only Mere."

"I know. I remember. The big, bad Earl. The one who disowned your husband when he married you. The one who doesn't care if you live or die. . . ."

"I have so little time." Samara would say stoically. She was a realist, a pragmatist. And a romantic until the end. She would stare dreamily at Francesca, in some twilight netherworld where wishes became realities.

"My beautiful sister," she would murmur. "You could . . . you could be my sister with that dark hair, those hands, those mysterious eyes. . . ."

Francesca would look in the mirror every time Samara said that, to try to see the similarities. Not the body. There were photographs enough of Samara, a younger Samara always outfitted in one of her sensational costumes, to know that she had been fleshy, voluptuous, and she, Francesca, was none of that.

But the long, thick dark hair, the elongated exotic eyes, the winged brows, the sensual mouth—from the neck up, she did faintly resemble the youthful Samara, she thought, before the excesses of Samara's life had caught up with her.

And before her body had wasted away to nothing.

"You do remind me of myself when I was young. . . ." Samara would whisper, reaching for Francesca's hands. "Those hands. I wove spells with my hands when I danced."

"So they say," Francesca would console her. "They said there was no one like you and that your dances were a gift of the gods."

"Yes, yes . . . I was born a temple slave, a daughter of the holiest of the holies, and trained all my life to be a handmaiden to the gods. . . ."

All of this and more, Francesca knew because as things worsened, and Samara slipped in and out of consciousness, she had spoken of her life, of her unprecedented successes, of her lovers, her wealth, her spectacular performances for Kings and Kaisers, and, at the very end, of her marriage to William Deveney, the youngest brother of the Earl of Mere.

Step out of the spotlight, Samara told her, while they still remember your name.

But Samara hadn't stepped: She'd jumped—right into an untenable liaison with an unstable younger son who adored her and saw nothing but the sensuality of her voluptuous body.

"A dear boy," Samara had described him in her more lucid moments. *"A tormented boy. I had to teach him everything. Imagine having such a brother as Mere. An unfeeling monster who cut him off without a farthing when he married me. And there's a middle son, who's a curate besides. Always holier than William. My poor darling. And then he died like that. . . ."*

Shot, four months earlier, and left in the streets; hauled off like a pauper to some charity ward before Samara could track him down.

When had she gotten entangled with Samara? Before the illness struck, Francesca thought, and very shortly after William's death.

They'd been living in the pension, Samara and William, on the floor below. Samara had still been performing for selected audiences and was still artistically revered. Their love had been noisy, dramatic, conciliating.

Francesca had seen them often from the window of her top floor studio, walking arm in arm down the *Heidestrasse,* Samara in her flamboyant clothes, William somber and sober beside her, solicitous and adoring both.

They had been nodding acquaintances initially, and in time, she and Samara had become passing friends.

William's shocking death had thrown them together in ways Francesca had never anticipated, not least her nursing Samara during the last days of her life.

Colm could have saved her, Francesca thought. If only Colm had come in time . . .

Samara's presence, Samara's scent still permeated the room.

ALL I DESIRE 19

"The clothes," she'd whispered with the last of her iron will. "Promise me, the persona of Samara Teva will never die. Promise me. . . ." Coughing over the words, barely able to keep down the hot broth that constituted all she could eat.

"Whatever you want," Francesca murmured, bathing Samara's hot skin. "Tell me what you want."

"The *Abtissen*," Samara breathed, feebly struggling to lift herself upright. "Take—me to . . . the *Abtissen*. . . . Take *everything*—" Her last words, as she slumped into unconsciousness.

She died as Kaiser Wilhelm II began his reign. She died alone, and no one but Francesca knew, no one but Francesca mourned.

And now this: The meager possessions of one of the most notorious women in Europe reduced to a heap of glittering gaudy costumes spread out on her deathbed, and the disposition of them squarely on Francesca's shoulders.

She wanted, she needed Colm.

This was more unsettling than anything she'd faced dealing with Aunt Ida. But she didn't want to think about Aunt Ida either. She could almost hear her aunt's abrasive voice: *Stupid scheme to bring you to Germany. Where has it left you? And what has it cost you? Cost me?*

With Ida it always came down to her, as if she were the moral center around which everyone revolved, with Aunt Clarissa a continual Greek chorus in the background.

What would she have done without Clarissa's support? Francesca thought. It had been hard enough in that house with Aunt Ida's gimlet gaze scrutinizing everything she did and dissecting every word she said.

It had been a nightmare when Colm finally left. She'd felt as if she were walking on eggshells. One misstep . . . And Aunt Ida constantly watching her, watching her—to catch her doing . . . what?

Colm's advice had proved oh so true. There was no other course in dealing with Aunt Ida. All had to be as she wished when she wished it. Francesca became Frances for the suc-

ceeding years, and she learned to live with it, and to be dutiful, punctilious, and to curb her tongue.

The only thing she would not do was suppress her artistic bent, and Aunt Ida grudgingly gave in on that point only because of Aunt Clarissa.

But she relentlessly tried to crush every other creative impulse.

So why she agreed to Francesca's trip to Germany, and her acceptance of this portrait commission, Francesca would never know. Perhaps it was because Colm desired it, and Colm, even though he was Aunt Ida's nephew, was the child of her heart. Or maybe Aunt Clarissa had pressed her on it and made her see that her objections were ridiculous, that it was an opportunity for her, and that Colm would provide everything necessary to protect and care for her.

If only Aunt Ida knew . . .

Colm had arranged for her to be met off the train and to be taken to the pension. He'd sent a note, some money, and vague reassurances that the moment he could get free he would come, but Kaiser Friedrich's condition, at that point, was so serious his doctors were required in attendance day and night.

But that had been two months ago. Friedrich had died in spite of all his doctors' best efforts, and still Colm hadn't come.

And now Samara was gone. . . .

Suddenly, she was all alone; all the intensity and emotion of taking care of Samara was gone, and she felt as if she were rootless, as if nursing Samara had been the sole underpinning of her life for the last several months.

Well, it had been. And getting away from Aunt Ida. But even Aunt Ida's presence provided a certain stability. Francesca had always known what to expect.

This—this was so different. There was nothing familiar here, apart from her strong certainty that Colm would come for her.

But still, it had been so long—it seemed like an eternity since she'd arrived, since she'd gotten the first and only communication from him, since Samara had become ill.

Had she depended on Samara that much?

Alone. It was the scariest feeling in the world to be in a strange country and have no resources whatsoever.

She had never expected to feel—to be—so all alone.

Oh my God, what am I going to do?

If only Colm would come . . .

Meresham Close
Somerset, England

There wasn't anyone who knew Alexander Deveney who didn't characterize him as austere at best, and rigid and inflexible at his worst.

But that was what came of inheriting the title and still having on his hands his impossible-to-please mother, his intractable brother, the curate, and his feckless younger brother, who'd gone and gotten himself married to an impossible woman and then killed in some tawdry encounter with a degenerate cutpurse.

A man could not grieve for those things; a man just stepped in and did what was necessary.

"Nonsense," his mother said, "you don't have to do anything except pay the baggage off. And make sure she doesn't drag the Deveney name in the mud."

"And how does one do that, pray?" Alexander inquired. It was another one of those interminable evenings when, after dinner, they gathered in the parlor, his mother in her corner chair, backbone stiff, embroidering still another piece of linen, busywork for a forceful, dynamic woman who could never find an outlet for her energy and her desire to manipulate everything in her orbit.

"Give her money. Make her sign papers. And prosecute if she oversteps her bounds." She moved the light closer to the frame on which she was working, and then she looked up at Alexander. "Kill her, if you have to."

He wasn't shocked. Judithe Deveney had always had an

outrageous sense of justice, and a tongue that kept pace with it. She was like a faucet, turned on and spewing anything that came into her head, no matter how vicious or venomous.

"Mother . . ." He wasn't shocked. "How bloodthirsty . . ."

Judithe ignored him. "Thank God, there wasn't a child."

Alexander ignored her. "I'm bringing her back to Mere."

"So you've said." Judithe bent over the frame and stabbed her needle into it. "I will not have that woman in the house."

"It's my house," Alexander said mildly.

"Yes, so you make plain every time I open my mouth."

"You chose to stay, madam. The Dower House is always an option, if you are so displeased."

The threat of removing her to the Dower House always made her both angry and conciliatory. To Judithe, it was the equivalent of sending her to a nunnery. She played always on her son's patience, guilt, and ability to close himself off emotionally.

And Alexander was never sure whether every complaint, every cutting remark wasn't her way to make him react viscerally. He'd witnessed enough of that between his father and Judithe. Judithe wanted so much to be loved, but she was not a loving or gracious woman, and she had not been an affectionate mother. How she could expect that he would be affectionate in turn was always beyond his comprehension. He couldn't even say he loved her because he wasn't sure he did. More often than not, he disliked her intensely.

"I might just as well stay here," Judithe snapped. "And you'd be better off leaving that woman wherever she is and letting William lie in the grave that he made."

"Indeed I might," he agreed in measured tones to hide his deep anger at her callousness. "But William is coming back to Mere, and so is his wife."

"You never listen to advice," Judithe muttered.

"Never."

"I don't know why I even try."

"I wonder myself."

She looked at him sharply. "This is the most foolhardy thing you've ever done, Alex. You are talking of bringing into this house a woman who is nothing more than a *femme horizontale*."

"I'm talking of bringing my brother's *wife*."

"Dear God, Alex—you're not arguing with Mother about *that woman* again?" His brother Marcus strolled into the room with his wife Phillippa in tow.

"I never argue," Alex said.

"No, he just rides roughshod over everyone's sensibilities," Judithe muttered. "Talk to him, Marcus."

"Don't bother," Alex said dismissively. "You've had two months to get used to the idea. William will not lie in a pauper's grave in some godforsaken cemetery in another country, and his wife *will* be welcome at Mere."

"Too bad you didn't act so precipitately when William married her," Marcus said as he guided Phillippa to a chair near his mother. "Cutting them off altogether . . . I told you, Alex, where it would end—"

"You *are* quite the seer," Alex murmured. "Such folly to have ignored *you*." But that wasn't far from the truth. With William's unexpected death, he had been plagued by a litany of *what ifs*. However, he was also cursed with the ability to compartmentalize the things he could do nothing about. All he could do was shelve his guilt, his grief, and the consequences of his inflexible nature.

And all the other factors did not enter into it. William wasn't supposed to have died, and it was a complication for which he would never forgive himself.

"My dear Alex," Marcus said conciliatingly. "Who can see better into the minds of men than a minister? Of course you must bring William home. The debatable point is the woman."

"She's ill."

"Let her *die*," Judithe spat.

"Not very Christian of you, Mother."

"You are the biggest heretic of us all," Judithe retorted.

"I revel in it, Mother."

"Marcus . . ." Judithe implored.

"It is too late to save his soul," Marcus said. "Have I not prayed?"

"I hope not," Alex muttered.

"And we mustn't forget how much we *all* are beholden to him," Marcus added. "Mother for a roof over her head, myself for a living, and William in particular for his parsimonious nature that precipitated the poor boy's demise. Yes, we are *all* eternally grateful to our elder brother for the blessings that accrue unto us."

"Marcus . . ." Phillippa this time, her voice sharp. Reminding him, perhaps, that the caustic words he spoke were the absolute truth. Phillippa was the most pragmatic of the lot: cool, assessing, logical. Alex had never been able to understand why she had chosen to marry Marcus, who was the very archetype of the lean, self-righteous country minister.

He'd always thought it was because Marcus was taller than she, because other than that, they had nothing in common, and he was certain that while Marcus pretended differently, Phillippa ruled him with an iron hand.

And in this, at least, she understood where her chickens roosted.

Alex stood up abruptly. He'd had enough of them all, and it hadn't taken a half hour in their company. A record, surely. "You are all free to leave Mere if it is so onerous for you to live here." His tone was deceptively bland, but they all heard the underlying irritation. And they also knew he didn't care one way or the other what they did.

They all froze. This time, their slings and arrows had produced the desired result—which they hadn't expected—and it made Judithe and Marcus even more furious.

Alex had no business painting them into a corner. They did not want to be grateful to him for anything. They wanted *him* on his knees to *them*.

"No rush to the door?" Alex murmured, making a little "tsking" sound. "Who would have thought that, after all that vilification, it would be so impossible for you to leave? I swear, I'm the most Christian among you." He moved to the door. "I'll be happy to be the one to go."

He'd made the arrangements, and, as always, his being able to take action gave him a sense of purpose that obliterated the grief. And the feelings weren't altogether buried. They crept up on him at the oddest times, a tidal wave of anguish and remorse that always culminated in the heart-wrenching desire to have one more moment with William alive.

Impossible dreams, compounded by whatever William had gotten involved in that had led to his death. Of this, Alex was as certain as his life.

His sole directive now was to get to Samara Teva before anyone else did, and there had already been an unconscionable delay, which was only mitigated by the fact that his sources were convinced that no one else knew where she was.

Dear God. And what if she had died in the interim while he was dealing with the petty tyrants he called family . . . ?

Enough. A man could only do what he could do. And if Samara Teva were not alive, he would cope with that when he arrived in Berlin. The only thing that had made his mission more urgent was the death of Kaiser Friedrich, the ascension to the throne of the militaristic Wilhelm, and the Queen's worries over what would happen to Friedrich's wife, her beloved daughter Vicky, who had always been perceived as the enemy by her very own son and his Prime Minister.

And the black box. The mysterious black box of which Kaiserin Vicky had written to Victoria . . .

But it was useless speculating over that until he got there.

Already Bismarck had taken steps to insure that Vicky would not abscond with what he called "state papers," and he had isolated her so that she could not form a court in opposition to Wilhelm's. And made it plain that Wilhelm was perfectly

*willing to do whatever he must to show he was not under
England's thumb, even aggression against his mother.*

*And somehow, William had blundered into all of that political
intrigue. No, William had blundered by marrying the notorious
nautch dancer, Samara Teva, who was believed to be an operative working undercover for the elusive German spymaster,
Heinreichs.*

*But none of this had been his concern before William's death.
His mandate had been to root out certain allied activities in
England, forced to a head by the Queen's fury that Wilhelm
had completed plans for a transfer of power before his grandfather's and father's deaths, and long before he inherited the
throne. Proof that was further reinforced by the way Wilhelm
had then schemed to wrest the seat of power from his critically
ill father and the way he had treated his mother since Friedrich
died.*

*It was therefore not inconceivable that Wilhelm had opera-
tives already in England, ready to step up at his command.*

*Heinreichs was casting his web in England as well as Ger-
many, Alexander was certain of that.*

And just as certain that Samara Teva had the answers.

Every single one of them.

Because she was exactly as he had pictured her, as he paused
just outside the mean little room she had shared with William
in the pension on the *Heidestrasse*. The door was ajar, and he
could just see her inside, and she was slender and voluptuous
both, with raven black hair in a thick braid down her long
straight back.

And she was holding up to her breast, with her long, tapered
fingers, one of the more revealing costumes that had made her
famous, and her eyes flashed to a place somewhere beyond the
door, a mirror, he thought, as she admired the filmy material
against her skin with a shimmering knowing gaze.

Samara Teva knew exactly what she was doing, he thought
venomously, but it was nothing more or less than he expected.

She was beautiful enough to attract his brother—to attract

any man—and callous enough to abandon everything when he died.

She probably had another protector already. She probably had a hundred different disguises.

But she couldn't hide herself from him. She'd begged for him to come save her, and he could do nothing less in William's memory, even if it looked suspiciously as if she'd already managed to find someone else to undertake the commission.

Perhaps she was even expecting him this evening.

Well . . . those plans were about to change.

He kicked open the door and barged into the room.

Chapter Two

Francesca whirled at the sound.

"Oh, you've come . . . !" she cried, her voice catching, and then she stopped dead, the diaphanous costume falling from her hands to pool at her feet.

She took an involuntary step backward just as a stranger moved toward her purposefully, angrily.

"Well, well, well," he murmured, suppressing his fury that his instincts about her were right on the mark. He wanted to shake her; he wanted to strangle her. He didn't want her to be the woman she was. Everything about her was dead on, from her glittering black eyes and wide sensual mouth to her curvy body—more slender than he'd thought from her protracted illness—but full-blown nonetheless.

Everything an exotic dancer should be—and more.

She looked as if she had been born in more exotic climes; her coloring was dark, her eyes mysterious, her mouth in repose just begging to be kissed.

No wonder William had fallen under her spell. How could

he have helped himself? How could any man, if he, who could resist any woman, felt her power?

Was there ever a woman like this, he wondered maliciously, born to reveal and conceal, dancing in homage to the temple gods she revered? How had William lived with it, the constant display of that body in the name of reverence?

And how could she simultaneously look like the most refined and restrained young society matron? he thought acidly. Like a woman who could have been William's wife.

The thought galled him. This trull had captivated his brother and God knew how many other men . . . and there was still something about her that seemed innocent and untouched.

Not likely. Women like her were better actresses than Sarah Bernhardt. Women like her brought men to their knees and brought down empires.

"Expecting Colm, were you?" he asked silkily and was gratified to see her stiffen, her dark eyes flashing. "Of course you were. A shame I came instead."

She found her voice. It was low, throaty, thick like honey, the queen bee luring the unsuspecting drone. But of course *he* knew who she was.

"And you are . . . ?"

"Suffice it to say I know who *you* are."

Oh God. She looked around frantically, feeling cornered. He was a lunatic, and she'd been careless. An open door was an invitation to any man. She didn't know how she could have been so stupid. Or how the landlady could have let this errant stranger in. Or what he knew about Colm.

Oh my God. Colm . . . !

Never show fear. She'd learned that lesson well at Braid-wood. Maybe you shouldn't reason with a lunatic, but that didn't mean she couldn't try.

"That is of no consequence to me," she shot back, hoping her tone struck the right note of insolence. "So you can just leave."

"Leave, Samara? When I've come so far to find you?"

Now she felt a wash of pure fear. He knew Samara's name. . . .

"*Who* are you?" *Omigod*—suddenly she knew. He had the arrogance and the heady aura of power. The awful Earl. The uncompromising monster living up to every inch of his name, with his excessive height, his hawkish face, his icy-gray eyes, and his thin, judgmental mouth.

He'd come—too late—and he thought she was Samara.

And worse than that, he *knew* she was waiting for Colm.

Her knees almost buckled, and she reached out to the nearby dresser to steady herself. She couldn't afford to give way in front of this stranger.

No, William's brother. If she thought of him as William's brother, she could pull her wits about her and try to understand why he thought she was Samara and how he knew Colm.

He saw the recognition dawn in her expressive eyes. "You know who I am."

"Mere." Her voice sounded like rusted iron, even to her own ears. She squared her shoulders and lifted her chin. "You're too late." As if she could bully him with her puny words.

She should have known that a man like Mere would never acknowledge a failure.

"I've come to take him home, Samara." No guilt there.

Oh God, why did he keep calling her Samara?

"And *you*," he added, his tone inflexible.

Her? It was like a little shock. What could Mere want with her?

No, he wanted Samara. He thought she was Samara because she was in Samara's room, she was handling Samara's clothes, and she looked just that little bit like Samara. . . .

Her heart started pounding. *He had no idea Samara was gone too.*

All she had to do was tell him. Easy. Nothing about that was scary. He'd probably pay her for her services and let her go—he was that arrogant.

Something stopped her.

Colm.

"You need not extend your specious kindness to Samara Teva now that William is gone," she said at length. That was the right note, the right tack. No admissions there. She was speaking truthfully, for her friend. "He won't know. And she doesn't care."

His icy gaze narrowed. "So Colm has come."

Like a knife to her heart. How could he know about Colm? She had to deflect him until she found out what Colm had to do with Samara. "I don't know what you're talking about."

He shrugged. "Do you not?" He gave her a long assessing look, up and down, right through to her soul. Obdurate, he thought, as only women of her class could be. And she would deny everything, because they always did.

But that didn't matter either. He knew how to handle women like her. Lack of time was his only problem. But he would handle that too as he did everything: with decisive action.

"As you wish," he said finally. "Now, this is what you're going to do, Samara. You're going to tell me where William is buried, and tomorrow I will make arrangements to bring him back to Mere with us."

Her voice caught again. *"Us . . . ?"*

"You begged me to come, and I am here. We leave Berlin tomorrow, and I fully expect you to be packed and ready to go by noon. And if indeed Colm hasn't come, it's too bad. He just won't find you where he expected you to be. Now, where is my brother interred?"

She felt as if she had been flattened by a juggernaut. "This is just a little high-handed . . ." she started to protest. Things were spinning out of control too fast, too soon. She hadn't counted on this complication about Colm. She needed time to think, time to plan. She *couldn't* go with Mere. And she didn't know how she could refuse.

Colm. Because of Colm.

"But you don't have a choice, Samara. You're coming back to Mere with me."

*   *   *

She had a headache that could fuel an engine, but by morning, she had almost convinced herself she could assume Samara's identity. She knew a lot about Samara's life.

Now she had to find out about Samara and Colm.

No.

Impossible. To pretend to *be* Samara? Stupid idea. Insensible.

Mere was mistaken. Colm had nothing to do with Samara; otherwise she would have mentioned him.

Her headache grew worse. *Why would she?*

She packed Samara's meager wardrobe and her costumes and all her own clothes. She would leave no trace; she would take it all with her.

This is insanity.

She almost couldn't see any other choice, especially since she had allowed Mere to assume she was Samara. How could she renege on that now?

Take everything. . . . Promise me—Samara Teva will never die. . . .

Samara wasn't going to die yet, Francesca thought, drawing a deep shuddering breath. She was going to do it. She was going to assume Samara's identity.

Was she? Was she crazy?

What if Colm came?

But Mere thought that he had, that Colm knew Samara. She had *to find out why. She* had *to.*

She'd tell the landlady. She'd give her a note for Colm—in case he came. If he hadn't come already . . .

She paced around her garret room, making a mental inventory of all she would be leaving behind. The expensive paints and brushes. The canvases. The easel. The half-finished portrait of General Von Abrungen. The landlady could store all that, she supposed. She had no money to pay her for that consideration and just barely enough to cover what she owed on her room, but perhaps Mere's generosity when he settled up William's expenses would more than compensate for the dearth of her own.

And then of course, she'd have to ask her landlady to lie . . .

Oh God. She felt weak as she contemplated what she was about to do.

Mere wasn't a fool. It wouldn't take him long to see through her subterfuge.

But maybe it wouldn't matter. Maybe by then she would have found out about Colm and what his connection was to Samara Teva.

Maybe Mere would kill her when he found out the truth.

And then what would she do?

There was only one thing she could do now that she'd chosen the course: She had to *be* Samara Teva. And Samara had not been a shivery, trembling virgin. She had been worldly, knowledgeable, and confident.

Everything Francesca was not.

There was no way she could carry off Samara's flamboyance and the sensuality that she exuded. That voice, low, husky, with a faint accent—but Mere hadn't even noticed that. . . .

She was insane.

But the thing she had in her favor was Mere had never met Samara. He knew nothing about her personally—only her reputation, her notoriety.

And because of that—maybe she could make it work . . . maybe—if she let go of all constraints—maybe . . . if she pushed aside twenty-four years of propriety and duty that had been drilled into her—maybe . . .

If she could stand up to Mere as Samara would have . . . If . . .

So chancy . . . so—but Samara had been ill. She wouldn't be her usual flashy self, especially on the heels of begging Mere to come. That was in her favor. She could pretend to be a more subdued Samara without it being questioned.

That was the tone, then. And she needed to cultivate an arrogance, a confidence to match his. That was the real sticking point, but she'd had years of shutting out and standing up to Aunt Ida.

How different could it be?

She could do it—she knew she could. She could do anything—for Colm.

And then—there was no time. Francesca hadn't expected him so early, but Mere barged into Samara's rooms well before noon, before she'd made arrangements, before she'd considered all the consequences, before she was really ready.

But that was probably how he operated in his own life, she thought fatalistically, sweeping in like a storm and whipping up everything in his path, and all she could do was try to replicate Samara's response to the man she most hated.

Harder to do than she thought, with his icy eyes boring into her.

"You're early," she said curtly. *Calm, calm. Keep moving. Don't let those eyes get to you.*

There wasn't much of a personal nature in the room, and Samara had given away what little there were of William's possessions after he died. Francesca had packed the rest: William's photograph; his few books that Samara had kept; a miniature of the house in which he'd grown up, in a golden frame; his pocket watch, cuff links and tie tacks; a pair of heavy silver candlesticks; linens; a brass paperweight; a tortoiseshell dresser set.

But the ring with the crest of Mere that Samara had worn as a wedding band was now on Francesca's finger, too large, too thick, too ostentatious, but the distracting touch to keep the overbearing Earl from looking too closely at *her.*

He paced around the room, looking in drawers and closets.

"It's never too early to make sure nothing is forgotten."

And too pompous by half. Or did he not trust Samara?

"Everything is packed," Francesca said coolly. "You've no need to check up on me."

He raised one well-defined brow. "Do I not?"

Arrogant beast. What would Samara have said in response to that?

"Your brother married me, did he not?" she answered in kind.

"You're curiously cold-blooded about his death."

Oh dear God, was she supposed to have been prostrate with grief all this time? Why hadn't she thought about all the nuances, and of Mere's expectations of Samara—and her relationship with William?

Samara had mourned, but perhaps her grieving would not have been up to Mere's standards. She would have been incensed by his arbitrary assumption. If nothing else, Samara had had a supreme sense of herself, and she, Francesca, must portray her with nothing less.

But oh, she wished she had given it more critical thought.

"I do not mourn publicly," she said finally, pointedly. "And I have been ill."

"You *are* thinner than I expected."

Exactly, Francesca thought. He had been prepared to come to terms with the fleshy, blowsy Samara, not someone as curvaceous and elegant as she. He was off balance, she comprehended suddenly. He didn't know quite how to deal with her because she was not as he had been led to believe. So she had the advantage of him, razor thin though it was.

"Bed rest and gruel will do that to you," she murmured. It was as good an explanation as any.

"Then we are ready to go." He grasped the two suitcases into which she had managed to pack everything. "I have a carriage waiting."

She longed to ask him about the financial arrangements—whether he had paid for the room, and if the landlady had said anything. For all she knew, he was already aware of the truth: that Samara was dead, and that his treating her as if she were Samara was some kind of trick.

But what would it gain him?

Colm. She hadn't blinked an eye when he mentioned Colm. . . .

The fear escalated again as she arranged the mourning veil over her face, and followed him down the narrow steps of the pension, and it ballooned into a wave of pure terror as she saw the landlady waiting by the door.

It was over. Her feeble attempt at deception was doomed. She could not be Samara Teva in the face of the landlady's knowledge.

The woman bowed to Mere and looked her straight in the eye. *"Frau* Deveney," she murmured deferentially.

Francesca's eyes widened. *Why? Why would Frau Dichter cover for her? Money? Had Mere been that generous?*

"Safe journey, madam," Frau Dichter added, staring at her meaningfully.

"Thank you," Francesca whispered. *It had to have been money. Frau Dichter would not have rocked the boat by telling a truth for which she would be paid in questions and suspicion. Landladies had to be practical, and what harm to Frau Dichter if Francesca Reay had been mistaken for Samara Teva? Mere had obviously paid her handsomely for all services, imagined and rendered, for the time that William and Samara had occupied those rooms.*

She touched *Frau* Dichter's limp hand briefly. "Thank you. . . ."

"Good luck to you." The words carried a double meaning.

"And you too, *Frau* Dichter."

Mere helped her into the luxurious carriage that was parked at the curb and signaled to the driver as he climbed in.

"William is waiting for us at Anhalt Station," he said, his icy gaze sizzling past the black veil she wore over her face.

Francesca started. *The coffin was waiting, he meant. And he meant to shock her by that statement. Ghoulish, to dig up a body like that. They had buried him decently, she and Samara, after they'd found his pauper's grave. What was it about these dynastic peers of the realm and their rituals? He cared more now about William than ever he had when William had lived.*

William might not have died if Mere had done something then.

She felt Samara's indignation and wondered how far she might take it. How far she could go.

"Indeed," she responded daringly, "William was always waiting on his family."

Ah! He didn't like that. Good. He ought to be reminded of his callousness every now and again, and that she, of everyone, was not fooled by his conscientious concern now.

"Was he?" Mere asked silkily. "Or were *you?*"

She stiffened. "*I* did not abandon him."

"No. You merely diminished him."

That stung like acid, as if she were Samara. "And you cut his legs out from under him," she retorted. "I made him a man. But you treated him like a child."

That made things worse. She cringed as his mouth thinned, his eyes narrowed. "You have not had the last word, madam. We are at Anhalt Station."

The building loomed to the left as the carriage crossed over a set of trolley tracks and turned left at the triangular park that fronted the arch-roofed station.

A porter came out to greet them and to load their luggage onto a wheeled cart. "All is as you wish, my lord."

Mere nodded and handed him some money.

"You and *Frau* Deveney will be in the next to last car."

The porter led the way, and Francesca marveled at the privileges of the wealthy. His own car. His own porter. Service unparalleled. All as he wished. This was the life William had renounced to marry Samara.

She stepped up into the parlor car. Wood. Velvet. Brocade. Gaslight washing it all with a soft golden hue. Tables, sofas. Porcelain. A replica of a room in some stately home.

His.

And two sleeping compartments, one at either end.

"Sit." He motioned to a table and chairs positioned at an angle to the central window. He took the chair opposite her, and they watched the bustle on the platform for a while.

Or rather, she watched it. He watched her, his expression impassive, his gaze incisive, and she was thankful for the veil that shrouded her face in mystery.

But apparently not enough.

As the train began to move, and the faces on the platform began to blur, Mere leaned forward across the table and caught her gloved hand, so that she was forced to turn and look at him.

But he wasn't content with just catching her off guard. He wanted more. He wanted blood.

"So tell me, Samara Teva," he murmured in that dangerously silky tone of his, "tell me: Who are you . . . *really?*"

Chapter Three

The traps, the traps, the traps . . . her life from now on was going to be lived in a perpetual state of fear. What to say to him? How much did he know of Samara's life? He was the kind of man who would have investigated Samara the moment William got involved with her. He probably knew more than she did about Samara. Dear God . . . her every response to any question had to be treated as if he did.

"Who is anyone?" she asked, keeping her swamping fear in check. "Who are *you*—really?"

"But you know that already, madam. I am the person most dangerous to you."

"To *me?*" She infused her tone with an overlay of incredulity, shocked that her voice wasn't shaking. This man scared her to death. "I believe you'd like to think so. I have nothing to hide."

"Don't you? How is it then that you speak German perfectly, and your English is virtually without an accent?"

Samara hadn't. Samara had had a faint accent, a flavor of Europe or East Asia, wherever she had claimed was her origin.

Of course he would notice. "The benefits of a convent educa-tion," she murmured, crossing her fingers.

"And where was that?" Mere asked idly. "At the convent of the Oriental temples where your mother supposedly danced?"

Quicksand. She averted her face. She had never done such a tightrope walk before. "You know my history as well as I do." There was a safe assumption.

"And yet there is much that is in dispute."

She had to deflect him. "The same might be said of you, my lord."

"Oh indeed. Nothing at all is known of *my* history, not where I was born or who were my parents, or even what my name is. You are absolutely correct, madam. The very same *might* be said of me."

The tone of his voice flayed her. She could not win in a game of wits with him, she thought, utterly dismayed. She had undertaken something that was totally beyond her capabilities. And if she had thought her best course was silence, he had decided his best interest was to goad her . . . to goad *Samara,* and he was truly a master at it, and his sarcasm made it all the more difficult for her to find the words to deal with him.

"Of course, I haven't your resources at my command, my lord," she said carefully, "but surely a man like you is the subject of gossip and innuendo—from time to time—that could be greatly exaggerated."

"Nothing to equal *your* notoriety, madam, I assure you. And yet you look like the veriest innocent. You are an amazing actress. But then, you've performed so often for so long on stage that you've honed your talents to perfection. Let me compliment you. Your bereaved widow act would fool all but the most jaded skeptic. Unfortunately, my dear Samara, *I* am he."

So, he was all knowing as well. A treasure of a man. How had William been able to stand it? Even Samara had wondered. But Samara would have known how to toy with him, whereas he terrified the unsophisticated and virginal Francesca Reay.

"But still you take me to England," Francesca murmured, parrying the comment that was meant to intimidate her.

"As you asked. You are William's wife."

"Widow," she contradicted. Surely he wasn't going to rewrite history as well? "And I asked only for William. I want nothing from you."

He applauded. "The tone is exactly right, madam. I marvel at your capacity to pretend. But I'm as certain as I live that you want *something* from me."

"As you do from me," she snapped, not even knowing where that comprehension came from. Nevertheless, her intuitive retort struck a chord. His face closed down. He leaned back in his chair and pinned her with his glacial gaze.

"We all want something."

She waited—the less she said the better.

"Why did you marry him?" He chipped the words out as if they were distasteful.

Not why did he marry you—Samara? Rather, he'd phrased his question as if Samara had had the control and the choice. What did he know? What?? What???

She gave him the only answer she could—what Samara would have said. "I loved him."

She saw the instant flash of irritation in his eyes.

"I adored him," she added for good measure.

"Damn you—"

"And he adored me."

"Bitch. I knew it would take no time before you showed your true colors."

"I hide nothing," Francesca said, awed by the emotion behind the ugly words. Mere hated Samara, pure and simple. And he wanted something from her.

What??

"By all accounts you don't," he said mockingly.

Francesca went still. This was just the beginning, she thought. Mere had so much ammunition against Samara. She'd cut a wide swath through Europe before she'd married William, and her infamous erotic dances had been the talk of every capital, every court.

Nor had Samara any compunction about removing her clothes in her exotic interpretations, and then overlaying the whole production with a specious theism that absolved her of exhibitionism and made her the darling of both Dukes and the demimonde.

Samara had been a phenomenon and artful enough to make the most cynical observer believe that she was a child of the gods, anointed to bring her kind of consecrated worship to the masses.

But all the fame, all the money had drifted and dribbled away, and probably Samara had married William on a tide of optimism that his family would provide for them, for her.

And instead, Mere had provided the wherewithal for them both to die.

Francesca felt a rush of rage that Mere—who had so much, to whom the small sum of money that would have kept William and Samara alive meant nothing—had chosen to do so little.

"There is obviously nothing I can tell *you*," she said furiously.

"Oh, my dear Samara, you haven't begun to tell me half of what I want to know."

She stared at him, appalled. But there was nothing to be read in his expression; only in his eyes did she perceive any nuance of emotion: They were hard as ice, incisive as a cut, and a mirror of his intention to attack and wound.

She turned her face away abruptly. *Calm, calm, you have to keep calm. That was just the kind of thing he would say to provoke Samara.*

And what would Samara do? She would be disdainful, she would act like the temple princess she claimed to be, and she would maintain that aloof air of mystery that drove men wild.

She took a deep breath to steady her nerves.

Think like Samara. Behave like Samara. You know enough about her to make William's family believe you are *Samara.*

*They have no reason not to, especially since they knew Samara
had been ill. Everything can be explained away by Samara's
illness.*

The thought reassured her. The rest was a matter of not biting
at Mere's insinuations. Of remembering that the less she said,
the more he would reveal. Of remaining calm, above all of his
insults, and making him look the fool.

She could do that. She *wanted* to do that. She had to do that.
And she would—for Samara.

No—for Colm.

Meresham Close

It was overwhelming—acres of shady parkland surrounding
a tall cream-colored brick house classically configured in three
stories, two wings, and a massive double staircase leading up
to the front door.

The minute the carriage drew to a halt, a dozen servants
flooded out from the arched entries beneath the staircase to
wait on them: two footmen to handle the luggage, another to
position the step so *milady's* skirt would not touch the ground,
a fourth to hand her down.

And Mere's eagle eye watching her every move, waiting to
fault her, wanting her to slip.

A formally attired gentleman awaited them in the shadow
of the arches, where Mere gestured for her to proceed.

"Wotten—this is Mrs. William."

Wotten bowed. "Mrs. William. Welcome to Meresham."

Mere took her elbow.

"Through the arch, if you please, Samara. We've installed
a lift. Mother isn't quite as spry as she used to be. Or Marcus
for that matter."

It was like a gilded cage, dripping vines and grapes in ornately
cast metal, and a quick shot up one floor to the reception room.

This was a long rectangular hall that stretched from the front
to the back of the house, with three doors opening on the

stairwell side, and two doors opposite. The ceilings must have been fifteen feet or more, Francesca guessed, and the walls were hung with ancestral portraits suspended from the thick moldings beneath.

The floor was covered with the most luxurious Persian carpet, as long as the hallway and almost as wide, and there were highly polished mahogany tables with priceless Chinese porcelain between the doorways.

The effect was subdued, elegant, tasteful, and it reeked of the kind of wealth that didn't ask prices.

Here there was still another battalion of servants waiting for them. It was stunning, how much William had given up to marry Samara. He could have returned to this haven with any bride he might have chosen besides Samara and lived a life of grace and privilege.

Mere introduced her brusquely; the women came forward and curtsied and withdrew until only Wotten was left.

"And where is Mother?"

"Madam is resting, my lord."

"I see." His tone was frigid. "And of course Marcus is shepherding his flock, literally or figuratively. One never knows with Marcus. But I expected nothing less."

"They are bringing Mr. William to the church, my lord. All will be in readiness for the service by tomorrow morning at ten."

"Thank you, Wotten. You may escort Mrs. William upstairs."

He turned away abruptly, as if he couldn't bear the sight of her, and Wotten indicated that Francesca should follow him.

It was an arduous climb—a punishment perhaps, when Wotten could just as easily have operated the lift for her—but Francesca didn't care. She was exhausted, emotionally and physically. She wanted nothing more than to go to sleep, because she'd gotten so little rest on the trip to England. Even when she was ensconced in her sleeping compartment, she lay awake, knowing that Mere was prowling the parlor car, waiting, watching, hoping to find her, catch her in the act of doing something untoward.

But Samara wouldn't have been that indiscreet—would she?

What would she have thought of William's ancestral home? She would have been the Queen of Meresham. Samara was a woman who knew how to manipulate the masses.

And she, Francesca, did not.

Samara would have had guests every weekend in every one of the ten bedrooms on the second floor. She would have had the very best bedroom all to herself and yards of the finest clothes all sewn up by her very own dressmaker in residence.

Samara Teva had known how to *live,* Francesca thought. Could she do anything less in her place?

She was gratified to see Wotten open the door to a room leading off the center section of the upper floor. It was a corner room with views to the east and south over the back lawns and fields of Meresham, and painted in a strong, deep wine color that contrasted with the heavy furnishings.

There was a huge four-poster bed with rope turnings, a mirrored dresser and commode, a substantial writing desk and chair by the window, and another large upholstered chair by the ornate mahogany fireplace mantel.

Two doors on the far wall opened into two built-in closets with drawers and cupboards, one of which was filled with men's clothing, and the other empty except for her two small suitcases sitting forlornly on the floor.

William's room, Francesca thought with a wave of relief. Of course they would give her William's room. A room of pure luxury, with the finest of linens and furniture. *William.* The young and ethereal William who truly had adored Samara.

If only they could have come here and lived the genteel life that Samara obviously longed for. . . .

Francesca paced across the thick carpet to the dresser and peered into the mirror. With her face shadowed by the thin black veil, she looked as mysterious, elusive, and aloof as Samara.

But when she removed the veil, she looked just like herself, and bone weary, too young and too innocent. Nothing like Samara.

She had to stop making these comparisons, she thought, panicked. But being in William's room only intensified her feeling of inadequacy. She knew nothing about this kind of life.

But then—neither had Samara, for all she had been showered with gifts and money from men of wealth and power. Samara remained till the end the woman she had obviously always been: worldly, flashy, practical, and plainspoken.

That was the woman William had loved.

And that was the woman she had to be, Francesca thought, staring at herself in the mirror. However it went against her nature. Whatever the cost.

No matter what she had to do.

His refuge was the library, always, among the leather-bound books that lined the floor-to-ceiling shelves.

It was the only place in the house where he could isolate himself from the poisonous presence of his family and know he wouldn't be disturbed.

But he *was* disturbed—about Samara Teva.

She was nothing like he expected. *Nothing.*

It shot all his thinking to hell, that she should be so cool, so competent, so alluring, and now Alex didn't know what he was going to do about her.

She was not cheap, tawdry, or coarse, as reported by his operatives when William had first become involved with her.

Nor was she garish, bold, loud, or showy. Rather, she was beautiful, mannered, and refined, the kind of woman William ought to have chosen for his wife—the kind of woman, Alex had to come to terms with it, he had chosen.

Damn her to hell. It would have been so much easier to deal with a piece of flashy trash. And easier to understand why a woman like that would choose to dance naked for admiring crowds of publicans and potentates.

Hell, *why* did he need to understand anything about her? She was what she was. An exhibitionist of the worst order. A woman who had no shame about using her body to get what she wanted.

She'd gotten William, bound him tight as a drum, to the pulsating sexual rhythm of her voluptuous nature.

It was inconceivable. That woman. That body. With what she did. And her sharp tongue, her fathomless black eyes, and her elegant, elusive air.

She was unknowable. Ladylike in life, an exhibitionist on the stage.

But that was a dichotomy that would challenge any man, he thought viciously. Even him. Witness the amount of time he had already spent thinking about it. Thinking about her.

There was nothing more to say or do. The die was cast now. He had her just where he wanted her.

"Is she here?"

Alex whirled. Marcus stood on the threshold, dressed in the garb of righteousness. It was too perfect, Alex thought, that Marcus had dressed up his intentions.

"Good God, Marcus, don't sneak up on a man. What are you doing here anyway?"

"What's the creature like?" Marcus asked as he came into the room.

"Unbelievable," Alex said curtly, turning back to stare out the window.

"That bad . . .? Our poor William. Well, rest easy, Alex. It will be my personal responsibility to save her soul."

"She'll probably corrupt yours," Alex muttered. "And you *will* stay away from her, Marcus. I don't think she has redemption in mind."

"Salvation comes in the least likely places," Marcus said loftily. "In any event, I came to tell you that William's coffin is at the church. Everything is as you directed, Alex."

"Thank you."

"Will she attend the service?"

"She will."

"Mother won't."

"But she will, Marcus." Alex had no doubt. No matter what Judithe said, she would do what was expected.

There was a long pause. Marcus hovered, consumed by curiosity, and Alex was very well aware of it.

"Is she common? Is she presentable?" *Is she the embodiment of sin?*

"You'll see her soon enough," Alex said dampeningly. "Is that all, Marcus?"

"Alex . . ."

"There's nothing more to be said. I expect you have a homily to write, Marcus, and don't wish to overstay your welcome. . . ."

Marcus started to say something, stopped, turned away, turned back. "You always get your way, don't you, Alex?"

"Always," Alex said. "You'd do well to remember that."

"My dear Alex, you never let anyone forget."

There was a knock at the door, and Francesca jerked awake, momentarily disoriented by the strange bed, the unfamiliar surroundings.

"Miss?" The voice was soft, low, feminine. "Miss, I've come to unpack your things."

A maid. One of the battallion to whom she'd been introduced earlier.

She scrambled off the bed and opened the door.

"Begging your pardon, miss—I'm Agnes."

"Yes, of course. Agnes." Francesca could barely concentrate, but she knew she did not want the saucy Agnes going through her things or Samara's.

Agnes's eyes widened. "Oh, did I wake you, miss?"

"I was dozing, yes. Let me ring when you can come and tend to my clothes."

"Very good, miss." Agnes curtsied, and Francesca closed the door, leaned against it, and shut her eyes.

Oh Lord. She was fully awake now.

All those servants. All those obscene costumes. What was she going to do with the costumes? And Samara's clothes? Bringing them with her had been the worst idea. No, assuming Samara's identity had been the worst idea. A disastrous idea.

She was never going to be able to pull this off.

She shoved her hands into her hair. What would Samara do?

But she knew already: Samara would have conquered the enemy. She'd be downstairs taking over the house, ruling the servants, secure in the idea that she was meant to live a life of luxury and ease.

Why, oh why hadn't William just stormed the castle and forced his way in? Mere could not have denied him, not with the rest of the family here, and presumably siding with William, the impoverished younger son, if not with his decision to marry Samara.

Samara was a performer. She could have played the gracious lady as well as anyone.

Maybe . . .

But not in those clothes. No, she had to hide those clothes. Why had she even brought them?

That showed how naive she was, not thinking ahead to all the small trip-up details with which she would be confronted as Samara.

Not the least of that was the way she dressed. Mere had been utterly thrown by her having dressed in proper mourning. He hadn't known quite what to make of her the whole trip.

He'd set her nerves on edge by his intense scrutiny, by his silence.

Silence was the tactic of a tyrant; she knew that well because Aunt Ida used it frequently. Of course that presupposed the person to whom you refused to speak cared at all about your speaking to them. It had always bothered Aunt Clarissa; but

Francesca had always been grateful for any length of time she did not have to listen to Aunt Ida's criticism.

But in Mere's case, the silence was meant to intimidate her. She was meant to fill the silence, to race to confession, to defend herself—Samara—so he would make no unwarranted assumptions.

And the gregarious Samara might well have rambled on in the painful silence for the time it took for them to travel to Meresham Close.

But she, Francesca, had used the silence as a wall, surrounded herself with it to protect herself against Mere's scathing comments and his ferocious desire to diminish the Samara she was pretending to be.

And now she was faced with the reality of the pretense. It was one thing to go up against Mere. Quite another to walk into the lion's den of his family with her lies.

This was such a stupid, ill-considered idea. It was entirely possible *her* Colm had nothing to do with Samara, and her whole masquerade had been for nothing.

No . . . it was too much of a coincidence, that. Colm setting her up in this particular pension, and then a pure stranger barging in and demanding to know if he'd come.

Yes, but to Samara . . . and that was the sticking point.

What if this turned out to be a fool's chase?

Colm would laugh at her. He'd say, 'You loved me that much that you went to those lengths to protect me . . . ?' And he would love her for it. . . .

The clothes . . . she forced her attention back to the moment. She couldn't waste time fantasizing about Colm. She had to do something about the clothes before Agnes returned.

The simplest thing would be to unpack everything and find a place to hide them. Only there was no privacy here for her. Nowhere to hide anything.

She wished she could hide herself.

Where in this room, where? Where wouldn't there be prying eyes, helpful hands?

She opened the built-in drawers in the closet. They were all empty, awaiting the belongings of William's wife. . . .

No, not there. Maybe among William's things?

She opened the second closet door to row upon row of neatly hung suits and frock coats and every drawer full to the brim with clothing folded to a knife edge.

She touched the precisely ironed shirts in the drawer.

No room for Samara Teva here either. . . .

Precisely ironed . . .

Oh dear God . . .

Too expensive and elegant for William, who had worn secondhand clothing bought at house sales and at the ragpickers. . . .

Not William's . . .

"My dear Samara," Mere said from across the room. "How perfect. I was hoping I would find you in the closet. I think it's time you took off your clothes."

Chapter Four

End of the game.

She hadn't expected it quite so soon. But then, she had underestimated Mere from the moment she met him. The tyrant's tactics included no mercy in ambushing the enemy.

Her.

He'd almost given her a heart attack. Her knees were still weak, and her hands shook. This was not the picture she wanted to present to him.

She had to get hold of herself. She had to think of this as act one of her performance as Samara Teva, who never let anything overwhelm her.

Except an incurable illness that wasted her away. . . .

She turned slowly, gathering her composure with an iron will she didn't know she possessed. For Samara. For Colm.

"My lord . . . ?" She knew just how to frost those words with an iciness that matched his own, learned from years of experience with Aunt Ida. "Can I have heard you right?"

Her poise floored him. He expected her to be furious at his presumption in giving her his own room. But this *lady of the manor* voice out of the dirty mouth of a brothel banger, was going way beyond Canterbury, and he wouldn't stand for it.

It was time to put the strumpet in her place.

He pushed himself away from the threshold. "My dear Samara, why else are you here?"

"The moment of enlightenment," she murmured. "Why *am* I here?" And at that, she was hard pressed not to say more. Even Samara, having appealed to him in desperation, had not known exactly what he might do or even that he might have an agenda totally apart from Samara's own.

It was the worst luck that he'd caught her in the closet. She needed to remove that advantage immediately. However, that meant she must move closer to him. And scary though that proposition was, the thought of being cornered by him was worse.

She edged, as gracefully as she could, out of the confines of the closet, while he watched her with his mocking glacial gaze.

"And now we are face-to-face, Samara Teva." But he liked that even less. In the twilight shadows of the room, she looked even more aristocratic, her body enhanced by her mourning dress, and her fine-boned features reflecting her distaste of him and the cat-and-mouse game he played.

Who *was* this woman?

"And what do you see, my lord?"

Cheeky, he thought impatiently; she knew damned well what he saw, what every man who looked at her saw: a ripe, taunting body clothed in propriety and bathed in lust.

She was right—it was time to end the games.

"I want what Colm gave you," he said abruptly.

That stopped her. *Colm again. Her Colm. Every fiber of her body knew it. Feared it.*

"I don't know what you're talking about." Did her voice shake—just a little? Colm. Why Colm? *What about Colm?*

"You are *such* a liar."

She wheeled away from him. "So—this is why you brought

me to England? To terrorize me over something I know nothing about?''

He clapped his hands. "Brava, Samara. Brava. A stellar performance. I would not have believed you had it in you— not from the reports I received."

Her heart plummeted. *Yes. Just as she'd surmised. Nothing escaped the long arm of Mere.* She kept her head averted.

"Reports . . . my lord?"

"Reports, Samara. I know all about you."

The scariest words in the world, and ones she could so easily refute by telling him the truth.

But then, she would never find out what the connection was between Samara and Colm.

She turned to face him then. "Do you, my lord?"

His face became set. His eyes hardened. This was how he faced down his enemies. This was a man to be feared.

"Let me count the ways. Sir Denis Beckwith; the Comte deFleuranges; Prince Vasili Guranov; Frederic, Duke of Farringdon; the Baron Blaust; General Von Abrungen . . ."

That jolted her. *Her general, one of Samara's lovers?*

"The King of . . ."

"Stop it!"

He allowed himself a small, knowing smile. "And I was just beginning. So it begs the question, my dear Samara, why, with some of the most powerful men at your beck and call, you settled on the youngest son of the house of Mere, a man who could offer you nothing, not a title, not a pound, not a home, not a name. . . . Why *William?*"

Now she was hard put to maintain her composure. Nothing escaped this man. Nothing. He was relentless, and she had no idea why Samara had married William or how she could not have been aware of all these things.

What could she say? What was believable? What would distract him from the questions and the illogic of the union?

Emotion would, she thought. *And passion. Amorphous things to which someone like Mere would not give credence.*

"I'll tell you why," she said, biting the words out. "He was young. He was tender. He was beautiful. He was virile. And he was all *mine*."

He slapped her. She hadn't expected that kind of unbridled rage from him, and it stunned her. She didn't think anything could move him, especially anything concerning William.

She stumbled backward against the bed, her ears ringing. It was enough. The question of *why* was met and joined and not even Mere could question the reality of it.

She looked up at him from under her lashes as she cradled her cheek.

"*All* mine . . ." she whispered, just to rekindle the fury in his eyes.

He could barely contain himself.

William—at the mercy of this harlot . . . He wanted to throttle her.

"Bitch." He felt a rage so blinding he didn't know what to do with it. "Trollop . . ." He wanted to kill her. "Whore . . ."

He got himself under control with an effort. "Your reputation, Samara, is justified."

She lifted her chin. "Indeed, my lord. So is yours."

"I want the black box."

"I know nothing of a black box."

He paced around to the side of the bed where she sat nursing her reddened cheek. "Miss Samara Teva knows nothing, does she, except how to corrupt the souls of men. . . ."

She set her chin. "And *love* . . ." she interpolated defiantly.

His eyes darkened dangerously; the muscles in his cheek knotted, and he flexed his hands as if he were forcibly restraining himself from attacking her.

"William always went for the cheap and the common," he retorted. "He was fair game for anything in skirts that walked the streets and back alleys. Love . . . !" He spat at her. "Animals rutting. Don't you impute any fine emotions to what went on between you and William. I know all about you, Samara Teva. You're a steeper of the first water, and you latched on to

William at the moment your allure started to fade and your power diminished. I had no sympathy for my brother—or you. And I know William never lifted a finger to earn a sou. But I know exactly how *you* got the money to support him.''

He loomed over her threateningly, and Francesca had to master her screaming nerves. *Calm, calm. Samara would laugh at him.* And she couldn't let him get to her. He knew so much, too much; he knew things that she didn't, clearly, and the time was ripe *now* for her to confess.

And she couldn't bring herself to do it. Too much was at stake, most importantly what it was he thought Colm had relayed to Samara.

She lifted her eyes to his and read pure vengeful fury in the icy depths. Mere would get what he wanted, she thought in a panic. And he would do whatever it took to accomplish it.

A loose-living nautch dancer was negligible in the scheme of things. Expendable even. What did Samara Teva have that he wanted so badly?

''My lord has been busy,'' she murmured to give herself a moment's distance. She had to get some answers. She had to discover what he knew. ''And I cannot think what you mean. My reputation is beyond reproach, my dances an expression of holy ecstasy.''

Yes, that got to him. It was exactly the right tack—to maintain that everything she—Samara—had ever done was respectable and aboveboard.

''Holy *ecstasy?*'' She was delusional too, he thought furiously, and her arrogance went beyond anything rational. Beyond reproach . . . !! It begged her sanity that she could even *think* that, let alone say it. ''God, you are good. But of course you have to be. You could not have sustained such a career if you weren't.''

She gazed at him so coolly, so unrepentantly, he almost lost control.

This was no volatile gypsy, as had been reported to him, and obviously his overbearing tactics were not going to work with her. He had to remember she was a performer, and she had an agenda, and she had reinvented herself to become the lady of the manor because that was what the role required.

Any good actress knew how to adapt to what the role required.

And so of course she had conveniently fogotten about Colm.

She was a chameleon, he thought, clamping down on his fury and his inability to rattle her, and she was much more intelligent than he had been led to believe. Nor was she ruled by passion or cowed by confrontation.

Everything she was contradicted everything that he knew, and he didn't like feeling impotent and powerless in front of her.

The only hold he had over her was that she wanted something too. And that *did* square with what he had been told about her. And that was the leverage he had to use.

Damn her to hell. Damn her, damn her, damn her to hell.

"Yes," she murmured. "I'm *very* good."

She was a master, he thought, in every realm. And now that he understood that he had underestimated her, he knew how to proceed.

"You're a traitor."

That jolted her. He could have sworn that she physically recoiled, that the look of horror that momentarily flashed in her eyes was not a lie.

Actress. Poseur. Liar. Harlot. He couldn't let himself forget. He still felt unbalanced by her, not in control. It was the face, the fine-featured, honey-skinned face, and the faint outline of his fingers fading against her high cheekbone. . . . He couldn't envision her in an erotic dance of rapture, but he could almost see her melting ecstatically in his arms. . . .

Goddamn damn damn damn her—what was he thinking??

She was speechless. She couldn't think of one thing to say in response to that bald statement.

What had Samara been up to????

"I *have* been ill, my lord. I thought I heard you say . . ."

"I did," he shot back brutally.

He was silent as a sentinel, watching every nuance of her expression. She felt cornered for the first time, boxed into a place from which there was no redemption. *A traitor* . . .

Tell him everything—NOW. . . . Throw yourself on his mercy . . . !

But—Colm . . . How could she? No! Because if Samara were involved in something that nefarious, so must be Colm. . . .

Oh my God—

Her whole body went weak. *Colm* . . .

Deny everything.

"You are mistaken, my lord." Her voice sounded shaky and unsure.

"You could be tried for treason."

She shook her head. "No. Whatever this is, it has nothing to do with me." A truth, yes, but not applicable to Samara. And he thought her such a good actress that the veracity of her statement became to him just another line in her ongoing performance to persuade him.

There was no way out but to tell him she was not Samara.

And then what? If he were in such a rage over Samara, what would he feel about her confession?

He'd still think she was some kind of traitor.

She resisted the impulse to cover her face. Truly, there was no place to hide and nowhere to go but forward—as Samara. Which meant she must attack.

She levered herself upright. "I won't listen to this. I won't. All these accusations. All these defamations. You seem not to know just who or what I am, my lord, so let me tell you once again. I am William's widow, no more, no less."

"*Black* widow." His eyes narrowed. "Spinning plots. Catching helpless men in your sticky web."

She had never felt so helpless. "I'm tired of these word games, my lord. I want to go to my room."

"My dear Samara, you weren't naive enough to think I would let you out of my sight? No, this is your room, your place, and you will be closer to me from now on than a Siamese twin—"

She started to protest.

"—unless indeed you are ready to be brought up on charges of treason."

She knew when she was defeated. "What do you want of me, Mere?"

He made a derisive sound. "Stop pretending you don't know. I won't go through this charade again with you, Samara. It's enough that I've allowed you to come here without calling in the authorities. Make no mistake: You are here on sufferance, because you have something I want. But I promise you, you will never be out of my sight. You sleep in my room. You go where I go. You do what I tell you when I tell you. And you *will* dance for me, Samara Teva, whether you want to or not."

She closed her eyes against the virulent hatred in his voice. But nothing could protect her against his violent fury.

"You have no choice," he went on inexorably. "You have no say. If you try to escape, I'll kill you."

He would—she knew he would. Her life was now at the mercy of one thin lie that she couldn't hope to sustain much longer.

Oh, Samara—my darling Colm . . . only for you—

She followed him with her eyes as he paced around the room, trying to contain the violence of his feelings. He wanted to crush her now, she thought. He wanted her out of his life already, and he had no choice, for whatever reason, to keep her at Meresham with him, and he hated it.

He hated her. And he had no great regret that he had struck her.

She was a *thing* to him. An object, just as Samara had been to her audiences, something to be desired and lusted after, even knowing it could never be possessed.

And yet now he possessed her, by virtue of threats and secrets, and he still didn't know what to do about her.

He stopped his furious pacing.

"Unpack your clothes." It was nothing less than an order, more words to strike terror in her heart. She should have destroyed everything that was Samara Teva's—*everything*.

"I'll attend to it in good time," she said defiantly.

"Now."

"Tyrant," she hissed.

"Then I'll do it."

He stalked around the bed and into the barren closet before she could raise a hand to stop him, and tossed the bags, one after the other, out into the room.

She jumped off the bed and sprawled on top of them.

"Bitch. As if that would stop me." He reached down and wrenched her up off of the suitcases as if she were a rag doll and threw her against the bed.

She crawled up onto it numbly, wondering what he wanted, what he thought he would find.

He ripped open the locks of the larger of the two suitcases and began tossing the clothing out all over the floor.

Samara's clothes. Velvets and silks and satins in varying hues. Hats and gloves and sheer stockings. And under all the flashy womanly clothes, the costumes. The glitter and gauze of the woman Samara had been pawed over mercilessly by the man who hated her most.

He threw them at her. He buried her in them as she lay shaking on the bed. He beat them onto the bed.

"This—this . . . and this . . . damn you damn you damn you . . ."

She buried her face against his awesome rage. She heard the dull thud of something dashed against the floor, Mere taking out his towering frustration on the empty suitcase.

"Get up."

There was no resisting that tone. He had already taught her that he could make her do what he wanted by the sheer force of his strength, his terrorizing threats, and his cutting tongue.

She eased herself into an upright position and dared to look at him. His hawk's face was still dark with that unfathomable fury and contorted with hate.

He held two minuscule pieces of one of Samara's costumes in his hands. "Put it on."

She had to resist this. This was madness, his trying to recreate for himself what it was that William had seen in Samara.

"*No.*" She knew it was the wrong answer even before she spat the word. He would make her, simple as that.

He took a threatening step toward her. "*Do it*—or I will."

Shattering to think of him manhandling her. He was capable of mayhem—she saw it in his eyes—and maybe just a moment beyond rational thinking because he hated Samara so ferociously, and he wanted—he needed—to plumb the riddle of *her*.

"I'll do it," she whispered, knowing there was no choice. *Maybe I can jump out a window. . . .*

Her heart pounding painfully, she edged into the empty closet and shut the door behind her.

No way out there. Nor could she lock herself in. And even if she could, she'd die in days in such an airless, stuffy, confined space.

"*Now*, Samara—" He was right at the door, waiting to pounce.

She was going to faint. She had never envisioned things going this far.

"I'm coming in."

"*Don't . . .*" The terror was in her voice, pure, high, strained, and desperate. He had to have heard it. No, he wasn't hearing anything but the rage and grief throbbing in his veins.

She had no strength to carry this off. Not an atom. And nowhere near the disposition to strut naked in front of a stranger.

But this was the only way he could defeat her—defeat Samara—and she couldn't pretend any longer. She couldn't take off her clothes and *be* Samara in the most essential way.

"And here I understood you *liked* dancing for an audience

of one," Mere growled from beyond the door. "They paid you well for it, those limp-nosed lovers of yours, didn't they?"

Her throat closed up. More Samara secrets—things that no one was ever meant to know, least of all her. She sagged against the wall, clutching the thin, transparent pieces of Samara's costume.

"I'll pay you too, you mercenary bitch. That's what you're holding out for, isn't it? That's what you've always wanted. . . . That's why you married William—"

He would kill her. He would choke the very life out of her, no matter what she did now.

Pay her . . .

Oh God, if she had some money, she would run so far, so fast no one would ever find her again.

She let the thought tempt her. Could she do it—for money? Was she that depraved?

He thought she was. He thought she was venal, sordid, and amoral.

No—Samara was.

The knob turned ominously, and she shrank against the wall.

"Give me a moment," she called shakily. He wouldn't wait while she wrestled with her conscience and a lifetime of sexual strictures. She either had to do it or tell him the truth.

Her limbs, her body felt boneless. She watched as if she were someone else as she lifted a tentative hand to the buttons on her dress.

She had to do it. Samara had to do it. Samara wouldn't have hesitated to do it.

And he would pay her. She would have something in reparation for his prurient voyeurism and his unbearable pain.

And then she'd go. The charade would be over. She'd sneak away and they'd never find her again.

She'd do it—this once—and then Samara could finally rest in peace.

* * *

The closet door opened slowly, slowly, slowly.

Alex stood leaning against the door, his arms folded across his chest, his blatant cynicism showing clearly on his face. But he had to hand it to her: She knew just how to make a man salivate with anticipation.

She used time-honored ploys—her denials, her reluctance, her silence, her pretense at a haughty pride—all of that in aid of provoking her audience and making him feel as if he would do anything, give anything to get more.

More of what? More of nothing until he'd offered her money, which he should have known would be a prime component of anything Samara Teva did, and now, finally, the performance was to begin.

She played it like a reluctant virgin, the way she pulled the door open by excruciating increments and gave him brief, tantalizing views of her bare arm, a naked foot, a long, bare leg snaking out and retreating, a glimpse of thin, transparent fabric edged with shimmering beads draped over her thigh.

God, get on with it, he thought impatiently. The Samara Teva he'd read about in the reports had been a woman who knew what she wanted and always got quickly to the point.

But on the other hand, there was something very enticing about watching her slither around the molding of the door as if she were making love to it, her long, strong body barely encased in illusion net and jetty beads that glistened in the subdued light.

He felt an instant powerful thrusting response to the curve of her naked buttocks and the thin line of beading that fastened to whatever scrap of netting she wore across her breasts.

She was everything, in the flesh, that he had been led to believe: shapely, bosomy, sensual, seductive.

Samara Teva knew exactly what she was doing, he thought, his rage building again, and knowing that, he should not have been so susceptible as he watched her naked hips writhe against the doorframe as if it were the most potent lover in the universe.

But his fury escalated in tandem with his arousal. He wanted to see more. And more. He felt as if she were keeping herself from him to provoke him beyond his endurance, and he was a man who prided himself on his stamina and his ability to wait out the enemy.

And she was the enemy. Because she knew how much he wanted to see her, all of her, naked and dancing for him, it seemed to him that she deliberately withheld herself until she enticed him to beg for more.

Well, he didn't do things like that. No woman had ever had him groveling at her bare feet, no matter how much he wanted her.

Especially a strumpet of the streets.

He knew how to wait. He knew how to endure. As painful as it was, as insistently as his body demanded his capitulation, he would wait. And he would win.

No woman's writhing naked hips had ever seduced him.

He watched, aloof, distant, and poker hard, as she whirled away from the doorframe and then backed herself up against it, as if her lover were holding her from behind.

She pressed her bare buttocks against the molding, and she raised her arms above her head as if she were wrapping her arms around her lover's neck.

Now her lush breasts were visible, barely encased in the thin netting, her taut nipples obscured by a swirl of jet beading. Riding low on her hips, a thin, beaded belt had suspended from it a length of netting and swirling beads that just barely revealed the enticing vee between her legs. And all he could see of her face was her long, exotic eyes, glimmering over the veil that obscured everything else.

Almost, almost . . . He found himself surging with excitement. There was something very potent about her concealing that which a man most desired to see. Something very expert and knowing in the way that she used her body to provoke and control him until all he wanted was for her to rip off the impeding costume and reveal herself to him.

Instead, she began the dance.

She didn't know how she'd gotten this far. Her nudity, her body's response to it, scared her to death. She had never removed that many of her clothes at one time, and she found it terrifying to be so exposed.

Thank God the room was dark. Thank God she couldn't see him. Thank God she had the doorframe to support her watery legs.

But she had to move from the doorway. She had to forget about her nudity. She had to perform the dance.

The dance, the dance. She had no idea about Samara's dances.

The hands, Samara had said. *She wove spells with her hands when she danced.*

Distract him with your hands. . . .

She was going to fall right on her face if she took one step into that room.

She forced herself to move; he expected her to move. And somewhere at the end of her abortive performance, there would be money. She'd make sure he gave her the money.

She could do it for the money. Anyone could do anything for money, especially when there was nothing to lose. All he wanted was to see some kind of dance.

She stepped into the room, the carpet rough beneath her bare feet.

Now what?

Move your arms. . . . Thrust your hips. . . . Shake your body—

She felt as awkward as a cow; she was nowhere near as graceful or as sinuous as Samara must have been. God, how had she maneuvered her body and her hands at the same time?

How did a temple dancer move?

She felt his intense, rapt gaze as she swayed and shimmied

closer and closer, weaving her hands and arms like two serpents twining around each other.

Oh God, so inept . . . so clumsy— He won't be fooled—a man like him would know about things like nautch dancers. He'd probably seen a dozen, a hundred, a thousand. . . .

She couldn't think of what to do; she did whatever came into her head that seemed exotic and erotic. But what did she know of eroticism? She knew Samara Teva in the last days of her life.

And there wasn't any primer for this kind of thing.

And she was so naked she thought she would die. She knew that he was focused on every inch of her bare skin and that the fragile netting that covered her intimate places would be like tissue in his hands if he chose to strip it from her body.

She wouldn't get close enough for that, but she had the distinct feeling he could see every inch of her that was covered anyway. A man like Mere knew about things like that too. There was nothing to hide from him, nothing he hadn't touched or experienced where women were concerned.

So how could she hope to fool him with her virgin's dance?

Oh God—what should she do next? Surely she could bring this travesty to an end now.

She whirled, lifting her arms over her head, around and around, the scrap of cloth around her loins flaring outward, the light catching the jetty beads in shimmering mystery.

And then she sank to the floor, her arms outstretched in supplication, her head bowed over her bare legs, her heart pounding from abject fear.

"You are everything they say you are," Mere said icily above her. "You deserve everything you get."

She lifted her eyes as he threw a handful of pound notes on the floor.

"And more." His hands were clenched and he looked as if he were about to strike her, as if something about her, about the dance aroused something violent in him.

So much so, he couldn't stand the sight of her, nor could he take the chance she would run.

She didn't dare breathe; she couldn't move. He could attack her on the floor, and she would be at his mercy.

He knew it and she knew it, but he wouldn't soil himself with his brother's leavings or force himself on a woman who had had by all accounts a thousand other men, no matter how lewd her dance and how voluptuous her body.

He wheeled around abruptly and exited the room, slamming the door violently and locking it emphatically behind him.

Chapter Five

But every propriety would be observed when they buried William the following morning in the family cemetery. Mere might lock her in the bedroom overnight, and let her stew in her shame, but he made sure, through Wotten, that she would be ready when the bell tolled, and specified that *he* would escort her to the church, and that she need do nothing more than clothe and veil herself properly and not say a word.

She felt like throwing things, but Wotten wasn't the person she wanted to maim. Poor Wotten was the unfortunate go-between who woke her obscenely early the next morning bearing Mere's tyrannical messages.

"I have a tray, Mrs. William, but you must stay on the bed when I come in. His lordship was very specific, and indeed, I am accompanied by his valet, if you understand what I mean."

That man! Francesca shuddered as she climbed onto the bed and wrapped her robe more tightly around her. As if she would try anything before breakfast or before she could think coherently.

She had spent the whole night wallowing in shame that she

had done the thing she had done. And now she was starving, and she wasn't about to attempt to escape Meresham Close before William was properly buried.

"You can come in," she called, her voice overlaid with just a touch of anger. Well, she was angry, at the whole impossible situation. And the fact they all thought she was a trollop and no better than she should be.

But of course, Francesca Reay would never have been alone, almost naked, in a man's bedroom performing a dance of seduction for a murderous Earl.

Wotten appeared at the door, holding a tray with a pot of tea, toast, jam, butter, and scones.

"On the desk," she directed coolly, just as if he delivered a tray for her every morning. "Tell his lordship I will be ready on the dot of nine-thirty."

"Very good, madam," Wotten responded, inclining his head, playing the game.

She jumped out of bed the moment the latch clicked, and tackled the tray. God, she was hungry, and that overrode everything else she was feeling. She drew back the curtains of the window beside the desk that overlooked the undulating fields of Meresham.

A gray day outside, with drifts of fog settled in the treetops like ominous little clouds. A wetness glimmering on the grass. A heaviness in the air.

A heaviness in her heart, and she wasn't quite sure why. She had pulled off her dance of the shimmering veil. Mere questioned nothing. He had believed it, believed *her* as Samara Teva.

That was what she had wanted, to buy herself another day, another chance to prize out Samara's secrets.

And she knew already that she would not take Mere's money and run. Not yet, not even if it meant a repeat performance of the night before. It would get easier, she thought, and she would feel more comfortable, she thought, because she did have the power to make him believe.

But what he couldn't believe, she comprehended with sudden insight, was that the respectable core of Francesca Reay could be a component of someone like Samara. That she could dance naked and still be a lady in the deep-most sense. This was the thing that infuriated him, and the thing he could not mesh with what he knew of Samara.

She saw it so clearly now. He could have dealt so much better, so much easier with the real Samara, who was truly a child of fantasy and make-believe. Who was every bit as dirty as he thought she was.

And he was doing everything in his power to make Francesca, as the embodiment of Samara, that dirty too.

But he couldn't. And that was the whole crux of his violent rage.

He couldn't, and now that she understood, she wouldn't let him.

Another day, she thought, munching on a scone and staring out the window. She'd stay just another day to see William buried, and to make Mere pay for his cruelty. Samara would have wanted that. Samara would have been happy to see Mere squirm.

And so he will. That is the least I can do for what he did to them.

She emerged from the room as stately as a Queen, shrouded from head to foot in black, just as she had been dressed on the trip from Berlin.

But he wasn't fooled now. He knew what lay beneath those layers of clothing; he knew exactly how that wanton body moved to a provocative rhythm all its own. He knew the shape of her legs, the flare of her hips into the sinuous curve of her buttocks. All of that he knew as she took his arm and they proceeded down the stairs and out the front door of Meresham with his body as hard as rock and pulsing with a carnal need that made him wary and crazy both.

The pony cart awaited them and he handed her up, saying, "The church is too far to walk." Except he walked alongside the cart as the boy Andreas drove it carefully down the track toward the village, where, midway between there and the house, stood the stately church of Mere's childhood, its spires shrouded in fog and reaching to heaven.

Francesca felt faint in the moist heat as Mere lifted her from the cart and roughly guided her into the church.

It was cool within, thank heaven. And bigger inside than she'd thought. She paced down the long aisle with its Gothic oaken pews and up toward the altar with its marble floor and its ornately carved nave.

The coffin was there, expensive, laid with flowers, and in the front pew, Francesca could see one blond head, one gray, all swathed in black otherwise, and up in the pulpit, the lean, sweet face of the prelate.

Mere pushed her into the pew opposite his mother and Phillippa. "Don't say a word."

She lifted her chin and straightened her back and ignored him as she settled herself in the pew beside him, noting that the priest was watching them avidly. Why?

Because of course this was the first time he had ever seen the notorious Samara Teva, and she must have looked nothing like a soul needing to be saved. The thought was amusing. And then it occurred to her that this must be William's second brother, the curate.

Holier than William, Samara had said. *Older brothers, a monster and a priest. No wonder poor William felt as if he had to get away from Meresham Close alive.*

And who could make him feel more alive than a nautch dancer who focused all her energy and sex on him?

She watched Marcus closely as Mere nodded, and Marcus began, "We are here to mourn the death and commemorate the life of our sweet but misguided brother William, who died too young."

Francesca stiffened. He surely wasn't going to give a homily on sin and seduction, not with her present. But then, who could tell what any member of this family might do?

But he didn't. "Poor William. It is the lot of a younger child to sometimes not know exactly where he fits in this life, and so it was with William. As we his family well know, his youthful nature could never be tempered with advice or instruction; his was a sensibility that had to follow its own volition, wherever it led. We can only hope that his soul, now having finally come home, can find the peace he sought at last. Let us pray."

The verses he chose for William's service were apt and not censorious; he was very conscious of propriety, Francesca thought, watching him, even though it was only his family in attendance. Still, it had to have been tempting to think about denouncing the woman who had brought his brother down in public and from the pulpit.

But he didn't, and he closed decorously with the Lord's Prayer, and preceded by the coffin on its bier, he led them solemnly from the church to the graveyard, which was above the church on a hillside overlooking the village, and conducted the brief service of interment there.

May the Lord bless you and keep you . . .

Francesca blinked away her tears. But she saw not a vestige of sorrow in either the stance or the face of William's mother. Her expression was as hard as a rock, and the glances she sent Francesca's way as penetrating as acid.

The woman hated Samara every bit as much as Mere did. And the other one—the blonde who must be the curate's wife— she merely slanted a brushing look now and again at Francesca's black-shrouded figure as if she were curious and nothing more.

The pony cart was waiting when they came down the hill.

Without so much as another look at Francesca, Judithe climbed in, and Phillippa followed, which left no room for Francesca, as Judithe had intended.

"Andreas," she commanded, and the boy snapped the reins.

Mere said nothing, but his fingers tightened on Francesca's elbow.

"We'll walk back," Francesca murmured conciliatingly. She wanted to walk, to work off her pent-up energy, which was close to explosive at the tension of the day.

She needed space. She felt so smothered by these people, by their fury and their snide curiosity about Samara. Their manners only extended so far, and Francesca was not anxious to get back to the house, because it was certain there would be some kind of scene played out there.

The mother wanted it and couldn't wait for it.

Another one who would as soon kill Samara as kiss her.

Dear God, what more had she gotten herself into with this masquerade?

She took a deep breath of the leaden air just as Marcus held out his hand. "I'm Marcus."

"Yes." She took his hand. "I know."

"We'll walk," Mere said, forestalling any further conversation from Marcus. "You'll join us later?" he said to Marcus.

"I could come now," Marcus said. "Perhaps I ought to . . ."

"Judithe will have a heart attack if she sees us both with the widow. Give us twenty minutes."

"As you wish," Marcus murmured.

"Come." There was no brooking that tone. Merc took her elbow and pushed, and suddenly she was moving of her own volition, as much to get away from his punishing fingers as to generate some feeling deep within her numbed consciousness.

The whole thing was going to be such a tightrope walk that not even the most skilled performer could avoid a mishap.

A misstep. A pretentious dance. A false move.

She had a hundred pounds in her possession—from his generosity of the night before. It was a truly eloquent statement of what he thought of Samara Teva, and Francesca in her place.

It *was* time to leave. Whatever more secrets there were about Samara, and about Colm, she could exist very nicely without knowing them. Or Colm would explain, once she saw him again.

She would go home, back to Braidwood, where dealing

with Aunt Ida would not be nearly as difficult as handling a murderous Earl. And she would wait for Colm, because surely he would come looking for her there.

That was the solution to the whole impossible mess, she thought, as they came up the long drive to Meresham with her still keeping pace with his brisk stride, which hadn't slackened in the half-mile walk from the church. And she'd always had the choice of telling him the truth, but now it probably was a truth he didn't want to hear.

He believed her to be Samara, and anything less would be, to him, every bit as much a lie.

Let him think she was Samara then. Let him have the memory of her bawd's dance, and her ladylike mien.

Let him stew in the mystery of it for the rest of his life. . . .

Wotten awaited them just outside the middle arch below the steps. "My lady and Lady Phillippa await you in the drawing room."

Mere grunted and pushed her ahead of him to the elevator. She wrenched her arm away from his proprietary grip, furious with the way he was treating her and panicked by what awaited her when she was finally confronted with William's mother.

"If you do not treat me with respect, they will not either," she hissed.

"As if anyone should," Mere retorted. "The whole family knows what you are, and indeed, there was one vote for even letting you die."

She was so shocked by that, she was almost speechless. He was the one, she thought instantly, the only one callous enough, insensate enough— But then—why had he come for her? Why why why?

No. The only one with the iron temperament to wish such a thing had to be the mother.

Which made this confrontation with her even more dangerous.

How they all despised Samara, whose love and affection had been the one thing that had made William happy.

But that was such a puny weapon with which to face down the amazon of a mother.

Still, the fact of that love had stopped Mere in his tracks. And it was something beyond anything his mother could or ever had given to William.

Perhaps she had more power than she thought, Francesca decided as the lift slid to a stop and Mere opened the gate.

"After you, my lady."

"As you wish, my lord."

She was curiously calm now. After all of Mere's slander, what more could the family say to her or do to her? Just knowing one of them—the mother—wanted her dead gave her a certain strength to face the woman.

And after all, she'd be gone by morning.

Be Samara. Say what Samara would say. But always remain a lady. That is the thing they all don't expect.

Wotten paused before a massive floor-to-ceiling double door in the center of the hallway, and turned to her. "If you wish, my lady, I will take your hat."

"Of course." She wanted them to see her face, her eyes, her manners. She unwound the veil, removed the pins, and handed the hat over to him.

"Very good, my lady." Wotten understood, she thought, more than the family, more than Mere, more than even Samara could have expected.

He opened the door. "My lord and my lady . . ."

Mere preceded her, and Francesca squared her shoulders and followed him in. And understood immediately what she was facing.

The room was huge and high ceilinged, and everything in it was dwarfed by the sense of space. It was a room for entertaining really, with light blue walls and moldings picked out in gold, a painted ceiling fluttering with cherubs and clouds, and spindly gilt-trimmed chairs and tables clustered against the walls.

The floor-to-ceiling French windows were open and framed

blue satin curtains that matched the walls, and at the far end, a massive marble fireplace was the focal point of a small intimate seating area consisting of a pair of sofas that matched the chairs and looked just as fragile.

Here sat Judithe Deveney, Dowager Duchess of Mere, a blot of mordant black against the fabulous Persian rug that picked up every celestial color in the room, awaiting the moment she could crucify the parasitic demirep who had had the temerity to marry her weakling son.

And her desire to receive Francesca here was a clear message of her intention to intimidate Samara and diminish her.

Samara would never have been cowed by such things, Francesca thought as she assessed the black crow, who was just waiting to peck out her eyes. Samara would have thought a room like this useless, while Judithe Deveney acted as if it were her throne room.

So be it.

The silence was deafening, and Judithe's virulent presence so compelling, that Francesca hadn't even noticed the blonde seated farther toward the fireplace, her manner more negligent, less negative.

Francesca was not going to speak first. This was the moment to take her cue from what she had learned living with Aunt Ida: Never give in; withhold all.

So she waited. And Judithe waited. And Mere said not a word, just watched them both, getting more incensed by the moment at the audacity and sangfroid of this woman, who was no more than a courtesan and no better than she should be.

Instead, she was as regal as a Queen. Her back was straight as a board, her body poised, her beautiful face serene, and her gaze disconcertingly direct.

And that in the face of his mother's relentless stare. Judithe wouldn't give up an inch to Samara Teva, in spite of the fact that she didn't know what to make of her. It didn't matter. Judithe hated her as if she were the devil incarnate. As if she were sewage from the gutter, which was exactly what they had expected. And if she'd been anything coarse and common, this whole episode would have been as dead and buried as William by now.

Judithe gave in first, because she didn't know quite what to do, short of murdering the trull, and that would have soiled her beautiful imported carpet.

"Alex." Her tone was frigid, underlaid by the demand for a solution, and even the words, that, for the moment, were beyond her.

"This is William's wife," Alex said composedly. "Our mother, Lady Judith Deveney, Samara. And my sister-in-law, Marcus's wife, Phillippa."

Francesca suddenly felt beyond speech as well. Whatever she did, Judithe would criticize her, so why give her the ammunition? Instead, she inclined her head.

"Does it speak?" Judithe demanded.

"She is *quite* vocal," Alex drawled.

"Proper English?"

Francesca's cheeks burned. Judithe was no lady, in spite of her titles and her wealth. She was a vindictive old woman, and she couldn't hurt Samara, or William, ever again. Francesca wanted to make sure of it.

"Indeed, my lady. Every bit as proper as your English, I daresay. But with much better manners."

Judithe looked startled. The voice was as smooth and rich as honey—obviously William had worked on her, or found someone to teach her to speak. Or something. Anything to explain the discrepancy between what she expected and what stood before her looking and sounding as if she *belonged.*

"Oh, you are the queen of yourself, Miss Samara Teva, but you fool no one here," she snapped, turning to Alex. "What do you intend to do with it now that William has had a proper burial?"

"None of your business, Mother."

"Take it away from this place."

"Not yet, Mother."

"Oh God, I'm going to die," Judithe moaned. "Why is He punishing me like this—first that inconceivable marriage, and then this perverted creature in my house—? And now Alex, working every which way to thwart me, and threatening to keep the reminder of his brother's sins constantly in front of our very eyes. . . ."

She rose from the sofa, an ominous expression on her face. "If you don't get rid of it, Alex, there is no telling what I will do. God could not want this piece of filth in my house. How William came to marry it I will never— Where is Marcus? *Where* is Marcus? Let him explain such a cruel son, such a heedless God—" She sank back onto the cushions with a theatricality meant to suggest that her legs could no longer support her and that her son should.

But Alex was immune to her histrionics. Instead, he started clapping and she glared at him.

"Brava, mother. Wonderful performance. You and Samara have much more in common than you know. Excellent actresses, the two of you. Perfect at manipulating your audiences. Peerless at causing havoc. You fool no one either, Mother, least of all me. William's wife is not your concern, as of this moment, and if you can't be civil in my house, please adjourn to the Dower House and make yourself comfortable there."

"I will not let it drive me from my house," Judithe said succinctly.

A new voice entered the fray: Marcus, who had been listening all along, entering the play precisely twenty minutes after they had left him at the church, and still dressed in his vestments, which lent him a height and dignity that made Judithe's hysteria seem excessively unladylike. "That is a very wise choice, Mother. And do dispense with referring to William's wife as an object. It really isn't worthy of you, no matter what you think of her."

He turned to Alex, but what he really wanted to see was Samara unbound.

She was as still as a statue, her face pale at the onslaught of his mother's corrosive temper. And she was beautiful as sin, as William's chosen wife ought to be. And elegant, the way she carried herself, even in the lioness's den. Thick black hair parted in the middle and tamed into a neat chignon at the nape of her neck. A dress of fashionable mourning, with no excessive touches. Graceful hands. Impeccable posture. Fathomless black exotic eyes that revealed nothing.

Francesca found his appraisal just a little off-putting, coming after Judithe's blatant attempt to bully her. Because there was no kindness there. He too was stunned by the anomaly of her and, more than that, would have liked to explore it if she would give him half a chance.

"I would like to retire to my room," she said, and she felt his reponse to the timbre of her voice. Nothing like he expected. Nothing.

"My room, you mean," Alex said baldly to aggravate his mother as much as anything.

Judithe flinched. "Of course. What did one expect? You can paint it over with a fine accent and expensive clothes, but in the end, it all comes down to whose bedroom it occupies and what depravities it practices in the dark. And now we know. William cold in his grave, and Alex already lowering himself to its level. You explain it to me, Marcus, because I just don't understand."

She levered herself off the sofa with some difficulty, real or pretend, Francesca couldn't tell, and she almost felt a shred of sympathy until Judithe stood before her, eye to eye, her hatred pulsating and palpable.

"If I could kill you with impunity, I would," Judithe hissed. "Just to keep you from destroying another of my sons."

"Mother—!" Marcus leapt after her. "Mother . . ."

They heard her voice trailing down the hallway as Marcus followed.

"It is a blight on my life. Tell him to send it away. Give it money. Make it sign papers preventing it from having a claim on Mere ever again. Promise me, Marcus—you'll talk to him. Swear to me it will be gone by morning—''

"I—can't . . ." Marcus's voice echoed back to them.

"Poor Marcus." Phillippa now rose indolently from her place by the fireplace. "He wishes to be so perfect as a priest, and he fails at every level, especially with his own mother."

She sidled up to Francesca. "I'm Phillippa. I have no opinion one way or the other. I hardly knew William. I do know Judithe. You'll never win her over."

"Nor do I want to," Francesca said stiffly.

"Then let him pay you off." She slanted a knowing look at Mere. "You could live forever on the kind of money they would pay you to get away from here. I wish they would pay me." Again that look that glanced off Alex like an arrow from its target. "Ah well. Perhaps you know more of heaven than Marcus knows of hell. Or maybe we were both meant to make Marcus's life hell, hmmm?"

And with that cryptic comment, she sauntered out of the room.

"What a bitch," Alex muttered.

"Which of us are you talking about?" Francesca asked, her tone deceptively sweet. Phillippa, in her own way, was someone to be reckoned with and deeply unhappy in her choice of Marcus as a husband. It could not have been clearer if she had baldly confessed it.

"Which of us has, in the end, sold herself to the highest bidder?" she added for good measure. "Indeed, which of us truly loves her husband? Do ruminate on that, my lord, while I go to—" She was about to say *my room,* but of course, she had no room. She had Mere's room. Mere's bed. Mere's will and Mere's whim.

Enough of Mere. Enough of them all with their malevolent bitterness and their underlying guilt about William. Give her an hour in that bedroom at most, and she would be gone. And they wouldn't even have to lay out their precious money to make it happen.

"You are going nowhere," Mere said, his voice deceptively calm. As if he could read her mind. As if he knew exactly what she planned.

"Where would I go, my lord?" she snapped. "Where on all the Meresham land would *I* be welcome?"

He said it without thinking. Or maybe he'd been thinking it, and wanted only the moment to be able to give rein to the desire that had been torturing him since he'd walked into William's room in Berlin. Whatever it was, he said it, each word like the drop of a stone, each word forecasting her fate.

"In my bed."

Oh now . . . oh now— She felt like running, and there was nowhere to run. Servants everywhere. Silence, discretion observed. This was the moment she had not wanted to come to, and it seemed suddenly as if it were as inevitable as air.

Of course, he would want Samara. Why would he not? How naive of her to even consider otherwise. What were his loyalties, after all? He had none to his family obviously. So that left only himself.

And then there was that matter of treason with which he had already blackmailed her. How much more forcefully could he use it now? This time he might give her all the particulars she didn't want to know: Samara details, Samara secrets that were better left buried along with William.

She *had* to get away from him.

She drew herself up, girding for the hardest battle of all. "I think not, my lord."

Once again, she confounded him.

"She thinks not," he mimicked. "My lady of Whitehall doling out favors like white papers. No, you're absolutely right, my lady. *I* think *not,* and since this is an autocracy, you are going nowhere."

"Fine." She dropped onto one of the delicate sofas. "I can rest myself here. The drawing room will be perfectly fine." She felt exhausted anyway; between his mother and him, any sane woman would be on the verge of having a fit of the vapors.

She just wouldn't be leaving quite as soon as she planned.

A hundred pounds. The thought of it was enticing, soothing. He thought she could be bought last night. She wondered what he would offer now—if he wanted Samara in his bed that badly.

How was she going to get around that, virgin that she was? Nonsense—it would never get that far. She wouldn't let it.

Really? When she had allowed him to bully her into performing a lewd dance half naked?

No. He had blackmailed her, and he would do it again to get what he wanted. She was in mortal danger from this man. He was ruthless, relentless, and she didn't have nearly the guile to outwit him.

And she would never know why she had thought she could.

He was staring at her so intently she felt a wave of heat rise in her body.

She bit back her trepidation and looked at him with the same intensity, the same scrutiny-under-a-microscope gaze that he leveled at her.

"My lord?" she murmured when she finally couldn't stand it anymore.

He debated with himself for one minute how much to say, even whether he should say it. "From everything I understand, you are loose, immoral, and avaricious, and you could have anything you wanted from anyone you choose to bed with. By every account, you are not particular, or even discriminating. They say there isn't a man who has met you who doesn't want to possess you, and now that you are free of the burden of a useless albeit young and tender husband, you can give full rein to your lascivious nature. I doubt if it was ever held fully in check, if last night was any example. So it begs the question of why you won't bed with me."

"Does it?" she asked frostily, her whole body shaking with his insults and insinuations. "Does it indeed, my lord? Well, you yourself read me the list of my alleged paramours. Consider—what is an Earl compared to a King? Perhaps, after all, *you* are beneath me—''

"Well, well, well, the little sharpie's claws come out and dig deep. But''—he rolled back his sleeve and held up his bared arm—''no blood, my lady. It's all about blood anyway, isn't it? Blue blood. Blood money. Or did you know William had a will? Oh, I wonder what you know—I do indeed. But one thing *I* know, Samara Teva, is that one day soon, *you* will lie beneath me. And that currency, my vicious-tongued lady, you can deposit in the Bank of England.''

Chapter Six

Not for a minute was Alex going to leave her alone. And Francesca was not going upstairs alone with him.

They sat in a mutually antagonistic silence in the drawing room while the hour ticked by, and she ruminated on all the stupid mistakes she had made since she had first become acquainted with Samara.

If she got out of this alive, it would be a miracle, she thought frantically. And what was this about William having a will? More complications that would make it harder for her to walk away?

Nothing would make it easier than that hundred pounds in her pocket, and the way William's family was treating her. Not that Samara would have buckled under, the way she, Francesca, was. Samara probably would have warmed Mere's bed already. . . .

Oh please . . . Francesca felt a wave of heat suffuse her body. No, she really had to give credence to the idea: Samara had not been shy, and with the constraint of her fidelity to

William removed, what wouldn't she have done—for attention, for the thrill of the forbidden, for money . . . ?

And how far removed from Samara's sensibility was she, if she had let Alex pay her to dance naked for him?

The wonder was Francesca could still present the picture of a cool, composed woman to him. But instinctively she knew the more she circumvented Mere, the less she said, the more intrigued he became. She wasn't sure she wanted that either, but it was better than his savagery and his threats.

They were on neutral territory now. If he ever got her back in his room, there was no telling what might happen.

Alex was thinking much the same thing. This was a woman of contradictions, a woman whose mind was as sharp as her tongue, which was why he couldn't—*still*—adjust his perception of the woman he had heard and read about with the woman she seemed to be.

There were so many inconsistencies there, not least her beauty and elegance. He found himself continually staring at her face, at those exotic black eyes in which a man could drown.

Not him, though. Never *him*.

And her skin, her warm tactile skin. He had seen almost every inch of her skin last night, and he ached to stroke it and make her moan at his touch.

She was everything a courtesan should be—

And not.

William . . . Alex felt an unexpected spasm of grief right down to his very vitals. He shouldn't be thinking of William's wife in these terms, but there was no other way to think about her.

She was pure enticement, and if he had ruthlessly used her last night, he felt no remorse whatsoever. Samara's sins would catch up to her eventually, but until then, he intended to take anything and everything from her and never regret the cost.

Even at William's expense.

But look at her sitting there so calm and cool across from him. He couldn't believe her damning sangfroid. Only a woman of the world operated like that, as if nothing had any meaning to her, not a death, not a life, not a lover. As if she were in control, which infuriated Alex all over again.

Samara Teva was in control of nothing, and she acted as if she was the mistress of Meresham Close, and as if his wealth and his titles were meaningless.

She could have had kings. . . . She'd settled for William.

Why?

That was the riddle of Samara Teva, and not least what Alex wanted to know about her. He wanted to know everything: He wanted *her,* to imprint himself on that sinuous, fastidious body so that she would never forget who possessed her, who *owned* her—

The savagery of his desire shocked him. He was thinking of her as if she were about to become his lover. His—no. *No.* There was nothing that seductive about Samara Teva. And all her radiance and desirability dimmed when he remembered her history, her salacious life.

And yet William had taken her, forgiven her, and made her his wife.

And he could see why: William had been as ensnared by the same paradoxes within her as he. William had probably thought he could save her. But he hadn't had the resources or the stamina to do it. And besides, you couldn't save a woman like Samara Teva; at best, you could bring her to heel for as long as you could satisfy her in bed.

If she could be satisfied.

If . . .

He could, by damn. And he would. He would pound her gyrating hips into the bed for as many hours as it took to make her scream for mercy.

He was the only one who could. He'd make her crawl. He'd make her beg. Samara Teva naked on her back, writhing, yearning, pleading for the one man who could ride her to oblivion.

That was what Samara Teva was all about. That one naked blast of pleasure with any man who could give it to her.

Him.

Soon.

Sooner.

"Still here?" Marcus's cool inquiry rocketed into Alex's reverie.

"Haven't moved an inch," Alex said lazily. "So you have that longed-for moment to get to know your new sister-in-law. Have a seat." That was good. The more Marcus talked to her, the more he could let his imagination roam. He was hot enough already, thinking about her naked in his bed.

And he was hard as a poker, and if Marcus hadn't come, he might be poking her now right in front of the fireplace. He couldn't believe how insanely he wanted her. Elusive bitch. That was the key to it, and she knew it and he knew it.

And Marcus sat there like a goggling fish and just let her reel him in.

"You mustn't mind Alex," Marcus was saying. "He's been king of the hill for so long, and William's death did hit him hard."

"Oh really?" Francesca slanted a considering look at Alex. "And why is that?"

"Because—as I told him, off and on—he should have done more."

Francesca smiled beatifically at Marcus, and Alex wanted to throttle them both. "You're exactly right," she murmured. "He should have done more."

"He will have to live with his conscience. But he can take some consolation in the fact he did go after you."

"Very consoling to both of us, I'm sure. But it strikes me that—Alex—never does anything without a reason."

"You are a very perceptive woman, Samara—may I call you that?"

"Certainly." Francesca smiled at him and leaned forward

to touch his hand. Alex gritted his teeth and clamped down on his urge to throw his brother out of the room.

"Very perceptive, and on such short notice."

"But we've been having some very intense conversation," Francesca said. "You can get to know somebody pretty well in a short time, don't you think, Marcus? I mean, if you're talking about meaningful things instead of just making social chitchat."

"You're exactly right." Marcus was falling like a star, burning already for what was utterly out of his orbit.

"And we talked a lot on the journey here," Francesca added musingly. "It was very—meaningful."

"Yes, indeed. Well, I hope we'll have time to get to know each other just as—meaningfully," Marcus said hastily. "In spite of Mother's somewhat understandable opposition, you are William's wife, and you are welcome at Meresham."

"Oh, yes—" Alex interpolated, "do tell us the disposition of Mother's *somewhat* negative outburst, Marcus."

"She can be made to see reason."

"She's capable of committing mayhem too," Alex said trenchantly. "You'd better keep your eye on her, Marcus. William's wife is my business only, not yours, not Mother's, and she'd better stay out of my way."

"Ungrateful beast," Marcus muttered.

"I am. As are you, my dear curate. Please try to remember whether your toast is butter side up or down, and that Mother's jelly-sweet wishes dissolve very quickly in the mouth."

"Fine," Marcus said stiffly. "We all owe our lives and livings to you. No wonder William left when he became of age. But"—he turned to Francesca—"did you know, there was money in trust for him—to be paid when he reached age thirty?"

Francesca's heart fell to her toes. "No," she said slowly because she knew Alex did not believe her and she felt that Marcus would. "No, I didn't."

"Ha," Alex rumbled.

"And on his death, half of his estate in trust goes to his heirs . . . ?"

Oh, my God . . . She closed her eyes. "I didn't know."

"Liar." Alex again, railing against her, against Samara.

But Samara could have known, Francesca thought with foreboding. She might very well have known. And she couldn't have known she would contract that disease and die.

But she might have known someone who would commit murder—

NO!! No . . . no . . . it was unthinkable.

Irresistible. She had sent for Mere after William's death . . . before the onset of her illness . . .

. . . no—

—no . . .

She wouldn't even think it. It just wasn't possible.

"Don't you want to know how much money?" Alex asked softly, insidiously.

"No." She said it succinctly, sharply, quickly.

"She's *such* a wonderful actress," Alex said to his brother. "Look at her. You'd *almost* believe all that sincerity—if you didn't know her history."

"People change," Marcus said a little sententiously. He believed her. He did.

"It's a lot of money," Alex said coaxingly.

. . . enough for someone to want William dead . . .

She felt sick. For once, she had no words for him, and nothing to combat the queasy feeling in her stomach.

A lot of money.

She thought a hundred pounds was a lot of money.

How could she even claim something that didn't belong to her?

He'd hand her over to the authorities first—she could see it in his eyes. He was waiting, like a tiger, for her to make one mistake.

"I didn't know," she said again.

"Stop badgering her, for God's sake," Marcus said. "She

didn't know. I believe her. William walked around looking like a ragbag's son. How could she have known?''

"Bed blow," Alex murmured silkily. "Samara must be very good at bed blow, don't you think? Wouldn't you love to listen to that honey voice in bed, Marcus?"

Marcus stared at him as if he'd lost his mind. "Really, Alex. You go too far, as usual. Damned tyrant. He does that just to shock us, Samara. If you understand that much, you can handle him. Listen, old Ackerly will be here at three to read off on it, and that will be the end: You'll know everything then, Samara. So don't let Alex make a mockery of it as he does everything else. Now, you must excuse me. But you must feel free to call me if Alex becomes too obnoxious. Or just come down to the vicarage to Phillippa and me.''

"I bet you'll dream of that: a threesome," Alex said nastily.

"As opposed to being lonesome—in *your* bed?" Marcus shot back. "Really, you are perverted, Alex. As if yours was the only bangstick in the world." He bent over Francesca's hand. "Till later, my dear."

The silence that followed was deadly.

" 'Till later, my dear,' " Alex mimicked snidely. She had charmed the damned cassock off of his unworldly brother and he didn't like it one bit.

Marcus didn't see her as needing redemption anymore. Or as the personification of sin.

No, Marcus saw her the same damned way as every other man: as a vessel for his bullshot as many times as he could get it up to do it for as long and hard as she could take it lying down.

And she was so experienced, she could milk a man for hours and still hang him out to dry before she gave anything for his corner.

But Marcus wouldn't see that. Marcus saw the siren eyes, heard the smoky voice, peripherally noted the smooth swath of black silk over her lush bosom, forgot he was married for

better or worse to that virago, Phillippa, and let himself dream
of a temptress who was far beyond his knowledge of women.

And that was the effect she had on everyone, and Alex swore,
as he watched her calmly watch Marcus exit the room with
that dark fathomless gaze of hers, that he would lock her in a
dungeon and have her all to himself, if that was what it would
take to wring out all her secrets—and he would have her treacherous body as well.

Sir Edmund Ackerly, Bart., barrister to the Deveneys for as
long as Alex could remember, arrived promptly at three o'clock.

"This is just a formality," he said, shuffling papers on the
desk in the library. "I'll want Lady Judithe to be present, since
all of William's financials devolve from her side of the family."
He looked up then, as she drifted into the room on Marcus's
arm, looking pale, angry, resentful. "My dear Judithe, I know
how painful this is going to be. It won't take but ten minutes.
I assume this is William's wife."

"That is what it presumes to call itself," Judithe said flatly,
seating herself the farthest away she could from Francesca,
arranging her chair so that Francesca was not even in her line
of sight. "Must we do this, Edmund? I'm willing to give it the
money, if only it would leave."

"We must observe the letter of the law, my dear." Ackerly
picked up a thin sheet and read William's last testament that
indeed specified that any heirs would be entitled to inherit half
of the estate extant at the time of his death, whether or not
he'd reached his thirtieth year. "The key of course is the word
extant, and the provision was set forth to protect a wife, and—
or—a child, should there have been one. However, Lady Judithe
had control of the monies during William's lifetime, and I'm
sorry to say, there is very little left in the trust for his lady
wife."

"*What?*" This from Marcus, whom it concerned not at all.
"How is this possible? Mother . . . ?"

"I gave it to him," Judithe said stonily. "Whatever he needed, whenever he wanted some money, I gave it to him. When he left for Germany. And after. The boy had to live, didn't he? I couldn't let him starve. Or see him in the hands of some ten-percenter."

Sir Edmund cleared his throat. "Exactly. The sum that remains comes to less than a hundred pounds."

"And," Judithe added imperiously, "I will increase that amount to the full inheritance if the creature will sign papers relinquishing any claim on my family, and if it promises to leave England."

Samara could not have known any of this, Francesca thought. None of it. They'd lived poor as church mice. What had William done with the money?

She felt dizzy with all these revelations. And certain as well that Mere would gainsay any plans Judithe had for getting rid of her.

"I have the cheque here," Sir Edmund said, "if Lady William would be so kind as to provide me with proof of the marriage."

They were among the belongings that Francesca had yet to unpack. If Mere allowed her to go upstairs alone, she would have a good fifteen minutes to pack and flee the house. "I have the papers," Francesca said, keeping her tone carefully neutral.

"If you would, my lady . . ."

"*We* will," Alex said. "I'm not letting her out of my sight."

Of course. Francesca rose stiffly to her feet. "I'll be but a few moments, Sir Edmund."

And as they climbed the stairs and she entertained thoughts of pushing Alex to a horrible, painful death, Francesca said, "This is humiliating."

Alex didn't think so. "You'll survive."

Samara had kept the papers in a green oilskin wallet. After they returned to the others, Sir Edmund opened the wallet, his expression mirroring a faint distaste for the cheap material; then he scanned the papers quickly with an expert eye. "Everything seems to be in order, Judithe. Any other arrangements you wish to make, you must do on your own.''

''The creature won't listen. Alex won't listen.''

''My dear—'' Sir Edmund said to Francesca. ''I don't presume to interfere in my clients' business, but perhaps it would be in your best interest to allow Lady Judithe to provide the wherewithal for you to live comfortably elsewhere. I hope you'll consider it.'' He handed her the checque.

Francesca took it, feeling like the fraud she was. And she liked Sir Edmund, who treated the woman he thought was Samara like a lady. ''I'll consider it,'' she whispered.

And why not? As Phillippa said, it would be a handsome sum, on which she could live a comfortable life for a long time. A hundred seventy-five pounds would never last *that* long.

''Greedy little baggage,'' Alex murmured in her ear. ''But no more than my feckless brother. Where *did* all that money disappear to, Samara? How much of it is on your body and in your belly?''

''Is that why you took so long to come when I begged you?'' she retorted, stung. Nothing about the way William and Samara lived in Berlin spoke of their having any resources at all. But now it was very clear why Judithe had been so anxious to pay her off. ''You didn't believe me that we were in need? How much money could it have been that William went through so fast? There wasn't a pfennig for me to pay a doctor's bill in Berlin. I saw none of that money—none.''

Alex sent her a skeptical look. ''Ah, you plead your case so fervently, Samara. But you know that doesn't work with me. I will find out the truth, you know. And it's yet another reason why you'll be going nowhere anytime soon.''

And now it was imperative that she get away from Meresham Close, from the enmity of Judithe, and the magnetism of Alex Deveney, and the mysteries surrounding Samara Teva.

She couldn't do it anymore; she couldn't pretend. For all

she knew, Samara had been a murderer, had plotted William's death to claim his heir's share of his trust fund, and had stolen all the money Judithe had given to him.

How could she know? And how could her nerves stand another minute of Alex Deveney's fierce scrutiny?

"You'll stay for an early dinner," Marcus was saying to Sir Edmund. "It's already arranged. Ah, here comes Wotten, his timing excellent as usual." He took Sir Edmund's arm. "Join us."

Alex gestured mockingly to Francesca to precede him, and she reluctantly followed Marcus and Judithe, wondering whether it would be more difficult to sit through this interminable dinner with Judithe's virulent presence across the table, or to be alone with Mere and the sole focus of his ferocious anger and suspicion.

But that would come later, no matter how she tried to circumvent it. For now, she must deal with the possibilities of Samara's treachery that had nothing to do with whatever reason Mere had come for her.

She had absolutely no appetite for the lavish meal that awaited them. Nor did Judithe, it was obvious. She pushed her food around her plate, shooting venomous looks at Francesca, then turning her head to speak to Sir Edmund.

Francesca sampled portions of the white soup *à la reine,* the partridge pie, the fricassee of duck. There was spinach in a crust, stewed onions, stuffed cucumbers, rice fritters. For the second course, biscuits, smoked tongue, apple pudding, blancmange and coffee cream. For dessert, fresh fruit, macaroons, a plain cake, and a cranberry tart. To finish, tea, wine, coffee.

Alex ate like a hussar. Judithe glared at him. Marcus and Sir Edmund made conversation, trying valiantly, each of them, to keep from touching on Samara's diminished legacy and sidestepping Judithe's hostility.

Judithe finally slammed down her spoon and rose from her chair. "If you gentlemen will excuse me . . ."

Marcus put out a detaining hand. "Mother—"

"I have a headache," she said stiffly. "I need to rest."

"I'll escort you."

"No need, Marcus."

"I'll take you," he said firmly, rising from his place and making his excuses as well.

Alex watched them both with a cynical look in his eye, not moving, not saying a word, sipping his wine, covertly and intensely aware of Samara across the table from him.

She was good, he thought maliciously. She was very, very good. Not by a word or a gesture or by anything in her expression did she betray any disappointment at Sir Edmund's news.

But of course, she had so many irons in the fire; she probably wouldn't even count the loss of five hundred or so pounds as worth the effort. On the other hand, he wondered what she had expected, if indeed her sole intention in sending for him had been to come back with him to collect that money.

You couldn't believe a word that cozening bitch uttered. It was perfectly plain to him: the whole damned thing was about money, had always been about money, no matter how she got it or what she had to do for it.

Why else would she have gotten involved with Colm? Why else had she danced for _him_? She was probably feeling desperate now: He had blocked her at every turn, and she hadn't expected it. No money from Colm. No money from William's estate. No way to get away from him to work her voluptuous wiles on other susceptible men . . .

He had her just where he needed her: all his, for however long he wanted her, for however long it took to force her hand, her body, and her cover.

Francesca dreaded going back up those stairs with Alex. Judithe was long gone by then, Sir Edmund had made his graceful exit after dinner, Marcus had disappeared to the rectory, and it was she and Alex Deveney, the wine, and the strained silence.

It wasn't as if she could bolt either, because there were three dozen servants wherever she looked, and then there was that *try it* look in his eyes that stopped her dead.

What was he thinking?

What was she thinking? That Samara was a conniving mercenary who had married William for the putative inheritance; he must have told her that if anything happened to him to contact his brother, that she would be taken care of, that everything would be all right—

But none of that squared with her reputation, her career, or her connection to Colm, whatever it was. Or the fact that up until William's death, she had been performing at private parties.

For money. That was the only conclusion. Until the disease felled her and she wasted away.

What was the truth about Samara and what was the lie?

Had she expected that inheritance, and would she have committed murder to get it?

Had William refused to apply to his family for funds because all the while he'd had access to the money he'd sworn he'd never touch, and he hadn't wanted Samara to know?

But why?

Had Samara known she was ill before William's death, and was that why she had planned to eliminate that which stood between her and the security and comfort that William had denied her?

All these questions. And all that laid over with what Alex Deveney knew about Samara that she did not.

That was why Alex looked at her like that. That was what he was thinking about: Samara, the temple dancer. Samara and her men. Samara and his brother. Samara and Colm.

Colm.

Her heart started pounding. She closed her eyes, picturing him.

All this for Colm.

She had to find out about Colm. At the very least. God, if she didn't, all of this would have been so futile.

She knew, she absolutely knew, that the only thing she had to combat Alex and his family was her silence, and she understood that Alex read it as something entirely different. Guilt, perhaps, or a tacit admission of all her sins, because Alex Deveney surely believed her to be the sexual siren that Samara was.

On the other hand, she had never considered the ramifications of impersonating a woman with Samara's reputation. There was only so long she could keep Alex at bay, especially now that he'd given her an inkling of his intentions.

. . . in his bed . . .

All the more reason not to be alone anywhere with him— and no earthly way to keep him away from her. As close as Siamese twins, he'd said, and if he could conquer his fierce animosity toward her, toward *Samara*, she would have nowhere to hide from him.

She was at a turning point, Francesca realized. If she were smart, if she were cagey, she would cut her losses and escape. The sooner she got away from these embittered people, the better. She didn't need them taking out their hostility toward Samara on *her*.

She'd already had a taste of that, and enough of it too.

The truth was, she didn't *need* to know what Colm's connection to Samara was; she *wanted* to know—she wanted to protect him and keep him safe the way he had protected her all the years they'd been with Aunt Ida.

But she felt helpless against the rushing tide that was Alex Deveney. She couldn't fight him, except with silence, and she thought how ironic it was that the thing that she had despised the most in her abortive years with Aunt Ida was the very thing that could give her strength and power now.

Silence it would be, then. And not what Alex was expecting of Samara, now that they were finally alone, Francesca thought.

Of course, she was cornered again. If she railed against

William's betrayal, he wouldn't believe her. And if she maintained her silence, it would lend credence to his certainty that she'd known William had access to the money and that she'd probably been the reason he'd wanted it.

Not possible. They'd lived like church mice, he and Samara, and even Alex had indicated that Samara had been their sole support by virtue of her *talent*. And Alex had cut William off altogether.

Where was the money?

No. That was the trap that she had fallen into to begin with: wanting to know what and why about Colm.

It was none of her business anymore. Let Alex solve the mysteries. Let him drown in the inconsistencies.

She'd had enough. She had a hundred pounds, which would fund whatever she needed to do from this point forward. All she had to do was get away from Meresham Close alive.

Alex rose from his chair, having spent a half hour scrutinizing Samara's composed expression and the calm way she ate her food, in small bites, concentrating intensively and ignoring him without a qualm.

And when his mother, Marcus, and Sir Edmund left, she continued her silent contemplation of the food, of the room, of whatever went on in that callous, mercenary head of hers.

He had expected a tantrum, not stolid acceptance of Judithe's perfidy. If he had had control of William's money, it would still be in the Bank and no skillful sexual predator would have seen a farthing of it.

Spilt wine. No going back now. He didn't even know how to proceed forward with the enigma that was Samara Teva.

But he needed her seductive skills. He needed what Colm had given to her. And he *wanted* something else he didn't care to define.

He rose from his chair. "It's time, Samara."

She jerked her gaze up to him. "Time for what, my lord?"

"Time for an accounting, a reckoning, an explanation. The truth."

"Your truth." She scrambled to her feet so that he wouldn't loom over her like that.

"I'm dying to hear yours."

"I have nothing more to say."

"Tell me another story." He grasped her wrist. "A bedtime story."

"I'm not tired." She was exhausted.

"I'll tell you one." He pulled, catching her off balance so that she was forced to follow him.

"I've heard enough fairy tales from you to last a lifetime."

"As if you haven't lived a life of fantasy, my lady." They were at the staircase, and he pushed her ruthlessly ahead of him. "As if you didn't deliberately set out to become the stuff of a man's fantasies. Now *move*—"

She moved, scurrying up the stairs barely a step ahead of him, and so aware of him behind her with his radiant hostility enveloping her as tightly as a noose.

He caught her and thrust her into the room and onto the bed. She fell flat on her belly, and she scuttled into a sitting position so that he wouldn't have the advantage of her.

He knew, the moment he looked at her with her tousled hair and her priggishly prim mourning, that he could drown in that face, in that body, and that if he didn't exercise restraint he would lose his soul.

He felt no different from any other man she had ever known. He cursed them all—that litany of men who had known that body, who had felt her caresses—and he knew that he was no better than any of them, that he was just as debauched, just as seduced by his own lust for something so readily available. And just as willing to condone her past to get what he wanted.

He, who had always had such contempt for the weaknesses of men.

"Bedtime stories," he said, his voice rough, contravening his hot desire to just throw himself on her. He began pacing to contain all that raw roiling energy. "I have such a fairy story for you, Samara Teva. How shall I begin? Once upon a time— but it wasn't that long ago, really—in a country not your own, there was an Emperor who was very, very old and a grandson who was . . . fairly young, who was also very forward thinking about the consequences of his own father's mortality and the chances of his succession to the throne. He had plans, this young Emperor-to-be, and to the dismay of his English mother, he mapped everything out in writing while waiting for history to take its course.

"And there came a moment in time when his grandfather died, and his father ascended the throne and shortly thereafter was diagnosed with throat cancer. The doctors couldn't save him, and when he was gone, and his son succeeded him, the Kaiserin put all the deceased Kaiser's private papers in a black tin box, which was to be sent to England in the care of the Queen.

"And lo and behold, the black box disappeared at approximately the same time an exotic dancer of ill repute appeared as the wife of the youngest brother of a peer of the realm, living in this country not her own.

"Now you might think that the connection between a nautch dancer and a King is very, very tenuous. But consider the career of this dancer who claimed to interpret holy temple dances of her native country.

"She had performed all over the world. She numbered among her friends and paramours the most powerful men in the world. She was a favored guest in castles and country houses.

"She was avid for money, knowing that her allure, her body, her mystery could only enchant a man for just so long.

"What would happen when the applause ended? Where would she go when her body could no longer seduce an audience—or a man? How would she live if there were no longer any generous gifts, jewels, offers of support and elegant and expensive apartments?

"What then would a woman who had always survived by her wits and with her body do?"

Alex wheeled around and pointed at Francesca, who was shivering on the bed. "What would you have done, Samara?"

Too close to the bone, she thought, holding herself tightly against the headboard for support.

Step out of the spotlight, Samara had said, while they still remember your name. . . .

What a thing to come back to haunt her. Truly, Samara would never be forgotten, not if Alex Deveney had his way.

But she, Francesca, was on the verge of learning some of the answers she sought.

Silence . . . silence was the only answer to any question Alex posed to her. And silent she was, which just made him simmer with frustration that none of what he said dented her composure, that she was not going to admit anything, especially to him.

He purposely let the silence lengthen and lengthen, and he watched her try to see the faintest nuance of recognition in her expression.

She was, he thought, so well schooled in every area of her life. She acted as if nothing about this story was familiar to her.

How soulless could she be?

A woman like that, who had sold everything she could get her hands on? She had no soul. She had no conscience. None. She was the kind of woman to whom you had to take the screws. Silence and sex were her weapons and she knew there were very few men who could resist her.

Even Alex, hardened as he was, found that combination hard to withstand. And she was experienced enough to push it to the limit, until *he* couldn't stand it any longer.

Bitch. He knew so much about her, and so little, but now he *wanted* to make her crack. And he would.

He resumed his pacing. "Always bearing in mind that this is a fairy tale, my dear Samara. This is what our notorious nautch dancer did: She began trading information for money.

Information she obtained from lovers, from admirers, from casual conversation and from the courts and courtiers she charmed in the places she performed.

"And as fast as she obtained the money, she spent it, living high and lying low as her sources caught on and turned their backs on her.

"But there was only suspicion; nothing could be proved. Nevertheless, her Intercessor was getting worried that her usefulness, at least in Europe, was coming to an end, and he needed her still for one last undertaking."

Oh God. Alex stopped short as a thought occurred to him, and he looked at Samara, at her beauty, at her lovely lying lips. At why, of course, William had married her.

Yes, that was why and he would bet his fortune his surmise was bang on. He couldn't wait to see her face when he elaborated on it.

But would she admit it? The bitch would die first, he thought, as he collected his thoughts and reiterated, "One last undertaking. She was to be the courier who delivered to an unknown contact in England some important papers contained in a certain black box that her Intercessor was to expropriate from an undisclosed place. And in order to do that, and to divert suspicion from herself and her commission, she was ordered to seduce and marry my brother William.

"You can almost guess what happened then. There was his money, which she stole. There was more, if he died. And there was myself, always available to bring a body and a destitute widow back to England in the name of family.

"What an insanely clever plan, Samara. How skillfully you pulled it off. If I had to guess, I would think that William never even knew Judithe was sending that money to him, and that you were the one who appealed to what there is of her motherly instinct.

"Am I there, Samara? Do I have the whole of it? Do we now know who Samara Teva is, and why she married my brother, and perhaps even why he was murdered?

"However, the only thing I *need* to know, my dear Samara, is where the papers you were given by your Intercessor are, and to whom they are to be delivered.

"And that is the reality that intrudes into this fantastical bedtime tale of mystery and intrigue. Because if you do not turn those papers over to me, Samara, you will be arrested and tried as an agent of a foreign country, and I won't lift a finger to help you."

Chapter Seven

Francesca's throat closed up. She couldn't bring herself to speak, she was so shaken. Everything could have happened exactly the way he described it; the whole thing was too gothic for words, invented and demented, and yet it made an awful kind of sense.

Even Samara's stealing William's money. She could have been hiding it away, waiting for the right moment, waiting for the signal to put the next stage of her plan into motion. The one thing she couldn't have planned was falling ill. And if indeed there had been any money, she surely would have used it all up in the treatment of the initial stages of her disease, because she had nothing left when Francesca had begun to care for her.

And maybe she'd never had anything at all.

Or the whole story was just a fairy tale, as Alex claimed.

No, the threat was real. Samara had received those papers from some source—Colm? Alex was too certain of that, and it was the thing that precipitated this fool's errand in the first place; it was the one thing *she* believed: that Alex Deveney had made a mistake, and whoever had given Samara these abortive papers had not been Colm.

. . . promise me—the persona of Samara Teva will never die. . . .

. . . take—me—to . . . the Abtissen *. . .*

Tell him the truth NOW—

Dear God, I can't . . .

"The Intercessor . . ." she said, her voice rusty with trepidation.

"A man named Heinreichs. In England, he is known as Colm."

"No—!" Her denial was involuntary and swift.

"So sure, Samara? I wonder why." His voice was silky, the tiger tempering his reaction to the scent. "*Where* are those papers?"

She gathered up every ounce of strength to ask, "How do you know him?"

"I wager you could guess."

She was hoping not. She was praying Colm wasn't involved in anything that had to do with secrets and spies. But of course that wasn't possible. He was as deep in this morass as Samara had been.

"Not in . . . Berlin?"

"That catch in your voice is perfect, Samara. I love the way you still pretend all of this is news to you." He was right on top of her now, looming over her as she cowered—yes, cowered—against the headboard. "You have nowhere to hide. Where are the papers?"

Now she was truly at the end of her rope, and she had no more tricks to pull out. She could just conjure up the truth or continue on with the lie.

There was no other way out, she thought desperately, and she might just as well keep up the masquerade as reveal her identity. But either way she was doomed because all she could do was pile more lies on top of the previous lies, and she'd never be able to untangle them.

And Alex would never believe her anyway.

How good an actress was she? She ordered her thoughts, focusing on what points she could lift from the story he'd told her that she could use to her advantage.

Not much. All of it was too damning to Samara. And all of it fell apart if—*if*—yes ... a thought occurred to her: She might be able to convince him of that, if she confessed to the rest, but even then, it was all a long shot.

She had to try.

"I don't have the papers."

"They trained you well," Alex observed, watching her as if he had her under a microscope. "But you'll break under official interrogation. They all do."

If he'd thought to scare her with that, he did. She couldn't think of two more terrifying words than *official interrogation.*

She had to distract him *now.* "Colm never came. He *never* came. He still has the papers." She sounded desperate; it sounded like the lie it was. Alex plainly didn't believe her, and she cast about frantically for something he would believe.

Last gasp. Last straw. Last lies. "You were right about the money. I took it. All of it. William never knew. I tried and tried to get him to agree to return home. I knew Colm was coming and I would have to transport whatever he gave me.

"But William wouldn't. He just refused to consider coming back here." *Omigod, now what?* she wondered agitatedly. Alex would never accept her confession that Samara had killed William. It had to be someone else.

"I sent word to Colm, because everything depended on William's agreeing to return to England. And then, before I knew it, William was dead."

That was good. Lay it at the door of the mysterious Colm— the Colm who was NOT her Colm.

"I didn't know what to do. I was already in the initial stages of the illness. I had no friends, no one to depend on. I certainly didn't want to tell Colm. He would have rescinded the commission—and I needed the money . . . for all the reasons you said, and more.

"Fortunately, one of the women in the rooming house took pity on me, and it was she who helped me recover William's body, and she looked after me until I got better. But by then, all the money was gone on doctors and medicine. I had nothing left, and there was no word from Colm. And, I'd been delirious during the illness. If Colm *had* come, I'm not sure I would have known it. But he never would have left anything with anyone else but me. Before I had time to send word to him again, you dragooned me into returning to England with you. So I don't know where those papers are. For all you or I know, someone else has them, someone else delivered them."

She stopped abruptly, out of breath and out of inspiration, and watched him pace the floor.

Bad . . . bad . . . there was nothing she could say to convince him; and reweaving his accounting into this tissue of half-truths only gave him more motive to shred Samara's story to pieces.

She couldn't rehabilitate Samara. It was stupid to try. Insane to keep up the pretense when things could only get worse. The only thing she could really do was save herself; and now that was impossible as well.

Alex wheeled and slammed his palm flat against the desk by the window. "I'm awed, Samara. I'm impressed. And I'm out of patience with your lies and your evasions." And he was; the lies poured from her mouth so easily and swirled and grazed around the truth like the moves of one of her dances.

Samara Teva, scared for her life, and still seductive even when she was rattled by threats and fear.

The question was what to do with her. If he turned her in, he'd lose what little ground he'd gained. And if he didn't, he'd lose everything else.

A Solomonic choice for an unquantifiable gain. But that was ever the way when you were working covertly. You took chances; you made decisions based on hunches, feelings, possibilities.

And on the truth in the lie. On a pair of cool black eyes. A glimpse of bare flesh.

Damn damn damn damn . . .

"I swear . . ." she started.

"Don't," he growled, thinking furiously. Whether he liked it or not, he needed her, and all his futile threats about trying her as an enemy of the people had as much substance as air. And if he browbeat her much more, she would know it.

She had never performed in England, he thought, assessing every angle. And she had a certain notoriety, even in England; perhaps her performances had been seen in Europe, and that would engender a lot of curiosity about her. That was good too. That would enable him to insinuate her into places he would not normally be invited.

This was no small consideration, given what he sought. The mysterious papers were the least of it. He needed that kind of free access, along with something to distract his targets, and smoke and magic besides.

She was it. She—with her lush body, cool gaze, and exotic dances—was the key to everything. It was stunning how neatly the plot fit together, once he considered every aspect. It would take time to arrange things, though, and he wasn't sure they had that much time.

And he needed her acquiescence, and her loyalty. And he wasn't sure that was something that could be bought. No, check that. Samara Teva could be bought. He'd paid her a hundred pounds for a dance.

He wondered what her price would be to topple an empire.

Francesca felt a lessening of tension in the room, as if Alex had decided to back off, as if he were giving her some leeway in some part of his mind. But there was no kindness in him.

He had no feeling for Samara Teva, other than how he might use her.

And she should not take hope from this conciliating silence. Alex was a bulldog; this was something he wouldn't let go. *Samara* was something he wouldn't let go. And he obviously had something in mind for her, something that changed his perspective, suddenly and completely.

But still, he had to wield his power over her, with that looming, menacing silence that was fraught with the unspoken litany of all of Samara's sins.

"So Colm never came. He arranged to get rid of my brother. There were no papers. You stole the money. And somehow you still managed to get back to England as was your original mandate. You are so very clever, Samara. Know this: I dearly want to throw you into detention, at the mercy of a jury who would wrest out your secrets. And I could still do that—toss you into prison, and let things take their course. Or . . . you could do something for me."

He waited; Francesca stiffened. He wanted her to ask, and she didn't want to. She didn't want to know.

. . . prison . . .

Maybe she did—

She found her voice. "And what is that, my lord? What could I possibly do for *you?*"

Once again, he was suffused with that frustrating rage. She was so self-possessed, so collected—but what did he expect? Samara Teva was obviously very used to bargaining—for everything. Her life would be no exception.

"You can dance," he said flatly.

It was the last thing she expected him to say.

"Dance . . . ?" she echoed faintly.

"Perform," he amplified. "Like you used to, for private parties, when and where I make the arrangements."

Dance? Like Samara? In those lewd costumes, half naked, in front of an audience*???? He must be deranged.*

And yet—and yet—it was a reprieve.

Dear God, she couldn't believe it. After scaring her half to death, he had actually offered her a reprieve.

A choice. A Samara choice, that, if she were Samara, she would leap on like a gazelle. And it would be horribly out of character if she didn't.

"You're crazy," she said, for want of making some response.

He shrugged. "Your choice. You can molder away in prison or you can dance. For myself, I'll get what I want eventually, with you or without you." He narrowed his gaze, pinning her dark unfathomable eyes, trying to read something, anything, in their depths. But there was nothing. They were the eyes of a gambler, assessing everything, revealing nothing.

"Maybe the question is, why do you need Samara Teva?" Francesca said slowly, carefully, feeling her way. There was something more here. Something Samara could provide that Alex Deveney needed, something that gave her some leverage.

What?

"I don't," he said heartlessly. "I need an alternate way to attack a problem. And it doesn't *have* to be you."

Now he was bluffing, she was sure of it. So the question was, as it always had been, how far was she willing to go in her impersonation of Samara Teva? She had already sold herself to Alex Deveney by dancing for him *and* accepting money for it. How far removed from that was what he wanted from her?

What did he really want from her?

Would he pay for it?

Her knees went weak. Samara Teva would have demanded her pound of flesh by now. Could Francesca Reay demand less? Did she have the nerve? Was she really considering his proposition?

Yes, yes, yes . . . until she could finally get away from Mere, yes.

"How *much* do you need Samara Teva?" she asked, keeping her tone neutral and her expression noncommittal, in spite of her wildly pounding heart and her trembling lips.

"I thought we'd get to that," Alex said complacently.

"Did you?" Francesca murmured, hating his tone, hating him. For Samara. Really. Not for herself. "And what exactly are we getting to, my lord?"

"You're much more subtle than I ever thought you would be, Samara. A hundred pounds a performance is what we are getting to. No more, no less. No bargaining. It's an extremely generous offer in light of the alternative."

Her throat went dry. Even if he were only talking one performance, it was a lot of money for someone like Samara. And if it were more, she could walk away with more than the sum of Samara's worthless inheritance and have earned every penny of it to boot.

And it would forestall prison and penury indefinitely.

If she got out of it alive.

An infinitely more alluring proposition.

If she could bring herself to prance around naked in front of strangers.

Samara could.

Samara *would*.

Francesca pulled in her roiling stomach and thought about the consequences. But she'd never had a choice, she realized. Alex wanted her to do it, and he'd put her squarely in a place where she'd have no choice but to do it.

The most she could hope for was to make him feel as if she thought she did have a choice. And perhaps, *she* had to feel that as well to justify going against everything she'd been taught and believed.

This was a huge step, becoming Samara Teva in fact as well as fiction. She was scared to death but she couldn't let it show.

"It will be my pleasure," she said coolly, because that was the only way she could operate from now on. Removed. Calm. In control.

If only he knew . . .

Alex's lips tightened, and for one moment, he looked as if he were intensely displeased. "My dear Samara, I never had any doubt."

* * *

So it was done. Alex had bought Samara Teva, and he had bought some time. But eventually, he would have to go after Colm. After he destroyed the corrupting evil that had been perpetrated. After he had taken care of Samara Teva. She of all of them was disposable, had always been, from the moment she'd married William.

Who would have thought that she would become the instrument of retaliation? And that, all because of his rebellious brother, at the mercy of forces of which he was totally unaware. One of a row of dominoes to be mowed down by the flick of someone else's finger, someone else's whim.

"I don't trust you," he had told Samara as he left her. "You'll be locked in my room when I leave you. You'll share my bed when you sleep. You go everywhere with me. You do nothing without me. I *own* you, Samara, and I can do with you whatever I wish."

"Not quite *everything* you wish, my lord," she had said insolently.

But that would come, he thought venomously. He knew it as surely as he had pinpointed what it would take to buy her. And he wasn't sure he wanted it to come, because she was the kind of woman who could enslave a man, and he was a man that needed above all things to maintain control.

Still, the thought of bedding her was irresistible, and fraught with images of the forbidden. A woman like that . . . He'd never stop thinking of her that way. Impure. Corrupted. Available.

For a price. Always for a price.

A man wasn't safe around her, knowing she could be tempted to spread her legs for a sovereign, hell, for a pound. The scent of it permeated the air around her like perfume.

It tantalized him now, and she wasn't even in the room.

Let her sleep. He'd had enough of her dispassionate acceptance of every demand he'd thrown at her today.

That kind of woman . . . she was accustomed to the whims

of men, trained to please and pleasure. Of course, she was
compliant. That was her stock in trade.

God, he had to stop thinking about her.

Alex stared at the blank page in front of him. He had much
to report and a foreboding feeling that he ought not put anything
in writing.

"Will she take the money?"

Marcus. Damn.

"She's not leaving yet," Alex answered.

"Are you crazy?" Marcus stalked into the room and came
around to plant his hands on the desk and lean into him.

"What happened to that holier-than-thou speech about William's wife being welcome here?" Alex set aside his pen,
and contemplated Marcus's angry stance. "And how does that
square with Mother supporting William after he went to Germany?"

"She'd pretty well drained the account by the time he married—that woman," Marcus said reluctantly. "Although it's
not clear how long it took him to tell her about it. Yes, we
went through all the gory details. If William had lived, she
would have replenished the account—she says. She did it for
the heir—not a wife, but the presumptive heir, if he'd ever had
one. Perhaps she wanted to give him some incentive. She is
distraught, Alex. You have to get that woman away from here."

"Not yet."

"Why?"

"My business."

"That's too damned cryptic for the kind of upset Mother is
enduring."

"What about you, O man of the cloth?"

Marcus straightened up. "What business, Alex?"

"None of yours, brother mine."

"You are up to something and into something, Alex. And
that doxy is part of it, isn't she?"

Alex considered Marcus for a long, long moment. Like it or
not, he had to make his family a part of his plan for Samara.

He needed Meresham as his base, and he needed a place to keep *her* where he could be sure she would be contained, because there was no telling what she would do if she weren't.

"Put it this way, Marcus. Samara Teva's career as a dancer is not yet over. She needs to appease the gods over the death of her husband."

Marcus blanched. "For God's sake, Alex."

"Believe me, Marcus. Everyone will clamor to see her performance. Mother's friends will line up outside the doors of Meresham demanding she come to them first. I will make her into a social coup, a celebrity, a legend."

"Damn it, that's nonsense, Alex. You have better things to do with your time. Why upset Mother and drag the family name in the mud? Why not just pay her off and send her away? This is crazy, Alex. *Why?* Just tell me *why.*"

Alex sent him a mocking smile, which he knew would exasperate Marcus beyond all measure and ensure he would stamp out and leave unasked all the questions he had.

"Because, dear brother, I can."

Now Alex had laid the groundwork. Marcus was prepared, and he would be the one to tell Judithe. She, it was devoutly to be hoped, would stay out of his way and nurture her ever festering resentments, which was fine with Alex. And he, meantime, could implement his plans without interference.

And that involved legitimizing Samara Teva and using the Deveney name to do it. William had been dead five months at least, Alex figured quickly, so a small private dinner party and an impromptu performance were not inconceivable, especially if it could be excused on religious grounds—Samara's religiosity, whatever that was. She could do a dance of mourning, perhaps. There had to be one in her repertoire.

The guest list was next, and that would require a great deal of thought because Alex's sole purpose was to attract attention and to lure certain select personages into engaging Samara for private performances for themselves and their friends. It had to be made to look as if they were importing a legend into their homes, something so rare and coveted that no one else could have her unless they could afford the price.

They had to *want* her, and Alex had no doubt that once she moved among them, with her aloof and elusive elegance, they would be storming the door.

"I will not dignify anything that you do," Judithe said flatly when he told her.

"That's fine, Mother. Just stay out of my way. Phillippa will be my hostess. You and Marcus can hole up in the Rectory and pick apart my black soul."

Judithe flounced out of the room. There was no talking to him. And no way she could stay away from one of the few social events of the season, especially if the creature were to be brought down, finally, by the censure of their neighbors and friends.

Phillippa, always eager to have something to do, went over the arrangements with him. "This is an odd lot of guests," she commented as she scanned the list he gave her.

"Nevertheless, these are the names of those I wish to invite."

"Of course. Whatever you say, Alex. I'll discuss menu and seating with you tomorrow."

"I knew I could count on you." Phillippa was always accommodating, Alex thought. Maybe a little too much. And he was never able to decide if it was because of her affection for him or her disdain for Marcus. No matter. Marcus was too occupied by sermons and sin and not enough by his duty to his wife. But that was none of his concern.

Phillippa would be a much less fractious hostess than his mother, but Alex had no doubt Judithe would put in an appearance, if only to catch Samara in some solecism that would discredit her once and for all.

He walked in on Samara just as she was eating her dinner.

"I asked Wotten to bring a tray up here," she said defiantly.

"There's no reason I should endure your mother's animosity with my food."

Privately he agreed; Judithe's sour expression could spoil anyone's appetite, but Samara had not seemed to him like someone who would become distraught over his mother's histrionics.

"I'm giving a dinner party in two days," he said abruptly, leaning against the door. "You will be introduced as William's widow, and you will find some reason to initiate a performance."

Francesca felt a shock down to her toes. A party? Her, dancing? This soon after William's death? It was insane, and beyond propriety; not even Samara would violate those rules. She didn't know what to say, other than she wouldn't do it, not yet. And it wasn't proper. But Alex would laugh at her. So she laid down her fork and looked up at him. "I beg your pardon?"

Those eyes. God, those eyes. Not a hint of emotion. Not a blink of an eye. It made him clench his fists in anger that this was just business as usual with her.

"You will dance, Samara. Not in costume. That would be too much for a dinner party. But something to express your deep sorrow at the loss of your husband. Something alluring and mysterious. Elegant. Dignified. I want every man in the room to want you exclusively, do you understand?"

"It's too soon in the mourning," she said a little desperately. "And I'm not ready."

"My dear Samara, *you* are ready. I can attest to that. And this is what you've agreed to do."

She closed her eyes. *Not this soon. She didn't expect him to come up with anything this soon.* "Your mother can't have approved of your doing this."

"Phillippa will be my hostess," he said coolly. "Mother of course will attend as long as her hands are clean of social impropriety."

"Of course," Francesca echoed faintly. *Judithe obviously*

lets everyone else do the dirty work. But that didn't mitigate the fact she would have to dance. He was really going to make her do it—and this soon.

She was so impassive. He went on. "There will be musicians."

"That will be comforting."

Now he wanted to shake her. "This is just the beginning of what you will have to do."

"I understand that."

And she didn't care, he thought. It was nothing to her. One of a hundred performances, a thousand, that she would infuse with her particular brand of sensuality, feeding off of the covert desires of her audience to possess her.

But for now, she was *his,* body and soul.

"I'll choose your dress, your music. You'll have a day to plan what you want to do. What do you have to wear that's even remotely appropriate?"

She was nonplussed by his question. There was nothing among Samara's things that was suitable.

"Never mind. I'll look myself." He strode over to the closet, where Agnes the maid had hung what little there were of Samara's clothes and Francesca's own minuscule wardrobe. The costumes Francesca had personally folded into the built-in drawers, hoping that Agnes wouldn't pry. Or Alex Deveney.

But that was a futile hope. Alex was ripping through the dresses and criticizing each one. "None of these will do. Phillippa will have something you can use. I want you to look expensive and unobtainable, but you've mastered the unobtainable part already. And you're to be overcome with sorrow. That might be a stretch. But you can do it, Samara, just as efficiently as you've done everything else."

But Francesca felt about as effective as a rag doll. This was Alex's production and she was only going through the motions, already turning over in her mind how she was going to perpetrate the fiction of a pagan dance of mourning on the kind of sophisticated guests he would invite to such a dinner.

He grabbed the bellpull and in minutes Agnes appeared. "Send for Phillippa please."

Phillippa happened to be in the house, and she came immediately, reserving her curiosity about why Francesca was in Alex's bedroom instead of her own, and what more Alex could possibly want of her.

"We need a dress. We need two dresses, actually, your best black dresses—I think you both are of a size. I want her to *look* elegant and wealthy. . . ." He eyed Phillippa consideringly, trying to determine just how much to reveal to her, but he had a feeling Phillippa would understand exactly what he wanted. "She should present the picture of a bereaved widow who is nonetheless exotic, eccentric, and sensual."

"Why is that, Alex? Are you intending to marry her off?"

"No. I'm relaunching her career."

That startled Phillippa. "You're joking."

"Maybe not."

"You know, Marcus said you were acting strangely. . . ."

"My dear Phillippa, Marcus always thinks I act strangely. Now will you help me?"

Phillippa sent Francesca an odd searching look. "Anything for you, Alex. You know that."

"Good. Could you take care of that now?"

He didn't waste any time, Francesca thought, feeling like a puppet. She couldn't make a move; she just sat there, limp, listless, wary, her mind an utter blank, waiting for Alex Deveney to pull her strings.

But he couldn't tell her how to move and what to do; he couldn't create a dance for her that would have the kind of restrained authenticity that would provoke a response from a jaded audience.

She had to make the dance, and she didn't have a single idea how Samara had done it.

She was sinking deeper and deeper into the maw of half-truths and white lies, and she could never go back now that she had accepted his terms and said she would dance.

She had given away every choice and all her autonomy when she agreed to his price, and there wasn't a judge or jury that would be likely to believe how shamelessly she had stretched the truth to encompass all her lies.

It was just she never thought it would go this far. But she'd reckoned without the dynamo that was Alex Deveney.

When he wanted something, it got done. It didn't take Phillippa a half hour to reappear with an armful of dresses, which he promptly laid out on the bed.

"Some of these look familiar . . ."

"Judithe's castoffs. A little too large for me, and too expensive to have a dressmaker alter," Phillippa said.

"Is that so?" Alex murmured, holding each one up in turn and discarding one after the other, and then setting aside one or two of the gowns that he thought had possibilities.

He knew exactly what he was after, Francesca thought, sliding her hands over the sumptuous materials of the heaped gowns. And each of the dresses was of a superior quality that she had never had the wherewithal to buy. Any of them would have done, but not for Alex. He wanted something very specific, very luxurious, very refined, very erotic.

"This," he said at length. "And that."

"I see," Phillippa said, with that knowing tone in her voice.

"Exactly. Just what I wanted, Phillippa. Thank you."

"My pleasure," she said, again with that faintly derisive note, and Francesca wondered what indeed would be Phillippa's pleasure. Attracting Alex's notice perhaps? Phillippa seemed very eager in her restrained way, and there was something about her that was both earthy and discontented.

Phillippa paused at the door. "Is she truly sleeping with you, Alex?"

The bold question didn't surprise him at all. "It truly isn't any of your business, Phillippa."

She tried to recover. "Marcus—"

"Will save all of our souls. I'm counting on it. Good night, Phillippa."

She took a deep, angry breath to control her emotions at his cavalier dismissal. "Good night, Alex." The door slammed behind her.

"And that's that," Alex murmured. "I was hoping it wasn't."

"Naive of you," Francesca said, rousing herself from her shock at Phillippa's brazenness.

"Ah, Sleeping Beauty awakens and bares her sharp little teeth."

"I bite too," she said, keeping her tone neutral.

"Do you?" His voice was silky, suggestive. "I can't wait to give you something to really chew on."

She wanted to back away from the sensual innuendos, but Samara in life had been nothing if not a creature of the flesh, fantasy, and illusion.

"Too bad I'm not that hungry, my lord."

There was no trace of interest or feeling in her voice, and again he felt the frustration of running into a wall. She knew how to keep everything contained and in its place, and while she seemed malleable, he knew there was fire beneath all that unruffled composure.

But in point of fact, it was this aspect of her nature that he wanted her to display at the dinner party, so that when she did let go and give vent to the Samara Teva of the carnal and voluptuous dances, it would be all the more stunning to her audience, and all the better for him.

"You will be," he retorted with sublime male surety. "Don't think I can't make you, Samara Teva. However, that's not your purpose right now. And until then, we have work to do."

Chapter Eight

It was time for her to take some control.

Above everything else, she needed privacy. She was tired to death of Alex Deveney and the whole situation. And she had to have time to figure out some semblance of a dance that would look legitimate.

And he wasn't going to leave her alone for a minute.

"This dress first." Alex held up a confection in severe black lace, high necked, clean lined with a long straight skirt, and underlaid by the barest hint of a blush-colored underdress, which would make it look as if she were naked underneath.

Francesca shuddered. He obviously had something very specific in mind.

"And this, after." This was an evening dress, trimmed lavishly in jet and feathers, formfitting and every bit as revealing as the first. But no one could doubt what kind of money had been spent on both.

And that was the exact effect Alex wanted.

"Agnes will loosen the seams on the first dress for the scenario you will play out tomorrow night. I expect perfect execution, Samara. Everything that happens to you after this night depends on it.''

He was bullying her again. And she was stupid to let him, now that his need of her was established. Silence and disdain, those were her weapons against him; that was the contradiction in Samara that gave her the power.

''You're paying me, aren't you?'' Francesca asked insolently. ''I need a full-length mirror. And I need some time alone.''

Blast her, and her haughty touch-me-not attitude. Alex felt the familiar hunger roar through him, and he ruthlessly pushed it away. There was time enough to deal with that.

He summoned Agnes. ''Madam needs a mirror and a bath. And then I have some sewing for you to do.''

''Very good, sir.''

That, Francesca thought mordantly, after Alex left her, was exactly what Alex Deveney really wanted: a servile woman whose every response to his *every* demand was *very good, sir*.

Maybe she herself ought to try it.

''Very good, sir,'' she said to the bedpost, making a mocking little curtsy. ''Very good, sir,'' she said to the desk, bowing lower this time because Alex Deveney would love such a display of humility. ''Very good, sir,'' she growled at the door, and she slammed her palm against it because she couldn't smash it into Alex Deveney's face.

The door swung open, and she stumbled backward.

''Oh, mum.'' Poor Agnes was on the threshold with two footmen and a walnut-framed pier glass.

''I'm fine. Thank you. Please.'' She gestured to the footmen, and they carried the mirror into the room, set it where she indicated by the fireplace, and then withdrew.

''Is there anything else, mum?'' Agnes asked anxiously.

There was nothing more effective than perpetuating her lady-of-the-manor attitude, she thought. ''Bring my bath in an hour, please.''

That sounded wonderful. That sounded *rich*.

"Very good, mum." Agnes murmured, closing the door softly behind her.

"Very good, mum," Francesca mimicked as she whirled around to face herself in the mirror. She stopped dead at what she saw.

Who was that woman?

She hadn't looked at herself in a full-length mirror since before she'd left Berlin. And the image reflected back at her was that of a stranger with a pale face, burning black eyes, and long, tousled hair that had escaped its bun and streamed down the back of a tight body-fitting black dress with a high ruffled collar and a long draped skirt.

She looked like what she was: a good, staunch English girl, raised in the country, and innocent of sin. But Alex Deveney didn't see that. He saw a temptress and the embodiment of sin. How much did expectation coincide with perception? How could anyone believe she was an interpreter of exotic dances? No one looked less like Samara Teva than she.

She stretched out her arms in a serpentine motion. A cow. She reached over her head and brought her arms down slowly, poising her fingers, twisting her wrists. Bovine.

She stared at her image. *How was she going to do this?*

She tried again, starting with her arms crossed over her chest, pulling her hands down over her breasts, unwrapping her arms from around her midriff to splay outward, and then holding them stiff, her fingers pointed.

Lethargic.

How could she ever replicate the fire and sensuality of a Samara Teva performance?

And yet, she'd danced for Alex Deveney and convinced him to the tune of one hundred pounds. What had she done not two nights ago that had been so persuasive?

She'd been half naked was what.

She ran her shaking hands through her unruly hair. She *had* to do this.

. . . I wove spells with my hands when I danced . . .

She could almost hear Samara saying it. And maybe that was her secret: nudity and her hands. What more did any performer have to do to win over an audience?

But tomorrow night, she, Francesca, would not be naked. She would be fully clothed, and in this scenario that Alex had yet to describe to her, she was to absent herself from the guests and perform a restrained ritual dance of mourning for William.

Could that pale-faced woman transform herself into a sorrowful siren overnight? *A sordid siren* . . .

She lifted her arms to try again. How would a grieving seductress move? With slow, sinuous movements, she thought, with her writhing body in anguish, squirming, twisting, tormented that her lover—*Samara's lover*—was gone.

Like that. And like that. Supplicating. Angry. Resigned. All those emotions, if indeed there would be any time to portray those emotions. That looked good: the twining arms, the repudiation of her body that couldn't have *him* anymore. The reawakening of passion with acceptance.

Yes. Better. She watched herself jerk and spasm and smooth out her movements until she thought she had the hang of it.

But it was a stranger within the depths of the mirror moving and responding to a bottomless imaginary sorrow. Someone who seemed apart from her, the puppet, the intruder, the fraud.

How did she ever think she could deceive an audience of Alex Deveney's worldly friends?

She stared at her white face in the mirror.

She would, she thought.

She had to.

But what Alex wanted her to do went far beyond what she imagined in the mirror that evening.

He outlined the whole program clearly and succinctly when he joined her after her bath and before she retired.

And he stayed the night, while she lay wide awake and horrified as she went over all the details in her mind, forbearing to ask him one single question about the performance on which everything in the future hinged.

Nothing was as simple as it seemed.

She came down the long staircase on Marcus's arm, dressed in the beautiful lace gown with the blush-colored underdress, scared witless that Judithe would recognize it and confront her in front of her guests.

Below, the reception hall glittered by the light of dozens of candles in wall sconces, and the guests who had already arrived stood around in conversation, awaiting the guest of honor.

Her.

They were dressed so opulently: the men in tuxedos, the women in gowns of satin and gold and bead-encrusted lace, in jet and diamonds and lustrous pearls.

Francesca paused on the bottom step and every eye turned to her as Alex moved toward her and held out his arm.

"Ladies and gentlemen, Lady Samara Deveney. Madam?"

She nodded and laid her hand on his arm and stepped down as he whispered approvingly, "Excellent, Samara."

"Indeed, my lord, did you expect otherwise?" she murmured. She felt like royalty in her beautiful dress. And great regret for what she was going to do to it.

Her hands were cold, her chin held high. Not by a word or a gesture would she betray how terrified she was.

They led a stately promenade into the parlor, where champagne awaited them, and Judithe, looking like some warrior queen. Alex ignored his mother and began introducing Samara individually to the guests.

Here was Crookenden, an old school friend, and his wife, Solange. There, Jasper Cardston, still a bachelor. Basil Edenbridge, Bart., and his wife, Hyla. And Allston Searle, the Earl of Barwick, another old friend, from Wellingborough.

A small select crowd not of his usual associates, but Samara couldn't know that, Alex thought, and she was handling herself admirably and eliciting from those sated aristocrats exactly the response he'd hoped: pure fascination with her beauty and mystery.

She carried herself exactly right, hardly spoke except if she were asked a direct question, lowered her eyes so no one could read anything into them, and otherwise displayed her body in that insanely tight, seductive dress, which was the model of the highest fashion and propriety.

And it looked as if she were naked underneath it. She moved with it, instinctively arching her body in ways that revealed the underdress, just the way he would expect Samara Teva to inhabit the dress of a temptress.

There was a faint blush of color on her cheeks, and she wore her hair parted at the center and sleek and tight at the nape of her neck. That dress. That face. That air of the unobtainable. She needed no other enhancements to have his guests drooling over her.

Of course his mother wasn't slavering, nor was Phillippa, but they each had the decency to keep their abhorrence in check.

But Judithe approached her son at one point. "Why these people, Alex? And why is the creature wearing a dress I gave to Phillippa?"

"Phillippa will explain it all to you, Mother. Perhaps it would be better if you retired for the night before we go to dinner."

"I will *not*," Judithe said through gritted teeth. "You try my patience, Alex, keeping that—that . . . *whore* in this house in spite of my wishes."

"Don't interfere. And don't make a scene, Mother. I can have it bruited about that you have become subject to hysterical fits, and see where that will get you with your precious society friends."

"You are an unfeeling beast," she hissed.

"I hope so," he said and turned from her. He felt her heated gaze burning him to a crisp as he caught Samara's arm to rescue her from Cardston, who was questioning her a little too closely. "Everything is prepared," he said, sotto voce. "After dinner, then, as planned."

She nodded. Her heart started pounding. She had seen him and Judithe. No one could have missed the animosity between them. She lost her appetite just thinking about the exchange between them and Judithe witnessing what was to come.

Judithe would never forgive Alex—never.

Phillippa eased by Francesca. "You have Alex in turmoil, my dear Samara. I should ask you to share your secrets. Or better yet, perhaps I should offer to buy them."

"You couldn't afford them," Francesca retorted without thinking, and instantly regretted her remark. She reached out her hand to Phillippa but Phillippa shook her off.

"We all know what you are and what you are doing here, sharing Alex's room and God knows what else. Don't expect us to be friends, Samara. I want you away from here as badly as Judithe does."

"I'm sure you do," Francesca murmured. "And no more than do I." But Phillippa didn't hear her. She'd already moved on, over to where Judithe stood, glowering like a miser.

Francesca was desperate for the evening to end. Another hour, perhaps, if dinner were announced soon.

As if on cue, Wotten appeared at the huge double doors that separated the front and rear parlors. "Ladies and gentlemen, dinner is served."

Immediately, Cardston came to Francesca and offered his arm. She sent a questioning glance to Alex, and he nodded imperceptibly.

Slowly, they paced through the rear parlor, with its gold-and-white furniture and accessories, and into the dining room, with its long burnished mahogany table set with service for ten.

The walls were paneled, and one of them was taken up by a mural of a triumphal battle scene painted in muted colors, which was reflected in the gilt-framed mirrors on the opposite wall.

Here, the chandeliers glowed with hundreds of candles, flicking muted light onto the golden flatware, the cut-glass goblets, and the gold-rimmed plates at each place. There were gold-filigreed holders displaying name cards and Phillippa unobtrusively directed each guest to his appointed chair.

Francesca found herself seated at the far end of the table, across from Cardston and next to Mere.

Worse and worse, she thought, as, from the gallery above, a cellist and violinist began to play. He would be with her every moment, every step of the way. He could signal and direct her; he could forestall conversation and circumvent any plea for help.

Cardston would have helped her. He was absolutely fascinated by her, and the more reticent she was, the more entranced he became. It was so obvious, so real.

It terrified Francesca all the more that any woman could have any man if she just played by Samara's rules.

Silence and disdain. Nudity and hands. All the secrets of Samara Teva coming into play on this weekend that would seal her fate.

The music was light, airy, unobtrusive. The food, served by liveried footmen and directed by Wotten, was superb. They began with a clear steaming consomme, which was removed by poached salmon in cream sauce, followed by roast capon, and a scallop of veal, which was accompanied by steamed potatoes and baby peas and spinach with hollandaise sauce.

Francesca picked at her food, her body shivery and tight with anticipation.

Alex fielded most of the questions directed at her. "My sister-in-law is still a little shaky over the death of my brother. This is her first dinner party, and she is understandably nervous."

He gave her a meaningful look, and she nodded.

But not yet . . . not yet—

"So difficult," Hyla Edenbridge murmured, her diamonds winking in the soft light.

"My dear, I don't know how you can bear it." That from Solange Crookenden, who was older than Hyla and more discreetly dressed.

Judithe glowered at Francesca from across the table.

"The Lord never sends us more than we can bear," Marcus said pompously. "Now where is the dessert?"

"Would you excuse me?" Francesca murmured shakily.

"Of course, my dear." Marcus again, and Alex deferred to him, watching her keenly as she rose and exited out of the door behind them.

Everything was in play now. No going back.

Francesca slipped into the adjoining anteroom, where a memorial to William had been set on display: a ledge covered in black velvet on which there was a gold-framed photograph of him, stiff and young, and candles burning on either side, pillars of rectitude.

Other than that, the room was empty, apart from the balcony that connected to the dining room, where the musicians played.

The prearranged signal was a change in the tempo and tenor of the music. They would have dessert first—some kind of strawberry bombe, and it would occur to Alex that she had been too long gone. He would ask the gentlemen to come with him, in case she was in distress, and that would be the cue for the music to change and for her to begin the dance.

This had all been planned out by him the night before and detailed to her. And there were to be two components to her dance, besides the actual movements: She was to remove her shoes and stockings; and in the course of the dance, she was to rend her dress and bare her breast.

And with these two seductive elements in place, no one would even be looking at her movements.

Francesca stood in her bare feet as she waited and waited for the music to change, her hands clenched tightly, her heart pounding wildly.

The candles flickered, exaggerating her shadow, the music a ghostly counterpoint far, far away.

She felt breathless, scared, powerful.

"But where is Samara?" The voice was Hyla Edenbridge's, and Francesca thought that Alex couldn't have timed it or wished it to happen better than to have a guest notice her absence instead of him.

She heard the rumble of his voice, low and reassuring. "I don't know . . . I think I'd better—Gentlemen, perhaps you could come with me in case she needs help . . . ? Marcus— you stay here. . . ."

And then the music shifted into something atonal and eerie. She began the dance as she heard footsteps pounding across the balcony. She turned her back to them as she heard someone whisper, "There she is . . ."

Francesca tore the pins out of her hair so that it spilled over her shoulders. She lifted her skirt and undulated her hips. She pirouetted away from them and dramatically dropped her head and pulled with desperate hands at her bodice. The dress fell apart, Agnes's expert handiwork draped in her hands.

Francesca shrugged it off of her shoulders and lifted her arms. In time to the wail of the violin, she began the intricate steps of a make-believe dance of mourning for William. She moved sinuously across the room so they could see her clearly. She offered her body, she pulled at her hair, she stripped away still more of her dress, she whirled around the room until she was dizzy, and she finally dropped to her knees in front of William's picture, her breasts bared, her body heaving with sobs, and one naked foot exposed.

The silence in the aftermath was thick, heated, charged with lust. And Alex was as aroused as any of them.

He spoke first, his voice hoarse. "Someone—get a blanket. Call Agnes."

She heard him land as he vaulted from the balcony; she felt his hands as he grasped her shoulders. "Samara . . . Samara—"

Francesca held back for a long moment, and then, as they'd arranged, she shook her head and asked weakly, "Where am I? Alex . . . ?"

"I'm here." He helped her to her feet, letting the dress slip to the floor so that they all got a long, hard glimpse of her voluptuous body and her naked breasts before he covered her with his jacket. "Ah, Agnes. Come, we'll help her to her room."

Alex glanced up at the balcony, where the three men stood, their gazes riveted on Samara's bare feet as he escorted her out of the room.

Sold, he thought triumphantly. *They wanted her. They could barely contain themselves. Samara Teva knew exactly how to make them salivate and beg for more.*

And they would. Soon.

Perfect.

Damn her, damn her, damn her, damn her. . . .

And then they protected her, all of them, by gentleman's agreement not mentioning the dance, the nudity, the hunger to possess her.

"She fainted," Alex said, as he seated himself at the dinner table. Judithe, Phillippa, and Marcus all turned to stare at him.

"Poor dear," Hyla Edenbridge murmured. "I hope she's all right?"

"She tore her dress unfortunately. Agnes has taken her upstairs to change. She'll rejoin us shortly. Please continue with dessert before we adjourn to the parlor."

"Perhaps tonight was too much for—the *poor dear,*" Judithe suggested maliciously. "We all know how much stress she's been under. Or is it—*who* she's been under? Isn't that right, Alex?"

He went rigid. Judithe never learned, but she wasn't going to put a crimp in his operations by her loose tongue. "Now,

Mother, I didn't think I'd have to mention the medication you've been on recently, but I think perhaps such injudicious comment deserves some explanation, don't you? Phillippa? Is it time for her next dose? That can be the only reason for her saying such a vile thing.''

"She's fine," Phillippa said stiffly.

"I think she should stay at the Rectory tonight," Alex continued in that same bland tone while his guests eyed Judithe warily. "She might need some counseling, and Marcus is so good with troubled souls."

"Alex," Marcus said warningly.

"Mother seems befuddled, Marcus. I thought the doctor said *this* medication would take care of things."

Judithe started to say something and thought the better of it even before Marcus waved her off.

"You're giving our guests the wrong impression, Alex," he said stringently.

"Am I? How could Mother say such a thing unless the dosage she's taking is not effective? Really, Marcus. Do I have the reputation of being a rake? No. Am I not always at Meresham when I'm not in London? Yes. For Mother to insult poor William's wife like that. . . ." Alex looked around the table at each of his guests, who appeared alternately shocked and avid to hear more gossip they could take back to their inner circle. "Ah well. I'm afraid Lady Deveney will never live down her reputation as an interpreter of sacred dances."

"Of course!" Jasper Cardston exclaimed. "I saw her on the Continent several years ago. Extraordinary performance . . . absolutely riveting—"

Judithe glared at him but Cardston didn't see her. Alex did. "Samara was well known on the Continent, Mother. A revered performance artist, sought after and acclaimed. William was lucky to have her."

"She was lucky to have *him*," Judithe muttered.

"She was extraordinary," Cardston said again, his expression mirroring the pleasure of his memory of Samara Teva and her dance of the veil. "Married to your brother, eh? Well, well—"

"But she didn't stop performing," Alex said. "No, William would never have deterred her from her sacred duty." He ignored the choking sound that came from Judithe's end of the table. "Ah, Wotten—it's time to adjourn to the parlor. Gentlemen, ladies . . ." He rose and everyone rose with him. "Wotten, you'll direct Lady William to the parlor when she returns?"

"Indeed, my lord."

"Marcus"—he grabbed Marcus's arm—"get Mother out of here."

"Nonsense, Alex. *Your* behavior has been boorish and insupportable."

"Don't cross me, Marcus. Get her out of here."

Marcus held his gaze as if he would defy him, but finally he thought the better of it. Alex held the cards and they all knew it, his mother as well. "Very well," he said, his voice brittle. "May I assume Phillippa and I may stay?"

"If you don't get in my way. But I would think that in this agitated state, Mother should have someone stay with her."

"Damn you, Alex."

"Not very noble sentiments for a curate, Marcus."

"You're up to something and I want to know what it is."

"There's nothing that should concern you except helping Mother before she embarrasses herself further."

"As you say," Marcus murmured, restraining himself from saying more. He stalked off toward the parlor to catch Judithe before anyone settled in with brandy and cheese.

Alex followed slowly. They'd done enough tonight, he and Samara. And it might not be a bad idea if she didn't appear again this evening, to add to her air of elusiveness and mystery.

He turned at the dining room door and his breath caught. Samara was poised at the anteroom door, fully clothed again, beautiful, cool, aloof, unobtainable. . . .

The essence of everything female and unknowable, and in

that instant he understood, that in spite of all his plans, he didn't want anyone else to have her either, and that the die was cast, and she could only be his alone for one more night.

He got rid of everyone within the hour and sat alone in the library nursing his brandy, feeling acutely the knowledge that he didn't have to go to his room, that even if he weren't there, she still was his alone, tonight, and for always.

If he went to her now, he thought mordantly, he would surrender all of his power. And she knew it. She played on it. It was all a game to her.

And that was why he sat brooding in the library. Samara Teva knew exactly what she was doing, and for all he knew, she'd deliberately set out to seduce him once William was out of the way.

But he couldn't be had, not like those tufthunters who were so easily taken in by a wriggle and a naked foot.

Samara Teva's seductive wiles wouldn't work on him.

He clenched the stem of the brandy snifter so hard it almost broke.

Cardston was the key, now that Judithe had almost ruined his plan.

Cardston would be the first because now he had seen her twice, and he wanted her. Her dance had rekindled memories for him, but unlike before, now she seemed obtainable, and what man didn't like to feel that a woman like that could be had?

Alex would invite the others, and those in his circle, perhaps to an all-male evening of entertainment with the famous exotic dancer Samara Teva.

Samara would become a sensation and be in demand everywhere.

Just what he wanted, just what he'd planned. Damn it all to hell.

He slammed the snifter down on the side table. Damn her perfidious soul.

No woman was going to do that to him, least of all a scheming, hardened harlot of indeterminate origins who knew how to play the right cards and call the right bluff at the right time.

Well, he was just ready to call hers.

He levered himself out of his chair and started slowly upstairs.

His scenario had worked. Francesca lay curled up on his bed still dressed and contemplated what she could remember of her performance. It seemed to her that she had accomplished the whole thing in a dream, that she hadn't stripped off her dress, and that she hadn't danced before those strange men half naked.

But apparently she had; the shreds of the beautiful lace dress lay on the floor, and Alex had sequestered her in order to tease them still more, so they would beg to see her again any way they could have her.

"You're so perfect for the part," he murmured, slipping into the room. "Look at you." He locked the door. "They couldn't keep their eyes off you."

"Neither could you," Francesca retorted, and the moment she said it, she knew it was absolutely true, and that because of it, she had so much more leverage than she'd ever thought.

And that she was in infinitely more danger.

Alex was startled by her perception, and he shouldn't have been. Of course she could read the evidence of a man's desire. She knew how to dissect every nuance of a man's behavior. She was trained that way.

"Cardston will ask for you first."

"Will he?" And he'd seemed so sane. And Francesca still didn't know what Alex was after, or what he hoped to gain. "What is the point, my lord?"

"You don't need to know." He reached into the inner pocket

of his frock coat and tossed a wad of bills on the bed. "As we agreed."

His gaze caught hers, and that rising fury gripped him again. A hundred pounds at her feet, and she let it lie as if it were nothing. And yet she'd bargained for it and chosen the path of least resistance—as she had done for most of her life.

What if he added another hundred to it and demanded her submission? He could live with that, having her and retaining the power and control over her, ruling her with an unlimited supply of money.

He saw precisely why men preferred to conduct their private lives this way. To buy what they wanted and damn the cost. It was because there were no emotional ties. No need to forgive the past. No need to plan for the future.

Sometimes a man liked to live that way: without love and betrayal clouding the issue.

Francesca stared at the money. Two hundred pounds now, and the blood money from William's estate. And more in the offing that would give Samara Teva the wherewithal to live like a Queen.

For what, exactly, had she sold her soul and any future she might have with Colm? "I do need to know," she said suddenly.

"All you need to know is what costume you will wear when Cardston offers for your services."

"Alex . . ." Her voice was urgent.

He stiffened. She had not heretofore called him by his given name. It changed something in the air. It made things more intimate just when he was trying to shut the door on her, to objectify her so that the thought of Cardston watching her dance wouldn't irritate him as much as it did.

"Don't develop a conscience now, Samara. It's a little too late for that, don't you think?"

"What about you?" she asked, with a catch in her throat.

"I have no scruples whatsoever," he said baldly. "The bargain is struck, you can't back out—and why would you, with all that lovely money to pave the way to a new and richer life?''

"Who's to say what kind of life I will have after this?''

"You know exactly what kind of life you will have," he said roughly. "More men. And more men. What other kind of life is there for a woman like you?''

"Or a man like you," she shot back, stung. But it was all about Samara, and the woman he thought Samara was. She was letting it become too personal, as if inhabiting Samara's skin diminished the woman who was Francesca Reay.

Maybe it did, if she was pretending to be someone else and taking money for dancing half naked in front of strange men.

She couldn't let it. But the Francesca part of her was keeling under the weight of Samara's iniquities, and she hadn't discovered one thing yet that linked Samara with *her* Colm that would justify this insane risk she had taken.

"Contrary to what you think, Samara, you have no control here.''

Francesca shrugged. "I controlled those men—your guests. If I wanted to"—oh, here was the biggest gamble of all, and a virgin's folly if ever there was one—"I could control you.''

He went absolutely still. *She could. She could. He wanted to plumb the depths of that impassiveness, that silence, that hauteur that was such a contradiction in her character.*

She had issued a challenge and no man could resist that kind of provocation.

He whipped out another handful of pound notes and strode to the bed.

"And tell me, Samara, how *does* a nautch dancer take control when a man pays for her favors?'' He pushed the pound notes into her face, into her hands. "How?'' He climbed up on the bed and straddled her. "*How*, damn you—'' And he lowered himself, pushing her back into the pillows. "Tell me now, Samara? What control? *Who* has control?''

Oh, dear God— She instantly saw the futility of fighting him with her body. Samara wouldn't. Samara would have instantly given into the pressure of that hot male part of him that bulged against her belly. Samara would have known just what to do.

Francesca chose to fight with words. Daring, provoking, infuriating words. She knew what he would do even as she murmured, "Who, my lord? *Who?* Why I do, or you wouldn't be on this bed with me."

And maybe she wanted him to, because the only response to that was his pushing her tighter into the bed and crushing his lips against hers in a wild, rough attempt to dominate her with his mouth.

What was this? What was this? He'd know in a minute that she had no experience whatsoever. He'd know everything.

Now she fought him, if nothing more than to save herself, the lie, her sins. And the more she writhed and bucked, the tighter he came down on her body and into her mouth.

She never imagined such kisses, so deep and thrusting and wet and tasting of the essence of him. And the strength of him, and his determination to have her and to remain untouched by her.

But he couldn't pull himself away from that mouth, those soft pliant lips, that luscious tongue—like the whore she was, she opened herself to him and let him feast, and that inflamed him still more.

He felt himself losing his edge, losing himself in the honey welcome of her mouth, in the undulating grind of her body. This was crazy. To let her get to him like that. To give himself over to the likes of her for the exhorbitant price of a kiss— when he had set her value, not she—

"Great goddamn it to *hell. . . .*"

He wrenched himself away from her and her tempting mouth and traitorous body and jacked himself up off the bed, scattering pound notes everywhere.

A hundred pounds for a kiss.

A hundred pounds for a whore's dance.

In another week, she would be offering up that voluptuous body for the delectation of yet another audience of strange men, and all in the cause of fighting corruption and the destruction of evil.

What was corrupt? Who was evil?

He was losing perspective. He'd let himself lose control. He moved away from the bed, where she had levered herself up on one elbow, her breasts heaving, her lips slightly swollen from the hard, unrelenting pressure of his.

And there was triumph in her cool black gaze. She had brought him down, just as she had so many other men, and it hadn't been that difficult after all.

And she wouldn't let him forget it either. He could see it in her eyes.

He hated her just then, and the surety with which she had exposed his weakness and his desire. Never again, he thought. He was stronger than she, and fully aware of what his surrender would mean.

Sometimes a man had to learn his lessons the hard way, with an ache in his groin and the taste of depravity on his tongue. He wasn't the first to be seduced by such a challenge—he wouldn't be the last.

But he'd never get that close again.

And he was glad as hell he had paid her first.

Chapter Nine

And now that he'd tasted her, he craved more, more, and more. She was a drug, luring a man with her opacity and hooking him with her submissiveness and her lust.

He hadn't imagined her yielding body and her utter capitulation. He felt it still, the soft curves rippling beneath him, supporting his savage weight, the ferocious acceptance of her willing mouth.

That lush body was quiescent now, numbed with sleep, as seductive in repose as in submission.

But who had surrendered to whom? Who had really been in command?

But he knew the answer to that; she'd thrown it in his face without a qualm.

He sat in the upholstered chair by the fireplace and contemplated his sins. Tomorrow or the next day Cardston would come, and Cardston would not be denied. Samara would dance for him; Samara would entice him and all with whom he chose to share her.

Exactly what he wanted. Exactly as he'd planned.

Distraction and diversion, with a born exhibitionist to pave the way. He couldn't have chosen a better spectacle than Samara Teva as a cover for what he needed to do.

He felt the telltale tightening of his groin as he thought about her. God, a man should not be at the mercy of a woman's nudity.

And yet, it was all he could think about: her sinuous sensual movements, her satin skin, the rending of her dress that portrayed the grief within. Acted perfectly, even to the moment of reorientation, as if she hadn't know where she was, or what she was doing.

What a treasure he had found in Samara Teva, he thought mordantly. And with his great good foresight, he was going to give her the wealth and freedom that would allow her to do anything she wanted anywhere in the world. Without *him*.

He folded his tensed hands tightly over the arms of the chair. *No. She'd never get that far. He wouldn't let her.*

He dwelled on the thought; it didn't shock him, but the intensity of his feelings did. Then he set that contradiction aside as well to contemplate a life of holding Samara Teva in captivity for his titillation and gratification alone.

That seemed infinitely viable in the dead of the night, in the silence and the sultry atmosphere of the darkened room.

He would get her a town house in London. He would keep her in chains.

He was going mad.

. . . To be so seduced by the pliant lines of woman's body and a pair of bottomless black eyes . . .

William had never had a chance.

Probably, neither had he. . . .

"This is just beyond anything you've ever done," Marcus said as he entered the breakfast room the following morning. "Mocking Mother's real concerns. In front of guests who weren't even real friends—and all for a woman like *that*. I can just imagine the tittle-tattle at *their* breakfast tables. Really, Alex, how do you live with yourself?''

Alex ignored him, dished out his eggs, toast, and tea, and settled himself at the far end of the table. Judithe would probably stay in bed all day to recuperate from his vicious vilification, and Phillippa looked at him over her cup with a cold assessing stare.

''But that's not the problem,'' she said into the deadly silence. ''The problem is, he's *sleeping* with her.''

Marcus's face turned pale. ''Let's not even think that, Phillippa.''

''What ought we to think, Marcus darling? That he's locked her up like a princess in a tower to preserve her virtue? I always wondered what it was like to have no virtue.''

''Phillippa!'' Marcus sounded scandalized. ''This isn't breakfast conversation.''

She sent him a scathing look. ''Tell me, Alex. Does it make a woman different? Free? Does she bear on her body the mark of a whore so all men can identify her and shun her? Or do they shun her? Does it matter, really?''

''Phillippa—I won't . . .''

She ignored him. ''Or are all men seduced by the notion of possessing such a woman . . . ? That's what it seems like to me. What do *you* think, Marcus? Do you have any opinion on the matter at all? Surely there's some doctrinal teaching on this?''

Marcus shot up from his chair like an arrow. ''Please excuse me. Everyone seems to be in a malicious humor this morning, and I refuse to be the one to cope with it all.''

He stalked out of the room, and Phillippa turned to Alex with a dreamy look in her eyes. ''What's it like, Alex? Is it better? With a woman like that, I mean.''

As opposed to a _good_ woman like me, she meant.

Alex reached for the jam pot. ''You wouldn't believe me if I told you, Phillippa.''

''I'd believe anything you told me, Alex.''

He stopped his motion in midair, mindful of Phillippa's sharp, assessing blue gaze. Poor, discontented Phillippa, swamped with jealousy at the pariah he had brought into their lives, and curious about everything she had missed as a country minister's wife.

She was lovely enough on her own, but too tall for fashion's standards, and too smart for any man to rule, too pale, blond, and aloof looking for anyone to want to try. And surely not the pattern card for a country vicar's wife.

Nevertheless Marcus had been instantly and completely taken with her, and she had reciprocated in the same measured, rational way she approached everything. So her emotional outbursts last night and this morning were utterly out of character for her and bespoke deeper feelings on other levels than anyone had been aware.

But that was Marcus's problem to solve, not his. He just didn't know what to say to her to ease that pain.

"Think of it this way, Phillippa. She was William's wife. What would Marcus have done in that situation?"

"Not shared her room," Phillippa retorted.

"I'm not married."

Phillippa's mouth softened dangerously.

"She's my sister-in-law."

"As am I," Phillippa whispered. "It's in the Bible . . ."

Alex shook his head, despairing of passing his behavior off as anywhere near explainable. "Phillippa, don't . . . There's more, but I can't tell you right now."

"Oh good—every man's excuse and absolution. There's always a reason. It's always a mystery. And it's something that can't be revealed. How far removed *are* you from *every man,* Alex, when you can secrete a whore in your room and then explain it away by the thing that can't be told. Oh!" She jumped up from the table. "Men are all alike. They're all stupid and they all fall for the common and the obscene."

She grabbed her cup and heaved it. It smashed against the

fireplace as she turned on her heel, her eyes brimming, and left the room.

Alex took the jam pot and liberally spread jam on his toast. Phillippa was in a dangerous mood, he thought. Samara Teva's impact was incalculable. If she'd looked different, if she'd acted different, that would be one thing. But obviously Phillippa could see no outward contrast at all between them, and if she hadn't been aware of Samara's notoriety, Samara could have passed for a London lady, no questions asked.

Marcus would have to handle it. There was probably some pamphlet somewhere on strictures for the wife who thought to stray, and Marcus was just the type to have it right on his Rectory bookshelf.

He summoned Wotten. "Has Lady William called for her tray yet?"

"Yes, my lord. She breakfasts even now."

"My mother?"

"My lady keeps to her room today."

"Good, she'll keep out of trouble. Have there been any messages, any mail?"

"As yet, no, my lord."

"All right. Thank you, Wotten."

So that was it. Now it was just a waiting game, and all he could do was choose the sheerest, most revealing, most eye-catching costumes in Samara Teva's collection, contain *her*, wait for Cardston's summons, and hope that his family didn't get in the way.

It was a wonder to Francesca that she slept. Alex's presence the whole night in the room was even more unsettling after that deep erotic kiss.

Dear God, how could he not have known that she was inexperienced, that she'd never been kissed, not like that, and that she'd never felt the lust-driven weight and the carnal intention of a man's body on hers, ever?

These were the things Samara Teva knew that Francesa Reay did not, and Francesca's masquerade was in deep danger of coming to an abrupt and well-deserved end.

Maybe, she thought tiredly as she sipped tea and bit into some toast, maybe it was for the best. She just didn't know how to do it. She couldn't dance. She knew no feminine wiles. She was too slender, too inhibited, she wasn't voluptuous, and she was as graceless as an elephant.

Why wasn't Alex seeing those things?

Men were insanely blind. Alex thought she was Samara. He *needed* her to be Samara; thus she was Samara. And to keep her Samara, he locked her in her room.

She wished she could order reality so easily.

The reality of Francesca Reay stared her right back in the face from that pier glass: the wild hair, the pale countenance, the huge dark eyes. The nervy mouth that had somehow uttered the words that enabled her to stand up to Alex Deveney.

But not to tell him the truth.

Here's the truth, my lord. I was Samara's neighbor who took care of her till she died. I know nothing about your plots, plans, papers, or purpose. I can't dance. I've never been kissed. I've never had a man. I want to go home.

That all sounded like the veriest innocent, like a scared child, seeking comfort from the only place it knew: home.

Berlin or Braidwood—not much of a choice. And no guarantee she'd see Colm, ever again.

She felt like burying herself under the covers forever.

I have to get out of here.

She now had a small fortune: three hundred pounds and that checque for seventy-five more. Probably she'd never cash it, since it belonged to Samara, but if she took nothing more than the money and the clothes on her back, she could easily fund a new life someplace else on the Continent.

She didn't have to go home.

It was both a terrifying and a tempting thought.

A single woman, alone, moneyed, dabbling in art. Wasn't

that what she'd been doing, to all intents and purposes, in Berlin? With no money?

And poor General Von Abrungen. She hadn't given him a thought since Alex Deveney had burst into Samara's room in the pension. What must he have thought of the capricious portrait painter who had suddenly disappeared?

Maybe he'd told Colm.

The thought caught Francesca unawares, and she just sank back onto the bed.

Of course. The commission had been arranged by Colm. If she just vanished, of course the General would have something to say to Colm. He'd wanted that portrait done, and just the way he fantasized it. So ... yes, it was possible that he'd contacted Colm. A contract was a contract.

And so—what if Colm were trying to find her even now?

She felt a jolt of hope. He'd find her. The landlady at the rooming house knew she'd gone off with the Earl of Mere. He'd know. He'd come.

Simple as that. For all she knew, he was on his way, and this farce of her pretending to be Samara finally would be over. He'd explain everything and take her home, and they'd be together.

Soon.

Colm could be that close. He could be in the village asking questions about the guest at Meresham Close.

He could be galloping into the park right now. . . .

Alex eased open the door and entered the room. And there she was, sitting on his bed as if she belonged there.

God, he had to stop thinking like this. Samara Teva belonged where he had put her—naked, in the spotlight, teasing and tempting men who were not nearly as strong as he.

"Get up," he commanded roughly. "I want to choose the costume you'll wear when Cardston summons you."

"You're so sure," Francesca murmured, covering her hammering fear.

"I want to see them on you."

That scared her right down to her toes. A private show for his lord high master? No, no. Not after last night. She couldn't trust him. She couldn't trust herself.

"Trust me to choose the right one," she murmured.

"Do it, or I'll do it for you." His hands itched. He would love to strip that thin muslin nightgown from her body and deck it out with the tools of an exotic dancer's trade.

Silence or disdain, wrap yourself in one or the other to deal with him; otherwise he'll eat you alive. . . .

She heaved a sigh, pretending exasperation at his bullying tactics. "What is it exactly that you want, my lord?"

"Nudity, without your body being entirely unclothed. I want your face veiled and your body revealed. Find something in that bag of tricks and let me see it."

"As you wish, my lord." Her gritty tone belied the fact she was scared nerveless. But it was another moment that Samara would have loved: putting herself on display for a private party of one.

God, what *was* there in Samara's heap of glitter and gauze that would cover her sufficiently and satisfy him?

And don't forget about the dance. . . .

Start with the costumes that conceal the most.

As if there were many—any . . .

The veil was easy. She took it from one of her hats, a velvet-dotted length of tulle that she could drape over her face, cover her mouth with, wrap around her neck, her waist, her breasts.

She took a deep breath. Now for the costumes. She had thrown them all together, and she had to separate the pieces to make some sense of them. And all they amounted to were scraps of netting, lace, gauze, and tulle held together by bands of beads, sequins, jet, and satin.

How was she ever going to dress herself in one of them and prance around in front of those awful men?

She shrugged into a satin vest that just barely covered her breasts and that was held together by a thin beaded chain.

She shivered. There was a matching cincture that bared her

bottom and dipped to an enticing vee between her legs, where strands of beads dangled and shimmered with her every movement.

But how she was going to find the nerve to show it to Alex she would never know. She just had to get a grip on her fear, close her eyes, and strut out into that bedroom as if Samara really inhabited her body.

Alex watched her as she sashayed out from the closet, all arms and legs and glittering beads. She turned as she came toward him, to give an unrestricted view of her derriere, and pirouetted back so he could see the little vest, the swell of her breasts, the fragile chain that held it all together.

"No." The word came sharper, harsher than he'd intended, a function of his unruly manhood reacting to even this covered-up display of her charms. "Show me something else."

She twitched back into the closet, while he clamped down hard on his burgeoning desire. Ridiculous. This was a dress rehearsal, nothing more, nothing less, to choose a costume that would so rivet her audience that no one would notice what he was doing.

She slithered into the room, wearing a sequined bustier from which were suspended matching garters that supported a sequined silk skirt that wrapped just around her thighs so that she moved like a geisha.

He felt a jolt of lust clear down to his boots. "No." His voice was hoarse, rough. "Try on something else."

She bit her lips and returned to the closet, and he wondered how many more of Samara's costumes he could stand to see without exploding.

She was perfect, a born exhibitionist who knew how to tease to please. Otherwise, why this selective and revealing array of costumes that ultimately would devolve into full nudity, which was what he expected, what he wanted, what he couldn't wait for.

But waiting was part of the temptation of her. He was her audience of one, no one else would have her—today.

He could wait.

She entered again, swathed in a sequined tulle cape that slipped off her shoulders—deliberately to entice him?—as she moved into the room. She wore a thin sequined belt around her hips with a long, translucent, sequin-trimmed panel suspended between her legs, front and back. Her breasts were covered, just at the tips, by two sequined cups, which were fastened around her neck and her back.

Everything was visible—and not—the most erotic combination of all. Alex felt himself stiffening still more, as if that part of him were utterly dissociated from reason and reality.

Maybe it was. It knew absolutely what *he* wanted. It pointed the way as surely as if he had lost it.

"No," he growled. "What else is there?"

She drew herself up, a movement that shimmied her breasts, and he felt himself surging toward her.

"I know what you want," she said in that haughty tone of hers.

"I always thought you did," he murmured insolently. As he'd thought, part of her game, part of the bait, the snare. "Why don't we just get to the point?" But he was there already, hard, hot, jutting, and lusting after every curve of her body.

"As you wish, my lord." She didn't know how she managed to sound so calm and sane as she turned away from him and glided back into the closet. She understood now what he expected her to do, how he expected her to perform.

Naked. He wanted her shimmying around in front of those men stark naked.

She leaned against the wall. She couldn't do this. She couldn't. Whatever he was after by using her to tempt and tease those men, she couldn't do it.

"Samara!" There was a note in his voice, keening, demanding, supplicating.

Samara could.

Naked. He wanted her naked.

She couldn't face him if she had to walk out there naked.

She didn't know what to do.

She knew what she had to do. She was Samara Teva. She couldn't—couldn't afford to be—anyone else. She removed the breast cups and stripped off the sequined panels and let them pool at her feet.

She wouldn't face him; she'd cover her face. She'd have to shorten the veil, but it was easy just to tear it to the length she wanted. There was some jewelry among Samara's costumes, a necklace she could use to secure the veil to her hair so that it would just conceal her eyes. There were thin golden anklets and armbands of thick-beaded gold. There were chains she could drape around her neck and let fall between her breasts.

She had to do it. The veil would make it easier, would make her feel as if she were dressed.

Francesca shivered as she stepped back into the room.

Alex was bursting with anticipation to see her final choice of costume, to see how much more she would remove and reveal. He'd never been so aroused, so hard, so inflamed by any woman before.

And she was taking her time, too, damn her, knowing exactly what that did to a man.

But he could wait, even if he were whipped into a frenzy by her tactics, he wouldn't be ruled by the lustful throbbing between his legs. She could take as long as she wanted, taunt him to eternity. Eventually he would take her.

But not yet, not yet. Business first.

And those long legs meant business. Legs like that belonged wrapped around a man, sucking him into her as deep as he could go.

And suddenly she was there, naked, on the threshold, the upper half of her face shrouded by a veil, her nudity accented by the thin gold chains around her ankles, her neck, her arms.

She was breathtaking, with that long, dark hair streaming over her shoulders like Eve, and that firm curvaceous body, those full, high, taut-tipped breasts, those long, strong legs, and that coy bush of pubic hair.

He couldn't move. The ache in him was that close to erupting. If he moved. If he twitched his hips. If he said one word . . .

"I take it that *this* costume is satisfactory," she murmured in that cool, disdainful tone.

As if she didn't know what her naked body did to a man. "It will do," he answered in kind, barely keeping his lust under control. "Do your dance, Samara. I want to see what Cardston and the others will see."

That was a jolt: She hadn't expected to have to improvise something so soon, and at *his* whim. It was going to be bad enough and hard enough to writhe and gyrate in front of an audience, *if* Cardston wanted her. Why did his high-and-mighty lordship need to see a command performance?

"But you'll be there, my lord."

He raised his brows. *"Dance."*

And now what? Once again, his desire superseded everything. The air was thick with it, and the rigidity of his body told her that he wanted her—he wanted Samara, the woman of mystery and experience—and he was very close to losing what little control he had.

What did he expect, if he wanted a naked woman prancing around him? No, maybe what he wanted was a blatant invitation to couple with Samara.

Which he would *never* receive from Francesca Reay.

God, she couldn't believe she was about to fabricate a dance for him. Naked. Shaking like a leaf. Pretending, pretending, pretending to be something she wasn't.

Something *he* was very willing to believe she was. And that was her greatest danger. He hadn't expected to respond to her. He couldn't have foreseen that he would feel a man's forthright desire for her.

He'd thought that was for other men—for the men he wanted her to seduce with her nudity and her dances.

And he had fallen too. How, how, *how,* in her inexperience, could she handle that too?

Clasping her hands over her head so he wouldn't detect her

agitation, Francesca stepped over the threshold and initiated a series of movements: stooping, her legs spread at an angle; circling her body downward and bending over her legs; up again, legs together, and then gyrating her hips downward until her arms touched the floor and all he could see was her bare, rounded bottom.

She rose up again, thrusting her hips back and forth, and then turning to the side and undulating her body, and her back, and the other side, so that all of her body was exposed to him as she writhed erotically in the sex-charged silence.

She felt her body responding to the heat in his gaze, to his unregenerated desire to possess her as an object that other men coveted, as a woman who could never be contained.

She understood, as she flaunted her nakedness in front of him, the power of a woman. A man couldn't live without her. He needed to see her naked and only for him. He needed to touch her body and know it belonged only to him. And he needed to nest in her most private place and know that no man had ever been there before.

And even though none of these things pertained to Samara Teva, Alex Deveney would have killed to strip off his clothes and pole himself deep and hard into the sex, the scent, and the mystery of her.

And the power and urgency of all those conflicting emotions in him were like dynamite set to explode.

Francesca sank to the ground, on her knees, as if she were the supplicant and he was her master. But even in her innocence, she knew, she absolutely knew, that she had him at her mercy.

The silence lengthened, thickened; the tension between them was so tight, she was afraid to move, afraid of what he might do, afraid of herself even, because he was so stiff, so unyielding, so unrelentingly *male*.

She'd never quite viewed him in sexual terms before. Always what he wanted of her was filtered through her perception of what Samara was capable of doing, and the amorphous, faceless men she was supposed to beguile.

But this was different. This was *him,* and her own naive responses to his mastery, his need, his hot tumultuous desire, and her nudity, and her unexpected power.

Over him.

Silence and disdain. Francesca had thought them her most potent weapons against him. But they weren't nearly as formidable as her nudity and her sex.

If she could figure just how to wield them to get what she wanted and keep him at bay . . .

She slanted a look at him as she rose slowly to her feet. No, she was not going to be able to put off the inevitable. He was a man in the grip of an insatiable hunger and he wanted to feast on *her.* On Samara.

This was insane. She had to distance him immediately.

"I trust that was satisfactory, my lord."

"It will do." He was ramrod stiff, every inch of his body; he could barely contain himself, he was so bone hard for her. She was the most luscious piece of cake. He wanted to burrow into her, into the heat and the wetness and creaminess of her.

They'd consume her, Cardston's set. They'd lick and chew every morsel of her; they'd suck her up like a Swiss roll. All she'd have to do was stand there looking at them like that, the glittering chains emphasizing her subjugation, her bondage to them, and they would devour her.

She was perfectly capable of taking them all, her glittering gaze assessing their prowess and skeptical of their stamina. She would ease from one to the other like a sinuous cat, swallowing their discharge, and dismissing them all.

Damn her courtesan's soul.

She stood like a statue, waiting on him. Not by a word or a gesture did she indicate she wanted him or that she would welcome anything he did.

He'd never felt so thwarted by any woman.

But this wasn't just any woman. This was someone who could have anyone she wanted, who wasn't ruled by unruly emotions or baser needs. Sex for her was a matter of *her* choosing the stallion who would rut in her. Of men begging her. Pleading with her. Buying her.

He couldn't see her eyes through the concealing veil. It was almost as if her eyes were inviolate, that he could look at all of her, any part of her, except her sacred eyes.

But he couldn't keep his own eyes away from her breasts and her tight, hard nipples. He wanted to touch them, squeeze them, and make her writhe and moan. He wanted to slide his hand between her legs, into that thick tuft of woman's hair; he wanted to feel her there, the wet, the heat, her woman's sex, all pulsating with need because of *him*.

And Samara Teva could not have cared less. And that infuriated him all the more.

But if he gave in to his every throbbing impulse, she would rule him forever. His body caved, suddenly, completely, without warning, sliding him into the backwash of his fantasies.

"Get dressed," he ordered harshly, as he held on to the last shred of control. "Get out of this room or I won't be responsible for the consequences."

"At your instigation, my lord." Oh, she loved the masking of her eyes. It made her bolder; it made her feel clothed in her nakedness. It gave her power. "Don't blame your folly on me."

"Get out . . . !"

"Or your decision to sell my talents off to Cardston and whoever else will pay . . ."

He rose up from the bed and she backed away. "Damn you . . ."

And backed away. "For some nefarious purpose you won't tell me . . ."

"Why should I tell a whore anything?"

And backed into the closet, and sagged against the inside wall.

Tell him the truth, the truth. You can't play this game. You can't compete with Samara. You can't dance naked in front of strange men. Why did you put yourself in a position like that?

Tell him—
TELL HIM. . . .
She listened, waiting to hear him moving toward the closet,
toward her, toward mindless culmination.
TELL HIM!
. . . I can't . . .

Cardston's note came that very day. Alex sat in the library,
turning it over in his hand, a piece of snowy-white stationery
slashed with Cardston's handwriting, brief and to the point.

> *I can't stop thinking about her. Bring me the fabulous*
> *Samara Teva, Friday night, at the stroke of nine, ready*
> *to perform for a select company of friends. All costs will*
> *be met.*

Cardston's friends . . . Alex ruminated on the list of honor-
ables and earls of the peerage who counted themselves Cardston's friends.
Spoiled every one of them, and seeking the easy up and out,
Cardston most of all, given his personal leanings. The political
barely entered into it. Cardston would always hew to the line
of least resistance and whatever would get him what he wanted
the quickest.
Money worked. Cost was no object for the coveted object
of the moment. Alex understood his mark very well.
The gathering was just two days away, a three-hour drive
deep into Somerset, but he wasn't sure they would stay overnight. Maybe. Depending on what he could do while Samara
was entertaining Cardston's friends.
His groin tightened instantly, painfully, as it always did when
he even thought her name. He clamped down ruthlessly on his
rising desire. If he let himself think of Samara, naked and
writhing, exhibiting herself to Cardston's friends, he would go
over the edge and off the beam.

"Spent the night with her again, did you?" Marcus stood on the threshold.

"Jesus, Marcus. Don't you have enough to do at the church?"

"What about the salvation of your soul?"

"Why don't you save your wife instead?" Alex snapped.

Marcus stiffened. "Phillippa is perfectly fine. But the village is scandalized by that woman remaining in the house."

"Is that so? And here I thought she'd won you over."

"Not if you're sleeping with her. Your dead brother's wife . . . ?"

"Wife seems too ordinary a word to describe her."

"Your dead brother's *whore,"* Marcus amended nastily.

"So much more *biblical,"* Alex said, holding on tight to his temper. "You can get so much more righteous, Marcus. God knows, you're excellent at that. Now, are we done? I'll say this one more time: Samara stays until *I* say she leaves."

"The servants talk," Marcus said.

"Let them."

"Mother is prostrate."

"The rest will do her good."

"You're a bastard, Alex."

Alex turned Cardston's note over again in his fingers. "Such language, brother. Very unsuitable for a minister. I'll tell you what: You tend to your own flock, Marcus, and leave me to mine."

"I won't dignify that by asking what you mean. You're making a huge mistake, Alex, taking this . . . woman . . . into our house and into our lives."

"You're boring me, Marcus. You haven't stopped on this theme since I left for Berlin."

"I can't wait till you leave again," Marcus muttered.

"Funny you should say that. Friday, Samara and I are going to Cardston's place."

"Good God, Alex. No! Cardston!"

"Cardston."

"One evening wasn't enough? You've lost your mind, Alex. How many times can you be told? I won't be responsible. . . ."

"No one asked you to be," Alex said coldly.

"You're up to something."

"Tend your own garden, Marcus. That's *my* advice. Take it."

Marcus turned on his heel and stormed out.

Alex held up the invitation. Searle would be there, without a doubt, and Crookenden, if he could get away. Otherwise, it would be a whole other set of single men. Single *lecherous* men who trolled the streets of London and the back roads of Somerset for any willing female.

And he was going to deliver one right into their hands.

He crushed Cardston's note slowly and deliberately in his hand.

Chapter Ten

The moment had really come. All her bluffs, all her lies, all her attempts to act like Samara had come down to this telling moment: She had to *be* Samara in every way, shape, and form.

That—or prison. Alex hadn't been loath to remind her; she had accepted *his* terms, and now, as his coach barreled down the dark and forbidding back roads of Somerset, he fixed his brooding gaze on her and unnerved her still more with his intensity and his silence.

How am I going to do this—how?

What was he after that he would use her like this?

A man like that—ruthless, selfish, merciless . . . God, she couldn't believe this was happening. But she should have known. She should not have left herself open for this.

She should have tried to escape before this, money be damned. Nothing was worth this . . . nothing, not even Colm.

She took a deep, shuddery breath. It was to be a party of a half-dozen men, including Crookenden and Jasper Cardston. She wasn't at all reassured that there would be two familiar faces; in wholly male company, who was to say whether any of them would remain civilized?

The carriage was coming closer and closer. It slowed and swerved around a curve, and there, suddenly, ahead of them, she saw the blaze of lights that signified they were approaching Cardston's house.

Cardston's Castle, Alex had called it. A rock pile of a ruin except for the main section of the house, and eerie as anything in a gothic novel in the dark.

Francesca squared her shoulders as the carriage drew to a halt at the iron gates, which magically swung open to give them admittance to the inner court.

Lights blazed everywhere, torches, candles, illuminating the grooms waiting to take the horses, the butler waiting to greet them.

A footman set a step by the carriage door and Francesca eased her way out and grasped his hand.

"They await you," the butler said stiffly and turned to lead the way into the grand reception hall. It was a wide square space, stone walled, high as the castle towers, with two stone staircases winding upward on either side, and three iron-girded wooden doors, two under the staircases, one directly in front of them, all of them closed, containing their secrets.

Flaming torches were chinked into the walls, flickering eerie light and ominous shadows across the marble floor.

The butler gestured toward the center door and went forward to open it for them.

Six men stood in a circle around a massive mantelpiece, sherry in hand, the lower murmur of their voices escalating with a thread of excitement as they heard her enter, and they turned to face her.

Oh my God. Not even the propriety of the moment and elegance of the surroundings could obscure the fact that she was the main event, the main course.

Cardston came toward her, his hands outstretched. "My lady."

What to do? How to act? Francesca inclined her head because she couldn't think of a thing to say. And she saw he expected that. That in spite of what they expected they viewed her with a kind of respect.

Behave like a Queen, they'll treat you like a Queen.

She could make the rules, she thought in amazement. She could set the parameters. Like little boys, they wanted that; they *needed* the discipline of someone containing their unruly male natures.

Cardston was making introductions. Crookenden, of course, she'd met; and here were Jamison, Hanscom, Sheffers and Fogg.

A minute later, Francesca couldn't tell them apart. They were all tallish, fleshy men, all in frock coats and evening dress. One of them—Hanscom—had disconcerting blue eyes. Sheffers had a beard. Fogg looked her up and down with the confidence of a man who could buy anything. But come to that, so did Cardston, who had seemed kind, at least, when he'd been at Meresham.

But there was no benevolence here. The air already reeked of provocation and lust, fueled by wine and the competitiveness of all that male virility in one room.

They wanted *her.* They weren't friends; they were foes, rivals for her attention, her notice. They could get obnoxious, offensive, obscene.

And Alex would be nowhere around.

"Some sherry, my lady?" Cardston asked solicitously—an excuse to get closer to her, to touch her, to flex his authority by virtue of his being the host. "A bite to eat?"

He looked as if he wanted to bite *her.* She looked uncertainly at Alex, as Cardston went on, "The musicians have set up in the gallery. You have only to ask for anything you want." And in an undertone, he added, "I haven't been able to get you out of my mind."

Alex heard him and glowered. Francesca removed her hand,

furious that Alex wasn't coming to her rescue. And Cardston obviously expected that she would fawn at his feet.

She'd have to handle these preening boobies herself with the magical combination of silence and disdain. It was imperative that she kept control and kept any salacious notions they had well and truly contained. "I'm sorry, my lord. I haven't given you a thought."

Cardston visibly cringed. "You will," he said, the tone of his voice, on the surface, light, but it was colored by something ominous. Something that told her her rebuff did not sit well, particularly in front of his friends.

She raised her eyebrows, which enraged him still more. "I believe you specified on the dot of nine, my lord?" The sooner she got this over with the better. "May we proceed to the gallery?"

Cardston held out his arm, sending a speaking look at his companions, as if to say, *Did I not tell you it was a ripe and ready piece?*

Alex made a sound under his breath, and Francesca allowed herself to be led through a pair of gilded doors into the anterooms of the lower floor of the castle.

All of them were sparsely furnished with a wall hanging, a chair, a table with a branch of candles, with the final door opening into a low-ceilinged room with a broad dais, a row of upholstered armchairs in front of it, and a balcony on which a violinist and cellist were tuning up their instruments.

Francesca swallowed hard. The staging area was too close to their lecherous thoughts, too close for her comfort.

"You can change in there," Cardston said coldly, pointing to a door behind the dais. "You might want to speak to the musicians first. There's a stairway back there. We'll be waiting."

"Excellent." She moved to the door, and Alex caught her arm.

"I need twenty minutes."

"For what, my lord?"

"For you to keep their minds occupied with sex and sin."

"As you wish," she said insolently. "Whatever you wish. You might arrange my sacred objects on the stage."

"I'll *arrange* to have someone do it."

"That will do." She disappeared behind the door, leaving him heaving with frustration at her cool, calm acceptance of everything.

He had no choice now; he had to go ahead with his plans, no matter what his feelings about leaving Samara with Cardston's debauched friends.

And why should he have such feelings? They all knew what Samara was, he most of all.

No, the thing was to accomplish the mission—if indeed there was anything to find. He would station himself behind the row of chairs and slip out the moment she made her appearance.

And he wouldn't even worry about her. She understood exactly what needed to be done.

Samara Teva could take care of herself.

The marble floor was cold, and the cold seeped up into her limbs as she stood wrapped in a black cape, waiting for that explosive moment between anticipation and desire.

For one electric moment, she'd thought that she was alone and that she could get away. But behind the ominous doors, a pretty little maid waited to assist her with dressing.

Cardston's idea—or Alex's?

Did it matter? There was no chance of ever being alone, of ever finding an opportunity to escape.

And where would she have gone anyway? she thought, letting the maid unhook her dress. She'd have gotten lost in the castle the minute she stepped foot out of the room. And she couldn't have thrown herself on Cardston's mercy. Or Crookenden's.

Cardston probably would have done the same with her as Alex: locked her up, punished her for her effrontery, and then used her for his pleasure.

Whatever was to happen, this scenario was better. She'd forestall them somehow until Alex returned. She'd figure out something to keep them in line. At the very least, she'd keep them waiting. Alex had hated every moment she'd made him wait.

It was yet another powerful weapon in her arsenal.

The cellist sounded a note. The maid opened the door to a darkened room lit only by candles on a platform on the dais.

Francesca paused on the threshold, waiting, waiting, and then she stepped onto the dais, holding her cape tightly around her with shaking hands, furiously trying to think of some way to take control.

Make it seem exalted. . . . Make it something consecrated. . . .

Maybe . . . maybe they would respect something that was portrayed as sacrosanct. . . .

She moved toward the edge of the dais to stand before her audience in a posture of humility.

"I give you a sacred dance of Eastern temples, where a woman is revered, and any man who dares to touch her is murdered in his prime by supernatural forces that no one has ever been able to explain."

That should make them think twice, she thought, swirling around so that her back was to them and gliding upstage to the platform and the candles.

No backing out now. She made a deep reverent bow to the artifacts on the platform. Alex had chosen them, little golden relics, encircled by candles, to lend a quasireligious note to the atmosphere.

She took a deep, shuddering breath. She couldn't put it off much longer. Girding herself, she let the cape slide down her back to reveal her long black hair and two transparent panels of silk, appended from a golden collar and two gold bracelets, caressing her bare buttocks. She lifted her arms to pull a veil over her eyes, and the panels parted like wings to reveal a gold chain nestling just below the small of her back.

The candlelight caught the glitter of the gold as she folded her arms over her breasts and turned slowly around to face them.

Francesca knew what they saw: her bowed head, her body enfolded in the sinuous silk, the golden chains that emphasized her neck, her arms, her ankles.

She lifted her head, and the music shifted into a glissando of atonal notes that was her signal to begin the dance.

She dropped her arms, only hearing the intake of breath, the guttural sound of lust, as she revealed her naked body, her high, tight-tipped breasts enhanced by a long golden ball and chain that fell from the golden collar almost to her navel.

She saw movement in the shadows—Alex?—and she whipped her arms over her breasts and began the stylized movements of the dance: back to front, front to back, revealing and concealing until she was almost at the edge of the dais, and then she held out her arms, angled her legs, and crouched down.

Now what? They were riveted by her nudity, the chains, and all she revealed. She shifted her weight from side to side and watched as their eyes followed her every movement.

Upright now, a little awkwardly, concealing her body, sliding away from them, and bending over to give them another view of her bottom.

Up then, her arms up, turning sideways, her hands on her hips, pumping her body, thrusting, arching her back so her breasts became exaggerated shadows against the light, the nipples tight and hard and mouthwatering.

She had no idea how much time had elapsed. She heard the men, panting and moaning in the shadows, as she swiveled her hips and ground downward to her knees.

Looking upward in supplication, downward in submission. Stretching out her arms, giving herself to her master. And folding her arms over her breasts, hiding herself forever. Lowering herself in obedience until her head touched the floor.

Waiting for an interlude as the music sawed on, feeling the excitement and the heightened anticipation, hearing their heavy breathing, inhaling the scent of lust.

They couldn't get enough of her; it was as palpable as a touch.

She lifted her head, still holding the concealing panels close, trying desperately to see if Alex had returned, but she couldn't see anything beyond the fog of voluptuous heat.

Damn. How did anyone get gracefully to her feet from this position?

Not possible. She had to use her hands. She lowered them to the floor, and shifted her weight onto her arms, and then lifted her body upright.

Now, she edged into the shadows, moving backward slowly, reverently, making obeisance to the objects on the platform that Alex had devised.

This was enough. She couldn't think of another thing to do.

She turned to the audience, lifted her arms to give them one last view of her naked body, and sank, overcome, to the floor.

Alex hadn't wanted to see one minute of her performance. He stood poised at the rear of the room, feeling the suffocating heat and the wolfish hunger that suffused the air.

This was nothing to her, just a way to earn yet another hundred pounds. And the money was everything to her. Easy money for someone who was accustomed to showing off her body.

Yes. And that on top of the price he'd negotiated from Cardston.

Cardston was desperate to have her. And after tonight's performance, there would be no holding him back. Or the others.

But Alex didn't want to contemplate the consequences of that. And anyway, it was Samara's business, not his, whether Cardston would get his way.

For all he cared, she could stay the night with Cardston, the week, forever if she wanted, once he'd accomplished his aim.

The door opened and she slipped onstage and boldly to the edge.

Her announcement was a brilliant trick, giving anyone who was her protector leeway to defend her virtue. And truly, for one moment, the audience looked taken aback.

And then she slipped off the cape, lifted her arms, turned—and began the show.

His cue—while Cardston and his friends slavered over her nudity, he slipped out the door.

It was over.

Alex crept back into the room just as Samara began her little back-to-front sashay around the stage.

All for nothing. He'd done what he could, but he hadn't really expected to find anything. His first mandate had been to eliminate possibilities. But all he could conclude was it probably wasn't Cardston, or if it was, he had the whole operation too cleverly concealed to be rooted out in twenty minutes.

He'd gone through Cardston's papers too, and even there, he had found no hint that Cardston was involved in anything more nefarious than keeping three mistresses, gaming at the worst hellholes in London, and running up debts with creditors he never paid.

His pockets were deep too, but he was notoriously tightfisted, even with his mistresses, except when he really wanted something—like Samara—and there was no sign that he lusted after anything more than a willing woman who would spread her legs. No one would ever think of taking him to stud even with his reputation, but Alex couldn't take any chances.

The topical details had to be scrutinized as thoroughly as possible without arousing Cardston's suspicions, and if what he saw was to be believed, everyone's eyes had been rooted on Samara Teva for the full twenty minutes he'd been gone and no one had even noticed his absence.

That dance would sear ice. Those moves, that body . . . Alex felt himself coiling up in the space of an instant as Samara raised her arms and gave them one last view of her nakedness.

The silence, as she slumped to the floor, was stunning. No one moved. No one spoke. Heat rose in waves, the air moist, thick, awash in the scent of sex and driven by an unslakable hunger.

They could never have her, Alex thought. No one could possess her. And she wouldn't want them. He knew that as surely as he knew she didn't want *him*.

He felt like slamming his fist into something.

He had to get her out of there, and he hadn't planned exactly how he was going to accomplish that. It would take a great deal more finesse than he felt at the moment to thwart Cardston's will.

He wished there were a curtain or some way to douse the lights. Samara had no easy way to exit into the anteroom without revealing herself and inflaming all of them still more.

He had to take some decisive action. Everyone else was still mesmerized.

He moved toward the dais, blocking Cardston's view. *Mistake.*

"How much?" Cardston's voice, rough with sexual hunger.

Alex leapt onto the dais and pulled the cape from the far edge, where Samara had dropped it, and draped it over her prone body.

"I said, how much?" The pampered aristocrat who would not be denied, Cardston bullnosed his way to the edge of the dais.

Francesca eased herself up into a sitting position, the cape wrapped tightly around her body so that nothing was visible, not even her feet.

No control here, she thought, panicked. Not when a man's pleasure was involved.

"My lord doesn't understand . . ." she started to say.

"I understand." Cardston ruthlessly cut her off. "Name your price—per man."

Alex didn't bat an eye. "She's not for sale."

"My dear Alex, don't go banging off over nothing. I thought I made myself clear about the arrangement." Cardston was nose to nose with him now. "And wasn't that what that little appetizer was all about two nights ago?"

Alex stared him down. "No."

"You're serious?" Cardston demanded in disbelief. "You prick-piss. She gets us all cocked up in the expectation of a good hard frothing and now we're supposed to give ourselves a mercy blow?" He doubled up his fists. "No, Deveney. The terms were clear, you son of a bitch, and I *will* have this ten-bob tart, and that's all I'll pay for her too."

He vaulted onto the dais and grasped Francesca's cape. "No more naffing around, you stupid buntrap. It's time to put and take, and no excuses from you." He pulled hard so that Francesca lost her balance and tumbled onto her side, and before she could react, he straddled her, confining her squirming body and flailing arms and legs.

"That's the way, my darling diddy," he crooned now that he had her, and he was so hotted up, his lust to possess her obscured everything else—including Alex creeping up behind him. "Just roll over and spread your legs . . . argghhhhh—" as Alex whipped his arm around Cardston's neck and wrenched it hard, and pulled him off of Francesca's shaking body.

"Frog's spawn. Blow bag. Cod wallop"—as he mashed Cardston down on the floor—"son of a madder's whore . . ." His fury went maniacal, coming from deep in his gut; suddenly he was choking Cardston, and banging his head against the floor, and even that was too good for that no-good Johnny Rutter.

He heard voices, recognized Crookenden's, but he couldn't let go, couldn't . . . the thought of Cardston, naked, and humping and pumping into Samara's body . . . his ham hands touching her . . . Cardston's mouth devouring hers . . . he saw red . . . he saw death . . . he saw, with the flickering sane part of his mind, that Samara was not on the dais . . . and only then did he loosen his grip and allow Crookenden to pull him away.

They left Cardston on the floor, holding his throat and cursing.

"If he had taken her, he would have died," Alex said, his voice rusty with some emotion he didn't want to define. "And I can't even promise he'll live out the night, because he dared to touch her. This isn't some tottie off the street, and you jerry-screws acted like humping gorillas in the face of a ceremonial performance that to her is devotional and inviolate."

That sounded good. He liked that. But he didn't fool anyone, by the looks on all their faces.

"Spit it up the wall, Alex," Crookenden said, without rancor. "You can tib and fib with the best of them, trying to pass that dolly-pot off as a nun. But you can't jigger us. We were offered some rub and gob, and no one mistook the invitation. The hell with it. Cardston said she had every man jack in Europe panting after her, and she took 'em on, one by one."

Dammit—dammit, dammit. Samara's reputation had just jettisoned him into a dead end.

"Until she married William," Alex reminded them as Hanscom helped Cardston up from the floor.

"She's a piss-pot," Cardston grumbled, still rubbing his throat. "And she's always been a tump slut. That's all they said about her all over Europe."

"She's a widow and deeply devoted to her sacred ritual dance," Alex said with a righteous note in his voice.

"Oh, poke it up your blowhole," Cardston retorted. "Get her out of here. I've had enough of this. A waste of my time and money. Bugger it. I need some jam tarts. Anyone coming with me?" He stalked out of the room.

"Watch out her guardian doesn't come after you," Alex called.

Crookenden looked at Alex and shook his head. "Nice jiggle and bob, Alex. But that's the last time you jerk anyone else around."

Alex shrugged. "I know what I know."

Crookenden threw up his hands. "I'll leave you to it, then. The butler will see to your carriage. Gentlemen—?"

Alex watched cynically as they followed him out, like good little gophers, all hot and eager to rut in the first available furrow.

. . . Samara . . . !

He leapt across the dais to the door and rammed it open.

The little maid cowered in a corner, looking like a rag doll, as if someone had punched the stuffing out of her. And there was no one else in the room.

God almighty—what if Cardston had come back for her? Alex felt his gut clutch with fear.

"Where is she?"

"Ar . . ." the maid whimpered, scared to her teeth.

He grabbed her and shook her. *"Where* is she?"

"G-gone, sir . . ."

He felt like killing her. What if Samara had escaped him? What if she were gone—forever?

"Where?"

The maid pointed wordlessly up the narrow steps to the balcony.

Alex took them two at a time, not in time, up into the passageway, not that much time gone; pounding his way back toward the dining room, not . . . not—not . . . if Cardston got her—

Not . . . not . . . not—

Where was she?

Down the steps to the dining room—through the anterooms, bursting into the parlor—and she wasn't there.

Wasn't.

He found a bellpull, and immediately Cardston's impassive butler appeared as if by magic.

"Did the lady call the carriage?" he demanded.

"The carriage has been called."

And could be gone.

Alex leapt for the parlor door.

* * *

Free . . . in minutes, freedom.

Francesca edged into the shadows in the courtyard as she heard the heavy footsteps of Cardston and his friends making their way out to the stables.

If they discovered her here . . .

If Alex came—her whole body swelled with the sweet thought of revenge. He'd be looking for her now, racing through the castle and down its myriad corridors and through its interlinking rooms, frantic to find her, in a fury because all his stupid plans had come to nothing.

When the carriage came, she would tell the driver to take her to Lincolnshire, to Braidwood, to safety.

Let it come soon, she thought, she prayed. She'd had enough of Alex Deveney, enough of mysteries and secrets and Samara's debauched career. Enough of everything.

She was horrified by Cardston's wrath, and appalled by her own imprudence. She would never recover from having displayed herself like that. She didn't even know where she'd summoned up the brass to actually do it.

What is wrong with me?

I don't want to go to prison for Samara's sins. This was a very bad experiment that is going to cost Alex dearly, including the hundred pounds he owes me. And then, I just want to get out of here.

I want to stop pretending to be Samara.

I'll tell him. . . .

"Samara! Samara!" Alex's voice in the distance, rocketing to the stars. "Damn it. . . ."

Samara Teva causing him no end of frustration, no end of grief.

She knew exactly how he would see it—Samara the temptress wreaking havoc among men who were helpless to resist.

No one felt more helpless than she.

"Samara . . ."

Alex burst out of the front doors of the castle just as the carriage wheeled into the courtyard.

Francesca had perhaps three minutes' advantage of him. She darted out to meet the carriage as Alex shouted to her, and pulled open the door.

"Keep driving," she hissed at the driver as she hooked her foot onto the fragile step, and with all her remaining strength, she levered herself inside and onto the floor, and lay there, panting.

Oh God, keep driving—as she heard the gritty crunch of Alex's mad dash toward the carriage, felt it sway as he grabbed on to the door and leapt onto the step, heard it crack under his weight, and felt him launch himself into the carriage as it swerved out of the courtyard gates, and had her breath knocked out as he landed on top of her.

The door banged against the frame as the carriage picked up speed on the desolate country road.

Neither of them moved. Neither said a word. Once again Francesca took Alex's unfamiliar weight and thrust, and she didn't know what to do. He was so supremely there, his elbows braced on either side of her shoulders, his face so close to hers as the carriage swayed and their bodies undulated back and forth with the motion.

Alex could read nothing in her eyes. Once again, she closed herself away from him, and he felt the familiar irritation, that even now, as she cradled his body in the aftermath of this disaster, she evinced no emotion and she neither accepted him nor pushed him away.

Because she knew she could have any man, she wanted no one.

After that sex-searing performance tonight, he wanted her to want *him.*

"Samara . . ."

"Don't—" she breathed, knowing full well he would not

be deterred. He was fascinated with Samara—with the *her* who was Samara—and she was not unaware, even in her innocence, of that banked, simmering desire in him. He wanted what Samara had given so freely to so many other men: He wanted everything she had given them tonight; and he wanted, on some level, a reward for having saved her from Cardston.

Francesca had no other choice but to deny him; she still considered that her virginity, her loyalty, her love had been pledged to Colm all those years ago, and she'd catapulted herself into this awful situation to save him.

Her weapons were still the same: silence and disdain. She stiffened her body and turned her head away.

But it wasn't going to work this time.

Alex lowered his head to get her attention, because she didn't want to look at him, she didn't want to hear anything he had to say. "You'll never, ever escape me. . . ." he murmured, his lips close to her ear.

She swiveled her head to look at him, to refute his arrogant declaration, and he crushed her mouth, her dark invader, plundering, dominating, giving her not a breath, giving her not an inch to all his suppressed desire, giving, giving, giving something she did not understand.

Kisses. She didn't understand kisses either. He devoured her virginal mouth, and each foray increased his hunger for more. What was it about a kiss? She was helpless under the onslaught; he took what he wanted and she let him feast his fill.

But kissing her didn't satiate him; rather she aroused him still more, and combined with the rock and sway of the carriage, the fretful movement of her body under his, and the image in his mind's eye of her naked body sinuously taunting and teasing her audience, he was primed like a blast cap and ready to explode.

"Samara . . ." His lips hovered barely an inch above hers.

Her impenetrable black eyes stared back at him, unmoved, unaroused, uncaring of his need, his frustration, his hunger, and her expression told him all he needed to know.

Samara Teva, who had once reveled in luxury and wealth, was on her high horse and wouldn't allow herself to be taken on the floor of a carriage. But she would allow herself to dance naked in front of strange men and show off the most private parts of her body.

And *show off* was the term. Right at the edge of the dais, letting them have a full, unobstructed view of her courtesan's body. Knowing what it did to them. Knowing they drooled over it. Knowing they'd pay to possess it.

Knowing she had the power to deny them all.

That was power.

Alex cursed. And she had the brass to act as if she were too good for *him*, when he was the one who had removed her from penury and allowed her the use of William's name.

She was an object of sin unto herself. And all she cared about was the next hundred pounds.

She had earned it tonight, he thought acidly, swallowing down his fierce sexual hunger. And perhaps, if he paid her, she would reconsider her position—although she was hardly in control at the moment.

. . . maybe she was—all she'd had to do was look at him with those eyes, and all his lascivious intentions shriveled into curses and resentment.

Oh, she was a master at it, he thought. *Let a man have a taste of her by strutting around naked, let him engorge his senses in her mouth, give him the feel of riding her surging body, and then politely say no.*

But not to him—no woman he wanted had ever refused him, and she, slum bitch that she was, would not be the first.

"I will have you," he murmured, slamming down hard on his anger and settling his mouth on hers again in a long, hard, harsh kiss that mirrored his resentment and defeat.

Still, he could barely force himself to pull away from her, and he despised himself for his growing weakness where she was concerned.

A man could only stand so much, and he still had hours to

travel with her, and hours to think how perfectly she had performed that naked, lewd dance for the most depraved audience in England. How perfectly she had carried out her orders, her mandate.

How perfectly she loved wriggling naked around that makeshift stage.

Damn and blast her.

Alex watched as she gracefully levered herself up onto the seat and smoothed out her dress, the second of the two dresses Phillippa had given her. And no less alluring than her nudity, the way it fit her. Or did she just look like a temptress in everything she wore? But then, he knew what she looked like naked.

There was only one way to combat her allure. He reached into his pocket and withdrew a folded wad of notes and flung them at her.

"You earned it."

She caught them with an expert hand and slanted an unblinking look at him. "Yes, I did," she agreed unflinchingly. Four hundred pounds now, enough to get away from him forever, in spite of his boasts and arrogant assumptions and plans.

She had never hated him more. The problem was, Samara probably wouldn't have. Samara would have reveled in his attention and the money, and the possibilities inherent in attracting a whole new wealthy, vigorous *male* audience.

And what did you revel in, Francesca? You didn't entirely hate that dance. You didn't entirely despise the fact that your nakedness made a roomful of men go wild.

Or that Alex Deveney is besotted with the idea of Samara Teva.

No—! Don't think that . . . don't let it even creep into your consciousness.

She stared out the side window of the rocking carriage. Nothing to be seen but darkness, and the looming eerie shadows cast by the carriage lights.

Like a nightmare; like her life since she had become Samara.

What was wrong with her, thinking that somehow she'd derived some pleasure from all the things that Alex was forcing her to do.

And soon, soon, he was going to catch on to the fact that everything about her contradicted the reality of Samara Teva. And then what would she do?

"Oh, don't even think it, Samara."

She jumped. *Good God, could he now read her mind?*

He leaned forward, in a posture of mastery and menace, a vision of her naked, undulating body firmly in his mind.

"Understand this: I will never let you get away. Never. Play your games if you have to. Pretend to be the virgin of the manor if you must. Ride your high horse, even though everyone knows you're a promiscuous mare. But make no mistake, Samara, I *will* have you, and the only one you'll ever ride again is *me.*"

Chapter Eleven

How did one seduce a courtesan?

Alex pondered this weighty question as the carriage traveled on through the night, and Samara Teva slept, an ill-conceived defense against his threats and his overt desire.

A gentleman would never take a woman against her will or while she was unconscious.

But he was beginning to rethink the rules where Samara was concerned. There were no rules. There was just her notoriety, that body, and a man's volatile craving to embed himself in it.

And that was the sum and substance of her fascination. Surely it would prove that owning her could not be nearly as satisfying as the *thought* of possessing her. Of bending her, filling her, and making her beg to come.

How many men had satisfied that body? His manhood seized up at the thought of it. His mind's eye pictured it: Samara recumbent on the dais and welcoming them all and taking them, as Cardston had so eloquently desired, one by one.

Who among those lickerish mollies was stallion enough to bring her to the gallop?

Me.
But first he had to get her to trot.

It was Marcus who barged in the next morning, and he didn't even bother to say good morning before he launched into the bad news.

"It will be all over the whole of Somerset by nightfall, Alex. Your damned amoral friend, Cardston, is boasting about her private performance last night. He's told Alastair that she danced naked for them and took them on, one by one, five times each, besides, and you know what that means. Alastair will send out his servants to spread that news. You've done the Deveney name proud, Alex, dragged it right down into the dirt with that . . . that— I'm so upset, I don't even know where to look, let alone what to say. My congregants . . . our friends . . ."

He sank into a chair opposite Alex, shaking. "You're demented, taking in that woman. She can't be saved. She doesn't want to be saved. And you've encouraged her *not* to seek salvation. I swear she'll be *your* downfall just as she was William's—"

"Good God, Marcus—" Alex interrupted, ignoring all the verbal hand-wringing. "Cardston says—*what?*"

"That they all had a piece of her—as you damned well know. My God almighty, is there a man born who was never tempted by sin . . . ?"

"Did he?" Alex murmured. "How perfect. Better than I could have orchestrated. A bonus, Marcus, and so timely."

"You've lost your mind. I can't *talk* to you. . . ."

"Alastair, you said?"

Marcus nodded mutely.

"He'll be next," Alex predicted. "They'll all want her now, but I think—I think we *won't* give them what Cardston got. I think I made a tactical error there. . . ."

Marcus stumbled to his feet. "I truly must pray for your soul, Alex."

"Sit *down,* Marcus."

Marcus sat. "You're up to something."

"Cardston's lying."

"Oh, and who is everyone going to believe, given that woman's reputation?"

"It doesn't matter who believes him."

"I will *never* be able to hold my head up in church this Sunday," Marcus moaned.

"It's Cardston who can't hold it up," Alex murmured. "It will do, it will do. Stop caterwauling, Marcus. I swear to you, on Queen and country, Cardston and his scrotes never touched her."

Marcus's head jerked up. "You mean—"

"Marcus!"

"Darling—" Marcus rose from his chair as Phillippa appeared on the threshold.

"Getting all the dirt, I see. Can't rest without knowing every last detail, can you?" She strode into the dining room. "Alex, you should be shot, bringing that woman into our lives."

"My dear, I was only telling Alex . . ."

"And I'm certain Alex was telling you—all the gory details." Phillippa sat purposefully in the chair next to Alex. "Where are your stupid servants? Or are they all waiting on *her?"*

"Oh, Phillippa, my dear . . . don't—" Marcus was at her side immediately, on his knees. "I didn't . . . you know how I feel—"

"I don't know anything," Phillippa said stonily, "except that woman has turned this whole house inside out and Alex has become her . . . her *panderer."*

Marcus literally fell backward. *"Phillippa . . . !"*

"What, you don't think a lady knows such words? Let me disabuse you of *that* notion. A lady knows those words and what that woman *really* is and what Alex is doing with her up in his bedroom—that's what a lady knows." Phillippa banged her fist on the table in frustration. "And every stupid *male* in the county can't wait to hear the lewd details. Including my own husband.''

"Phillippa, *no* . . .'' Marcus was patting her hands, her arms, and she slapped him away. "Alex . . . ?''

"You have your hands full," Alex said. "I don't get in the middle of family altercations.''

"Indeed," Phillippa retorted, "you've never been known to take anyone's side—except that *slut's*. Which proves just how much power a woman can wield over a man. I wish I had understood that before you went off and imported your own high-priced whore.''

"Phillippa—'' Marcus protested, trying to wrap his arms around her.

Phillippa raised her hands to push him away—and froze. "And there she is, perfect timing, perfect entrance. Good morning, Samara. Don't you look rested—and sated. I wonder that Alex is confident enough that he's letting you prowl the grounds like a bitch in heat.''

That was too much, even for Marcus. He looked at Francesca, who stood dead still in the doorway, her face preternaturally pale against the severe black dress she wore, and he got to his feet.

"I apologize, Samara. That was ill considered of my wife." He grasped Phillippa's arm to pull her to her feet. "You'll excuse us. We must be going.''

Phillippa wrenched away and stood up. *"Don't* apologize for me to that party piece, Marcus Deveney. No, you stay, since you're so fascinated by sin. I'm sure Samara would love to go over every salacious detail with you—in the guise of her confession. I'm sure you'll find the time and good reason to expiate *her* sins.''

"Phillippa . . .'' Marcus called futilely as she jostled Francesca and stalked out of the room.

"Let her go," Alex said.

Marcus sank into his chair. "I don't know what to do with her.''

"You'll figure it out," Alex said. "Take a seat, Samara. Breakfast is served."

"Or maybe I'm the main course," Francesca murmured, still a little shaken by Phillippa's rage. "I'll have Wotten bring something to my—your room."

"Sit down."

She sat. A maid immediately came forth and poured her a cup of tea.

"Tell Marcus—nothing happened last night."

She lifted her cup, sipped, and looked at Marcus over the rim. "I wouldn't go so far as to say that, my lord."

Marcus flushed, and Francesca could see that her answer was meaningful to him. But everything this morning was slightly out of kilter, including Wotten's delivering Alex's invitation to join him for breakfast.

She wasn't naive enough to think that Alex trusted her. Or that he felt any guilt about anything that had happened last night. Rather, it was likely he wanted something.

And in fact, he trusted her not at all: If she'd thought to try to escape, her hopes were instantly dashed. She'd seen any number of servants stationed covertly all through the hallways as she'd made her way downstairs.

And she'd heard most of Phillippa's diatribe as well.

But she liked Marcus, even if he didn't like *her*. He looked too distressed at Alex's candor, and almost didn't know quite what to do with his hands or his eyes. And he was, beneath his robes and his religion, insatiably curious about her.

Phillippa, she reflected, was not too far off the mark.

"Let me reassure you . . ." she started, and then wondered just how she should phrase it. *None of those pigs wallowed in me*. No. That didn't quite work.

She saw Alex, waiting impatiently.

Silence. Disdain. Make him wait.

But then she took pity on Marcus. "Let me just reiterate that whatever Alex told you is true. I danced for the gentlemen, as we had arranged. Nothing more."

Marcus looked slightly relieved. "They say there was much more."

"I see," she murmured. Why hadn't she expected that? She should have, especially after she'd spurned Cardston. He was too fragile, and there were too many witnesses. Of course, he would claim he had conquered her. Ten times over, he would claim, and probably that she groveled at his feet.

It nauseated her, and she put down her tea. Obviously, this episode wasn't over yet.

She picked up her cup and directed her gaze at Alex. "All right, Alex. You don't fool me. You certainly can't distract Marcus. What more can you possibly want of me?"

It started to rain as Phillippa stormed out of the house, and she felt a searing sense of the unfairness of things. Rain. Whores. Ineffectual husbands. It was all of a piece. Nothing ever went right for *her*.

How could a proper, virtuous, and seemly minister's wife compete against a beautiful, voluptuous, exotic *foreigner* who danced naked on tabletops for anyone who tossed her a groat.

Just the thought of it must turn any man's nether parts to stone.

And God knew, Marcus wasn't immune. He was titillated and fascinated by the creature and willing to spend time speculating about her and listening to her.

A woman like that commanded every man's attention, of which Marcus had given her precious little in the several years they'd been married. He was truly a man of the cloth, sacred, gentle, caring.

Boring.

Phillippa had married him because she wanted Alex. Desperately, fiercely, intensely, and she always thought she had more time.

Time to make him notice her, time for him to be kind. He'd look at her and see the body of a goddess, the woman he wanted to possess, and he would take her somewhere in the vast parklands of Meresham and make violent love to her, just as she'd always dreamed.

But Alex, in all these years, had never once looked at her like that, or treated her like that. She was Marcus's wife first, moral, upstanding, protected, and secure. And he never heard the need in her voice or saw the hunger in her eyes.

And now he had eyes only for Samara Teva—the slut, the strumpet, the whore who spread her legs for everyone—and he treated her like a queen. He took her to his bed, and he did luscious, forbidden things with her in the dark, and she let him, and she was naked for him, and she wanted him to.

How did a good woman defend herself against that?

But Phillippa wasn't good, deep in her heart. Way down there, it was her most secret wish to be the kind of woman who could make men grovel for her favors. In her dreams, they put her on a pedestal, they worshiped her. They spent themselves at the mere sight of her ankles, her leg, her bosom.

And sometimes, when she let herself, she had lascivious dreams and lewd yearnings and a ferocious desire to compromise her husband's brother and get him in her bed so he would do all those delicious sinful things to her.

It was clear now that, with Samara Teva in residence, none of those things would ever happen, that she would die never knowing what it was like to exercise that kind of power over a man. Alex Devency would never want her, and Marcus would bore her forever.

Where was that wild desire she'd daydreamed about in her youth? She felt twice her age and more, up against a wall of rectitude and sanctity, and surrounded by tempting, thrilling, provocative sin.

Phillippa didn't know if the wet on her face was the rain or her tears. Her body ached with the need to be touched, to be desired by a love so overwhelming it would just sweep her away.

But none of that was in the stars for her, the minister's wife.

None of that, ever, now that Samara Teva lived in her world. Samara was the one every man desired. Samara with her body, her dances, her nudity, her knowing, insufferable, insolent smile . . .

Oh my God, I've got to stop thinking like this. I've got to, got to, got to. . . .

She barely knew where she was. She had deliberately veered away from the Rectory—how could she go home with all this wickedness on her conscience?—and she saw that she had come to the fenced-in edge of one of the far fields.

. . . places she'd dreamt that someone would ravish her . . . Alex . . .

She grasped her head in anguish. She could never *be* Samara Teva, could never be the seductive creature that she was in her mind. She had to let it go, let all of it go. Let Alex prostitute himself for that . . . that wanton. Let Marcus drool all over what he couldn't have. Let her resign herself to a dreary, tedious, lackluster life with Marcus. . . . Let everyone just go to—

"My God, you're tall." The sound of a deep, resonant male voice in the depths of the drizzle and her despair was shocking, almost as if she'd conjured it up out of thin air.

Phillippa wheeled around, her heart pounding, to find the man just dismounting his horse. And to find that he was everything she wanted him to be.

I'm dreaming. I fell asleep somewhere in the rain, and I'm having this wondrous fantasy. . . .

She pushed her damp hair away from her face to get a better look at him. Oh, he was beautiful, with blond hair, and deep blue eyes that roamed all over her and made her feel warm. He had a firm muscular body and he was tall, like her, and elegantly dressed even for a day's riding in the rain.

"I don't speak to strangers," she said haughtily, devouring him with her gaze, and then abruptly turning away. Too tempting, too dangerous. Too redolent of sex and sin. She couldn't do it. She thought she could, but even in this dream, she couldn't; even with a man like him, she couldn't.

He caught her arm. "But we're not strangers anymore, my love."

She stopped in her tracks. "Then what are we?"

"Whatever *you* want us to be," he murmured, pulling her close.

Oh, this was an excellent dream, perfect perfect perfect....

Phillippa leaned against his chest, feeling his heat, his urgency, reveling in his height, and the hard feel of his body against hers.

"Who are you?" she whispered.

"You give me my name," he murmured, his lips against her ear. "I will be whoever *you* want me to be."

Oh God, it was so tempting. She could call him the name of the man who inhabited her dreams. She could dare to take a lover who would enact all the forbidden sins.

Did she dare?

"You are so beautiful." He slid his hands down her shoulders. "So desirable. An enchantress in the rain. A goddess." He encircled her midriff. "How did I ever find you?" He cupped her breasts, brushing her nipples with his thumbs, and she trembled. "How can I ever let you go?"

"Don't," she whispered, arching herself into his hands and turning her head to invite his kiss.

His mouth settled over hers awkwardly at first, and then with a shuddering, devouring urgency.

Phillippa had never been kissed like this, never been fondled like this. A dozen contrary sensations streamed through her body; willingly she allowed him to turn her toward him, to unfasten and push down the bodice of her dress, to rain kisses on her mouth, her neck, her shoulders, her breasts. And finally, to fasten his mouth onto one and the other nipple, in a hot, hard sucking motion that made her whole body weak.

Phillippa hung on to his shoulders—his broad, broad shoulders—as he backed her up against a tree and fed on the tight nubs of her breasts, pulling, licking, sucking until she was breathless and begging for more.

"I want more and more and more of you," he whispered. "I want you all to myself. Tell me it's possible. Don't walk out of my life now."

"How could I?" she moaned. *How could I, when in five minutes you've given me more of myself as a woman than Marcus has in five years?*

"Listen. This is not how any man wants to be with his lady—outside in the cold and rain." Tenderly, he removed himself from her breasts and dressed her, kissing her all the while, murmuring the words she had always yearned to hear. "Tell me you'll come with me now. I want you. Only you can ease my torment, Goddess. I need to know you want that, that you want me right where I want to be. . . ."

Oh, yes, yes, yes—I want that. I want you. . . .

"I want you," she sighed.

"Come."

Come. That was the whole, true secret of what she always wanted. A man to make her come, to drive her so hard and relentlessly that she screamed with pleasure, and then promptly did it all over again.

She didn't know his name. She didn't know how long she spent in the village cottage that he had rented for the summer. She didn't want to know details or anything.

All she wanted was the pure, bone-dissolving pleasure of this man desiring her in the most elemental and primitive way.

For hours, she lay flat on her back, naked, as he pummeled her, pushing and pounding in raw, hot possession of her. And she reveled in every minute of it, playing the coquette, coaxing, pouting, teasing, and arousing him until she got her way.

He was huge, long and pulsating, tactile and hard.

Phillippa couldn't get enough of him. It was like a dam had burst within her and she was making up for lost time.

And he was equal to the effort, with the stamina of a bull, coming at her and coming at her, riding her waves, making her moan.

"I have to go," she murmured sleepily late in the afternoon.

"You have to come," he contradicted, posing himself once again between her legs and just pushing the tip of his rock-hard erection inside her.

"Make me," she taunted, and he pushed and pushed, torturously, an inch at a time, watching triumphantly as she spasmed in waves until he was buried to the hilt.

"Don't go."

"I must."

"I won't let you." He rammed into her again. "I can stay right here forever."

"I know you can. But I can't. I can't." *Oh God, I can't. . . .*

He heard the note in her voice.

"Are you—married . . . ?"

Phillippa turned her head away and moaned as he eased himself out.

"You hate me."

He shook his head. "I'd hoped against hope that my goddess was free. But how could such a luscious creature as you not be taken? How can I hope to see you again?"

"You can hope," Phillippa whispered. "I want to. Do you?"

"Must you ask?"

"Tell me when," she begged, a little desperately. How would she get through the night without his forceful coupling with her?

He gave it a moment's thought. "Tomorrow . . . here, the same time. Can you? I won't be able to bear it until . . ."

"Neither will I," she whispered.

"One more time before you leave me. . . ." He was stiff and raring to go, a testament to how much he desired her body, her sex, *her.*

Phillippa felt potent, powerful. Desired.

She opened her arms and spread her legs. "One more time, my stallion. And then maybe one more time again . . ."

*   *   *

Alex wanted Francesca to dance again. Lord almighty, after last night's fiasco, after the wildfire gossip, and all the salacious speculation yet to come, he still wanted her to dance.

She closed her eyes just so she wouldn't have to look at him. And she had an ally in Marcus.

Marcus said exactly what he thought. "You're insane, Alex, and you're pushing this way too far; you're upsetting everyone. Mother hasn't come down from her room since Sir Edmund was here, and now you've brought all this gossip down on our heads. The sensible thing would be to pay her off and let her go, and whatever you're involved in, take it on another way."

"But you know I've never been sensible," Alex said.

"Put it this way: You've always done what you wanted and gotten your own way," Marcus snapped.

"And I intend to keep on doing so, brother. The Deveney name will survive, I promise you. Mother will survive. And I'll thank you to keep any more of your opinions to yourself."

"Fine. Obviously, as always, there's no talking to you. I'll pray for you, Alex. I have a feeling that only God can reach that soul." He nodded at Samara. "I'll pray for you as well, Samara. I hope you can mend your unseemly ways."

Francesca turned her head away as Marcus left the room. Lies upon lies never ending. She ought to confess to Marcus. She ought to throw herself on his mercy before the next time she would have to dance.

But she had to consider the real Samara, and what her response would have been. And the real Samara would never have turned down the chance to earn some money, or to show herself off in front of a crowd.

Samara would have danced.

"The only thing the Cardston gossip will do is whet their appetites still more," Alex said into the heavy silence. "I would make book that I'll receive some inquiries today."

"I'd rather go to prison," Francesca muttered.

"No, you wouldn't. You'd rather dance, Samara. Trust me. You'd rather do anything else, even with me." *Especially with me.* "With all the comforts and all the admiration you could possibly handle. And think of all that money."

Yes, the money. She couldn't discount the money. Four hundred pounds worn close to her heart—her passport to freedom and whatever kind of life she wanted to live.

If she could ever escape him. If she could ever find Colm.

"You've yet to tell me what is so important for you, my lord."

You, he thought and immediately repressed the thought.

"Why should it matter as long as you're paid, and you are provided with everything you could want—for now?"

Francesca opened her mouth to say it mattered and closed it again. It shouldn't matter. It wouldn't matter to Samara.

"It doesn't," she said coolly. "I just like to know what I'm risking my virtue for."

Alex thought of ten things instantly, not the least of which was his mission to root out the wellspring of corroding evil that festered somewhere in England, somewhere close, perhaps nearby.

But what he said was, "Me."

"Not worth it," she murmured.

He closed up instantly. She had dismissed him again. "It will be."

How did you seduce a courtesan?

She shrugged. "Whatever you wish, my lord." Somehow she would circumvent him. She did not ever want to dance again.

Alex wanted to shake her. That blank, uninterested look on her face just drove him wild. She cared nothing about anything, at least on the face of it. She was his puppet, his doll, his to manipulate for the best effect, the most arousing response.

He wanted to take her and maneuver her into his arms, into his bed. To make her *see* him, respond to him. Even after their standoff last evening, she did not indicate by any means that anything he'd said had made any impression.

And that galled Alex still more. Samara was such an expert at feeding a man's fantasies. The more she withheld herself, the more rabid he was to possess her. It was hell having her in the house, in his room, in his bed, but he would have no other arrangement.

She was his for the duration, and if it took the threat of prison to keep her in line, it was enough. For the moment.

"I think we understand each other, Samara. You're free to roam around Meresham, if you want to. But do understand that someone will always be watching, so any attempt to escape would be futile."

"My lord plans for everything except the vile nature of men."

"To which you must be very accustomed, Samara, mustn't you? Don't play the coy virgin with me, my lady. Every man knows what you are, and they've ogled your naked body and demanded your sexual favors from Paris to Marrakech—and gotten them, by all accounts." He was getting steamed up now, thinking about all the men who had tasted, who had plumbed the contradictions of her.

"You love displaying yourself for them, you loved how you got those men in a lather last night, and you'll love it tonight and every succeeding night you can get them hot and boiling and bring them to their knees."

There it was in a nutshell, his whole perception of Samara Teva, and in his blindness, he was missing all the clues that she, Francesca, was nothing like her. He still believed what he saw on the surface.

"Maybe one gets tired of all that, my lord."

"A pretty sentiment from someone as infamous as you. You know, of course, if they'd caught you with those papers, there would have been no mercy."

So the whole business about the papers was still simmering in the back of his mind. He'd forgotten nothing, and he was tightening the net around her at the very minute she thought she could possibly break free.

"Oh—those papers again," she said dismissively because she'd allowed herself to forget about them.

"You said that just right. Nice touch, but you know better than any of us that there's a price to be paid for smuggling state secrets out of a country."

"As opposed to the price I pay aiding and abetting you," she retorted.

"It's a damn sight safer," he shot back, and probably, she thought, it was. But no one, having come upon her in Samara's room, would ever have taken her for an exotic dancer. They would have asked who she was and what she was doing. They never would have mentioned Colm, and she would have carried on in Berlin, finishing out her commission with the General and returning home to Braidwood to wait for Colm.

That was how things should have played out. But instead, this lunatic had shanghaied her for the express purpose of using her—Samara—as entree to the homes of some very prominent peers for some purpose he would not disclose, and he was keeping her close because, whatever those papers contained, they were still a factor in whatever he was involved in.

And he still believed sincerely that she had them. That Samara had them.

Francesca was living a scenario out of a penny dreadful.

Only every moment of it was real.

"Samara . . ."

"What?"

"You're not stupid."

"No, my lord. And thank you. But I wonder about you."

Alex slammed his hand down on the table in frustration. "All you need do is hand over the papers."

"I told you, I don't have them."

"No one believes that, not after everything you've done for Colm."

She froze. *Oh God—Colm again . . .*

"He never came. I was ill. Why are we going over all this again?"

"Because I'm not getting what I want—any which way."

The words hung there, fraught with every possible meaning. Francesca broke the festering silence. "Because—?" Her voice was abrasive, raw with something akin to anger.

Alex levered himself out of his chair to lean over the table and into her face. "Because I want what I want—and I want *you.*"

"And like the animals last night, my lord doesn't like his desires to be opposed," she countered brazenly.

"But unlike those animals last night, I can restrain myself. But from what I saw, it's impossible for *you.*"

So he would give Samara no quarter, even as torn as he was between anger and desire. Well, she knew how to play that game now. Words had power too.

Wait—don't toss some irresponsible promise of retaliation in the air because you'll have to make good on it.

I don't care. I feel like attacking him. Whatever it is, I'll do it. And how bad could it be, after last night?

"Last night, my lord? You thought last night was self-indulgent and indecent? Just wait till the next performance. There for the first time you will see Samara Teva—unrestrained. Now, is that all, my lord?"

Alex wanted to wrap his hands around her neck and crush that arch, mocking tone in her voice. He almost did it too. He flexed his hands, he bent toward her as she rose defiantly from her chair, he pulled her toward him violently, and he crushed her mouth under his instead, swallowing her hateful words, swallowing her lies, falling down down down into obsession and lust.

And she, opening herself to him like the obedient seductress that she was, giving him her heat, her wet, her tongue, giving him the power, for one provocative moment before she pulled away, softly, lingeringly, as sweet as a virgin.

He felt his whole body under attack, pricked everywhere by his unconsumed desire for her.

Dangerous. More dangerous than he'd given her credit for.

Samara Teva had much to answer for, he thought venomously. She thought she had him whipped into a froth and at the mercy of his lust, and she had yet to learn he was so much more powerful than that.

And that in this contest of wills and sex, she could never win.

There was something to be said for good works being rewarded, Phillippa thought, as she completed the last of her charity rounds of the morning and made her way back to the Rectory.

Marcus was there, of course, immersed in some text from which he hoped to divine a profound thought to use in his next sermon, and he sat bent over his desk by the window, intent on every word.

"Marcus dear," she said softly, coming over to him and laying her hand on her shoulder.

He patted it. "Yes, dear?"

Her heart started pounding because this was the first lie, and she didn't know if she could do it. Oh, yes, for what she had experienced in the arms of that stranger, yes, she could do it.

Her heart pounded painfully as she said, "I'm finished for the morning, and it's such a nice day, I'm going to take a walk."

"Exercise is an excellent idea," he murmured abstractedly.

"I'll be gone—oh, perhaps an hour . . . maybe more—"

"I'll be fine, dear."

Oh, I know you will. I know. . . .

Phillippa slipped out of the room silently, carefully, not even taking time to change her clothes. There wasn't much time. She had to take the most circuitous route to the cottage, to be certain no one saw her.

And if someone did, it had to look as if she were out for a casual stroll. So she couldn't hurry, when every fiber of her being demanded she race to the cottage and into his arms.

Him. Him. Sent by the Fates to light up her life.

Unless it was a dream. And even now, even after her unconscionable slide into debauchery, she thought maybe it had been just the sum total of all her fantasies and she'd dreamt the whole thing.

She almost missed a step as she came to the cottage. Wismer Cottage, as it was known. Let to city people who wanted a taste of the country far and away from their peers.

Who was he? Did she even care?

Phillippa was shaking as she made her way around to the back door. Which was as it had to be. Never could she go to him proudly, honestly, and proclaim him her lover.

And sometime in the future, he surely would have to leave.

She touched the doorknob, her hand shaking. She still didn't believe.

The door swung open, and she stepped into the dim recesses of the kitchen. Past that, into the parlor, where the drapes were drawn and atmospheric candles burned.

A place of their own, where nothing intruded, not even real life.

He'd made one major change. Gone were the stiff sofas and chairs that had furnished the room.

Now, in front of the fireplace, he'd placed his large ornate bed with its thick, sheltering mattress, on which he'd pummeled her willing body to a rough and pounding pleasure.

And there he awaited her, naked and throbbing.

"This is what you've done to me," he told her, his voice laced with the violence of his need. "I haven't slept for wanting you, and I've been so hard and hot I'm ready to burst. I'm begging you—come touch me, my goddess, and show me how much you care."

She swallowed hard, her whole body seizing up into a wet, hot need of what he could do to her. "What did you say?"

His eyes darkened, his body contracted. "I'm begging you. Have pity on me." His hips jerked and she felt an answering call deep between her legs.

He was begging her. He wanted to bury himself in her sex. How could any woman resist that appeal?

But still—to have him at her mercy, and so thick and pulsating with wanting her . . . Her breath caught as she contemplated him, the lover of her dreams.

No, there was no time for this, no time. She could either salivate over his turgid length, or let him put that huge bangstick deep inside. She could tease and tempt him some other time; she knew which she'd rather do.

Phillippa lifted her skirt and climbed onto the bed, granting him the privilege of doing to her every obscene thing he knew.

Chapter Twelve

Francesca had bolted for the fresh air, and Alex followed her slowly out of the breakfast room and into the hallway to be certain that she was heading outside.

He'd been waiting, as well, for a moment to search her things. It was time. He couldn't stand to spend another night in the room with her without knowing the truth about those papers.

He took the stairs two at a time. The bedroom door was ajar, Agnes having come and dusted and swept and made the bed, and it seemed strange not to find Samara waiting for him.

Had it been only a week since they'd returned from Berlin? It felt like a lifetime, it felt as if he had coveted her forever, and he wondered how William had been able to stand it.

Poor besotted William. Taken for his money, taken for a ride, and used callously by the most hardened of women as a cover for her clandestine activities. It was so likely that Colm *had* had him killed, given everything Samara had said. And if Colm had used her as well. . . .

He didn't want to think about the ramifications of that. He

wondered why he persisted in wanting to believe that she was innocent somehow, that everything she'd told him wasn't wholly and completely a tissue of lies. She had confessed to knowing Colm and working with him. She had expected delivery of the papers. She had coldly and deliberately seduced William to use him to take her to England for the express purpose of delivering them.

And over and above that, she was a temptation, a siren, an illusion.

A dream.

That was the part about which a man had to be ruthless, Alex thought implacably. That was the thing he couldn't allow to get in the way.

He yanked open the drawers of the built-in cupboards where Samara had folded away her costumes.

Illusions made of glitter and gauze. Revealing and concealing. The sum and substance of Samara Teva.

He took them out, one by one, the ones he recognized, the ones she'd tried on for him, the one she'd worn dancing for him, and he ran his hands roughly all over the fragile material.

There was nothing to find, unless the sequins and paillettes contained some secret code, and he was skeptical enough to think it was possible; otherwise there was nowhere to hide anything on those bits of net and gauze.

Then, there were the ones she hadn't yet shown him, one with tiny cups and sheer trousers split up the middle, which immediately sent his imagination soaring; a belt and bustier made of open conjoined satin circles that couldn't conceal a mole, let alone an inch of skin; a shrug of lace to wear over her shoulders, presumably with nothing else; a garter belt and breast cups made of lace and thin, swagged golden chains; and a camisole of fine, fine netting embroidered with swirling passementerie that concealed just the tips of her breasts.

Those beautiful hard nipples—he rubbed his thumb over the embroidery, his body instantly shot through with throbbing, urgent heat.

He forced down his erection and shoved the costumes back into the drawers. The last thing he could afford was to spend the day ruminating on Samara Teva's nipples, for God's sake, when they were available to anyone—for a price.

Her clothes were next, redolent with the scent of *her*. Everything black, prim and proper. Nothing in the pockets. Nothing hidden in her skirts, her shirtwaists, her underclothes, which were plain and made of muslin and cotton. Nothing fanciful or erotic here, everything the complete opposite of the woman who inhabited those costumes and strutted her insolent nudity in front of audiences who paid.

So why was he in high gear, throbbing like an engine and hard as a bone?

He ravaged the suitcases next, looking for secret hiding places under the linings, under the locks, between the layers of the thin worn cardboard.

Nothing rich or luxurious about Samara Teva. If she'd had money and luxuries, it was all gone now. Everything pointed to a woman who would sell herself to keep her myth and her reputation alive.

Everything about her story fit—and didn't.

In the upper drawer of the dresser, Alex found all of her jewelry: the golden chains that she'd worn close to her skin, dangling down her back, on her arms, between her breasts. He could feel the pulsating warmth of her, as if he held her naked body in his hands.

He wanted to wrap her in those thin, thin chains of bondage, chain her to his bed, to his body, to his soul. God, he was lost. All he could see was her beautiful naked body undulating across a stage.

NO . . . Goddamn it, *no!* He had no business, he had no right . . . he had *nothing*— And then, his body caved— *noooooooooooooo*—spurting and spending itself on the unobtainable fantasy of *her*.

* * *

"Oh God—it's been *hours*," Phillippa groaned. "I have to go. I *have* to go. They'll be looking for me."

"I'm looking for you," he growled, tumbling her onto the bed again. "Don't you adore this new arrangement? We don't have to move. We don't have to go anywhere."

"I have to go." She scrambled to a sitting position and grabbed frantically at her clothes.

"What kind of man is he, your husband?" he asked idly, and then he stopped himself. "No. I swore I wouldn't ask any questions. . . ."

"He's very quiet. Very kind," Phillippa said. "Very . . . unimaginative."

"Of course, I could have guessed."

"But fascinated by the idea of sin."

"Really. And he knows nothing about the hidden depths of you."

"I think it would cause him to have a heart attack."

Phillippa stood up and smoothed out her dress. She could do nothing to make it look fresh, when it had lain on the floor for hours, crumpled in a heap. "He likes knowing things at one remove."

"Well, your sins are nothing to what I hear about a guest in residence at Meresham Close," he murmured. *"There's* a ready piece. You're a saint next to that one, if what I've heard is true."

"I'd warrant it's true," Phillippa said, keeping her tone neutral. She didn't want to talk about Samara; she didn't want him to know she had any connection to Samara.

He sensed her withdrawal and levered himself to his feet to take her in his arms. "You're an angel. An amazon."

"And you"—she reached down to cup his manroot—"you're a bullock, my love."

"Oh God, don't go."

"Don't make it harder. . . ." she begged.

"You're making it harder," he whispered, backing her into the far wall. "Lift your dress, my amazon. You can't leave until I have you one more time."

Away from *him,* that was how Francesca thought of the half hour she had already spent wandering the grounds of Meresham Close. Just away from him, but followed everywhere by unseen eyes.

But not him. Not him.

She knelt beside a little pond, and splashed some water on her heated face, and took a minute to look around. Everywhere, to the rise of the hill she'd just come down, there was an expanse of emerald green lawns and blue horizon.

It was the most perfect day, with a bright, hot sun and not a cloud in the sky. A veritable painting of an English summer afternoon.

Francesca clenched her fists. Over that hill lay the traps and tricks of another woman's life. And now she had imprudently committed herself to propagating them because she couldn't stop herself from going nose to nose with Alex Deveney in defiance of his threats and edicts.

In the bright light of a summer's day, everything she'd done over the past week seemed impulsive, irresponsible, and indiscreet. And this morning was no exception. There was something about being in that house with that man. There was something about inhabiting Samara Teva's skin.

She wasn't immune to it. She wasn't. She was just beginning to understand the power and the passion that someone like Samara provoked.

Especially the power.

God, the power—of dominating all those men with just the movement and motion of her body. It was heady. It was arousing, even to someone as inexperienced as she.

And then, to bring a man like Alex Deveney to heel . . .

She didn't think she could take him kissing her, not one more time. She hated him.

But those kisses ... those kisses made her feel things that she didn't expect. Those kisses coaxed and teased and dominated and made her want more.

What did she know about kisses? All she had learned was how to flaunt her body. And that she was driving him crazy over it.

That was probably a good thing. But whatever had possessed her to fight him this morning and put herself in the very same position all over again?

Him. His arrogance. His dominating nature.

And all that secret business about Colm—

One more time, she thought, getting to her feet. She could stand to expose herself like that one more time. Another hundred pounds' worth. Just to show *him,* just to prove she was every bit as depraved as he thought she was.

Was she crazy? Did she really want to provoke him that way?

He was on a thin edge already, walking a fine line between fascination and obsession. Over Samara.

No, over her, *Francesca.*

The power of a woman ...

She started back toward the house. Over the hill, she saw a figure shifting in and out of the shadows of the trees, moving so furtively that it gave her the shivers.

And then that figure emerged as a woman, striding briskly from that same direction. Phillippa—hiding? Or just trying to avoid her?

Phillippa's step faltered as she caught sight of Francesca. But it was a momentary lapse. She had nothing to fear. Samara couldn't possibly have noticed the direction from which she'd come. But still, she started trembling. What if she had?

Oh God, oh God—she couldn't bear a scandal now. And if anyone interfered with her visits to the cottage, she'd kill him.

Better to distract Samara than to have her ask questions.

"Good afternoon, Samara," Phillippa called. "Such a nice day to be out rutting with the animals." And rather than join Francesca, she pointedly veered away.

Always a viper in paradise, Francesca thought disgustedly. Always a snake hiding in the grass, waiting to bite. But she expected nothing less. Phillippa hated her, hated Samara.

Except—except . . . there was something different about Phillippa today. Francesca wheeled around to look at Phillippa's receding figure. Something different, but she couldn't tell what, not at that distance.

And really, she didn't care.

And Judithe, right in the entrance hall when she returned from her walk.

"Dear God—" Judithe sagged against the newel post. "It's still here. It haunts me. Go away! Go away! Alex! *Alex!*"

Wotten appeared, agitated and concerned. "Madam, madam—"

And Alex, racing down the steps. "For God's sake, Mother . . ."

"I thought it was safe. I thought I could go to the parlor in my own house and spend some time with my embroidery— and look what walked in the front door. Explain this, Alex. Why is the creature still in my house? I thought you'd paid the baggage off."

Alex looked disgusted. "Take her to the parlor, Wotten, and get her some tea. Send someone to get Phillippa to keep her company. You"—he pointed to Francesca—"come with me."

She immediately stiffened. "Must I?"

"You must." Alex grasped her arm and propelled her down the hallway to the library. "Sit down. You can't be allowed out of the house by yourself. You're dangerous."

"I hope so," she muttered. "What do you want?"

. . . *You* . . .

He clamped down on his baser instincts. "Some notes in the

mail, my dear Samara. Alastair has been nothing if not efficient. Have I not mentioned Alastair? He can't stand to be behindhand on anything, our Alastair. His efficiency at relaying the gossip has brought forth a choice of invitations.''

Francesca lowered herself into a chair. ''What are you after?''

. . . You . . .

''We're going to Tuftonborough tomorrow night. Selfridge's house.''

And in fact, Alastair was arranging everything. Alastair wanted to be in the front row, in spite of his inverted nature. And that was only because he always had to be first with the news. He was appalled he had missed the debut of Samara Teva. And he was playing right into Alex's hands by doing everything to remedy that.

''Why won't you tell me?''

Alex shuffled the papers at his desk, and then he looked up at her. ''Because there's nothing you need to know.''

She stared at him a long minute. ''No, that's not it. It's because you think I know everything already.''

''Do you?'' he asked carefully. Because even though his search had turned up nothing but his own weakness, he still believed that was true.

''How often do we have to have this discussion?''

''We have lots of time to keep having this discussion, Samara. You're not going anywhere. And I will find out the truth.''

She cringed. ''Your truth.''

''Ah. A truth. What, indeed, is Samara Teva's truth?''

Oh, here was the moment: the perfect opportunity to tell him. What would he do if she said she wasn't Samara?

No. It still wasn't the time to tell him.

''Samara dances. That's all you think she knows how to do.''

''That's not all,'' he murmured and instantly his mind was awash with images of Samara bending, twisting, undulating as she danced, and open to her lovers, in every conceivable lascivious position.

This woman, in her demure and decorous mourning, could turn a saint into a sinner.

"Oh, yes. I know what you believe," she said acidly.

"I know what I know, Samara, and this is just the calm before the storm."

Which storm? His vacillating emotions or the furor she would cause by her dance? The two, she thought, were inextricably linked. And there was nothing she could do about either.

Nothing she could do about him.

And he still didn't know quite what to do about her and that cool, aloof air of self-possession that infuriated him. She was an enigma he couldn't solve; and he knew he ought to leave it at that, but he couldn't.

How did one seduce a temptress?

He had nothing else on his mind as he began to pace the room.

"And yet the sun still shines, in spite of the dire predictions of Sir Alex of Mere," she said caustically. "What are you looking for in Tuftonborough, Alex? What could be so dire that you need *me* to distract those men?"

He stopped by her chair and stared down at her. "I'm looking for *this*—" He bent over and touched her lips, and when she didn't demur, he murmured, "And this . . ." He deepened the kiss and she opened to him like a flower unfurled. "And this—" He cupped her face and went deeper still, pulling her into the most innocent, the most dizzying manifestation of his passion for her.

He felt as if he were drowning; as if he were being pulled into the backwash of something powerful, he had no control. It was her, and her black formfitting dresses, and her tight, high breasts, and the blatant invitation of her mesmerizing mouth.

Alex felt the enchantment all over again, and this time, it was solely for him, wholly from her, from the reluctant desire rising in her kiss.

As if she couldn't help herself any more than he.

Wishful thinking. She was the most in control of any woman he'd ever known. All he could do was revel in this moment of complete possession of the only part of her she would freely give.

He cupped her face and pulled her gently toward him. She didn't resist, and he felt a crowing triumph deep in his gut as he folded her against his body.

She was perfect for him—perfect. She felt as if she were made for him, molded to fit every hard line of his body. *Made for any man . . .* The insidious thought crept into his consciousness like the tide.

She could make a man forget everything . . . for the moment. But when the moment passed, reality hit like the blast of a gun.

He eased himself away from her, feeling the siren pull of her full soft lips, and still keeping her imprisoned with one arm.

She looked slightly dazed, her lips parted, her eyes shimmering with a sensual, knowing light.

"Did you find what you wanted?" she whispered, suddenly very aware of his height, his heat, and the weight of his arm around her shoulders. Aware of the light streaming in the library windows and the sound of voices beyond the open door.

Wotten's voice, and Phillippa's, and Marcus's, braced with concern.

But in the magic circle of Alex's arm, she was invulnerable. In the light of that dazzling kiss, she became Francesca Reay and free to desire all the things that were possible for *her.*

But not for Samara. A kiss like that, to Samara, was like a piece of candy, to be taken, savored, and swallowed whole.

And Francesca Reay could not let herself be sated by it.

She stiffened her shoulders as if to shrug off Alex's kiss and any hold he had on her. He moved his arm downward, over her upper arm, her breasts, her forearm, her wrist, a proprietary motion that claimed everything that she wasn't willing to give.

"Did you?" he murmured as she stepped away from him

and the danger he represented. She slanted a puzzled look at him. "Find what you wanted," he amplified.

Yes, she thought, raising a quizzical Samara-like eyebrow, as if to say she had no idea what he meant. *I found you.*

Now Alex couldn't help himself. Now that he had the taste and feel of Samara branded in his consciousness, he had to be alone with her whenever he could.

"Perhaps my lady would like a tour of the grounds," he suggested when Wotten came to announce that luncheon was served. "Do you ride?"

But he didn't expect an affirmative answer, it was almost as if some demon in him wanted to punctuate the chasm between lowborn wanton and a peer of the realm. Wanted to distance himself from the relentless violence of his feelings about her.

Wanted to isolate her and ravish her.

Or at least get her out of Judithe's and Phillippa's way.

"You know I don't," she said coolly, as if she were very aware of all his intentions.

"Pity," he murmured. "We'll take the pony cart. Wotten— see to it, will you?"

"Very good, my lord."

"It's a most excellent thing to have a butler," Francesca murmured. "What would one do without him?"

"I expect you know," Alex said.

She met his glittering gaze with the same dispassionate look she'd given him before. "I expect I do." Aunt Ida hadn't believed in such a frivolous mark of status. She believed in a cook, a housekeeper, an upstairs maid, seasonal help, and everything else done by Mrs. Beeton's book.

And she doubted if Alex had ever heard of such a thing; her statement put an end to that avenue of conversation, but he still kept looking at her as if he couldn't keep his eyes from her, and she felt as though she were pinned to the wall.

Thank heaven Wotten was quick about his duties, shepherding Judithe, Phillippa, and Marcus into the dining room and simultaneously ordering the cart to be brought around so that the family would avoid seeing Francesca altogether.

There was even a straw hat for Francesca placed thoughtfully on the seat.

"No driver?" she murmured, wedging herself tightly against the very low sidepiece of the cart.

"I'm not so cack-handed I can't handle this old girl," Alex said, patting the patient mare hitched to the cart. He climbed in next to her, overpowering the narrow, tufted leather bench and smacked the reins. Immediately they set off in a sedate trot toward the far corner of the house, and then around and out toward the back fields.

It was a lush and wondrous holding, meticulously maintained, and comprising hundreds of acres of land, farmed by Alex himself and a dozen tenants who lived in neat, thatch-roofed houses that dotted the landscape. Long before, they'd passed the little pond to which she'd walked, and they were now on a track going deep into Meresham Park.

It was like something out of a fairy tale, dark and light, foreboding and sane. And his shoulder jammed against hers, tight, hard, dangerous. Alone with him in the magic of the woods, with the evil witch Judithe still captured in the castle. Who knew what spells she cast, what incantations she chanted, what wizards lurked in the trees?

Alex was the sorcerer, with his wicked mouth and his skeptical eyes. He wanted one thing, he believed another, and he never stopped trying to fuse the disparate pieces into a whole that he could understand.

And Francesca was the enchantress, falling under his spell.

The last thing in the world she could allow herself to do.

The silence was deafening, underscored by the rustling of leaves, the flap of wings, the chirrup of birdsong, the trickle of water on stone, the clip of the mare's hooves.

And he was too close, so close. He didn't need words. She

could well see what was all around her: the landed wealth of generations and pride of place, privilege, and birth.

He was trying so hard to diminish his fascination with her, to exorcise her out of existence. For one fanciful moment, she imagined that he intended to dispense with her in the woods.

But Samara would haunt him—even he knew that. He was so aware of her next to him, with her covert curiosity and her impassive face, and he was irritated all over again that she couldn't care less about heritage, land, or family pride.

And none of that mitigated his desire to possess her, because by that act, he would fill her with all those things. He could contain her and know her and then send her away.

He could not come to terms with his contradictory feelings about her. He felt an explosive male urgency to mark her, to make her *his*. And the equally conflicting desire to just leave her alone, because he knew that to him she was more dangerous than Eve.

Treacherous, beguiling . . . sinuous as a snake, digging deep into his soul with her poisonous fangs, immutable and in his blood forever . . .

He could not let it be . . .

His hands tightened uncontrollably on the reins; he wheeled the cart around abruptly and pointed the mare back the way they'd come. Or did the darkness and inevitable pain lie that way?

The sky had darkened considerably. There was a feeling of menace in the air, and a storm break slowly rising.

If he kissed her again, as he so urgently wanted to do, he might be struck by lightning.

Omens and portents—and Samara was the locus of it all.

She felt it too, wafting across her skin, moist and heavy in the air, palpable as a touch. And she knew what it was: Alex, burning, resisting, coveting her soul.

Combating her ineffable need to oppose him, to protect herself, and maintain her own secrets of Samara, no matter what the cost.

She was going to pay dearly, because she already had a price for which she had suborned every moral principle by which she'd been raised. It was too short a step from there to flat on her back and becoming Samara in action as well as deed.

But she had made her bed; the trick was to keep him out of it.

Which was not what Samara would have chosen to do.

How long could she forestall the reckoning?

Maybe not even as long as the time it took to return to the house. The scent of sex and danger was sharp and clear, and there was no protective coloration behind which she could hide.

She felt frantic, suddenly—stalked. And he hadn't made a move or said a word.

"I want to walk," she said, her voice sounding strained in the silence.

"Why is that, Samara? It's a good two miles back to the house still."

She couldn't look at him. "I feel cramped." Closed in, contained, and helpless was more like it. "I need to stretch."

"That's not what you need."

She cringed. It was starting already, the inevitable, unbearable clash between his obsession and her resistance. And if she would but admit it, that was not what she wanted either.

But she still didn't know if she wanted him.

He could have been fused to her body—he was that close, that threatening, that hot. He could take her here, in the vast dead silence of the woods, and no one would hear her moan.

But that wasn't an option either, and she had run out of ways to fight.

Silence and disdain—weapons of the scared and the devious.

"And what do *you* think I need, my lord?"

Now he turned, and she knew there was no escaping those burning eyes and his relentless hunger for Samara—for *her.* And that he'd brought her here precisely to entice her and coerce her through his shameless seduction of her mouth.

He took her chin in one hand. "This," he murmured, sliding

his fingers over her pale soft skin. "This"—and across her
derisive lips—"and this"—slanting his mouth over hers and
giving her a whisper of a kiss, which sent little darts of pleasure
clear down to her vitals.

So distracting, a kiss.

"What I need," she said clearly, succinctly, "is to take the
money I've earned and get away from you."

That wasn't what he expected in what was almost a romantic
moment; but it was, he thought acidly, just what he should
have expected from *her*. She gave nothing—everything was
for sale. He'd caught her by surprise before, but she'd already
started calculating the profit on his need and had come up with
a very nice sum indeed.

He felt the familiar fury wash him from head to foot. "I'm
not done with you yet, Samara Teva." His voice was gritty
with suppressed rage that the infamous lady of the night would
not even grant him a kiss in broad daylight. "This is only the
beginning." He snapped the reins and the mare pushed herself
into a trot. "And I swear to you, Samara Teva, you'll *beg* for
it not to end."

Chapter Thirteen

Now Francesca was counting the hours until they were to go to Tuftonborough. The assignation hung over her like a sword. Samara Teva would dance again. Would face those men or face prison. And put another hundred pounds in her pocket or die.

It was in the air between them throughout the evening, through the disaster of a dinner, from which Judithe pointedly excused herself, and to which Phillippa sauntered in late.

"Oh, the lady Samara is dining *in* tonight. And Alex looks as if he wants to dine on *her*. My dear, what have I missed?"

"And where have you been?" Marcus inquired mildly.

"In the village, dear. Did you finish your sermon?"

"It's increasingly difficult, given what's going on in my own family," Marcus said peevishly. "One cannot take the high moral ground, can one? I've done what I can. And I'll probably change it all tomorrow. Pass the vegetables please."

"Dear Alex," Phillippa implored, "can't we end this farce? Haven't you embarrassed us enough?"

Alex raised one brow. "I can't think what you're talking about. Can you, Samara?"

It was obviously going to be *that* kind of night. And Francesca still had all those hours between darkness and dawn alone with him and his edgy, unspoken demands.

She was exhausted, from both the effort of being Samara and keeping everyone—Alex—from finding out she wasn't.

She couldn't exist in this kind of high tension much longer. She had to end it before tomorrow night.

She looked longingly down at the empty hallway as Alex shepherded her up to his room.

Not a servant in sight. No one watching, as the clock in the library struck nine. If she had time . . . fifteen minutes' time . . . ten . . . she wouldn't even pack a suitcase. She would just grab the money, and with the clothes on her back, she would be out that door faster than lightning.

No time . . .

Wotten appeared from beneath the staircase, ever vigilant, always watching. A wonderful thing, a butler, whose loyalty could not be bought.

Tonight, Francesca knew, everything would be different. In the space of two days, everything had changed.

She had changed.

And Alex had discovered the kind of savage desire that Samara the femme fatale would have owned.

She didn't know how to be that kind of woman.

Alex thrust her into his bedroom and shut the door meaningfully behind him.

She didn't *want* to be that kind of woman. She sat down wearily on the bed.

One more night. One more awful, lewd Samara dance. It seemed utterly impossible right now. She watched in dismay as Alex locked the door and went into the closet, to reemerge a moment or two later with one of Samara's costumes in his hands.

He tossed it on the bed, the belt and band of circles made of satin cording.

"This is what you'll wear tomorrow night. And this is what you'll wear tonight for me."

Francesca closed her eyes in surrender. And opened them again, startled, as something substantial fell in her lap.

Money. He was willing to buy what he wanted from the woman who would sell everything she owned.

Now what was she going to do? This wasn't a moment of tease and tempt and bar the door. Not after this afternoon. Not after those kisses.

She went into the closet and began to undress. There was no way to hold him off now, no way for a known femme horizontale to tell a prospective customer no. All she could do was make him wait.

How did you seduce a wanton?

Alex felt the same shuddering excitement as the first time he'd made her dress for him. Only now, he knew the feel of her sinuous body against him and the honeyed taste of her tongue, and his imagination ignited at the thought of her naked body encased in those revealing satin circlets.

For him. First and foremost for him.

Francesca edged around the closet doorway, feeling, as she always did, utterly exposed on every level. The circlets hid nothing; they rode her hips and breasts like big golden chains, emphasizing her creamy skin and her nipples as they peeked out all hard and luscious from the pressure of the circlets against her breasts.

She didn't know what next to do, so she climbed onto the bed, fully aware that the stretch of her legs revealed that much more of her to his devouring gaze.

Samara had worn this costume, danced in it, made men crazed. Francesca could feel the power of it working on Alex, and he was standing across the room. She could feel it working on *her,* filling her mind with all kinds of voluptuous notions about enslavement and control.

Her body tingled. This truly was what Samara was all about: capitulation and control. And she could feel all of that roiling around within her as the tight bands of the circlets pressed into her bare skin and she sat immobile as a sphinx and let Alex look his fill.

But he wanted more than that. The thrust of his body told her that, emphatically. This time he wasn't going to keep his distance. It was only a matter of how long he could stand not to touch her or kiss her.

And she thought if only she didn't move maybe he wouldn't either.

But that was a naive hope at best.

Slowly he started walking toward the bed. *His* room, *his* bed, everything in it, on it belonged to him, he thought, reining himself in. *Everything.*

Her.

Those cool, deep eyes watching him. That touch-me-not expression on her face.

Oh, he wanted to touch her. He wanted to surround her, imprison her, and make her beg. Samara was on her knees already, brought there by his threats and his demands, but her cool, calm expression told him she would never submit.

No matter what he devised, no matter what he said. If he conquered her, she would never be his.

And he didn't care. He would vanquish her anyway and damn the consequences.

She watched him with those calm black eyes as he mounted the bed. Now there was truly nowhere to go. Alex Deveney meant to claim what had been given freely to so many other men.

She read the purpose and determination in his eyes. Not a word needed to be said: This was inevitable from the first moment she had danced for him, and now truly there was nowhere to hide.

He cupped her face, his hands flexing with the tension of his desire. Her mouth first, he thought. He would take it slow, slow, savoring how she managed, with all her skill, to purvey a kind of frenzied innocence in her kisses and a sultry invitation for him to feed on her long and slow.

He wasn't sure he could last even that long. She was a vessel, offering herself up to him to take whatever he wanted, and he ached to discharge himself into her in one rampant, spuming stroke.

That was all it would take.

Instead, he moved his hands downward, from her face to her shoulders, and still further down to her rounded breasts protruding from the breastplate of circlets to her hard prominent nipples.

And touched them. Felt her body shudder.

Squeezed them, and she spasmed right in his hands.

Yes. Yes. He felt as if he was her master, if he could make her respond so strongly to just the compression of his fingers on the tips of her breasts.

Such pleasure. The heat of her mouth, the hard nubs between his fingers. Maybe it was enough.

Maybe it wasn't.

He pushed her down on the mattress and climbed over her. This he needed above all: to feel her naked body aligned with his, taking his weight, feeding his carnal hunger for her.

This—all in his kiss and the way he sprawled all over her, prodding her, urging her, making himself known.

She had never been used like this in her life: the sensations in her breasts streaming through her body like silk; his deepening, demanding, burning kisses.

She felt overpowered, inundated, tiny, and alone; she couldn't do anything but *let* him do whatever he wanted to do. The weight of him suffocated her; she had no control.

And she was everything he wanted her to be . . . and not. She was pliant, quiescent, open—but she goddamned wasn't *there.*

He had never felt such frustration in his life. The infamous Samara Teva was nothing more than a rag doll to be propped and prodded and used whatever way a man desired. *That* was the secret of her notoriety.

And men bought it, obviously, and the illusion she created in her dances that she was a creature of the senses who couldn't wait to get a man into bed and just let him have his way.

But having his way and having *her* were two different things, and he was beginning to think that she was so jaded that nothing could touch her and that she derived all of her pleasure solely from making a man beg for her favors.

God, what kind of woman was this? How had his brother borne it?

He eased himself away from her, mindful of the delicate state of his jutting member. He should not have allowed himself to surrender to the allure of this woman. She was a fantasy, a delusion, a phantom, a mirage.

Men died pursuing mirages, slaking their thirst in the desert on nothing more than a handful of sand.

And that was Samara Teva: a handful of hair and skin and mouth and bone. A man could die of hunger trying to possess her.

It was the most shocking rebuff. She lay rock still trying to make some sense of it, and his anger, and his abrupt reversal of desire.

"Get up," he said roughly, levering himself off the bed. She was a picture, she was, her body laced with those circlets, and her expression as knowing as Eve's.

Yes, she knew what she had done, what she still did to him. He could see the exultation in her eyes. The bitch thought she'd brought him down.

Goddamn her all to hell.

"The fun is over, Samara. You got what you wanted and you brought me to the brink. But I won't let you have the satisfaction of making me submit. I'm on to you, my lady. All your clever tricks and manipulations. Most men wouldn't care.

But you can't bamboozle me anymore. You look foolish, Samara, with that innocent expression on your face. Get up. Get ready for bed. And enjoy lying in it—alone.''

Phillippa had never loved the mornings. There were days she would lie in bed and contemplate all the charity work she was required to perform as Marcus's wife and wonder whether it was even worth getting out of bed.

How much her life had changed in just three days. And all it took was a hard, thrusting man with the stamina of an ox and a firm sense of the order and importance of things.

Her things.

And she felt so dependent on him already, she didn't know what she might do when he would go.

But that was a long way into the future. Even he had said so, and that all he wanted was to spend every afternoon rocking between her legs and he would die a happy man.

Every time she pictured in her mind the stallion rise of him, she trembled with excitement at the knowledge it all belonged to her.

It had taken but that one first visit for her to comprehend that the faster she stripped naked, the faster he could mount her and ride her home.

And how many times a day? She'd never imagined a man who loved shooting his seed the way he did. Three times, four. That many times a day, and more, as he encouraged her to think up new and lascivious ways to arouse him and bring him to peak.

Phillippa dressed for him today, slipping on a loose, long dress and an apron over it, and bundling her hair into a topknot. The errands she must run took a shorter and shorter period of time now, because she was learning how not to linger without being rude.

All she could think of was *him,* and she tossed and turned

beside Marcus at night, imagining him in his bed, hard as a
bone and tortured in his body for want of her.

Quickly, more quickly than yesterday even, she raced through
the calls and commissions that Marcus always neatly wrote
down for her every morning.

Was her face flushed? Did her impatience show?

She didn't care; her body was responding to him already
and she wasn't even there. But soon she would be . . . she was,
creeping up on the enchanted little cottage with all her bedrock
dreams.

She started unfastening her dress before she even got to the
door.

It swung open, more magic, and as she entered, she let her
dress fall to the floor. He was there, waiting, primed, pushing
her against the door, ramming himself into her without a word,
without a sigh, hard and hot and throbbing in his lust for her.

She made a little sound, as he rode her, wide, high, and wild.
His mouth was brutal on hers, savaging her tender lips, making
his need known by his hot, harsh, guttural breaths.

Once, twice, three times, he shoved himself into her tight to
the hilt. Once, twice, three times again, pinning her, pounding
her, giving her no room. Once, twice, three times still—as she
moaned and clutched and whimpered his name, he blasted
himself into her, spewing his seed.

"Ah, ah, ah," he murmured as they sank together to the
floor. "Ah. Shhh. Ummm . . ."

He knew just what to say.

And just how to fondle her to arouse them both again. He
took her this time on her knees, the next on a kitchen chair,
thick and hard and forceful and *there*.

After that, they lolled for a while on the bed, in idle love
talk, as she played with his head.

"You wear a man out," he whispered.

"Not you. Look at you. . . ."

"You are the most surprising woman."

"Why?"

"You know things a man would only expect from a woman like that—that Samara woman that everyone is talking about."

Phillippa felt a flash of pleasure—and jealousy. "She's nothing special."

"They say she's beautiful. But she couldn't possibly compete with you, with your hands, your body, and what you have between your legs."

She spread her legs, inviting him, and he inserted his fingers.

"They say she's going to dance tonight," he went on, his voice hoarse. "But I'd rather watch my amazon dance for me now—" He thrust his fingers inside her, hard, and she ground her hips down against them. Immediately he stiffened and she moaned. "Dance for me, amazon. Show me your harlot's moves. . . ." She shimmied downward, hard, and he went rigid as a rock. "Yes, yes, that's the way to tease and torment a man. To make him want to stuff himself into you. Tempt me some more. Make a man forget that whore. Just like that"— she swirled her hips in a mating dance—"like that. Look at me—beg me . . . Show me how you do it better—"

He drew a hissing breath as she grasped him, moved on him the way he was driving her. "God . . . you're a born courtesan, my amazon."

"Then put yourself between my legs, and let me pump you dry."

He pulled out his fingers and climbed over her, positioning himself for the hardest possessive thrust. "You instinctively know a whore's most fervent desire, my amazon," he murmured, as he rammed himself in, "the complete . . . exhaustive . . . pleasuring . . . of her . . . man . . ."

Phillippa couldn't bear to leave him. Any man who thought that she was more seductive and enticing than the most coveted wanton in Europe was someone she wanted to be with forever. And that was in addition to that bulldog sticking power of his, which was truly to be prized.

She wanted to know everything about him, and he just wouldn't tell. "What would be the point, my amazon? To make us both ill if it should happen you must leave me? You will, you know. Because under that courtesan's skin, you're probably the prim and proper wife of . . . oh, a minister or something."

That swiped too close to the bone. "Or something," she murmured.

"It would kill me to make you part of my life and then have to cut you out altogether."

"But we're part of each other's lives now."

"No. This is a fairy tale. A slice of time when we found each other just when we needed most what each of us can give. You needed a lover. I needed an amazon naked in my bed. And here you are. What a gift." He nuzzled her breasts. "That's all we need to know about each other."

But it wasn't. She wanted more and more. She wanted to know about all his other women who had honed his endurance to such a rock-hard resistance. She wanted to know about his other life.

"No other life right now. I have all I want: your whore's instincts and my pole between your legs. You couldn't be more ripe for me than that naked dancing bitch. And if you were honest, you'd admit that's what you want too."

Almost. What she really loved the most was that he admired her sex above and beyond that of the woman she hated most. He—a man who must have had hundreds of women and could have had anyone he wanted in the village—had chosen *her* as his vessel and his whore.

"Tell me what you want," he whispered insinuatingly in her ear. "Be a good little whore and make me big and hot and hard for you."

These were the dirty, shocking, arousing words that someone like Samara was accustomed to, and they stoked her like a fire, and he was already hard as stone.

Phillippa wrapped herself around him and pushed him home.

* * *

This time, Francesca wore the costume under her dress. It seemed like a reasonable thing to do in light of Alex's explosive rejection of her last night.

Once again, Samara's reputation had saved her—but she didn't understand what it was about her that so infuriated him.

Well, it mattered little. *She* was getting away from Meresham Close if she had to climb out Judithe's window and burn down the stables.

There was a knock at the door. "Lady William?" Wotten, precise, punctilious, polite, come to escort her downstairs and to the waiting carriage.

"Thank you, Wotten."

What was most wrenching, she thought as they walked down the stairs, was that the servants all knew where she was going and what she was going to do. Judithe knew, as did Marcus and Phillippa. William, in heaven, probably knew.

And certainly Alex, with that scurrilous and hateful expression, had already envisioned the whole show in his devious mind.

Wotten settled her opposite Alex and gave the signal to the driver.

"This is the last time," she said, and Alex let out a short barking laugh.

"Ha."

Other than that, there was silence. The same loaded portentous silence thick with carnal awareness.

It must have radiated from her skin. The circlets of satin pressed against her like a brand, suffusing her with heat. She was intensely aware of her body, her breasts, the place between her legs, and she was fully clothed up to her neck.

She felt a creamy kind of lassitude, as if the costume itself had magically remade her into the sensual persona she pretended to possess. This costume, even more than her flaunting her nudity, made her feel sensual, swollen, in carnal heat.

Tuftonborough wasn't all that far.

Francesca's stomach knotted as they came ever closer. She closed her eyes, but she couldn't shut out the reality of what she was going to do. Again.

Why did he need Samara Teva to divert and distract?

Tuftonborough was not a three-hour drive. Too soon, the carriage swayed and turned off the road and into the park grounds of Selfridge's estate. Down a long road overhung with trees they went, and then, in a straight line before them, Selfridge's house, the lights glimmering through the leaves.

This house was bigger and far less ostentatious than Cardston's castle. The entry was on the first level, right at the carriage stop with its little stone stoop for the ladies. All the main rooms were right on that lower level and laid out sensibly off a main hallway that was furnished with chairs and console tables against the wall, luminous paintings, and warm candlelight.

They were greeted as if they were arriving to attend a ball. And indeed, it was up to the ballroom that the butler escorted them, a room that encompassed one whole side of the house on the second floor.

Nothing intimate here. Just a vast expanse of parquet floor, warm blue walls, a ceiling frosted with thick, cakelike moldings that were replicated on the walls, and a hundred chairs piled and situated against the far wall.

Toward the front of the room was a stage, and here, it could be inferred, Selfridge's family were entertained by musicians, or performed their own plays.

Or maybe they imported exotic dancers when they became bored.

There were a dozen men seated near the boards, and four of them were men she now knew: Crookenden, Hanscom, Sheffers, and Fogg. The tall one was Selfridge, the others strangers. One of them, whom Selfridge singled out by the elbow, was a flashy dresser and as flamboyant as any man she'd ever seen.

But what did she know of men?

"Miss Samara." Selfridge was ever the gentleman, acting

as though this were a tea party instead of a male smoker. "This is Alastair."

Alastair bowed. "Miss Samara—" He took her hand. "Everyone's agog. Amazed. Amused. Adrift. You're a dream. I can't believe the way . . . *that man* treated you. I promise you, you'll find only friends here. And all your secrets will be safe with us. And nothing will ever pass from *these* lips."

She smiled uncertainly, recalling instantly everything Alex had said about him. *The biggest gossip. Didn't like to be behind-hand about anything.* Which meant everything that happened here tonight would be tattle fodder by morning.

What to say to *him* that wouldn't be misinterpreted by the light of day?

"I appreciate your discretion," she managed finally.

Alastair patted her hands. "Ah, I see the others are seating themselves. *I* want the best view. So nice to meet you, my dear, and I will see you after." He scuttled off to join the others, who had already chosen their chairs.

Alex felt his insides seizing up again as he watched her with Alastair, charming him all to hell before she put herself on display for him.

Damn her all to hell. She could make a nancy boy go straight. Alastair was popping out of his trousers for her. Every last damn one of them was. How did she do it? Alex could not separate the whore from the woman, and all his contradictory feelings.

Selfridge was saying to her, "We brought in the same musicians—they're behind the curtains, thought you'd feel more comfortable, you know."

Francesca didn't quite know how to respond to this when she was the most uncomfortable of all. "Thank you." It seemed sufficient.

"And there's one of my girls waiting to help you. Behind the curtain."

"Oh. Behind the curtain." A little dressing room there, actually rigged up out of matching curtains, and a maid who reminded Francesca of Agnes, lively, pretty, and eager to help.

"Oh mum . . ." the girl murmured as Francesca peeled off her dress. "Oh mum. I ain't never seen nothing like that in my life."

"Me neither," Francesca muttered as she tugged the pins out of her hair.

"Let me help brush it, mum."

Francesca stood still and gave herself over to the girl's willing hands. "Ay, now, that's good. Anything else, mum?"

"A mirror."

"Oh yes. Master said I was to prepare one. Just pull the curtain here."

"Thank you."

"Master said to stay until you was done."

Her spirits sank. Wherever she was, Alex had her covered, and even though she was pounds stronger than this girl, she couldn't cope with hurting her and launching herself half naked out the door.

The maid pulled the curtain to reveal the mirror, and there she stood, Samara Francesca, the embodiment of smoldering, reeking sin.

There was nothing remotely theistic about this costume or her dance, and this time, there were no quasireligious artifacts and no announcements of supernatural reprisals.

But she had had the forethought to take with her one silk panel to use as a veil so that this time she would not get stuck on stage without some kind of covering at the end.

Not that it concealed much. But it did and could cover her whole body, front to back, and there were interesting ways she could use it as a prop.

Her maid peeked out between the curtains. "The gentlemen is seated, mum."

Twenty minutes, then, of sensuality and sin, courtesy of the famous, the infamous Samara Teva.

She told the maid to signal the musicians so the show could begin.

Francesca stood, shrouded in the silken panel, with a bowed head. As the low bass notes pulsed through the room, through everyone's consciousness, there came a shimmering high note from the violin. Another, and another, and she raised her head, and slowly, slowly, slowly she pulled the silky panel over her head until it slid like a caress down her body and into her hands.

The music was soft, insinuating, like the movements of her hands as they fluttered before her, subtly revealing the golden satin circlets pressing into her naked flesh, emphasizing her round and pointed breasts.

To the formless soft music, she moved, crouching, sliding, speaking with her hands. Pulling the softness of the silk into a winding band. Up her body and down, pulling it slowly, letting it caress her body in concert with the flowing, shimmering music.

Long, slow, stretching, languorous moves, one side to the other, harmonious, stately, revealing, slow. A story in them, for only her to know.

The music, sliding like water; the silken panel, sliding like a lover, over her breasts, her nipples, her body, her legs. A rich, deep cello note of hot male yearning.

She uses her hands to tell her story. Never let them forget her. She was the most sensational, most lovely thing, most coveted body, most adored woman—the circlets only enhance her carnal soul—

She feels her nipples puckering and pointing as she pulls the silken panel over her body again. The temptation is to pull it right between her legs . . . and every one of those men would hand her his soul.

The power . . . so hot in her body she could feel it . . .

The violinist began a glissando of short plinking notes, quick step quick, here, there, hands, restless movement, can't rest, want want want a man—

Samara inhabiting her body, hot, ripe, ready—where—different from before . . . nothing between this heat and desire but the thin rhythmic plink-string melody on the violin . . .

Quick step quick . . . power—they were all leaning forward in their seats, watching her restless hands, lapping up her carnal impulses . . .

This was how a woman learned. . . .

The cello came in, swamping the strings with a dominant note, humping and grounding it, in a primal male plainsong.

That was her cue. She whirled around the stage, wrapping herself once again in the silken panel; around and around she went until she was almost dizzy, and then she fell through the curtain and dramatically disappeared.

A much better finish, Alex thought cynically, as he used the moment of high drama to slip back into his place. The instincts of the woman were infallible. She had them all stunned at her sudden withdrawal, and panting for more.

But the auction for her would be a lot more subtle. Selfridge would act as the middle man, and draw him aside to disclose any offers. He had already settled Samara's fee with Alex. That was how a gentleman worked it. That was how things should be done.

Nevertheless, Alex hadn't felt the slightest twinge of conscience as he searched the house and grounds. There was as much land here as at Meresham Close, and room enough to build another town—all of it a statement of Selfridge's stature and wealth, none of it relevant to what he was seeking—yet.

What he found of interest was that Selfridge was uncommonly generous to improbable causes. Which meant he was either foolhardy or a visionary, and dangerous or benign.

It was, at least, a place to start down a long, frustrating road, which heretofore had provided too few markers to guide him.

"Alex." Selfridge, on cue, slapping him on the shoulder.

"Alex, Alex, Alex . . ." Alastair on Selfridge's heels. "Why didn't you *tell* me! She's a goddess. She's unbelievable. She almost makes me wish I were . . . well—no, I'm not sure I'd go that far. But her . . ."

Alex raised his hands. "Spare me the euphemisms, Alastair. The picture is painted."

"We have business," Selfridge said pointedly.

"Do you?" Alastair murmured. "Oh, I *must* know who."

Selfridge looked disgusted.

"I count four," Alex said. "What about you?" This, to Selfridge.

"If she would."

"And the others?"

"Morality prevails. Or else they don't think they can get it up with her."

"Maybe they can with me," Alastair offered lightly, maybe even half seriously.

"Down, boy. Go back to your seat and lick your wounds. There are no ready morsels around here."

"Pity." He moved away, and Alex watched him through narrowed eyes. Dear Alastair. As predictable as rain, and right where he wanted him doing exactly what he expected him to do: make a delicious melange of gossip out of Samara's dance.

"I'll tell her," he said to Selfridge and moved toward the stage.

Crookenden intercepted him. "No devoted supernatural guardians tonight?"

"I got your message," Alex said. "I'll tell her. Take note, Crookers—*this* is the way to handle things. And then no one is embarrassed."

He vaulted onto the stage and slipped behind the curtain, not at all sure he'd find her there, not at all sure he would go to the lengths he had previously to find her if she were gone.

Yes, he would. He would go to hell and dammit if she ever disappeared.

But she was there, and dressed, which was a clear message what her intentions were.

"What do you want?" she asked ungraciously. "When do we leave?"

"I have offers."

"Oh God, not that again."

"The Cardston four—and Selfridge. And probably Alastair, if he could."

"Whoremonger," she hissed.

"They like what they see," Alex said impassively. "It's a damned lot of money on the table."

"So they can put *me* on the table? I don't think so. I never liked pig wallows, Alex. I have *some* pride."

And he'd thought for sure that this time she'd take the money, and he'd absolutely shielded himself from his own deep-down feelings of rage.

"When did you develop a sense of integrity?"

"Since meeting you, Alex. Since meeting you."

That was the end of it; he almost snapped, and he had to go back to Selfridge and relay her regrets.

"You can do that," she said nastily. "Tell them I'm sorry Samara won't let you indulge yourselves in her body. She's saving herself for better things."

And that was the truth of it, he thought, steaming. The less she gave the more they wanted. This wouldn't be the end of it for any of the five of them who had seen her dance tonight. It would just whet their appetite for more.

She was the most brilliant tactician he'd ever met.

Or those men were the most gullible on earth. Alex couldn't decide which, as he stared broodingly out the window the whole ride home. Because the whole thing was perfectly understood by them, there were no hard feelings, and some heartfelt good-byes.

What was the link forged between patron and whore? God help him, he couldn't figure it out.

Or figure her out.

She stalked up the stairs the moment they arrived home.

She didn't want to ever dance before an audience of men again. She wanted to get her money, including the hundred pounds owed for tonight's performance, and she just wanted to go.

Damn it! She struck the bed with her fists. What was so impossible about wanting to go? There was nothing more Samara could do for him. Whatever he was seeking, he hadn't found it yet. And her prancing around as Samara wouldn't give him any more time or access to any more places or people than he had of his own accord.

This stupid charade had to end.

Had to. She struck the bed. *Had to.* Again. *Had to.* Again.

She felt tears streaming down her eyes. Every good intention had turned into a nightmare, and all on the whisper of a name.

Colm.

Never, for anyone, would she go through something like this again.

All she wanted was to go home to Aunt Ida and to things she understood.

Well, she would.

How would he stop her, if everyone else wanted her to leave?

Resolutely, she pulled open the closet door.

All of the clothes, hers and Samara's, and every single one of the costumes, lay cut and hacked to shreds all over the closet floor.

Chapter Fourteen

She was so stunned she could only sink to the floor and lift the tattered pieces of gauze and net in her hands.

Oh my God, my God. This is so vicious. So hateful. It almost felt like an attack on her, on Francesca.

Who would do this? Who would slash Samara's things to pieces? Who hated her enough?

Who was fed up with her enough?

Everyone.

Everyone in the house.

Francesca slowly got to her feet, tears stinging her eyes. Poor Samara. She reached outside the closet door for the bellpull.

A moment later, Wotten appeared.

"Would you—?" She didn't even need to finish. He looked at her face, saw the hacked-up pieces of net and silk on the bed, and instantly withdrew.

A minute more and Alex came running.

"Look . . ." Her hands were shaking, her body trembling. Looking at the sordid remains of Samara's life was heart-wrenching. Whoever had wielded that knife could just as well have hacked Samara to death, had she been there.

It was too terrifying to contemplate.

And there wasn't one person at Meresham Close who wasn't capable of doing it.

Alex pushed her onto the bed and picked up the rest of the remnants.

Jesus. The destruction was positively wanton, and it proved beyond all doubt that Samara had never had those papers.

Now what?

And who in his house was vicious enough, amoral enough, and desperate enough to wreak such devastation?

Who? Judithe. Marcus. Phillippa. They all wanted her gone.

She was crying. "Look—look, this is all that's left of . . . of . . . of Samara Teva's life. Look—" The hurt was acute, for herself and Samara; someone hated Samara with a passion.

Someone wanted her dead.

So he killed the one thing that was wholly and completely her: her costumes and, with them, her dance.

Alex had sent Wotten to summon Marcus and Phillippa, and then Judithe, and they crowded into his room now, protesting and complaining that he'd roused them from sleep.

"What is so important, Alex?" Marcus demanded testily. "I swear you think the world revolves around you and that woman . . . oh—" He blinked as he caught sight of the shreds of costume. "Oh. Oh dear. Well. So?"

"You tell me," Alex said coolly. "Mother?"

"What?"

"This isn't a prank."

"Thank God, someone took a hand to those ungodly things," Judithe muttered.

"You, Mother?" Alex asked silkily.

She pulled her robe around herself more tightly and made a distasteful face. "I wouldn't touch those . . . *things*—I can't believe I'm even in its bedroom—ooof . . . Alex, I can't bear it. I must go. . . ." She edged toward the door.

"Phillippa—?"

"Leave her alone," Marcus and Judithe said simultaneously.

"I see," Alex murmured. "So you're telling me that none of you know a thing about this vicious act, all of you are innocent, and it must have been some mysterious prowler who somehow got by the servants and mistook Samara's clothes for the family jewels."

"That's not funny," Judithe said.

"Who couldn't tell one glittering object from another," Alex pressed on.

"I don't like what you're saying," Marcus said.

"And cut them all up when they proved not to be Mother's diamonds."

"I'm going to bed," Judithe announced. "I won't be insulted. I won't be accused of doing something someone should have done the moment the creature stepped foot in this house, and I wash my hands of it altogether." She paused on the threshold. "Maybe it was a warning, Alex. Maybe now the creature will go away."

They all stared after her.

"Maybe Mother is right," Marcus began.

"Who got in this house that the servants didn't see, Marcus?" Alex was amazed at his self-control. He wanted dearly to shake his mother, and throttle Marcus, but none of that was permissible, and he had to maintain some control. The wonder was, he sounded so calm. "The answer is *no one.* So who does that leave, Marcus? Why don't you sleep on it, because I sure as hell am going to find out *who*—and there will be no mercy when I do."

"Always so melodramatic, Alex, and over a piece of trash like her. Maybe Mother's right. Maybe it's a warning. Maybe it's time for her to accept the money that we've offered and go."

Alex felt a flash of real thumping fury. "Maybe I'll pay you off—and *you* can go."

Marcus finally saw the red roiling rage. "Now, Alex—"

"Not done yet, Marcus? Go pray for your hypocritical soul."

"Martyr," Marcus muttered. "Come, Phillippa. He'll get over it."

But he wasn't sure he would; someone had committed two heinous and violent acts against him: Someone had violated his room and destroyed property. The niceties didn't matter. And everyone in the house knew where he'd gone with Samara, for what purpose, and even how long.

Anyone in the house had had enough time to sneak into his room and cut her clothes and costumes to ribbons. And who would have taken notice of Phillippa or Judithe in the upper hall? Phillippa was always visiting his mother in her bedroom for one reason or another. Judithe was always giving her advice or clothes.

And nobody hated Samara more.

Judithe. Phillippa.

It wouldn't have taken much strength to shred those clothes. Or much time either.

But there wasn't enough there to warrant calling in the authorities. There was just a wanton act of hate directed against someone that everyone in the house despised.

He gathered all the pieces up and put them in the cloth bag that Wotten had provided, and placed them on the closet shelf.

"They hate me," Francesca said dully. "I never should have come back to England with you. I should have stayed in Berlin and let Samara Teva die."

Later, Alex wondered about the way she had phrased it. Deep in the night, with her curled up and restlessly moving about on his bed, he thought about all the incidents and all the strands that tied him and Samara Teva together.

William was the least of it. William was to have been one cog in the wheel of a vast apparatus that moved men and mountains for subversive purposes. So if he hadn't come to

Berlin, and William still had died, the implication was that Samara Teva would have disappeared forever.

It was positively diabolical of Colm to have murdered his brother to get Alex to come to Berlin. Colm wanted those papers in England, and Alex knew why. It was because the thing was already done, its approval tacit, covert, and not by fiat.

Until now. Now there allegedly existed in one secret, coded document the architecture of a bold new world.

And Colm had been confident enough to entrust it to one streetwise lowborn exotic dancer whom no one would suspect. Except he hadn't come in time, and Alex had gotten to her first.

God, if she had had it . . . The earth would be turned upside down.

The Queen's daughter, *Kaiserin* Vicky, had been certain it existed, that it had been in the planning stages long before Wilhelm became kaiser, and with his implied consent. No wonder she'd been frantic to get all of their papers out of Germany before Friedrich died. In that notorious black box that had disappeared in the chaos after Friedrich's death was the blueprint for domination and death.

Webs. Fragile, strong, interconnected. And somewhere in England, the prime mover, the one he sought. That was what he called him: the prime mover. The one who'd formulated the philosophy and set up the grid on which evil and corruption could fester.

And all this he knew because he had been privy to *Kaiserin* Vicky's letters to the Queen. And nothing about it was simple. Victoria was to have held the box, nothing more, until Vicky got out of Germany. She never dreamt that the Prime Minister would have her detained, or that he would demand the deceased Emperor's papers, including those in the black box.

It was as if her son had severed himself from his mother, amputated her, and all things English.

Except one.

Alex had been looking for the prime mover ever since. It had been like chasing a shadow. But somewhere, among his friends and foes of the peerage, the prime mover moved and waited and plotted his little world.

He didn't think the prime mover was Colm. Colm was too important to the government on other levels, a man who moved easily between the two worlds, a not inconsiderable talent. He shared it himself.

No, the prime mover was here, had always been in England, waiting for the moment, the word, to launch his world.

And his mandate was to find him. Soon. Samara had given him his first opportunity to prowl the homes of men of substance and discontent who would be ripe for the prime mover to take in hand.

A farfetched scheme at best, desperate at the worst, and all for Queen and country who feared Wilhelm's militaristic tendencies and his envy of the British navy.

And so now there was a beautiful courtesan in his bed. And somebody somewhere wanted her dead.

It wasn't possible to creep out early in the morning. Phillippa could never be sure that Marcus wouldn't return to the house because of something he'd mislaid or forgotten.

She was beginning to hate Marcus, who plowed her body sometimes with gentle, secular disinterest that left her cold as stone. If she could give rein to her one true desire, it would be to spend every waking hour with her lover, the one man who yearned for her.

He now had a name. She called him Apollo—her beautiful, perfect god of the sun.

She was never going to be able to live without him.

It was getting harder and harder to leave him, insanely difficult not to ask questions of a personal nature.

"But you mustn't," he cautioned her. "What good would it do?"

"And you can be happy knowing nothing more about me?"

"I know the only important thing—what's between your legs."

She melted every time he said that, and when he whispered in her ear, "You *are* the best whore I've ever had." She loved the erotic wordplay and the pretense that she was coveted by every man but chosen by him. "If you ever sold yourself, my amazon, you'd be more notorious than Samara Teva."

She loved those words. "What do you mean?"

"I mean there isn't a woman to compare with you, your body, your heat, your instinct for pleasure. A man looks at you and just wants to rut in you."

She shuddered with desire at the thought.

"I don't know how they all keep their hands off you. Thank God, I don't have to, do I, my harlot? I can put my hands anywhere I want. I can pole your naked body right up to the wall and plow you. But those other men, how can they resist you?"

She thought of one especially who did.

"Maybe I resisted them. Maybe I was waiting for you."

"Maybe I was looking for *you*," he whispered. "I can't believe where I found you and what you let me do."

"I'll let you do anything," she whispered back, "ten times a day if you want it."

"Will you?"

"I want it."

"You're so much better than her," he whispered, mounting her. "Samara Teva couldn't handle a man ten times a day. She's not whore enough. But you are." Her body spasmed with pleasure and he murmured again, "You are . . ." as he drove into her. "You are—" as she convulsed beneath him, "a born . . ." and again, "whore . . ." and again, "born . . . whore . . ." as if he had found the magic code, the secret words that would bring her to endless culmination.

And maybe they did, those words. Maybe she'd always wanted to hear them. She couldn't get enough of them, and he gave them to her with every coupling, every thrust until they were both limp and wrung to the limit.

"She's still in the village," Phillippa said sleepily as she lay on his shoulder. "She's still here, causing trouble wherever she goes."

"When she leaves, you'll take over, my amazon, and you will be discreet. But you'll always know that I was the one who saw the whore in you first and who told you, you're so much better than her. . . ."

"We're going to give a ball."

"Excuse me?" Judithe looked at Alex over her glasses and clutched her embroidery frame. "We're doing *what?*"

"Giving a ball. I'm giving it. For Samara. It's time she met our friends and neighbors."

"Oh my God, I'm going to faint."

"You don't have to do a thing, Mother. I'll do it all."

"*You'll* do it all? What will you do except cause more grief, Alex?"

"So I won't invite you. I just wanted you to know. In two days' time."

"But you can't organize . . ."

"It's an informal ball, Mother. Trust me, in the dead of summer, when there's nothing to do, everyone will come. *Everyone.*"

"Even all your new friends?" she asked, stung by his confidence. Surely *her* friends wouldn't, not if the creature were the guest of honor. She shuddered at the thought of it.

"Every last one of them."

"Why, Alex? Haven't you done enough for her?"

"No. And actually, she hasn't done enough for me. She's the honey and we've got all the bees, and now all I have to do is get them to the hive."

Judithe clenched her fists. "You're so vulgar."

"And yet you still care about me."

"I won't come."

"Of course you won't."

"I'm going upstairs."

So that took care of that problem. Wotten, the cook, and the housekeeper would do the rest. His only real problem was to find Samara a suitable dress.

Phillippa had so many of his mother's castoffs, she surely had another one Samara could use.

"Tell me again why you're humiliating me?" Francesca asked.

"I thought we needed something to lighten things up."

"I know something that will accomplish that with the speed of a bullet. I'll leave."

"You are never leaving," Alex said.

"What, am I to be immured as William's widow forever? Why don't you just build a mausoleum next to his and incarcerate me? You've as much as done it in the house anyway. What is the company of ghosts and ghouls compared to a murderer skulking around your house?"

He still wasn't sure it wasn't Judithe—or Phillippa—who had destroyed her clothes. She had now only the one mourning dress, and every night, Agnes rinsed all of her clothes, dried and ironed them, and returned them in the morning.

Judithe refused to give Samara any of her clothes. "Taint my belongings?" she shrieked, horrified. "I'd kill myself first."

And Phillippa was nowhere to be found.

Alex put Samara to work with Wotten, planning the event. She moved around the house as if she owned it, sure and secure in what was wanted and what was superfluous.

He watched her from the library as she and Wotten and the housekeeper discussed the invitations, for which Alex had already given him a list, music, flowers, and food.

As if she knew exactly what she was doing. As if she'd been doing it all her life.

The curious inconsistencies of Samara Teva.

He had been ruminating on them last night, as he watched her sleep.

Somewhere there was someone who knew her as Colm Heinreichs's pawn. Someone who had been primed to make contact with her when she reached England.

Where? The question jumped at him. He had always assumed it was here, but the significance of it hadn't struck him before.

Her orders had been to convince William to take her to England, and where else would William have come?

Whatever sixth sense had prompted him to bring her back with him instead, he'd been right on the mark.

Her contact was here—somewhere in surrounding Somerset. And his instinct to use her to gain access to unfamiliar places had been absolutely bang on.

Even if he hadn't unearthed very much worthwhile.

So, he thought, *why not bring all those familiar and unfamiliar faces together here, and see who tried to contact _her_?*

Which made it seem appropriate to throw a midsummer ball.

Of course sending invitations on such short notice *was* a little dicey, but he had little to lose, and something real to gain.

And it wasn't as if he was doing all the work. Obviously Samara and his servants could take care of that.

The real question was, where the hell was Phillippa when he needed her.

Phillippa was in bed with Apollo the following night, stretching languorously after a long, rough session of lovemaking. Every day, her stay with him seemed to get longer and longer, as if both of them were prolonging things so she wouldn't have to go.

Oh, how she wanted to stay. Imagine spending the whole rest of the night, every night with that sinewy, gorgeous length. She got shivers just thinking about it. She felt as if they were Adam and Eve, and always on the brink of discovery of some new taste, some new secret pleasure.

Surely there was nothing about this that could be wrong.

And besides, she was furious about the whole idea of a ball honoring Samara. "It's the most insane idea Alex has had yet."

"Still hasn't sent her away, has he?" he murmured. "You have to wonder what she has that keeps her by his side. What is she doing for him that he can't live without? And now he's hosting an informal ball in her honor? Oh, my dear amazon. I think I've underestimated the whore."

"You have no idea," Phillippa muttered.

"Don't be jealous, my darling. I would host a ball for you if I could."

Why can't you? Phillippa thought resentfully, but she squashed it. She couldn't afford to lose him, not now, and not over some surly, petty jealousy of someone like Samara, who wasn't nearly as randy as she.

And Samara didn't have Apollo, who had spent the past hours licking, sucking, and banging her to a fare-thee-well. She wasn't jealous of Samara at all—just the fact that Alex wanted her.

If Alex even had an inkling of her wanton's heart, he would want her too and want her more than he had ever wanted Samara.

Phillippa's breath caught at the thought. Prayers did get answered. Apollo had come to be her teacher, to show her the path to enslaving Alex and making him her own.

"You host a ball for me every day," she murmured, cupping him between his legs. "Why should I be jealous of that bitch when I have *this?*" She squeezed and instantly he popped to life.

"You know all the whore's tricks," he said, rolling her on her back and nudging her with his heat. "Look at what you've done."

"Just what I wanted," she whispered. "Dance with me, Apollo. Make me come."

* * *

And now altogether she had seven hundred pounds, which were scattered in thick wads of banknotes all over the bed. People killed for money like that, Francesca thought. People died.

And money like that set people free.

She wasn't the same Francesca who had come so innocently to this house under false pretenses. She didn't have to go back to Braidwood when this was over.

And it would be over soon because she was going to tell Alex the truth.

It was the only way, especially after all the plans and schemes he had concocted for Samara. There was nothing more she could do for him; the one sure thing she knew was that she would never dance as Samara again.

Well, even that wasn't strictly true, given tonight's impromptu ball. She supposed she would have to dance at that.

On the bed Agnes had laid out the most beautiful dress, one of Judithe's castoffs and a charity gift from Phillippa's closet.

"You can have it," she said nastily. "It's out of style and out-of-date and it doesn't fit me, but it won't make *you* a lady."

Oh, but it would, Francesca thought, with its long, sleek bodice of lavender silk that was trimmed with bands of dove gray lace gathered at the neck and at the waist, and draping into a soft bustle low at the back, and finished off with matching pleats at the hem. There were elbow-length gloves, and dove gray shoes, which didn't fit.

She'd never owned anything like it in her life. She felt like a princess through and through.

But the money—what was she going to do with the money while she went to the ball?

Cinderella, losing her fragile life instead of a slipper . . .

And not even willing to trust it to Prince Charming—because Prince Charming was really the Big Bad Wolf.

She'd never considered the ramifications. There was nowhere on that formfitting dress she could carry all that money. . . .

Nowhere to put it in the room either, with a houseful of guests and a mystery marauder who desecrated clothes.

She didn't know what to do and she was running out of time. And it was just about time for the guests to arrive.

This was very different from the dinner Alex had given a week before. This was a crowd and a crush and an atmosphere of excitement and pleasure.

Light, wafting music underscored the conversation as the guests arrived and entered the reception hall.

They had opened the parlor and moved out the rugs for the event, and there were footmen stationed at both doors and in the hall to point the way.

Inside, where hundreds of candles burned in the chandeliers, waiters moved among the guests with trays of champagne. On a little balcony at the far end of the parlor, a string quartet played.

"Such a good idea," one of his guests murmured to Alex. "Just the thing. Love to get dressed up on a summer's night. Lends importance to the thing, don't you think?"

"Dear boy, wonderful idea, getting together all these new faces. We need new blood. Somerset is getting just a bit insular after all these years. . . ."

"Alex . . . you sly thing." Alastair at his elbow. "Would you believe I had exactly the same notion myself? A big party, lots of new people, lots of good new gossip—oh, I wish I'd been the one to pull it off. Where's the beauteous Samara?"

"About to make her debut, I hope. Why don't you hold on to my champagne for me, and I'll go get her."

Alex didn't have to go far. She was at the far end of the second floor landing, gazing with all the delight of a child at the color and chaos below.

Nothing like Samara Teva, the temptress. This was a lady

so far removed from Samara's excesses, he could hardly believe it.

She was properly dressed in lavender and dove gray, with the most elegant posture in her elegant gown. Her luxuriant hair was gathered into a topknot trimmed with flowers, and in her gloved hand, she carried a lace fan.

And she was leaning over the banister like a hoyden and keeping time to the music with her fan.

"Samara."

She jumped, turned, straightened herself up, and squared her shoulders. "My lord?" The mask of indifference was back in place.

His lips tightened. "It's time to go downstairs."

"Of course."

They were a pair walking down those stairs as if they belonged together. Everyone stopped and stared and counted every step until they reached bottom.

"Everyone, our guest of honor, Lady Samara Deveney."

Oh God, Francesca thought, reeling a little. Those words made her pretense seem more real than anything else she'd done in the guise of Samara Teva.

"Oh my *God*—" Alastair, limpid as a butterfly and instantly by her side. "You—I . . . it's just—I'm speechless."

Everyone around them laughed.

"Not tomorrow," someone said, and everyone laughed again.

"Well, I know something you don't know," Alastair said in a singsong voice.

"You always know something we don't know," another voice chimed in. "Until you tell everyone."

"Don't listen to them, darling. To hear them talk, you'd think my reputation stinks. Well. Maybe it does. But I'm in love with you. Take my arm, Lady Samara, and a-waltzing we will go."

She didn't have to say a word; Alastair conducted a fast,

funny one-man conversation all with himself, asking questions, answering them, making her laugh.

"Well, do let's have a toast in memory of William," he said at last. "Mustn't forget poor William."

"No," Francesca murmured. "If it weren't for William . . .' "

"Oh, indeed. You've landed on your feet, dear girl. What a smart thing that was." He tipped his flute and sipped.

"I can't imagine what you mean," Francesca said lightly.

"It's our little secret, dear," Alastair said, lowering his voice. "I promise I'll never tell."

"Good," Alex said, moving in on them. "Then if word gets out, I'll know who to kill."

"Oh God, you sound so *serious,*" Alastair said in mock horror. "Worse and worse—I think you *are.*"

"Let's not keep him from his friends," Alex said. "Come, there are lots more people you have to meet."

So many people, her head was whirling. People who had known William, who'd gone to school with him, had been his friends, who wanted to offer condolences. And that was just the beginning.

Alex had also invited the men for whom she had danced. There was Selfridge, Hanscom, Fogg, and Crookenden—all with their wives. And Basil Edenbridge and Hyla, and Allston Searle.

There were neighbors and friends and acquaintances from farther away. Phillippa in feathers and deep blue satin, and Judithe hiding in the hallway, still as a stone.

And the music, sweeping them up, sweeping her away. Alastair first, propelling her around the room. Alex next, so tall and forbidding and holding her too close.

And after that, everything was a blur, from dancing to dinner *en buffet* and dancing some more. There were stuffed eggs, marinated cucumbers and mushroom toast, crisp puffed shrimp and sliced pork roast; there was liver pâté and spinach tarts, cheeses, fruits, coffee and tea.

Alex watched her like a hawk. If there was anyone among

the guests who wanted to make contact, he had ample opportunity. And in point of fact, Alex had to admit, he wouldn't have known one way or another. There was just no way to tell who was a friend and who was a foe.

And then there was Alastair, who had wrapped himself around her like a veil. It was almost as if he had discovered her, and she was *his* creation, *his* triumph.

And she was. There was nothing about her tonight that wasn't perfection, and it was jolting to watch her among his guests when only two nights before she'd danced nearly naked among a half dozen of those men.

"Mother."

"Yes, Alex. I am here."

"I never doubted you would be."

"You take too much for granted. The creature is wearing one of my old dresses."

"She does very well too," Alex murmured.

"Get rid of her. Pay her off."

"Old song, Mother. I'm not ready to do that."

"You'd sooner bury me," she said trenchantly. "But what child ever followed the wishes of its parent?"

"Indeed, Mother. She acquits herself very well."

Judithe followed the hated figure with her eyes. "An act. Totally an act, artificial and false to her soul, Alex. And corrupting our family on top of it all. I don't know how I bear it, I really don't."

"You give a ball, Mother. And you see old friends. There's Alastair. Go pry him away from Phillippa."

"Hmmph." But she did.

Phillippa sauntered over to him. "She looks passable in my dress," she said, eyeing Samara as she waltzed around the room.

"Thank you, Phillippa."

"Anything for you, Alex," she murmured, stroking his sleeve.

He pulled his arm away. "I think Marcus is looking for you."

"I'd rather it was you."

"Never." God, he hated this back and forth with her.

"Don't say never too soon, Alex. Things can happen."

"What things?" he said sharply.

"I mean, maybe there's someone of your acquaintance that's more of a woman than Samara Teva could ever be." She watched him closely for his response, but all he did was search the room to pinpoint where the whore might be.

And then he raised a brow. "I daresay."

"Exactly. Would you like to dance with me, Alex?"

"No. I'd like to find Samara." But he had found her in fact, and Phillippa with her edgy conversation made him uncomfortable. He abruptly wheeled away from her and left her standing alone.

"Ohhhh ... someday, Alex Deveney—someday," she swore, on the verge of angry tears, "I will get you alone. . . ."

"Get who alone, my dear?" Marcus asked, suddenly beside her.

She lifted her head and blinked back her tears. "Why you, dear. Tonight. Us. Alone."

"Oh," Marcus said, turning the thought over in his mind. He was so tired, so drained from keeping up appearances, he didn't think he could keep anything else up as well. "Alone. Of course. Together, you and I."

It had been three hours since the festivities had begun, and now the guests were leaving and things were winding down.

Francesca stood in the hallway with Alex, bidding the departing guests good-bye.

"Dear, dear Samara."

"Alastair."

"I'll never forget you." He kissed her hand.

"Nor I you."

"Till next time, my darling."

"I'll count the hours."

Alastair blew her a kiss. "She's perfection, Alex. Keep her around."

"Just for you, old boy."

"Oh, I hardly think—well, it *is* a nice thought—*au revoir, my dear.*"

He was the last, lingering on until he couldn't, in good manners, stay anymore.

Alex closed the door behind him. "He can wear on you."

"He's delightful," Francesca said.

"He knows you very well too."

"That was mean." But it was true: Clothes made the woman and all vestiges of Samara's sinfulness seemed to have been washed away by a length of proper lace and silk. "Everything else though was very nice."

And it all had gone excellently well too, and none of it had proved that the prime mover's contact was anywhere in the vicinity; and Alex could have sworn he had invited every family for ten miles around.

It had been a long shot at best, and even now he wasn't sure that somewhere some kind of contact had been made. Maybe something that even she didn't know.

Alex gestured toward the steps, and Francesca reluctantly preceded him up to the bedroom, pausing on the landing to look down in the hall, ghostly now, with no trace of the ball.

He opened the door and motioned her inside.

"Oh, my God, Alex—oh my God—"

He was beside her in an instant with a bracing hand on her shoulder as they both stared at the carnage of his mattress and bedding, which had been slashed and cut to pieces and dumped all over the floor.

Chapter Fifteen

"Someone really doesn't like me," Alex murmured, nudging the mattress with his foot. "Unless you hid all that money in there?"

Francesca froze. "No. I didn't." She'd hidden all those bills on herself, pinned to her corset, her petticoat, and the underside of her dress. No, this was the same person who had slashed Samara's clothes.

There was such fury there, as if the person wielding the knife had been blinded by rage. The cuts were uneven, deep, animalistic in the way the stuffing had been torn out.

She couldn't stay another moment in this room, and before it went any further, she thought, she *had* to tell Alex the truth.

He rang for Wotten. "The mystery man has struck again. Prepare the guest room and have someone come and clean this up."

"Very good, sir."

"I don't suppose you saw anyone enter this room?"

"No, my lord, but I can check with the maids. Perhaps one of them saw something."

"Thank you. I'd appreciate that." But Alex was certain that no one had seen anything. There had been too much noise and commotion in the house tonight. A guest going upstairs to refresh himself, or to tidy up a dress, would not have seemed all that remarkable.

And there were really only two viable suspects, and both of them had vilified Samara yet again tonight. And what about Phillippa's cryptic, double-edged comments? She seemed so much more brittle lately, as if she were walking on the edge.

As if Alex hadn't always known that Phillippa wanted him. That was a sorry story there, but he refused to feel pity for her, or sympathy. There were rewards that came with being Marcus's wife, as well as crosses to bear.

But she might despise Samara enough to try to scare her away. And she in fact was more likely than Judithe, who didn't have the strength to wield a weapon this way.

Or did she? Who knew what his mother was capable of in a red-hot rage? The thought was horrifying, but no more so than the debris on the floor.

"Come, the guest room is ready. Agnes will have brought some tea."

"Truly? And how will I be able to sleep, knowing how much someone in this house despises me?"

"I think you can do anything, Samara. You did tonight."

She opened her mouth to tell him—and closed it again. "I need a nightgown. I need privacy. I need to go away."

"No. No privacy. And you'll never leave here. A nightgown you can have."

"Then tell me, just when does this little arrangement end?"

"My dear Samara, it cannot be that you have enough money to satisfy your greedy little soul."

"Maybe it can," she muttered. "Maybe I don't want to die."

"If I'd left you in Berlin, you would have died," he said, watching her carefully.

"Yes," she said, "for certain Samara Teva would have died."

"Why?" he asked sharply.

She looked up at him with her dark, cool, luminous eyes. "I was ill, my lord, or don't you remember? There was a woman in the rooming house who helped me. I could have died."

"That's not what you said."

She gave him a long considering look while she castigated herself for her carelessness. Or maybe she'd wanted him to catch that slip. She was torn now between wanting to confess or accepting the other consequences.

"If you hadn't come," she said finally, "I never would have danced again."

"What would you have done?" he asked curiously.

These were questions to which she didn't have the answers. And she was much too tired to think.

"You would have continued working for Colm, wouldn't you?" Alex said. "You would've come to England anyhow, once he'd given you the contents of the black box."

Colm again. Every time she thought she had finally gotten clear of Samara's deceits, Alex brought up Colm.

It could not be her Colm.

"Oh, fine and good, my lord. But you saw what was left of my costumes. I couldn't have hidden a comma in there, let alone these mysterious papers. And why do you keep harping on them? He never came."

"He would have," Alex muttered. "He probably did, after we were gone."

"So maybe he brought these infamous papers to England himself."

It was a possibility that he had only peripherally considered. Colm certainly would have known where Samara had gone. So why hadn't he tried to contact her? Because it was dangerous, and in certain circles, Colm was too well known. And he couldn't be certain of Samara's loyalties.

Because Alex knew better than anyone, Samara could be bought.

"Maybe," he said noncommittally, "but he probably wouldn't take the risk. Here you go. The room is right at the front of the house."

"The *guest* room, you said."

"And you *are* my guest."

"I'm your prisoner, you mean."

"Don't split hairs. Ah, everything has been made ready. Have some tea."

It was a smaller, cozier room, at the front of the house, as he'd said, and to the left of the stairs. It was papered all over in roses and contained the same kind of burnished mahogany furniture as in his room: a dresser, a washstand, and a half tester bed with a tufted bench at its foot. There were two chairs by the fireplace and a table to be used as a desk or as a place to serve a steaming pot of tea, which Agnes had left there on a tray.

Long silk draperies picked up the green leaf color from the wallpaper and gold silk cording draped the curtains, the bedspread, and the cushions of the chairs.

This room too had its own dressing area, not nearly as commodious as Alex's, and the built-in cupboards were nearly bare. But hanging neatly inside was one mourning dress, just her size; and folded neatly below were all of the undergarments she needed, and a flowered muslin nightgown. Tucked in a corner was her suitcase, inside of which was the one remaining costume, the satin circlet belt and breastplate, to commemorate Samara Teva's career.

Alex poured a cup of tea and handed it to her.

"You'll be safe here."

"You would have thought I would be, under such vigilant surveillance," she said, adding sugar, stirring with a miniature silver spoon, and then sipping lightly.

Tell him now. How much more are you going to enmesh yourself in Samara Teva lies?

It was almost the right moment, almost.

Francesca felt soft, vulnerable, scared. And Alex Deveney sometimes seemed invincible. Even in the midst of destruction all around him.

She looked up at him. "Alex—"

There was something about Samara Teva, so many aspects, so many faces, he still couldn't quite merge them all together. She was soft now, and altogether feminine, slightly hesitant, going slow. No hint of the abrasive, seductive, impassive femme fatale.

And something in him, despite all his caution, responded to that.

"I like when you say my name. . . ." he murmured.

She backtracked. "My lord—"

"Too late." He cupped her face. "I like it when you're just a little off balance too."

"As anyone would be to see his bed slashed to ribbons. Or is that an everyday occurrence with you?"

"I will find the person who did it."

She believed him too. "My tea," she murmured.

"Put it down."

She groped for the table and set the cup on the edge. The way she was on the edge with his closeness, her fear, his desire, her lies.

Nothing about her deterred him. As angry as he had been the last time, he wanted to kiss her that much now. It was as if he were responding to Samara, the lady, the mistress of his house.

And wouldn't that be a feat: Samara Teva, chatelaine of Meresham Close?

What was she thinking? She was trying to block out everything about Samara Teva, not embrace it.

And yet here he was, trying to embrace in her the essence of everything Samara could never be. And then of course, there were Alex's kisses—the ones he was lightly raining all over her lips before he pulled her inexorably close and swallowed her. Just devoured her, a man hungry and full of pain.

And here finally she wanted it, she felt it, because tonight she had been herself. Tonight, he set her free.

And he felt it, the give in her, the quickening of body, and her avid response. No more secrets. No more lies. Samara Teva could not hide from him anymore. She was his tonight, eager, pliant, wholly and completely there.

In his arms, on the bed, letting him touch her everywhere. Something somehow had changed, and he didn't want to question it. All he wanted was that woman, that mouth, that body wholly in his control.

He nurtured it. He approached her like the lady she had been tonight, with reverence and a hot, burning need that she plainly understood it was hers to feed.

Her kisses were wild and out of control, seeking him boldly, and teaching him what she wanted, what she liked.

It was the kisses, she thought in a haze. They just made her flare up like tinder. And she was vulnerable and scared. And on the brink of telling the truth.

Not yet, not yet. Kisses first, confessions later.

She swooned in his arms, swamped by a storm of sensations assaulting her that inflamed her all the more. This, this, this . . . She felt incoherent at all the fire and fury within her. This was what Samara knew . . . this—

This excitement, this hunger, this gnawing feeling between her legs—this . . .

She undulated against him, like a pagan in her dance, and he pulled her tighter, closer, more perfectly aligned.

That . . . what nestled hard and hot and tight at the vee of her legs—that . . . was what Samara knew—

But she wasn't Samara, God—she *had* to tell him. *She had to.*

He was nuzzling her neck and unhooking her dress. And she let him; in her sensual fog, she wanted him to. She heard her dress whisper as it slid to the floor.

"Oh my God," he murmured with a trace of suppressed laughter in his voice, "all your money . . ."

She stopped him with a kiss. Sweet, slow, heady kisses, endless kisses, sustaining her, supporting her, warding off the blow.

"Samara . . ." he whispered against her lips.

Now—tell him now . . . !

"What . . . what if it turned out that I'm not Samara?" Her voice quavered, her knees went weak. She didn't fall only because he was holding her so tight, and even then, she thought she might die.

Or he might kill her because of the lie.

He laughed. He just laughed and began working the fastenings of her chemise. "Who the hell else would you be?"

Me.

But he didn't care. It was *this* Samara he was obsessed with, *this* one he wanted to possess.

Why hadn't she ever understood that?

And now she felt fear. All the heat dissipated from her body as he removed her underclothes.

Now it was really time to pay for her folly. She stood naked and uneasy before him, the Samara of *his* dreams.

He lifted her so so easily and carried her to the bed, all soft, quiescent, and willing in his arms.

This was a Samara he had never seen before; it was almost as if she had transformed herself into the Samara he'd dreamt of—the one who was knowing, accomplished, reserved, and shy.

Just the way he wanted her, her body supple, flexible, smooth as satin, her nipples tight and hard with excitement.

This was not the Samara of the exotic dances. This was the Samara begging to be loved. And he didn't want to wait another minute, or give her time to change, to harden, to distance herself from the explosive excitement he felt.

Kisses first, hot, hard, long and slow as he mounted her with the efficiency of a stallion, and subtly removed as many of his clothes as impeded him.

And she helped him. God help her, she helped him, his kisses making her forget everything except this hot swamping desire—and him.

And suddenly he was there, poised at the brink.

Francesca stilled, feeling him probe, feeling the weapon, the power of men. Everything that Samara knew and she didn't pushed at that point between her legs.

In and out, gently, restraining himself from the possessive thrust, content at the moment to just insert himself at the crown of her velvet fold.

The sensation was exquisite, bone-melting. Her body responded as if she had been waiting for him, waiting to envelop him, because that, she understood suddenly, hazily, was the purpose of a woman. To contain and connect with that hard hot part of him even as he sought to possess her.

When had it come to this? She couldn't think as he continued to shift himself into her inch by rigid inch, and her body ground down on his hard heat almost of its own volition.

This was what men paid for, died for, and why, once they'd seen her naked, men lusted after Samara.

Or maybe it was inevitable that to know Samara's secrets was to give up her own. Maybe there had never been a choice, and the only way to confess was to surrender.

Maybe it was too late for anything—for everything . . .

And maybe, Alex thought, as he cradled himself between her legs, this was all he desired; just this long, slow, hot push into the essence of Samara Teva.

It was almost enough, almost—the dream, the thing he couldn't allow himself, the pleasure he didn't want to feel.

But now, this night, this time, this woman—whoever she was—she was every man's fantasy, and tonight she'd become what he had—in his deepest, darkest dreams—wanted her to be.

And all he wanted to do was bury himself in the deepest,

darkest part of her. Pushing and pulling, in and out, exquisite torture at the very most tip of his sex almost as if he were ambivalent about taking what he wanted most from a woman who had no reluctance to give.

His imagination flashed with images of Samara naked, Samara dancing, Samara girded in golden chains, and only then, as he felt a rolling wave of possessive excitement, did he thrust forcefully, deeply, and meet the one obstacle to his obsessive desire.

And even then, he didn't believe it. She who couldn't count the number of men who had possessed her was tight and hot and denying him?

No. He pushed her legs wider to open her more and gathered his body for the final plunge.

She felt it; she braced herself for it, because it meant the end of everything and the death, finally, of Samara. And it was a fitting death at that.

Oh God, I shouldn't have done this, it shouldn't have come to this, he should have believed me-e-e—

She cried out at the sharp tearing lunge, and he froze, but he couldn't stop himself, he couldn't, and he exploded into her like a rifle blast.

"Je-e-sus *God . . .*" He felt like a stone. . . . *What if it turned out that I'm not Samara Teva . . . ?*

What if . . . he couldn't begin to turn over the ramifications in his mind.

It took a long, long time before he could move, and then he eased away from her as gently as possible, covered her up and put himself to rights.

By that time, she was curled up in a corner of the bed, her fathomless black eyes staring at nothing.

And he was left with a potent roaring anger that this body that he had lusted after for the past two weeks, this body that had allegedly cradled hundreds of lovers countless times, that was the most notorious body on the Continent, that had danced

naked before public and private audiences including his own—
this body belonged to a virgin.

And he wanted to know with every fiber of his soul, how
the damn hell that had happened, and when it was he had lost
control.

He handed her the muslin nightgown. "Get dressed." God,
he could barely get out the words. "I'll turn my back."

"It's a little late for that," she said.

"A little late for everything," he growled.

"I told you." It was such a pathetic defense. A dozen days
had gone by along with too many other offenses, and she could
have told him any time before then. But he forbore to remind
her of that because he was still stunned, and he was furious.

He poured her another cup of tea. It was lukewarm by then,
but it was something she could hold in her hands and use to
wet her throat and her lovely, lying lips.

Who was this woman who haunted his dreams?

"I wager you've got *some* story to tell. Samara—what is
your name?"

Francesca sipped at the tea, moistening her mouth and the
dryness in her throat. God, why had she let herself in for this?
Why hadn't she just continued on with the lie? She could
have fended him off otherwise and kept him out of her bed.
Somehow.

He settled himself near the bed in the one of the chairs.
"Whenever you're ready—Samara. . . ."

"I'll never be ready," she retorted spiritedly. "Samara Teva
is dead."

Shock again. *Dead?* He went still and silent. "The hell.
When? How?"

"A week before you arrived in Berlin. I was the woman I
told you about, the one who nursed her—all the months after
William's death—when she became ill."

"Jesus." He ran it through his mind. Samara dead, and this

stranger for some ungodly reason stepping into her shoes. How? Why? He could barely find the words to ask, "What's your name?"

"Francesca. Francesca Reay."

Not even a relation or someone remotely connected to Samara. He couldn't quite grasp it or take it all in. Virginal Francesca Reay taking on the role of the most notorious courtesan on the Continent? If there was any remotely rational explanation for *that*, he wanted to hear it.

"Francesca." He rolled it around on his tongue. Her tongue, the one he knew so well. God almighty. Hell. "So—you nursed Samara during her illness?"

"There was no one else. There was no money."

"You knew William?"

"In passing. And I came to know Samara extremely well, after he died."

"I see." Alex didn't see anything, least of all how she'd pulled off this trick. She looked like a scared child right now, not like the sophisticated, sensual being that Samara had been. *She* had been.

"And so—Samara died, and then?"

Francesca turned to look at Alex straight on. "*You* came, my lord, and what transpired but that you thought I was Samara, and so Samara I became."

He digested that for a long moment. "You could have mentioned that you weren't at any time."

"I suppose I could have. But suppose," she said daringly, "I had my reasons."

"Anything you'd care to share?"

"I'm thinking about it."

"I have all the time in the world." She looked so young and so vulnerable, huddled in his bed. How on earth had she pulled this off? And where had she found the brass to dance in Samara's revealing costumes in front of an audience?

He thought of a question, a nice, safe, neutral question. "What about your family?"

"They're here, in England. I was over there working on a portrait commission, and waiting for a . . . friend."

He caught the note in her voice. "A *male* friend." Of course, it couldn't be anything else.

She nodded.

"And so for some unspecified reason, you let me believe that you were Samara—and you became Samara."

"With *great* difficulty," she said stringently.

He couldn't wait to hear her reasons. It was time to be blunt. "Why?"

She shivered. Oh, now he wanted the why of it.

Why. Such a slick, all-encompassing word, short and to the point. The ineffable, inexplicable why. The one word, the one explanation that would catapult her right back into her web of deceit and betrayal.

But conceivably she could also find out the truth.

Why . . .

"Colm," she said bravely into the silence before she lost her nerve.

And she shocked him again. "Colm?"

"*I* was waiting for Colm."

That statement rocked him and set all his perceptions spinning top over tail. One thing at a time, he thought, trying desperately to get his bearings, because he really needed to understand.

"Waiting for Colm—why?"

"Because he'd arranged my stay in Berlin. So we could be together. He's my cousin, you know. We were raised by our aunts at their house in Stonebourne. We had always planned to be together. So of course when you asked if Colm had come, I'"—her voice faltered as she saw the expression on his face—"I had to do what I could to protect him—if indeed you were speaking about *my* Colm, which I never did believe."

Betrayals every which way. Alex felt as if everything he'd built was crumbling, that he was crumbling over his unwarranted lust for this woman. But women were ever the downfall of men. Why should he be immune?

"I was," he said brutally. The real hit was the cleverness of Colm: how he'd gotten Alex Deveney, the most skeptical of men, to go haring off to Berlin and then bring back into his house Colm's very own personal operative, who, even though she had limited access to the important rooms, nevertheless had been an integral part of his plan to unmask the prime mover.

Colm had played him like a chess piece, and Alex had fallen right into his nemesis's hands. Maybe he'd been looking too far afield for the motive power and the answer had always been right under his nose.

He saw it all clearly now. And it wouldn't even have surprised him to learn that Colm had arranged Samara's death too, just to put his little cousin in her place. What wouldn't she do for the man she loved? She had proved herself to him again and again by everything she had sacrificed of herself to play the role of Samara.

The loyalty of the woman. And he'd thought she could be bought.

He was the naif, and she—she was every bit as dissolute as Samara, and a virgin besides. And that was one thing he could take from Colm, something precious and rare, and now, he had no regrets.

It still boggled his mind. William dead, Samara dead, and Colm's own spy in his house by his invitation.

To distract and divert him from his purpose until the papers could be brought to England.

Alex sat back, stunned. The enormity of the plan was staggering, and how each little piece had to work, from Colm's successfully getting rid of William, to his getting Alex to Berlin, and getting Francesca to take Samara's place.

And how could he have counted on Francesca's wholehearted participation in the role of Samara Teva?

The man was a master puppeteer, and they had all been running in place.

"*Your* Colm," he said flatly.

"No. I don't believe it. That's what I came here to prove."

"Have you?" he asked curiously.

She looked away. "No."

"How did he get you to do it?"

"What?"

"Take on being Samara."

"He didn't. It was my idea, and your bullying."

"Good story . . . Francesca. And meantime, we're his pawns and Colm rules the day. Well, we've come to an impasse—"

"You've gone over the impasse," she interrupted acidly.

"And you've burned your bridges, no matter what you say."

"You don't believe me," she murmured.

"Oh, I think some of it's true. Maybe all of it, but just not the way you tell it. How could it be with Colm, the master planner, moving the pieces?"

"Then who destroyed my clothes and your bedroom?"

"One of us, none of us. I don't know. And maybe the vandal's instincts were right, and you *are* the viper in our midst."

"Because of Colm?"

"Because of Colm. And don't pretend you don't know what he is."

"I do know what he is," Francesca said staunchly. "And he's not the Colm you claim you know. He's the man I love."

Alex felt as if he had taken another body blow. All Francesca had done for Colm in Samara Teva's name, and she had been preserving herself for him too. Her loyalty to Colm and his cause was stupefying, monstrous, because she had to have known all along what she was involved in and what she was intentionally doing to Alex.

And what was the line between innocence and desire? She

had known that too, conning him with her kisses and stringing him along, until the very moment that it was too late.

All the pieces finally fit, and Alex himself was the dupe, gulled, like every other susceptible man, by the promise of sex and sin.

Unforgivable, and almost irreparable. The prime mover at work. And he, who knew all the dangers, had fallen hardest of all.

Francesca. Her name was Francesca, and she wasn't foreign or lowborn or exotic and she'd grown up in the company of a traitor.

And he had threatened to imprison her for treason . . . well he might—

He still was having trouble coming to grips with it and his own culpability. He started to pace the floor.

"So this is the story: William dies. Samara Teva dies. And you are conveniently installed in the very rooming house where they live, and instructed by Colm to get to know Samara intimately. Find out everything about her in preparation for your mission, and then when she dies, step into her shoes. And your sole purpose is not to transport those abortive papers to England, as I had originally thought. Your mandate first and always was to spy on *me*. Such a sublimely ingenious plot. And you—so resourceful, Francesca. So inventive. So shrewd."

"That's not how it happened," she protested, futilely trying to fight his black rage.

"That's how it happened," he said succinctly. "It could be no other way, knowing Colm, and knowing what I do. This smoke screen of innocence only goes so far with me. But the magnitude of this deception is stunning. I haven't even touched the surface of all the ramifications. Nor have I decided what I want to do with you."

"You're already done with me," Francesca muttered, her voice tinged with bitterness. How in God's name had he misinterpreted the situation so drastically?

He gave her a long, assessing look. "I never want to see

you again. But my wishes right now aren't paramount. And everything *you've* ever said has turned out to be a tissue of lies. So what was it you were going tell me?''

"Nothing," she said stormily. There was no talking to him now. Everything she'd told him, everything she'd done belied her version of the truth. And what indeed was the truth, if even half of what he said about Colm were true?

But how could it be? How could she, who loved him the most, not know these things?

She knew very well—because none of it was true. *Her* Colm was a respected physician in service of a king and not some cold-blooded traitor. And that was what she knew and Alex Deveney could never shake her faith.

Everything else—he had turned upside down. In the aftermath of his breeching her, she had barely been able to assess the consequences of it. He had taken her because he wanted Samara, and for some reason, this night, she had not wanted to run.

The most calamitous decision of her life: to open herself up to him and confess her sin.

It was throwing a rock in a pond, the kernel of truth radiating outward into dozens of concentric circles that, like lies, grew larger and larger until the kernel finally disappeared.

And now her truth and her virginity were buried in this maw of mysteries and deceits and there was no going back and no retrieving her innocence.

But that was not her problem right now. Alex Deveney looked fit to kill and all his wrath was aimed at her. But there was yet a third story going on here—one that involved him, covert activities, and secrets she had yet to learn. *That* was what Samara had been involved in, and it had nothing to do with Colm.

"That was the right answer," Alex said. "You did right well for yourself, Francesca Reay. You've got a bundle of money on the closet floor and that will buy you the best lawyers when I throw you in prison for treason.''

She felt a cold chill wash down to her toes. "Oh no, no. We made a bargain. We had a deal. I'm not involved in this. You have to let me go."

"I don't have to do anything, Francesca, not a damned thing about you. You can rot in hell for all I care. And I'll make sure your Colm joins you there too. Rest in peace, my lady. You put on a most excellent show." He paused at the bedroom door as though something cataclysmic had occurred to him, and as if this, above everything, was the last straw.

"Good holy God, Francesca Reay, you goddamn faked your virginity too."

Chapter Sixteen

Francesca knew for a fact that Alex had stationed two foot-men outside the bedroom, and there were two more patrolling outside back and forth underneath her bedroom window.

Wotten brought her her meals, and Alex had for all intents and purposes disappeared.

Judithe and Phillippa must be happy as clams, Francesca thought mordantly. Samara Teva would plague them no longer, and sooner than that Francesca Reay would vanish from their lives as well.

Dear God, *what* had she gotten herself into?

She had spent the night wide awake, numbed by Alex's accusations, his mistrust, and the perversion of all her lies.

And one thing was absolutely clear: Alex meant to get rid of her any way possible. And that meant what? Prison? Incarcer-ation somewhere Colm couldn't find her? If indeed the object of the exercise *was* to keep her from Colm. The *other* Colm.

She had to get away from there. In the deepest part of the night, she began to plot and plan. It was imperative she eat to keep up her strength. And to keep watch on how Alex rotated the footmen and whether they were present when Wotten brought her food.

And to see if Wotten showed any sympathy.

Alex hadn't appropriated her money—yet. Good. That was one positive action she could take—unpinning all those bank-notes she had so laboriously placed all over her clothes. But worth it, on the heels of that violence that someone had perpe-trated in his room. She could just as easily have placed her stash beneath the mattress—and lost it all to a vicious stranger.

The money was all there. She packed it all in her little suitcase, and then she washed and dressed.

There wasn't much time to really think about this. She had to act—and fast.

Of course the most likely time to escape was at night. But then she'd have the disadvantage of not knowing where she was going. On the other hand, she might be under deeper surveillance at night, when there were more bodies to stand guard.

So her best bet was daytime. Early morning, perhaps, when no one but the servants—and Alex—were about?

How early? With the stars.

It was so, so good not to be thinking about Alex, or Samara, or Colm. To be planning instead to direct her life toward safety, security, and home.

Home. She had never thought of Braidwood as home, but there was something about the consistency of it that beckoned her. She could always count on Aunt Ida and Aunt Clarissa to be exactly the same.

And Colm most certainly would be there or would have left some kind of message for her. Probably he had only just told the aunts that he just missed her in Berlin. Yes, that was the kind of thing he would tell them to allay their fears. And that Francesca was on her way home, by other means.

She felt a growing, gnawing tension in her as the day drew to a close. She had reckoned the times, the places, the changes of all of her guards. She had her suitcase positioned just by the door. And now all she needed was that one sweet opportunity to set herself free.

But what if Alex came?

No. He was finished with her; he'd made that plain. It was only a matter of him making some kind of arrangements for her. But she was not going to wait for Alex to dispose of her.

Early the next morning, she waited, cold and dressed. Debating. Calculating. Everyone was asleep, and only her watchdogs about.

She tapped gently on the door. It opened inward just a crack and a footman's burly face appeared. One guard? Only one?

"Yes, mum?"

Francesca gave him her most beguiling smile and murmured, with a modest little catch in her voice, "I—I need the . . . to do—you know . . ."

"Yes, mum." He opened the door.

One. Act now . . . !

She kicked him in the knees, and as he bent over, suppressing a howl, she got him in the vee. And then she grabbed her suitcase and *ran.*

Around the landing, down the steps, his angry voice calling for help. God, she hadn't had three minutes to make her escape, but she would, she would.

Another servant came running up the steps—she held out the suitcase and pushed and he toppled back down the stairs.

Pounding footsteps and shouts that woke the house.

Down to the reception hall—another servant coming up from below. Francesca grasped the suitcase with both hands and swung it at him—and down he went.

The door, the door . . . oh, God, if the door was locked, it was over. . . . It opened easily on silent oiled hinges. . . . Down the steps into the moist gray dawn with shouts and footsteps behind her.

Where in all of Meresham Close could a fugitive hide?

She skirted the corner of the house, keeping to the shadows, and doubled back underneath the entrance steps.

They were out in force already to find her, streaming out from under the arches where she hid, and from the servants' quarters above, Wotten at the lead.

They spread out as they ran, covering every conceivable angle from the house, going farther and farther afield until they were dots in the distance.

Only then did she creep out from under the arches and dart into the shadow of a nearby stand of trees. And slowly, bush by bush, shadow by shadow, she made her way up the drive and toward the road.

From his room above, Alex and Marcus watched her.

"For God's sake, Alex—don't let her go."

"The servants have their instructions. They'll let her alone. I know where she's going, Marcus. And I'm going to use her to kill two birds with one stone."

Phillippa didn't know whether to feel anger or relief. The bitch was gone, out of Alex's bedroom, out of their lives, away from the house to places unknown.

She slipped down to the cottage earlier than usual to tell Apollo the news.

It never ceased to amaze her that he was always there, always naked and waiting for her.

"Don't say a word, my darling. Tell me about the ball."

"It was very, very . . . nice." She had told him she would be in attendance.

"And you looked beautiful," he whispered. "I know you did."

"How?" she demanded, frightened. What if he had seen her with Marcus? What if he had deduced . . . concluded . . . What if her idyll ended?

"More beautiful than the harlot, my amazon. No one could miss you in that bright, bright blue. But then, you love that kind of attention, don't you?"

He had her naked already and flat on the bed.

"I do." Phillippa pulled him inside her. "You know I do."
She reveled in the feel of him, rocking, nestling. "She's gone,
by the way."

"Who?" he asked abstractedly.

"You know. *Her.*"

He stiffened instantly. "Is she? How did that happen?"

"He—" she started and amended, "I'm told he finally sent
her away."

"Well, well. So the great Alex Deveney has his limits. And
it's true, the whore can wear on a man. The only time a man
likes to keep one around is if she can wear him *out.*"

"As I do you, Apollo," she murmured with confidence, her
body rippling to entice him.

"Oh, but today is another day, my wanton. So why don't
you try?"

"Well, Alex, I suppose we can say you finally came to your
senses."

"Well, Mother, it *was* a lovely ball, thank you."

"And did it get you what you wanted?" Judithe asked.

Alex shot her a quizzical look.

"You never do anything without a purpose, and you had
something in mind for that creature."

"Nothing more than to introduce her to our friends and
neighbors. To accord her the respect she deserves as William's
widow."

"And that's why she ran away."

"Something like that."

Wotten was serving a late breakfast, all the servants having
been involved in chasing after Francesca, and Alex's mother,
on hearing the news, had deigned to join him for some toast
and tea.

"You're a wretch, Alex. You do as you please."

"Yes, I'm happy you understand that, Mother, because I *am*
going after her, later this week."

"I swear to God I'm going to have palpitations. Whatever for?"

"My business."

"We have had this conversation," Judithe said pungently. "I refuse to discuss it anymore."

Nor did Alex want to. He was still raw from all the revelations and betrayals.

"You'll do whatever you want to do," Judithe said, completing the ritual. And it was rather comforting to have things return to normal.

But Alex couldn't diminish the scent of Francesca's sex fogging his room. Never again would he allow it to cloud his vision. He had been taken for a long, torturous, sensual ride that no man in his right mind could have resisted, neatly set up by a master at the game.

Well, everything now was diamond clear, and he was prepared to face Samara Teva—Francesca Reay—one more time.

But he'd give her time enough to get back to Stonebourne. Time, indeed, for contact to be made.

Chess pieces. He was counting on it. Colm wasn't the only one who played the game.

Money eased the way for everything. A pound here, a shilling there—no one looked askance at a woman with a suitcase who flashed some ready money.

And even as Francesca boarded the coach at the Mereton Pub, she was still sure that Alex would catch up with her. But no such thing happened. She traveled safely, albeit through most of the day, until they reached Rillston, where she changed for another coach to Vernon Vale.

It was a long, dusty ride, broken by an evening meal at the Inn of Vale and an overnight stay, eased by all that lovely money.

It was another full day before she reached Stonebourne, and suddenly she felt slack with fear. There were so many hurdles, suddenly, not the least of which was how long it had been since she'd been home. Six months? No, more like close on a year.

And she had so drastically changed. And then all the other permutations relevant to Colm. And had she stupidly told Alex where her people were?

God, she thought she had.

Well, too late for any of that now. She was going home.

Alex was a patient man. He knew how to wait. But he found himself growing impatient to track Francesca not two days after she'd left.

He hadn't yet exorcised her from his craw. Even now, alone in his bed, all he could think about was *Samara Teva*, and all her contradictions explained.

But it was just not possible that Francesca's story was true. He could not let himself fall for any piece of it or he'd be whipsawed all over again.

No, the thing was what it was: She was Colm's puppet, lover, agent, and her express purpose had been to seduce and spy on *him*.

Any day now, he'd start out for Stonebourne. It took time to get there, going by coach. Time for her to assess what had happened, and to make her plans. And he was certain Samara— no, Francesca—was good at making plans. She'd brought him down like a rotten oak tree.

And you didn't do that with naivete.

It was one reason he didn't like the silence: Thoughts grew there. And memories. Of kisses in the dark.

He was relieved the next day when Alastair called.

"You really let her go, Alex? How brutal of you."

"All things must end."

"Oh, but really, dear boy, she was something else, end to end. I just came to say, lovely party. Lovely whore. I was hoping to get her for a private party of my own."

Alex raised an eyebrow. "Really? Well, I'm sorry to tell you—she retired."

"Go on, Alex. Retired? That feisty piece? I don't think so. Truly, where has she gone? I'll negotiate myself. Same terms as Selfridge. You're invited of course."

"I wish I could tell you. I don't know."

"Oh, Alex, Alex, Alex. Keeping her to yourself. Tsk. Tsk. Well, the thing will work out one way or another. Ta, dear boy." And with a twitch of his frock coat he was gone.

Still, they wanted her. And Alastair too. She was becoming a parlor game, for God's sake. Come for an evening of *dance and spread your legs*. It's a new card trick that utilizes one pretty harlot who's willing to take off her clothes.

Damn it, damn and damn . . .

Another day gone. Tomorrow, he would begin the journey, all alone.

But tonight, there was an unaccustomed light in his room—Wotten, probably packing.

"Close the door, Alex."

Phillippa, properly unpacked, and naked on his bed, her body ripe and full of shadows and hollows in the dim candlelight. And her breasts were large, well shaped, taut. Her blond hair streamed in a fine golden glow down her back.

She moved against the pillows, patting the space by her side.

"Phillippa, this is a big mistake."

"Is it? Why? You have needs, now that the creature is gone. I have needs, because we all know that Marcus is *not* a creature of the senses. So who would know?" She shifted her hips to give him a better view. "You know I've wanted this for a very long time."

"But I haven't."

"You're still besotted with that bitch. But that will pass, and meantime, you'll have come home." She rose onto her knees. "Come to me, Alex. I'm willing to please."

And he wasn't immune. His groin tightened. His imagination flamed. He envisioned Samara on the bed, her body enchained.

"Phillippa, don't make me say this twice. I don't want you. I won't take you. You're Marcus's wife."

Now she felt a tremor of desperation. This was not how it was supposed to work. Her naked body was supposed to be irresistible to men—hadn't Apollo told her so?

Phillippa swung her legs off the bed and bent one knee. "I'm Marcus's beast of burden. Alex, think. What could it hurt? How can you refuse me after having *her?* I can service you better than she ever could. She was a luxury. I get in your blood."

Not a saint, he thought, a muscle flexing in his cheek. Not a monk. And not possible with the woman who was his brother's wife.

And Samara Teva didn't count.

"Get dressed, Phillippa, and give it up and go home."

"You don't know what *you're* giving up."

"Maybe I do," he said, trying to ease her pain a little.

"Try it then. Try me."

"Phillippa—"

Her mouth crumpled, vulnerable and in pain.

"I won't forget you did this." She marched across the room in a jerky movement to pull her dress and shoes out of his closet. "I won't forgive." Tears were streaming down her face.

"But can you face me across the dinner table?"

"Don't make light of it. I offered you *everything.*"

"It's time for you to go home."

But she didn't. She didn't. She felt so humiliated by his rejection, she raced past the Rectory, not caring who saw her.

She needed her sun god, her Apollo, the one who had willingly chosen her above everyone else.

She raced through the village and down the long, winding road to the cottage, all in the dark. It was like a magnet—it drew her.

But it was dark.

"Apollo—Apollo—" She rattled the knob. "Open the door—"

She twisted the doorknob. It was locked.

Omigod ... "Apollo ..." Her voice broke as she edged around to the front of the cottage and tried the front door. Locked.

She peered in the front window, to the parlor lit by firelight. The bed had been moved from in front of the fireplace, and the chairs and sofa restored.

She knocked frantically on the door, and it slowly swung open.

An old woman stood there, as bent and crooked as a witch in a fairy tale.

"The man who was here ..." Phillippa said desperately.

"Gone, my dear. Left yesterday. I just mind the house until it goes to let again. But he—he's gone. And didn't leave no other address."

Aunt Ida received her exactly the same as if she'd just come back from an errand to the village.

"Oh, it's you. Come in, Frances."

"Francesca," she said militantly, perfectly willing to reengage in their old battle. She set her suitcase by the coatrack.

Aunt Ida led the way to the parlor. Not much had changed at Braidwood. The room was still curtained in thick velvet drapes that were closed to the light and air. The furniture was still as stiff and unyielding as her aunt. And altogether, there wasn't much inviting about the room.

"Sit down," Aunt Ida said.

Francesca sat, giving her aunt a critical but covert once-over. But Aunt Ida too looked much the same, except that it seemed to Francesca that every line in her aunt's face had crept downward. Certainly those around her mouth, which were noticeable as Aunt Ida pursed her lips and considered what to say.

"Well, Frances—"

"Francesca."

Aunt Ida ignored her. "Is this a visit, or have you finally

come to your senses, given up that frivolous idea of becoming a painter and come home for good?''

"Both. Neither. I don't know.'' She felt ten years old again, and she mentally shook herself to get a grip. This kind of continuity was *not* why she'd come back to Braidwood.

"I see,'' Aunt Ida said. "So what exactly are you doing here?''

"I'm home. I just don't know for how long.''

"My dear Frances, this isn't a boardinghouse, although I imagine you're fairly used to that by now. You're either here or you aren't, Frances. There are no in-betweens.''

"Francesca,'' she said automatically. "Well, then—I'm here, for now.''

There was a long silence, almost as if Aunt Ida were thinking it over. Which was curious, to say the least.

"Well,'' Ida said finally, "I suppose since there's no money I'll have to take you in.''

Francesca opened her mouth to dispute that—and closed it again. Her aunt didn't need to know anything about the hundreds of pounds she concealed.

Well, maybe a little lie—

"There was some money, actually. The general whose portrait I was painting?'' Aunt Ida sniffed. "He was very generous, and I managed to save some money. So I won't be a burden, Aunt Ida. I thought you'd like to know.''

But Francesca rather thought that Ida didn't want to know, and that Ida would have much preferred that Francesca come home on sufferance rather than independent and not in need.

"Well, thank God for small mercies. Very well. You'll have your old room. Meals are the same. And I expect you'll pitch in and help.''

"Of course.''

"And make up your mind finally whether you want to be a bohemian or a wife?''

"They both sound rather distasteful, Aunt Ida.''

"Still the same smart mouth, I see, Frances. A year away from home hasn't broadened your outlook."

"Or narrowed my ideas. Thank you, Aunt Ida. It's nice to be home. By the way, where is Clarissa?"

Ida looked startled for a moment. "Oh, Clarisssa. She'll be along in a moment, Frances. She's probably in the garden. Or somewhere. Why don't you get settled in your room? You still have some clothes in the closet. I hope you'll change out of that debilitating black."

"Yes, Aunt Ida."

She picked up her suitcase in the hall.

"But you left here with far more than that one suitcase, Frances. Where are your—"

"Francesca. All in good time, Aunt Ida." She was halfway up the steps, and the familiar scents and smells assaulted her: must, mothballs, perfume, stale air.

Ten years old all over again. Francesca pushed open the door of her room, one of the narrow hall rooms that faced the north light in the front of the house. And still the same as she'd left it, with its narrow bed, its painted dresser, its burned-down candlesticks. Her easel stood, propped by the window. A bookshelf full of cracked and hardened paints. Experimental miniatures she'd done of the house, her aunts, and Colm's face.

Oh God, oh Colm . . . why didn't you come?

She opened the closet door. A handful of plain cotton dresses hung in a neat row. Her shoes, her boots. Her underthings. Colorful ribbons and laces spilled out of her box of *pretty things*. Her desk, by the bed, seemed excruciatingly small.

Or had she grown since she'd gone?

She needed a hiding place for all that money, because as sure as a lightning strike, Aunt Ida would snoop and find it.

But for the moment, she shoved the suitcase into the back of the closet, as she heard footsteps pattering down the hallway and Aunt Clarissa's tootling voice, "Francesca! Frannie dear . . ." before she came bursting into the room and folded Francesca into her arms.

"There you are," she murmured, patting her everywhere. "Oh, we've been so concerned about you, but here you are, and everything's all right."

Her aunt held her away for a moment and gazed on her face. "You're thinner, my dear, but I think it becomes you. And you look so mature."

Aunt Clarissa always made her feel happy. "I'm a year older, that's for sure. I'm glad to bc home."

"For how long?" Clarissa asked shrewdly.

"A while."

"Good. Well, Ida tells me you're going to change out of that funereal black dress and then you'll come downstairs for tea."

"For the inquisition, you mean."

"That too," Clarissa said, laughing. "Go on, Francesca. Hurry up."

And she left her niece alone.

Now—the money . . . no, change the dress first. That made more sense, and it was so much more easily and quickly done. But Francesca's old dresses didn't fit her quite the same any more. They were a little shorter, or she was a little taller? She didn't know which. She chose one in navy blue serge with a deep hem she could let out later.

Ten years old again.

Now *where* could she hide that money?

There was a little screened porch off the breakfast room at Braidwood, and it was there they repaired for afternoon tea during the summer. All against Aunt Ida's most stringent objections. Aunt Ida didn't seem to like fresh air, and Aunt Clarissa did.

Aunt Clarissa wanted to know everything.

"So tell us how things went in Berlin? You traveled there fine. We got your card. And we know that Colm arranged your accommodations. Were they decent? And how was the food? And the general. Was he pleased with the work you did?''

"Pleased enough that Frances was paid," Aunt Ida said, almost as if she didn't at all like the idea of it.

"Paid! That's wonderful, Francesca," Aunt Clarissa said, using her name pointedly. "Paid. Oh my. What was he like?''

"Well, he certainly had a perception of himself that was a little different from mine," Francesca said, "but we ironed that all out. Money is always a persuasive factor. The rooming house was clean and came with meals. And the boarders pretty well kept to themselves."

"And Colm—?''

"I never saw him. He never came. I was hoping you would tell me he's come back here.''

Aunt Clarissa shook her head. "Well, isn't that strange? Ah well. He's a man, and I suppose he'll come when he will. Have some tea, dear."

It was actually a rather pleasant interlude, and Francesca found herself having some very fond feelings, at least for Aunt Clarissa. Ida just sat there and glowered, almost as if the fresh air distorted her face.

Francesca talked about the sights and sounds of Berlin, and the ease of her comprehension of the language, with a dutiful bow to her aunts for their foresight in giving her lessons.

She told some amusing stories about the general and mentioned the ongoing confusion in the aftermath of the Emperor's death.

"I daresay Colm is still involved with some of the details about that. They still haven't stopped trying to blame the doctors," Aunt Clarissa said indignantly. "Ah well. Colm is the best of them all and he'll surely be home soon."

Exactly, Francesca thought triumphantly. Colm had nothing to do with manipulating agents and missing papers. He was busy taking care of the tail end of the problems that had resulted in Friedrich's death.

She felt vindicated. Elated. And finally home.

After Ida excused herself, Francesca spent the afternoon on the porch, talking to Aunt Clarissa, relieved and amused that everything was just the same.

"I wonder what we'll have to talk about at dinner," Clarissa said. "I think we've exhausted every topic. Go upstairs now, and rest."

Oh, but she'd been resting since she walked in the door, and who would have thought the home that had so unsettled her would seem like a haven now.

But the thing she most feared she found right in her room: Aunt Ida was snooping around.

"One dress? One nightgown? One suitcase? Where are your art supplies? Do you know how much money we spent on that paint? And what is that awful pile of circles on the bed? Really, Frances. Being away from home has gone to your head. No appreciation at all for anything anyone's done for you."

"I left everything at the rooming house when I came home. The landlady is holding it for me. You didn't lose anything."

"Oh? Are you going back?"

Damn, painted herself into a corner. "Maybe."

Aunt Ida sighed. "You haven't changed one whit, Frances."

"Francesca. Well, neither have you, Aunt Ida. Would you please leave my room?"

This was the kind of draining encounter Francesca had run away from. She moved the circlets and lay down on her narrow bed and folded her arms behind her head.

Thank God she'd hidden the money before she'd gone downstairs.

She'd found the perfect place: behind the crown molding over the doorway, where there was a little space between the wall and the doorframe. A place that Aunt Ida couldn't get to easily. And couldn't go poking around.

But everything else, and more if she'd had it, was fair game to her aunt.

Francesca jumped up suddenly. The circlets!

The last remaining vestige of Samara Teva. And nothing she

needed to keep with her to remind her of what she had done. Or to raise Aunt Ida's suspicions.

It was time, she thought, to bury the dead.

She picked up a pair of scissors and started cutting the belt apart, surprised to find that the cording was soft and pliable. She poked a finger inside one thin satin tube.

Not cording. Not cotton batting either. She picked and pulled at it and snipped the satin sheath away.

Curious.

It was a length of tissue-thin paper, rolled into the satin tube. Carefully she unrolled it and lifted it to the light.

All kinds of numbers and letters were written on it in sharp, tight ink.

Her hands trembling, Francesca snipped open another of the circlets and with some difficulty, pulled out another tube of paper. And another. And another.

Not every circlet contained the rolled-up paper, but she found enough so that when she laid them out on the bed, she had no doubt what she was looking at: the infamous black box papers that Samara had allegedly never received.

Chapter Seventeen

Francesca ran a shaking hand over the fragile papers on the bed. Each one was printed with indecipherable letters, signs, and symbols. Altogether the papers made up one sheet about the size of a business letter.

Papers . . .

God, the disputed papers. Which meant that everything that Alex had accused Samara of was true.

Now what was she going to do? One thing—no one could see those papers. Whatever they contained, people had been killed for them. And there was nothing to say that the vandalism at Meresham hadn't been linked to them. A sane person would burn them on the spot.

When had Samara been given them? It had to have been after William's death.

But why speculate. Francesca had them now and she wasn't going to destroy them, not yet. Maybe.

She stared at the mess she'd made ripping apart the satin circlets. That too had to be disposed of and in a way that her aunts wouldn't see and ask questions.

God, she'd been home less than a day and already she was involved in subversive activities.

Just as Alex had said . . .

She shuddered. Webs tightening everywhere, sticky with deceit. And she was about to weave another one.

What if someone walked in on her now?

She had to get these things out of the way.

She began piling up the delicate transparent papers one on top of the other.

Here and there, as she examined them, something familiar caught her eye. A number. A word. A cross. Nothing that made sense.

How many? Twenty? Fifty? A breath and they'd blow away.

And she hadn't even finished examining the costume. No, she had to hide that too.

She needed something to weigh the papers down. Glass and paper, maybe. Or . . . behind one of her miniatures—she reached for the one of Colm. A minute later the portrait was on the bed, and she was fitting the pile of papers flat against the sawn-wood backing. And then Colm's portrait over that, and back into the—

. . . wait—

On the topmost paper, she saw something—a word. She took it to the light to examine it more closely.

Abtissen.

She knew that word.

How?

She placed Colm's portrait over the papers and compressed the whole back into the frame. One thing taken care of.

Abtissen.

The circlets next. They could go right back into her suitcase, but Aunt Ida would probably want to know why they were still there, and why they were all cut up.

This subversive business was very tricky.

She found an old stretched-out canvas under her bed with a partially finished painting. The frame on that was deep enough to conceal the costume *if* she could find some kind of backing. Wood or cardboard would do. Even another piece of canvas—wait—surely there were some old canvases stored in the attic.

Up the dusty steps to the attic, rummaging quickly in the stale air, she found what she wanted: a piece of cardboard she could jam between the wood braces of the canvas, and then she propped it up on the easel in her room.

Good effect. Terrible painting.

Abtissen . . . *why was that word so familiar?*

A gong tolled somewhere downstairs. A sound from her childhood, to summon them to the table. It resonated inside her, heightening her dread.

But this wasn't a house of horrors, and she herself had brought the incriminating papers with her.

Just because she was hiding things didn't mean she had anything to fear. It just meant that she didn't want Aunt Ida's all-seeing eyes prying into her business.

Abtissen.

Something about that was meaningful—what?

She ran down the stairs to the dining room, where her aunts were already seated.

"You're late."

Typical Aunt Ida. "I beg your pardon."

They were served typical household fare, redolent of her childhood, plain and uncompromising: lentil soup, chicken pie, potatoes, salad, and an orange cake.

Truly she was home again.

But now what? In her younger years, she used to go to her room and either play with Colm, read a book, or sketch with her paints.

"Come, dear." Aunt Clarissa now. "We'll sit in the parlor and read some magazines."

That was new. Francesca followed her aunt back into the dark room and Aunt Clarissa pulled a handful of periodicals out of a drawer. "There you go. All within the month. We pass them around the ladies' circle, you see. This is our week."

No, this wasn't quite what she wanted to be doing either. They were all spiritual and *uplifting* magazines. "These don't really interest me."

Aunt Clarissa looked down at them. "Oh. Oh. Well, we've enjoyed them. Perhaps you'd like to read?"

"You really don't have to entertain me."

Clarissa looked at her consideringly. "No, I suppose I don't. But—a game of chess, perhaps?"

"I haven't played in so long." Since Colm had left, she realized, remembering how they used to race to the library for that hour before the fireplace with the chessboard. *We're his pawns . . . Colm, the master planner, moving the pieces . . .* She shook her head to get Alex's voice out of her mind. "You'd have me checkmated in ten seconds flat."

Clarissa smiled. "I'm not quite that proficient." She thought for a moment. "I know. A game of cards. We used to have so much fun, remember?"

So much fun in a house of gloom? Aunt Clarissa had been the one who'd made it bearable. And Colm.

"We can stay right here." She reached into another drawer and withdrew a deck of cards. "Hearts?"

They sat for perhaps an hour and played, and then Clarissa prepared some tea and warm milk. "Always good before you go to sleep."

It was all of nine o'clock. Francesca drank the tea, kissed her aunt, and having no reason to stay, went upstairs to sit on her bed.

Now what?

Maybe coming back here was a bad idea. A *really* bad idea. Aunt Ida still snooped. And there was never anything to do. Dear Aunt Clarissa, trying to keep her occupied as if she were still ten years old.

A book probably would be more the thing.

She started back downstairs again when she heard the low murmur of voices.

"Tonight, we begin the program."

That she heard clearly. The second voice's response was garbled, and then they faded away.

Francesca ran down the last steps and down the hall into the library.

It was like going back in time, this room particularly, with that monster of an altar dominating one wall. Aunt Clarissa had saved all their childhood books, and Francesca browsed with pleasure, inhaling the childhood scents of old books, perfume, and a faint musk.

What little pleasure they'd found in their childhood, she and Colm, they'd found here. Books were their companions, and they could sit for hours inventing stories and pretending new lives.

But she remembered some of the not nice things too: Aunt Ida chasing her when she was disobedient, and hiding under chairs and desks, and behind curtains, and in the space between the wall and altar, and under a bed. Anywhere her aunt couldn't find her whenever she'd been disobedient.

All those things came back in force as she stood in the library and was inundated with childhood memories.

Enough of this. She shook off all the old feelings, selected a book, and went back upstairs.

"Fran-ces . . . Fran-CES—"
The voice was there, inhabiting her dreams.
She jerked awake, finding herself still in her little, narrow room, her body almost falling off the bed.
Fran-ces . . .
A demon in a dream.
She settled back again, and the voice immediately came.
Fran-CES—
A bohemian like her mother—punish her . . . take her to the Abtissen. *Take everything to the* Abtissen—
Fran-CES . . .
Promise me—Samara Teva will never die—

Step out of the spotlight while they still remember your name. . . .

She awoke the second time in a cold sweat.

Samara! Haunting her dreams . . . Take everything to the Abtissen, Samara had said. Everything. Clothes? Costumes? Clues . . .

Lord. She couldn't sleep.

And what good did it do her to remember?

Francesca got up and got her robe. Tomorrow night, the warm milk instead of tea.

Maybe tonight, the way she was feeling.

She crept downstairs to the kitchen and prepared it.

There wasn't a sound, a soul in sight. But then, her aunts had always been early risers; they were probably fast asleep.

She was just halfway up the stairs when she heard a faint sound.

The house, creaking, she decided. Braidwood was as old as the trees that dotted the landscape.

Another step up—and she heard it again.

Stupid to put herself in harm's way, but she couldn't ignore the sound. She sipped deeply of the milk, set it on the step, and went back down.

Braidwood.

He only knew about her being at Braidwood from making inquiries in town, but now that Alex had found the dilapidated old manor house, he was loath to turn around.

Deadly eerie place, he thought, reining in his mount. And both of them had been raised here, among the turrets and the towers.

The moon was full and made the landscape seem unearthly and still, as if ghosts prowled the shadows, and evil was in the air.

Francesca Reay had come back to this ungodly place for a

reason, and it wasn't just to escape him. Somehow Colm had made contact, and she'd come here to meet *him*.

Alex had wagered his life on it, his soul.

It was steamy quiet when he finally dismounted in the small copse of bushes from which he could clearly see the house. The moon was high, the night was old, and there was something about that house.

Maybe because it was the home of the unholy pair.

How long had they been collaborating? he wondered. Probably ever since they could talk . . .

But Francesca had come later, when she was older, after the death of her parents. From everything he'd been able to find out, Colm had lived there from birth, the ward of his aunts, and latterly having had a successful career rising through the ranks at Fenchurch and then into medical school in Scotland. All of that was well known about Colm.

What was not understood were the intangibles. The things in Colm's life, and in his upbringing, that had turned him into a spymaster in a time of peace—and perhaps the prime mover in a catastrophic initiative that was only a whispered rumor in the halls of power of the elite.

That was why there were people like Colm. They took care of the things with which other people did not want to dirty their hands. And Alex Deveney took care of people like Colm.

There wasn't a breeze or a sound, just an owl and the moon. Alex hunkered down and prepared to spend the night.

Francesca paused at the bottom of the steps. And then she heard it again—a long, sawing sound from somewhere to her right.

The library . . .

She darted down the hallway again, and then flattened her back right outside the library door.

Quiet . . .

A high-pitched squeak, almost unheard.

This was insane. It was probably mice.

She started back down the hall—stopped, listened, moved forward into the library, where the lamplight still burned low.

She was hearing something, somewhere. Or was it her imagination overblown?

Forbidden . . .

The word, ringing into her consciousness, made her jump.

It was almost as if she heard Aunt Ida's voice.

Forbidden . . .

A thousand and one things forbidden in this house . . .

She moved toward the altar—that huge, ungainly, carved piece of wall-to-wall wood.

Something about the altar?

Francesca touched the wood and pulled her hand back as if it were burned.

And then she heard the squeaking sound of the clock's minute hand moving inexorably toward midnight.

Of course. The clock. The shifting weights. The cricking sound of an ancient minute hand.

She picked up her milk from the step and headed up the stairs just as the clock struck midnight.

It looked as if it was going to be a repeat of the previous day. Breakfast with her aunts, she and Clarissa in the garden picking flowers, arranging them in the dining room, and then some free time to spend by herself.

Francesca walked to the village; there was nothing else to do, and already she could see this wasn't going to do.

And in fact, she thought, she was perfectly free to leave now. Her aunts were both certain where Colm was, and that was the major thing.

If she were smart, she would go back to Germany and get on with that commission. At least it was something for her portfolio, and the money was good.

But she'd never have to worry about money again for a long,

long time, and she rather liked the thought of being a bohemian who lived a touch above herself.

There was nothing to stay here for. But with any luck, in Berlin, she could reconnect with Colm.

All those years ago, he'd promised, and she'd lived on that dream. And even if it didn't work out, didn't her returning to Berlin seem like the most logical course?

And she could forget all about Samara Teva as if she'd been a bad dream. No, she'd never forget about Samara, or her dances. Never.

Or Alex Deveney, at the end, breaching everything, including her trust. But that was a memory left behind and a bridge best burned.

All in all, it was better this way. Spend a little time with her aunts, and then go on her way. She didn't much care what Aunt Ida would say.

She felt she had reached a calm and reasonable decision by the time she returned to Braidwood. Another week or so with the aunts should suffice, and then in good conscience, she'd be able to go.

The afternoon and the evening passed much the same: dinner, cards. A book. Warm milk taken up with her to bed.

Drowsy, and snuggling down in her bed . . .

Fran-ces . . . Fran-CES—!

Tell the Abtissen *you have to go. . . .*

She bolted upright in bed.

The *Abtissen* was haunting her; Samara Teva haunted her. And Alex's kisses. *No, why was she thinking about that?*

She jumped out of bed and grabbed her robe.

Every sound seemed magnified as she glided down the stairs with the intention of preparing another cup of milk.

Wait—a sigh. A squeak. A creak. A moan.

She was imagining things again.

No—wait—

Again toward the library . . . the damned library was haunted, she thought, once again entering, as the lights flickered low.

A sound behind her, a low-sawn note . . . her hands out in front of her, groping for air.

Why had she come here?

Francesca touched the altar—made a sound as if burned. Came that close to forbidden things.

She backed up and stared at it, a massive piece of carven wood. Nothing hot about that. Why would it burn?

But she couldn't bring herself to touch it again and she just stood staring at it.

Alex watched her from the shadows, from the place of comfort where he'd established himself, easily entering by the kitchen door. For a place that was the home of a master planner, he'd thought, security was awfully lax.

Careless of Colm. But Colm wasn't careless. He was a brilliant tactician, logical, bold, and ruthless. There was something else going on here. Or else he wasn't yet in residence, and when he got there things would change.

But for now, there was Francesca, and the look on her face was strange, a combination of fear and disbelief, and no understanding in response to what.

She was hearing the noises, the same as he, the subtle, low basso moans, like ghosts haunting your dreams.

But they were coming from behind the altar.

And she knew it too. She reached out her hand again and immediately snatched it away as if it were burned.

She was determined. She tried it again and again and again, finally sticking her hand to the brass handle that opened the door and pushing it open, with a silent scream.

And then wrenching her hand away, and nursing it, she stepped inside the gate.

She was remembering this. Many, many, many years ago, there was a bad little girl who remembered this. Down she went, down some narrow stone steps, not the heroine of a fairy tale. And into the room with the bed, full of forbidden things.

She remembered the bed, hiding under the bed from the wrath of Aunt Ida. The place only she and Aunt Ida knew—
The Forbidden Room . . .

She felt a sheer slide of pain as she remembered, and it almost crippled her. Instantly, because she was grown-up now, it was clear that the thing to do was to not remember the words. She could think about the things, but she shouldn't remember the words.

Because one day, Aunt Ida had found her there.

And then, oh then, the pain . . .

That was assuaged by the perfectly pleasurable sigh.

She walked on into the furnished room that, yes, she remembered.

"The program is working."

The words, a whisper, inside her brain.

She kept going forward in that room, urged on by mysterious memories. There was another door, on the far wall, that seemed to suddenly appear, and she knew it was one she had never opened.

And behind that door was the answer to her every question.

Without hesitation, she opened the door and found herself at the gate of a new city. She stepped out onto a parapet and looked down.

I'm dreaming. This is a horrible, awful dream.

Or was it?

She felt frozen. She couldn't move a muscle.

She counted twelve naked women prone on their opulent beds.

The light below was subdued, lit by flares, so that the women's bodies seemed sculpted of hollows and curves.

"The program works." Guardians pronouncing a benediction.

She stepped down off the parapet, down one step at a time. Her subjects were spread out below her, each on her own bed; and her King moved among them, mounting each in turn.

She wasn't imagining this, was she?

Horrified, she watched as he continued on, with each of her subjects welcoming him in turn. He was a piston, an engine, with a full head of steam.

"The program works. . . ."

It was a dream. . . .

"The seed is King."

Aunt Ida?

And all the captive women murmured: "Long live the seed."

Chapter Eighteen

And then, shockingly, she was in her own bed, it was morning, and she had such a feeling of well-being, she thought there must have been something in the milk.

"Did you sleep well?" Aunt Clarissa asked.

"I think so. It's almost as if there were some kind of potion in my milk last night. Did you . . . ?"

"Ah—you caught on to my little secret," Aunt Clarissa said. "I thought you might need a deeper rest."

Had it been a deep rest or a sleep troubled by strange dreams?

Francesca supposed she was never to know, but she had the distinct feeling, as she did some chores around the house, that Colm was near.

Now isn't that a strange thing to feel?

Or was it that she wanted him there so badly, she'd even conjure him up in a nightmare?

What made her think of that?

A visitor came later in the day to exchange some village news, which meant the aunts would be occupied for a good full hour.

And that should give her enough time, Francesca decided, to finish pulling apart the rest of Samara's costume. The sooner she disposed of that the better, she thought, because with it she'd destroy the last vestiges of her adventure as Samara, and the papers would be safe.

Safe for whom?

Safe from what?

Safe, period. She would take the painting, behind which she had concealed the remnants of the costume, and go up to the attic and pick it apart. And then hide it under the floorboards or something.

But she had the uneasy feeling, as she climbed the steps up to her room, that things wouldn't be that easy. She hadn't been meant to find the papers or to even know what they were.

And she was scared to death that because of it, she would have to make some kind of choice.

Nonsense. There was no choice. Colm would explain everything when he came, and that would be the end of it.

And meantime, she wouldn't do anything foolish. She'd keep the papers and bide her time.

That was sensible, rational. There was an explanation for everything.

But there was no explanation for why, when she got to her room, the painting was gone.

Aunt Clarissa was at a loss to explain it. "Nobody's been up there except you. Was it there this morning when you awakened?"

"I don't know."

"Well, you see. Maybe you did something with it that you don't remember."

Aunt Clarissa dealt in simplicities. If a thing wasn't one place, it had to be another. If you couldn't remember seeing it, then you must have done something with it.

Now Francesca felt frightened. That on top of the strange

nightmare, and the sense she had of both burning her hand and feeling Colm's presence, was enough to spook anyone.

But as long as her money was still where she'd hidden it, she felt less trapped. She checked that, and then she got out of the house and went for a walk.

The evening replicated the previous day. She and the aunts dined together, and then she and Aunt Clarissa played cards.

"I'm afraid this isn't much of a life for you," Aunt Clarissa said.

"I've been thinking that myself," Francesca admitted. How kind and sensitive of Aunt Clarissa to perceive it. "I'm thinking about going back to Berlin to continue on with my art."

"I would support that," Clarissa said, "although you know Ida would probably put up a fight."

"Well, maybe she won't, if she understands I have enough money to do it on my own."

"How resourceful of you, dear."

"Well, what does a woman do when she's alone? Can I really count on Colm—or any man?"

"No, dear, I'm afraid you can't, and he's so busy. . , ,"

"Exactly my thought," Francesca said, dealing a round.
But why do I feel he's close?

After, Aunt Clarissa brought her a tray with a glass of milk. "No powders tonight, dear. I know you'll sleep."

Did she? Francesca knew she went upstairs. She remembered undressing and getting into bed. She had a sense of time passing, clouds and sun and the darkened sky, and then suddenly she was wide awake, pulled by some force outside herself, and eager suddenly to explore that strange, beckoning nocturnal netherworld.

He had made himself quite at home in the library, Alex had; he couldn't have asked for a more perfect location from which to survey the house of Colm.

There was something a little eerie about the place, with its faded furniture, its dark, airless rooms, and the fussy atmosphere created by Colm and Francesca's aunts.

It was too bang on the mark, too much exactly what they were: two spinsters who hardly ever left Braidwood, except to go to church.

Even in a day, Alex could see that they had strict routines they followed throughout their day and, Aunt Ida especially, carried out an absolutely rigid regimen of daily chores.

They even retired at the exact same time every night.

Francesca's arrival must have thrown everything out of kilter, Alex thought. They hadn't had her home for a year. She'd been accustomed to being on her own, before he'd carried her off to Meresham Close.

From what he had seen so far, she was exercising remarkable constraint. And all of them were probably trying to find a way to solve the problem of this outside disorder living with them.

Aunt Clarissa was handling it gracefully. Ida was not.

And all of them seemed to be waiting for Colm.

Last night, Alex had watched, mystified, as Francesca crept into the room in the dead of the night and approached the altar as if she feared it. Sinking down in front of it as if she were praying, as if she were seeing ghostly visions.

As if she weren't seeing anything at all.

It was the last thing he expected to see: Francesca sleep-walking and acting as if she were horribly injured and seemingly utterly unaware of it all.

It was he who got her back to her room, and he'd fully expected her to come back, awake and aware, in the morning.

But no, she came again instead, in the depths of the night to feed her secret fear.

Alex watched her again from the shadows as she stared at the structure a long, long time, as if she were trying to figure it out, as if she was sure that she would get hurt again. And then she put out a trembling hand to the altar door, and with a moan of pure pain, she pushed it open, and then she disappeared inside.

Down the steps to the *forbidden room* she went. Over to the far wall, to the door she came.

And this now was the hardest part, the strangest part of the dream. Resolutely she pushed it open and gazed down at the scene.

It was completely and exactly the same: twelve nubile women stretched out in bed, welcoming the sexual attention of the one and only man.

And as if he sensed her there, he turned and he looked up. *Colm!*

"Ah," he murmured, "here is my Queen." He held out his arms. "Francesca, my love, come to me here."

"Colm—!" A stricter voice. "You have work to do."

"Ah yes, Abtissen. *So I do."*

Francesca froze as Colm covered each of the three women closest to her, pumping and humping and discharging his seed.

"Long live the seed," they murmured when he withdrew from them.

"The seed is King," said the voice of the *Abtissen.*

"The ceremony is over," another voice said.

Ida?

Colm was looking at Francesca from down below. "Look at her face. She's not ready yet."

"It's too late to take it slow," the *Abtissen* said. "If she can't come with us, we'll leave her behind."

"And it will be so," a chorus of voices murmured.

And suddenly, violently, Francesca awoke from the dream.

She was back in her bed, cradled in the eerie shapes and shadows of the room, shivering with fear and horror, and the sense that there was an unknown presence there, hovering beside her.

Not Colm. *Not Colm . . .* She would have known *him—*
She knew this one. . . .

—kisses . . . the heightened awareness of his scent, his body, his fearsome fury . . . He'd tracked her down, just as she'd feared.

"Who's there?" she whispered sharply, her whole body tensed, her arms braced against the bed as if she could defend herself from anything in the state she was in.

Even Alex. If he'd come for her, if he intended to carry out any one of his threats, she would not go easily. She'd scream the house down before he got a foot out of her bedroom door.

"Shhh . . . it's Mere."

"I knew it," she muttered, faintly relieved to have her worst suspicion confirmed. "Don't come near me. You're not going to take me. . . ."

"The hell, I'm not. I just brought you upstairs to your room for the second night in a row."

"What?!" Oh, God—now everything was confused. Her nemesis was here? And part of her dream? She had no sense, no memory of anything, not even of leaving her room, let alone going downstairs.

"Shhhh . . ."

"I just . . ." she began, but then she didn't know how to go on. There was something—now he reminded her of it—the feeling that she had experienced something real. She noticed suddenly her hand felt blistered, and she had the distinct feeling Colm was near.

Alex didn't seem any more real, cloaked as he was in the darkness, a disembodied voice next to her ear.

"I'm going back to sleep," she whispered pettishly. Not likely, but God, what was he doing there? How had he gotten in? "What are you doing here?"

"Counting sheep," he murmured. "Move over. I'm sitting next to you so we can talk."

"I don't want to talk. You talked enough the last time I saw you. You called me a liar and traitor and all kinds of romantic things. Go away."

She buried her head in the pillow. *What exactly had happened tonight?*

"Listen to me," Alex went on, barely above a breath. "I

brought you upstairs yesterday, when you collapsed in the library.''

"I didn't . . ."

"*And* today . . ."

No. Yes. A flash of a moment, as she stood on a parapet . . . NO . . . but everything seemed so real . . .

It couldn't be real. . . . She couldn't let it be real.

"I'm hallucinating . . ." she whispered. And she wondered how she even knew Alex was there, if everything else was just a bolting memory that slid away like rain from the roof.

And then, Alex. Why was he there? Why was he haunting her with his anger, his kisses, his certainty about Colm? He could be a ghost in the night, a figment of her imagination.

Or maybe she was a figment of his. Her thoughts tailed off as she considered the implications of his presence there. "You . . . bastard—you let me escape, didn't you?"

"Maybe."

Then she understood, and it was like a hammer at her heart. "You want Colm."

"Maybe he wants me," Alex murmured.

"He's not here." That was valiant, especially when she had seen him—in her dreams?—and she kept feeling as if he were near.

"He will be."

She clenched her fists; she wanted to pound on his chest— she wanted to fend him off, get him away from Braidwood, and save Colm.

Save herself too, she thought, *because right now he was being too kind for a man who had vilified her, nearly had her arrested as a traitor, and had wanted nothing more than to let her rot in hell.*

What if she told him she'd found those papers?

Ha. He'd say she'd had them all along, and wasn't it convenient they'd suddenly turned up at Braidwood?

After the fact.

He'd think it was another ruse. Like her virginity.

Oh my God. And that was the good part. . . .

She started shivering. *What* was going on?

"Clarissa says he's still in Germany."

"He may have been, oh, a month ago." Which coincided with Alex's browbeating her—Samara—into returning to England with him. "But he's here now. He's waiting for something, Francesca."

"I'm not going to let you get near him," she said fiercely.

"He's not waiting for you."

"No, you are. God, if you don't get out and leave me alone . . ."

"I've been living in the library for the past three days, Francesca."

She sank back into the pillows, feeling on the verge of hysteria.

"Any damn body could take up residence in this place."

"I'll tell Ida," she threatened. "She'll—she'll—"

"She'd kill me. She's capable of it. But you're not going to do that, Francesca, because you know I've watched out for you these past two nights. There's something about that structure down there—what is it?—that scares you beyond reason."

There was nothing about the altar, she thought. Whatever he thought he'd seen, whatever she'd dreamt, it had nothing to do with the altar.

"It's an altar and confessional. Some itinerant relative who didn't have a permanent home found it in the Far East and shipped it here. And there's nothing about it. Someone sometime attached it to the wall, and nobody dares to say they really want to get rid of it."

"What's behind it?"

"Just the wall . . ." *Forbidden* . . .

"You went into the confessional door both times and vanished."

"There's nothing behind the door."

"That's what it looks like, but there must be, because twenty minutes or so later, I'd find you there, on the floor."

"Oh." Dreams? Screams? Punishments? "It's not possible."

"But during the day . . ."

"It's just a wall, Alex. You imagined everything else."

"I didn't imagine you." But sometimes he thought he had, especially the few days after she'd fled Meresham Close. But he hadn't wanted to examine that too closely, or how he felt being this close to her in her narrow virgin's bed.

"I can't talk about this."

"All right, we won't talk."

"You have to go away."

"No," Alex murmured, "I think I have to stay."

Francesca slept finally, and Alex wedged himself into the uncomfortable slipper chair that was the only upholstered piece of furniture in the room.

A narrow, little room for a person with narrow, little dreams. But if Francesca's version of things were true, there was nothing contained about her. She was an artist, for one thing, and she'd been alone in Berlin. And her finicky, critical aunts could not have been happy about that.

But then there *was* Colm. By all accounts he had been their fair-haired boy—literally. He'd installed Francesca in that rooming house, though that coincidence was way too hard to swallow, and she'd been waiting for him there just as she'd said.

Everybody waited on Colm. It was a function of his super-intelligent abilities. The gamesman always directed the play. His whole philosophy was not unlike that of an exotic dancer: *Make them wait.*

Alex crossed his legs in front of him as he hunkered farther down in the chair. Such an innocuous room. He could almost believe Francesca's story now that he'd seen Braidwood. And if Colm didn't exist.

But Colm came from this very bedrock. Which was evidence,

if nothing else, that the mundane could foster malevolence as well as the commonplace.

And evil festered everywhere.

It was Alex's job, the mission of his life, to stop Colm.

And to let nothing, and no one, get in his way.

She'd dreamt him too, she decided, when she awakened the next morning to find that there was no one in the room. The whole thing was macabre—her nighttime forays; her realistic dreams; Alex's ghostly appearance; his obsession with Colm and coincidences—

There was nothing coincidental about him being here. Alex Deveney could plot and plan with the best of them, and he'd given her up so she could lead him to Colm.

If only she could see him, she could warn him.

But you did see him—last night . . . didn't you?

Noooo . . . awful—noooo . . . She felt herself growing agitated. That wasn't Colm. That was something different. Something about the mysterious Abtissen *that Samara spoke about.*

That's right. It was about that—and seeds.

Francesca felt calmer. *Planting seeds.* Which she'd always loved to do as a child, and the result was the cutting garden where she and Clarissa had gone to pick flowers these past two days.

She'd be going to the garden with Clarissa today, for sure. It would be a repetition of everything they'd done yesterday and the day before.

But that was all right. That was reassuring sometimes, to have things always the same. And the rest was a product of her dreams.

Alex crept down from the attic, where he'd hidden in the early hours of the morning, so Francesca wouldn't find him in

her room when she awakened, and he stood surveying her room,
which was still redolent of the scent of *her*.

It was such a small room, with vestiges of the girl she had
been, and the woman she had become. Nothing frivolous here
either. But that was a function of her aunts' strict upbringing,
which, he thought, must have been hell.

Still, there was an easel in the corner, so they hadn't denied
her that. And those miniature paintings on the shelf. He picked
up the one that was obviously Colm.

Colm, seen through the eyes of her unconditional love, his
light eyes clear with the optimistic vision of youth, the lines
of dissipation and discontent not yet etched in his face.

But he had not been born out of the air. There had to have
been something in his innocent childhood that created what
he'd become, something that had molded the charismatic ideol-
ogist who could move legions of men—and women—to do
his bidding.

Alex didn't see it in that raw miniature portrait. He saw,
unwillingly, Francesca's hand, and the partial truth of what
she'd told him.

It would be so easy to believe after the two episodes in the
library, after seeing the aunts.

And maybe, Alex thought, a part of him wanted to believe
her because he still wanted her, and still couldn't believe that
she was part and parcel of Colm Heinreichs's objectives.

And that was the weakness of a man.

He was wasting time, Alex thought impatiently. But there
was something about that little painting of the enemy in the
country of innocence that held him rapt. That gave him a flash
of insight into the magnetism of a man like Colm, when he
had been meticulous, exacting, and romantic.

Colm radiated beauty and confidence . . . and an unconditional vision of what the future could be. And he'd made it
come true.

There were a thousand reasons that a man like Colm emerged
from the crowd. And one overriding reason to smite him down.

Alex's fingers tensed on the frame of the painting as he set it back down. And picked it right back up again.

Something was not right; the backing felt thick and padded. *In the country of the enemy, all things are suspicious.*

He prized it open, and a wad of tissue-thin paper fell into his hands.

He didn't have to lay them out and decode them; he knew exactly what they were. But the worst part was the betrayal: He felt it as keenly as a knife at his throat.

Francesca had had the papers all along.

Samara was never going to die, Francesca thought mordantly, as she took breakfast with her aunts. Not while Colm was still alive. Or did Colm have to die first?

The idea was so unnerving, she couldn't swallow her toast. Alex would hunt him and haunt her forever, and in the end, someone *would* die.

I have to protect him. . . .

Who—?

"Oh, my dear, you're so distracted this morning," Aunt Clarissa said sympathetically as she dispensed the tea. "I know how wearisome country life can be. Perhaps you'd like to talk about your intentions?"

Francesca drew a blank. "My—intentions?"

"About going back to—"

"Oh. Going back. Yes. I thought—" She took a sip of tea to avoid looking at Aunt Ida.

"I see everyone's up to the mark on this but me," Aunt Ida interjected sourly as she looked from Francesca to Clarissa with a disapproving stare.

"I *intend*," Francesca amended, thinking she might as well make it a statement rather than have Aunt Ida believe she was asking her approval. "I intend to return to Berlin to continue on with my commission and to study there."

"Do you?" Aunt Ida asked flatly. "And how much is this bohemian exercise going to cost me, Clarissa?"

"Nothing," Clarissa said hastily. "Nothing. Francesca has saved a little money of her own."

"Ha," Aunt Ida interpolated. "It's just as I always told you; it's bred in the bone. She has bohemian blood coursing through her veins, and it proves over and over again that education will never cleanse it."

"It's settled then," Aunt Clarissa said. "We have no objection if you want to go."

"Faithless, ungrateful child," Aunt Ida muttered. "Never tried to reorient. Fought me at every turn. Her father's blood betrayed her. You see that, Clarissa. If Lily had only married—"

"But there's never any going back," Aunt Clarissa interrupted. "And Francesca is old enough to decide what's best for her."

"I should have beat it out of her," Ida said. "I never should have let it get as far as it did. Artistic bent. No one will ever marry her with that bohemian blood. It makes me sick." She got up abruptly. "I did my best, Frances. You have no appreciation of all I tried to do." She turned to Clarissa. "The thing is done. I wash my hands of the matter." She pushed out her chair and stalked out of the room.

Francesca stared after Ida. "She never changes. I guess that means I can go."

"We both think that's best," Aunt Clarissa said gently, and Francesca had to wonder to whom her aunt referred. "How long do you think it would take to arrange everything?"

"I don't know," Francesca said slowly, wondering why she suddenly felt as if she were being banished from Braidwood. "I don't know. I should probably go up to London and make my travel plans from there."

"Excellent idea. Well, you decide when you're ready, dear. Please don't feel like we're pushing you out. I just don't think you're very happy here right now."

She wasn't. Nothing had changed, not Aunt Ida's attitude or her penchant for snooping, or her aunt's hatred of her father. Why had she thought anything would change? Or that Aunt Ida would be pleased she'd come back to Braidwood?

Or that by then they would have heard from Colm?

Francesca moved slowly down the hallway from the breakfast room to the library, without even consciously thinking about where she was going.

Alex had been hiding here for two days. Doing what? Spying on whom?

She paused on the threshold, barely able to force herself to go inside. Two days ago, she'd had no problem whatsoever entering and choosing a book. Now, she trembled as if the place were inhabited by a ghost.

She couldn't bring herself to step within; so what did that say about her that she could be so intimidated? And by what? She didn't even know.

Aunt Clarissa was right: She had to go.

But one thought almost crippled her as she hovered on the threshold: There was not one vestige left of her childhood hope and dream of being with Colm.

No, how could she think that?

Because if he had cared at all, he would have sent word, he would have come, he would have been here . . .

Then why are you going to Berlin?

Because he's there?

And if he's not—?

She whirled away from the door and raced out of the house.

. . . If he's not, if he's not, if he's not—

She would be utterly without a home. . . .

For every skirmish, an army must be prepared. It was a simple matter for Alex to slip out of the house by dawn, and back in under the cover of darkness.

It was so simple, it was suspicious.

And there had been no sign of Francesca all day.

Which was, perhaps, for the best, because right now, he felt like killing her too.

He stayed hunched and hunkered in the shadows behind the library shelves and wondered when Francesca would sleepwalk again.

Another morning, and this time without the disturbing dreams.

Francesca awakened slowly and naturally, stretching and elongating her body, feeling rested and full of well-being.

It struck her as odd, as she dressed for breakfast, especially in light of her full, complete realization of the futility of her wanting to be with Colm. She ought to be morose, she thought. She ought to be mourning the death of a dream.

But instead she felt a keen sense of anticipation, as if her ongoing love for Colm had been a yoke from which she'd broken free.

She suddenly comprehended that he'd become utterly mysterious to her, a shadow, a cipher. It would make eleven years now since she had seen him, and she wondered fleetingly why he had even sent for her to come to Berlin.

Unless Alex was right, and he'd wanted her there.

But for what purpose? Surely *not* to become Samara Teva. He had delivered the papers and was long gone by then. He couldn't have known Samara would die.

But had Samara known when she'd enlisted Francesca's aid in recovering William's body? Had Samara been so forethinking that she plotted how to get that costume back to England and into the hands of . . .

Of . . .

Her mind balked. There was a piece of the puzzle here, something just beyond her grasp.

Why would Colm have brought her to Berlin?

It was probable he had murdered William when William had

refused to come back to England. Samara had sent for Alex, but there was nothing to guarantee that Alex would obey her summons.

By that time, she was nursing Samara, and Samara must have known who she was because Colm would have told her. By then too Samara had hidden the incriminating papers and must have been frantic for a way to get them out of Germany.

. . . take everything . . .

No!

Why had Colm arranged for Francesca to come to Berlin? Because they were going to be together as he'd promised—

No!

—to the . . .

Colm needed a courier. He was far too well known to smuggle those papers, whatever they were, out of the country.

And when Samara knew she was dying, she designated her, Francesca, to be her proxy.

Why?

Why—

. . . why . . .

No—no—no—no—no . . .

Yes.

I don't want it to be—

But there was no other reason than Samara knew she would eventually return to Braidwood . . . and—the . . .

She heard the sound of clapping behind her and she whirled.

Colm!

Chapter Nineteen

He looked just the way Francesca remembered him—and
not. There was still that same cool, pale, youthful beauty and
the same fire in his eyes. But there was something more to it,
now—a ferocity she had never seen. His face was still beautifully proportioned, but the lines were sharper now, deeper, and
there was a kind of contempt in his smile.

She felt as if she were rooted to the floor. The one moment in
her life she'd been waiting for, and she couldn't even galvanize
herself to run to him so she could feel the reassuring strength
of his arms around her.

And if she asked the obvious question, she thought, she
would turn to stone.

"You have grown up quite beautiful, Francesca *mia*." Colm
moved toward her. "It was vastly amusing to see you pretending
to be Samara Teva. . . ."

. . . *See you* . . . ? *She was riveted by shock.*

He was standing right in front of her, smoothing her hair
back with his hand. She'd always loved his hands, but now
she was scared to death of them. She shuddered involuntarily

and she knew by the look in his eyes he had felt the tremulous movement.

"But the thing is over now, Francesca," he went on, his voice silky. "She's gone, you're here. She was more clever than I ever gave her credit for—but then, so were you. The two of you were quite the pair." His voice changed suddenly and his face hardened. "So, my dear Frannie, where are the papers?"

"The—papers?" she managed to whisper.

"The papers. I need them now. You know, I honestly tried to save you the trouble of *giving* them to me, so we could preserve our little secret. But"—he pulled her head back by the roots of her hair—"there's nothing behind that painting but garbage, Frannie. Nothing more in those satin tubes but cotton batting. So I was forced to conclude that you found the whole document. Am I right?" He wrenched her head. "Am I?"

So Colm had taken the painting, Francesca thought, fighting the terror she felt. But if that were so, it meant he had been in the house days ago. *Or weeks ago. The mysterious Colm . . .* She almost gagged as she choked out, "I don't know what you're talking about."

His expression turned ugly. "Fine. Do it that way, if you must." He thrust her, hard, down on her bed. "I'll just tear your room apart ceiling to floor. But I will find those papers, Frannie. I promise you I will—"

"Co-olm . . ." Aunt Clarissa's voice sang through the upstairs hall. "Co-olm . . . where are you?" She skidded to a stop outside Francesca's room. "Oh, there you are. Oh, I was so hoping we could surprise Francesca."

Immediately Colm's face smoothed out and he turned to Clarissa with a smile. "But my dear aunt, I did," he said smoothly. "She's just a little shocked by my sudden appearance, aren't you, Frannie?"

"Stunned," she managed to say.

"We all are," Aunt Clarissa gushed. "Can you imagine, he

just walked in the door this very morning, not a half hour ago, and the first thing he wanted was to see *you.*"

"Well, of course I did," Colm murmured. "My beloved Frannie—" He held out his hand. "Come. I came to escort you to breakfast. We'll have a party. Smile, Frannie—I've finally come home."

And there he was, the depraved monster, the suppurating evil. And the wonder of it was, Alex thought, he looked just like a man.

But this was a man who had conceived of a dominion of like-minded dogmatic intolerants whose sole purpose was to create a superior blood lineage that owed none of its origins to the peerage of England.

It was an ugly concept, drafted from excerpts of a philosophy of racial supremacy that had been interpreted to mean the purification of the blood by selective mating. And there had been more than one disciple of the idea, but Colm had been the first to understand that the ruling power was after nothing less than the colonization of England by disseminating the seed of those chosen specifically for the purpose, and that he was the one handpicked to lead the way.

All of this was known about Colm Heinreichs for the last eleven years, and that he had earned his medical degree more to further his purpose than out of any desire to aid his fellow man.

And it was whispered in some circles that Dr. Heinreichs had been called in to attend the ailing Kaiser solely to make certain that he would *not* recover, and in exchange all he asked was official sanction of his domain, his universe.

And he, Alex, had been seeking it all over England, and it had always been right here, at hand.

"Well, my dear aunts," Colm was saying, "we're all together at last."

Aunt Ida humphed. "And what are you going to do about it?"

"Well, I don't know," Colm said consideringly. "I never could have predicted things would turn out this way. Francesca, you should still have been in Berlin. I was sure the Von Abrungen commission would keep you there for at least a year. He was *supposed* to keep you there for a year."

Brave Francesca. She found her voice. "And why is that, *dear* Colm?"

"No!" Ida said sharply. "Enough of this. You have to make a decision, Colm, and you have to make it now."

He looked at Francesca for a long, torturous moment. "Well, we couldn't have Samara Teva, curse her soul; we'll have Francesca in her place."

Francesca bolted up from the table. "What do you mean? What does that mean?"

"But she can't be the mother of a country," Ida spat, grasping her arm and pulling her back to her seat. "She's got all that bohemian blood."

"No, I don't want her for that," Colm said. "She's learned so much in the past six months. She's learned all the exotic arts, like how to dance naked and sleep with other men. You *were* supposed to save yourself for me, Frannie; I thought you knew that."

"I knew that," she whispered.

"And then you sleep with my worst enemy, my worst nightmare. Well, I fixed you, my darling, didn't I? Cut up your provocative costumes and cut up your bed. . . ."

"You—?!"

"And seduced his brother's wife. The self-righteous, sanctimonious curate's wife. It was a joy to turn her into the sex-starved slut she really was, to make her as dependent on me as a drug, and then to drop her cold . . ."

"Colm!" Aunt Ida again. "We have work to do."

"You think you're so smart, Francesca. I've outwitted you and the Lord of Mere, who's been on my tail for years. He'll never find me now. The colony is almost in place; my work is set to begin full force. It only remains for you to deliver the papers.''

"I don't have them.''

"You do. That cut-up costume is proof of it.''

"Then find them,'' she said defiantly. "You're so smart, you find them.''

Colm lunged at her.

"Stop!" Ida again. Ida in full control and command. "We'll find the damned document in due time, Colm. But now, we have to do something about her.''

"Then do it,'' Colm said mercilessly. "I'll take care of her room.''

Aunt Ida nodded and reached over and clamped an iron hand over Francesca's wrist. "You'll come with me, my girl.''

Francesca tried to wrench her arm away. "I won't—!''

But Aunt Ida's grip was like a manacle. She hauled Francesca to her feet; she looked at Clarissa, who hadn't said a word, and Clarissa nodded, and then she propelled Francesca out of the room.

Quickly, Alex stole back into the shadows and down the hall to the library, not a minute too soon.

Ida came marching into the room, pushing Francesca before her, with Clarissa following in her wake.

Francesca stopped so abruptly that Clarissa almost fell into her.

"Where are you taking me?''

"Where do you think?'' Ida said, pulling at her, pulling her toward the altar.

Francesca's eyes dilated with fear. "No. No. I won't—''

Clarissa moved to open the confessional door, and Francesca screamed, "DON'T— Oh my God—you'll get burned—!''

Ida turned to Clarissa. "Stupid to have given her that sleeping powder. All it did was make things worse.''

"We had to make sure she would sleep,'' Aunt Clarissa defended herself.

"Well, she didn't, did she?" Ida said nastily. "Instead she remembered everything. All our work unraveled because of one stupid mistake."

"We couldn't have known."

"But now she remembers."

"Be that as it may," Clarissa said, "we must continue. Take her down."

Francesca reacted like an animal at bay, pulling and snarling at Aunt Ida. But Aunt Ida had the grip of a prison matron, and eventually she got her way. Francesca went through the confessional door, and Aunt Clarissa looked around, then stepped inside behind them and disappeared.

Alex edged out of the shadows of the library shelves, and, armed now, he followed in their wake.

This was the nightmare, and now she was awake and aware and everything she had dreamt was really true.

There really was a secret room . . . *forbidden* . . . beautifully furnished—*under the bed—footsteps, hiding . . . Aunt Ida's voice* —and the door on the far wall—*the program is working* . . .

Aunt Ida's hands were like two vises, holding her immobile, pressuring her forward into the nightmare.

Aunt Clarissa opened the door, her eyes so sad and understanding.

Aunt Ida pushed Francesca onto a parapet.

Below her was the scene she remembered from her dream. All those beds, made up with opulent bedding of satin and lace. But now she saw more details: a hall-sized Persian rug spread across the floor; golden candlesticks on high ledges to give the room a smoky, shimmery atmosphere conducive to sex; mirrors hung over each headboard to reflect the light and the prowess of a man; an anteroom closed off by a brocade curtain, hiding—what?

Francesca couldn't move; she felt paralyzed. She had been

here before, and she had seen the depths of a man's putrid soul.

"Yes, my dear Frances." Aunt Ida, accurately reading the expression on her face. "Yes. Nosy little tut, you were. You found this place when you were very young."

Francesca started shivering. It was the cold: It started in her veins and it was working its way into her very soul.

"Your stupid vagabond father, getting himself and your mother killed. Do you know what a wrench you put in our plans, you stupid girl? Can you *conceive?* Well, we took care of you, we did."

Ida stared out over the parapet. "So now you know."

"What do I know?" Francesca whispered. "What? What did you do?"

"Hypnosis," Aunt Clarissa said gently. "We had to, you know."

Francesca wheeled around to her sweet aunt. "Why? What did I do?"

"You found the forbidden room and you saw what we—what Colm did here."

. . . the program is working

Long live the seed—

She isn't ready to hear it yet. . . .

The seed is king—

Horror washed over Francesca as she began to comprehend "Colm was involved—even then?"

Aunt Clarissa nodded solemnly. "Even then. A kind of practice for what was to come. We made sure you never evinced any curiosity about the altar ever again."

"Until you dosed her," Aunt Ida interjected sarcastically.

"Well. Yes. Until. But—we thought you were still in Germany, my dear. We had no idea you'd show up at the very moment the program was to begin full force."

"The program . . ." Francesca said faintly, turning to look down on the beds, all of them invitingly turned down. She felt shudders of fear up and down her spine. All those years of living with the aunts, and she'd had no idea.

"The new order, the new day," Aunt Ida said reverently. "A new population selectively bred. We have worked long and hard toward this day, and nothing is going to stop us now. The wheels are in motion. Colm has begun and he will never have to leave the colony again."

. . . the seed—is king. . . .

Colm is king.

Long live the king. . . .

"The colony—it's not here?" Francesca managed to ask.

"Don't be naive, Frances. This is the breeding farm. This is the genesis of the new order."

Francesca was going to die—she knew it. No one could know these awful secrets and live. And her aunts were not bound by any duty or loyalty to her. Even Aunt Clarissa, with her kind and knowing eyes, had that exalted look on her face like the one on Aunt Ida's, as if they had both found a new religion, a new god.

The breeding farm.

She closed her eyes and saw it—saw Colm, moving among them, servicing them, impregnating them one by one by one, and she almost collapsed from the horror of her realization.

Colm—Colm was the god—Colm was the seed.

And who gave benediction to this obscene worship?

. . . take everything to the Abtissen *. . .*

. . . take the fiat and the blessing of an emperor—

She could barely get out the words. "The *Abtissen*—?"

"Is me." And the speaker was her beloved Aunt Clarissa.

Aunt Clarissa had enshrouded herself in ceremonial robes, and she stood at the edge of the parapet, like some holy object for her followers to worship.

"Sound the gong," Aunt Clarissa commanded, and a low

sawing sound commenced in a steady rhythm, one for every beautiful naked young woman who entered from the anteroom.

One, two, three, four—they filed into the forbidden room and eased themselves up onto the bed. Five, six, seven, eight— all perfectly formed and eagerly awaiting the next stage of the ceremony.

"The program begins," Aunt Clarissa intoned and raised her hand.

Ida pushed Francesca forward. "An education, Frances, so you may understand the purpose of untainted blood. There's a symmetry, a synchronicity. Everyone bred to the same under- standings, the same purpose, the same superiority of nature. And he is the one. Watch him now. All these years, he has been in practice to perfect that stamina that will allow him to propagate his seed. And you never even knew. Watch him, and know that you can never have him. You can never be good enough, pure enough. Your gypsy blood taints your veins."

The scene was so fantastic, Francesca couldn't even close her eyes. There was an awful fascination in watching Colm and knowing that he had never been an innocent boy, that his whole life he had been indoctrinated and moved toward this one moment: to be the father of this freakish nation.

It didn't seem possible that a sane man could believe it. Or that women who awaited him with their legs spread and outstretched arms could want it.

But want it they did, each fresh-faced beautiful woman, with her milky skin and exalted expression . . .

. . . *the drawing—the girl* . . .

Francesca had a vague recollection of the girl. Impressions bombarded her, disconnected and discordant. For one terrifying moment, she thought she was going insane.

Below her, Colm was pumping away like an engine, without any thought to his partner. Once, twice, spew, and then he withdrew. And he tumbled onto the next waiting woman, almost as if he had trained himself to ejaculate only so much, and not more, so that he could conserve himself to mate more than one time.

It was worse than a nightmare—it was reality, it was her family, and it was the man whom she had adored for so long.

He was a monster and a deviant, and no one could stop him.

One by one he serviced the women, and one by one he warmed them up, spurted his seed, and left them moaning and cold.

The sawing gong sounded again as he removed himself from his final insemination.

"The program is working," Aunt Clarissa intoned. "The seed is king."

And the women answered in benediction, "Long live the seed."

A breeding farm for a new world order ...

It was an obscenity. It was beyond pornographic. It was almost beyond words, Alex thought, flattening himself against the wall outside the parapet door.

And this excrescence had been mandated by an ambitious young emperor aching to get his tentacles into virgin English soil.

Never. On his life, and on the soul of his Queen and his country—never.

If it was the last thing he ever did, Alex swore, *the seed would be destroyed.*

Francesca was that close to fainting. The air was redolent with sex and sin.

Aunt Clarissa removed the robes and left the forbidden room, left her without a word, and in Aunt Ida's care.

"What are you going to do with me?" Francesca whispered.

"Not what I want to. Your Aunt Clarissa has a soft spot for

you—isn't that rich? She, who is the driving force behind the
new world order, wants to think about what to do with you.
Well, I know what I'd do. I'd hand you over to Colm, let him
have all of you he can stand—for recreational purposes, mind
you—and then I would throw you into the Thames.''

Francesca shuddered. ''And meantime?''

''She wants you chained to the wall.''

There was no fighting Ida. She was strong as an ox and filled
with the power of her purpose, and she forced Francesca down
the steps to the fornicating floor.

Colm sauntered in, buttoning his shirt, as Ida clicked the
second of two locks into place.

''So there she is, a veritable martyr for our cause.''

''You can use her if you want,'' Ida said callously.

''I might,'' Colm said, tilting his head to look at Francesca.
''Or I might think of something else. We still don't have the
document, and she won't tell me where it is.''

Evil. Colm glowed with a rampant evil, packaged in a beautiful face. An angel could look like this—both radiant and
debased.

Francesca twisted and turned futilely, pulling at the chains.

''We could gag her too,'' Colm suggested. ''Perhaps a night
spent down here imprisoned and alone would convince her to
speak. You know, we must convince Clarissa there is no room
for sentiment in our work. Truly, Frannie, if you'd just kept
out of Samara's business and stayed in Berlin—none of this
would have happened. But on the other hand, you look positively seductive in chains.''

*None of it. It was too ghastly to contemplate how much
different her life would have been if she had just told Alex
Deveney she wasn't Samara.*

*All that she had done for Colm. Colm and his vicious, creep-
ing evil empire.*

*And it had all been for nothing. There had been nothing to
protect him from. And every reason for her to run.*

She could die now, she thought, *because she knew things*

*and she'd done things that she didn't know how she could live
with the knowledge.*

Or how she could allow Colm to live.

The seed must be destroyed. Any way she could.

Francesca lashed out at Colm suddenly, swinging her foot
up and out and connecting right between his legs. He howled,
his knees buckling, and she had him at her feet. Before Ida
could react, Francesca kicked him in the face.

Ida tackled her legs, and a shot rang out.

Alex, with a rifle, up on the parapet. Ida screamed and cursed,
and then she fell. He aimed again, at the limping Colm. The
shot went wide as Alex saw Ida lever herself up with superhu-
man strength to attack Francesca—and then Colm was gone.

Alex lifted the rifle again. The woman was a monster: She
was drowning in blood and on she came, choking Francesca
with what was left of her life's blood. All he needed to do was
loosen that death's grip.

He aimed at Ida's legs, one last shot through her matron's
dress, and she dropped to her knees. And then, like a resurging
monster, she made a macabre move to attack Francesca again,
and then, stunned, she crumpled to the floor.

The silence was deathly, the odor of smoke mingling with
the fecund atmosphere and the cloying scent of sex.

Alex raced through the brocade curtains, knowing full well
that Colm had made his escape. But a man couldn't be too
careful with a bastard like Colm, even if Colm had been fairly
immobilized by Francesca's kick.

"He's gone," Alex murmured. "You're so resourceful."

He hunkered down as he rolled over Ida's body and searched
for the key. But Francesca had forgotten all about Alex. She
watched, as if from a distance, as he set her free, mindful of
pounding footsteps in the distance, and the need to escape. And
a rifle—the key to freedom, balanced against his knee.

"Ida!" Aunt Clarissa on the parapet. "What's going on
down there?"

Alex grabbed the rifle and cocked it. "We don't have time for explanations," he said softly.

Francesca shook her head. It was not for her to give him permission. How could she?

"I heard shots. . . ." Aunt Clarissa said plaintively.

That little old lady, Francesca thought, every pore in her body suffused with the evil of a cause.

Alex aimed at Clarissa.

"Ida?"

Francesca had loved Aunt Clarissa best of all. How could she let Alex take her aunt down in cold blood?

"Ida . . . ?" Now Clarissa sounded worried, and like her usual frantic, fluttery self.

But she wasn't—fluttery, sweet, or kind. She never had been. She'd been the progenitor of an evil too colossal to comprehend.

. . . *The* Abtissen—

The shot was explosive.

. . . *is me* . . .

Clarissa grabbed her chest. "Francesca?" she moaned in a high, little voice, and then she toppled over the parapet, dead.

Francesca looked like the walking dead, herself. Her face was pale, her gaze unfocused. It was as if she had been exposed to all the wickedness and depravity in the world, and it was too much for her to take in.

But Alex didn't have the luxury of cosseting her. "Francesca?"

She didn't hear him.

Lightly, he smacked her face. "Francesca . . . !"

She focused. "I hear you, Alex."

"Your aunts are dead. We have to find Colm."

"Where?"

"I don't know, but he can't be long gone. He was virtually crawling when I shot at him."

Francesca swallowed hard, swallowed her fear, her horror, her apathy. "All right."

"We have to destroy the seed."

So he'd heard all that. "Yes," she murmured. "We have to—" Her eyes widened. "I smell smoke."

Damn the bastard's soul to hell. Great minds did think alike; he'd wanted to burn down the cell too. "So do I," he said, keeping his voice careful and calm. "Don't move. I'm going to check upstairs."

But he didn't need to; he knew exactly what Colm had done: He'd torched the altar and it had flamed up like a tinder box, giving them no place to go.

"We can't go that way," Alex said, but Francesca had already figured that out. And she felt surprisingly calm. Or maybe she was the one who was dead.

"Look. He got out of here somehow, and he didn't go up those steps. We have a little time to figure it out. Grab one of those candlesticks." Alex took one too and parted the brocade curtains for Francesca to go through.

"Those women—where did they come from?"

"They just appeared through the curtains," Francesca said, but of course they too had to have come from somewhere. But the anteroom outside the curtains was just a small stone-walled place with seemingly no egress.

"There has to be something. Maybe a secret wall. Or a lever." Alex knelt down at the opposite wall and began moving his hands over it, inch by inch.

Francesca examined the curtains.

There was nothing.

But there had to be something, because the smoke was getting thicker and thicker and somehow Colm had escaped this room.

"Wait. . . ." Alex was at the curtains, holding his arm up to block the smoke and looking at something in the stone. "I see . . ." He reached up and yanked hard on the curtain rod, and it moved downward, and behind them they heard the sound of stone scraping stone, as a narrow door creaked open.

"Hurry—" He could barely hold his breath a minute longer, while Francesca was coughing and hacking as she stumbled through the door. The minute she was through, he launched himself after her and fell on top of her, taking deep convulsive gulps of the clear night air.

Braidwood burned.

They stood on a rise a short distance from the house and watched it flame up into the cool night air, a fantasy of red and orange fire and billowing smoke.

All the evil demons but one called to hell, Francesca thought. And that one, somehow, would be called to account.

Everything was gone. Every vestige of her life, her hopes, her dreams, her family . . . her money . . . oh, God—all that money that might have assuaged every loss . . . The enormity of the whole, of everything that had happened, and everything she'd seen, just staggered her.

It seemed almost superfluous for her to ask, "Now what do we do?"

But Alex knew. "We find the monster and we kill him too."

Chapter Twenty

Secrets. Everywhere there were secrets.

Phillippa didn't know how she had borne it. She was wasting away for the love of Apollo. Her beautiful radiant stallion, Apollo.

And she knew she had a baby on the way, and she couldn't tell. But then, there was nothing to see.

And worse than that, no one seemed to notice. Neither Marcus, so busy, busy all the time, or Judithe, who was still crowing with glee that the creature had gone.

Only Alastair noticed that she looked pale and wan since he had taken to coming around. But what he wanted was a glimpse of the creature, and on that score he made himself plain.

"A goddess, I tell you. Bursting, ripe. Next to her, Phillippa, you look like sticks and bones. Tell me true, does Marcus even *look* at you anymore?"

That was the kind of bluntness that made her burst into tears, which was the one thing that Alastair hated.

"I won't have you cry," he chided, looking for the delicious moment when she would confide in him. "But you *could* tell me what's wrong."

Phillippa knew his reputation. She knew he would tell. Maybe in the end, that was what she wanted. For everyone to know and to get some attention. Because living like this was sheer, unremitting hell.

"I met a man a month or two ago. . . ."

"Oh— *oh* . . . !"

"He . . . um—left unexpectedly."

"Oh dear." That wasn't quite the thing a woman would want to confess, but Phillippa looked like a desperate woman. "How deep?"

"As far as you can go," Phillippa whispered. "And beyond."

Alastair shook his head. "Oh, you are rowing in troubled waters, my dear, and you will sink sooner than you will swim. Why did you do that? And look at what it's brought you to."

Phillippa took a deep breath. "That's not the whole of it."

"No," Alastair groaned.

She nodded. "And no one has guessed."

"How could they? *Look* at you?"

Her eyes filled with tears. "Tell me what to do."

There was no man, Alastair reflected, whether he was a man or not, who could resist such an appeal.

"Put yourself in my hands, my sweet. I'll take care of you."

At twilight the next day, they arrived at Meresham Close, Alex having hired a coach and pair and driven them himself. It was the most practical thing to do under the circumstances, although he was certain Judithe would have a spasm or a palpitation—or something.

"My lord—" The stable boys came running as he drove into the stable yard and pulled to a halt. "Let me—"

He felt as if he had been gone a year as he handed over the reins.

"Francesca—" He held out his hand just as Marcus came running out from the archway beneath the house.

"Who on earth was driving like a drunken batman?" Marcus stopped short. "Oh my God—Alex . . . ! And . . . and—you both look like hell."

"Is Mother home? Phillippa? Come on, there's a lot to tell."

But Judithe certainly didn't want to hear anything mitigating about Francesca's convoluted circumstances, and Phillippa looked as if she couldn't care less herself.

"So you're going to do the whole thing all over again— take the creature to your room—"

"She'll have the guest room," Alex said mildly. "I can't even begin to explain how it came about that she was here under a false identity. Suffice it to say, I believe her now, and I hope in good grace you will too."

"You have really got him twisted around your little finger," Phillippa said in a nasty undertone. "I would kill to know your secrets."

"A couple of delusional aunts," Francesca murmured. "It does wonders for galvanizing a man."

Phillippa stared at her.

Francesca stared back. Phillippa looked gaunt, her eyes glistening with malice and a kind of subverted anguish, as if she had gone all to hell.

And she had, Francesca suddenly realized. She'd been so caught up in her feelings about coming back to Mere, she'd nearly forgotten about Phillippa, and that she had also been the cat's pawn.

Colm had even told them—he'd taken the vicar's wife; he'd kept her bed nice and warm.

Oh my God, oh my God . . . he'd tracked Samara right here from the rooming house in Berlin. Insinuated himself into their lives by seducing Alex's kin. Looking for the papers, all the time; and seducing Phillippa for no other reason than she was ripe, available—and he was a master at interpreting exactly what a woman needed.

Poor, bloodied Phillippa. A receptacle for the seed . . . and what if it were to bear fruit? What if it had already? But she didn't look as if she wanted sympathy or commiseration.

Francesca tentatively reached out a hand, but Phillippa squared her shoulders and shook away her pity.

"So we'll be just one big happy family," Phillippa said caustically. "How nice." She felt like crying. But a minister's wife never cried.

And in the end, Samara or Francesca or whatever her name was would get what she wanted. And Phillippa would wind up with a brat born of her faithless lover's seed. It just wasn't *fair*.

"Come, my lady. His lordship wishes you to take your rest." That was Wotten by Francesca's side. She kept her eyes on Phillippa as he escorted her upstairs to the guest room, and she felt deeply disturbed. Phillippa looked small, low, haunted. And no one could help her now.

"Agnes will see to your needs, my lady. A bath now, if you wish. A tray in your room? You have only to ask."

She opted for the bath—a hot, soapy, soaking bath that might wash all *her* sins away. And food. And a fresh, clean nightgown in which she curled up in bed to try to sleep a dreamless sleep.

"I have been gone but five days, and Phillippa looks like a trull from the streets. What's been going on, Marcus?"

"Damned if I know," Marcus said, running his hand through his hair. "And your giddy friend Alastair has been keeping her company of late. I tell you, Alex, this is too tame a life for someone like Phillippa. Why in heaven's name did she ever marry me?"

"I don't know. You'll have to ask *her* that."

"I can't talk to her at all anymore."

"Well," Alex said brutally, "you can't talk to me either. I have bigger fish to fry."

"That woman—"Marcus said.

"Is not Samara Teva."

"I thought I heard you say that. After everything you've put her through, you're telling me that she was just *pretending* to be what that woman was."

"I bull-nosed her into it. She didn't have a choice. And by the time she came here, it was too late. Her name is Francesca Reay, and I'd appreciate it if you would treat her with a little less antagonism than you did Samara Teva."

"Yes, of course, of course. A mistake has been made; we all understand that. One can only hope . . ."

"One lives for hope," Alex said, cutting him off. "Go find your wife."

While he wrestled with the problem of what to do about Colm.

He'd almost had Colm. Almost. The catch of a lifetime, the man who would spawn a new world. He was the kind of man whose lust for power could never be quenched. The only solution for Colm Heinreichs was death.

And Alex wanted no more blood on his hands. It was enough that he had destroyed the only family Francesca had really known. Enough he had put her through her own little hell.

But the vision of her dancing as Samara Teva still haunted him. And her elegance and cool grace.

"The little bitch owes us seventy-five pounds," Judithe said from the doorway.

"It got burnt," Alex retorted. "So it's as if it never was, as they say. Come in, Mother. Make yourself at home."

"Is it really true, Alex? Is she really *not* that god-awful exotic person?"

"She really is not."

"You're not trying to pass something off on me."

"No."

"And yet—she danced. . . ."

"I threatened her. I blackmailed her. I forced her to," he said bluntly.

"I don't understand this generation. I don't understand *you*.

Why can't you stop what you're doing and set up your nursery?''

"Maybe I can, Mother."

Judithe swooned. "Not with the creature?"

"God help me, she might not have me."

Judithe moaned. "With the creature."

"Roll it around in your mind, Mother. You may come to get used to it."

"Never."

"Good night, Mother."

"Never." Her voice wafted down the hallway.

Never. It was an inconceivably endless time. What if they never caught Colm?

Alex leaned back in his chair and closed his eyes. All of a sudden he felt bone weary. He had been chasing Colm for years, ferreting out every hint of the monstrous evil he perpetrated, never once coming across a hint of the aunts and Braidwood and their tainted niece.

How well Colm had kept the secret; and he'd done that simply by throwing everyone off the trail by the diversionary tactic of simultaneously maintaining a dual life as a counterspy.

And all these years, he had been preparing and exploiting events. And moving Francesca around like a chess piece to keep her out of his way.

The mania of a man, so all-encompassing he would master and manipulate everything in his path.

The high-powered indoctrination he must have had at the hands of two of the most innocuous-looking spinster ladies Alex had ever seen. Colm must have seemed like a god to them when he came into their care. And it was evident by the books on the shelves in the library, their ideas, at the least, had been nurtured there.

What kind of mind and iron will had pulled something like that off? Who had planned it, chosen the women, *convinced* them that mating with Colm would be heaven on earth?

It was so bizarre it was unthinkable. Unspeakable.

And yet—it had been.

And it was over—with Braidwood burned to the ground and nothing left of the opulent mating room but char and ash.

But that didn't mean that Colm couldn't start the thing over anew.

A breeding farm, Ida had said. With women willing to let Colm root in them, impregnate them, and what—? Take the child?

It wasn't the colony, Ida had said. It was the breeding farm.

Which meant—which meant . . . he himself had been on the right track.

And that Colm himself could be anywhere.

But way back before all this happened, Colm had known Samara would have to come to Somerset. It was the only choice if Alex went and got her from Berlin. And he had already deduced that was where Colm had intended her to go.

Therefore, it was rational to infer that Colm's new world order could exist right . . . under . . . his . . . nose.

There was a chilling thought. That somewhere in Somerset Colm's acolytes lived, and Alex had been that close to them, with Samara as his entree. He felt it in his bones.

And that Colm was here now, in the country, close to his allies, and sheltered by a friend.

. . . it's the child . . .

In the rubble of Braidwood a baby cried, and its mother picked her way through the detritus of Francesca Reay's life, looking for the father of her child. But no one was there to acknowledge her, and so in a while she left. And so did the next one and the next one and the next, until they had all gone away. . . .

Francesca bolted awake from the maw of her dreams. Such realistic dreams; she was trembling with fear for all those sad, lonely women rooting through the ruins. . . .

Rutting in the ruins . . .

She swung her legs over the bed, feeling as if she wanted to run, as if Colm were behind her, reaching for her, touching her skin.

It was too horrific to contemplate. She grabbed the wrapper and slippers that Agnes had provided, then made her way downstairs.

There were lights on everywhere, as if they could hold back the terrors of the night.

Francesca walked down the hallway in a house where the servants were no longer watching her, and she still didn't feel free.

She veered toward the light in the library and paused at the door. Alex was there and she had a long moment to look at him without his being aware.

He sat at his desk, his head buried in his hands, a man who had not hesitated to destroy a cancerous growth, and now felt remorse. But he was also a man who had no compunction about using any method he could get away with to get what he wanted.

He was not so dissimilar from Colm, she thought. *And not so dissimilar from me.*

He looked disheveled and weary down to the bone. His shoulders slumped; his whole body looked as if he had just collapsed where he was.

Francesca felt a little dart of compunction attack her vitals. For the first time since she'd left Meresham, she wasn't seeing him as the enemy or the man from whom she had to save Colm.

What a farfetched, self-serving notion that had been.

She wrapped her arms around her midriff and leaned against the door. She felt safe there, as if she didn't need to make any kind of commitment. She could have one foot outside the room, and one foot in, hovering between the world she'd left, and the world of Mere.

The differences were incalculable; and for all his fascination with her when she had pretended to be Samara, she wasn't nearly sophisticated enough to handle the consequences of his breaching of her body. She barely remembered it, she thought;

more, she remembered his kisses, and the heightened feeling of power every time she became Samara and danced.

That was the way to tame a man. She knew all of Samara's secrets, and, perhaps, some of her own, but she didn't have the wit or guile to know how to use them.

Alex looked up suddenly and saw her standing there, an angel waiting to claim him. He needed her then; he wanted to bury himself in her, in her contradictions and her innocence. He wanted the elegance and the earthiness of her imprinted on his skin.

He got up from the desk the very moment she moved into the room, and without a word, she came into his arms, and he enfolded her there.

They stood this way for a long moment, and slowly he settled his mouth on hers, drinking from her like a thirsty man.

This time, her response was true, and she clung to his strength, and let his kisses sweep her away.

Hunger. Now she could allow herself to feel that deep feminine hunger that was so connected to the sensuality of Samara. In him. In his heat and hardness, in his strengths and weaknesses.

And in herself, in that little hollow between her legs. All the unfamiliar feelings pooling there, swelling, drowning her in need and pleasure.

This was what she still didn't understand: this building, burning excitement, this connection, this molding of mouths and bodies into a sinuous whole. Why she needed it, wanted it, found herself clawing at his clothes.

And he, taking her and taking her, feeding on his fascination with her, and his comprehension that her maddening elusiveness had been nothing more than virginal fear.

This was the most tender moment, the bridge between her desire and his need. His weariness vanished, submerged by his cataclysmic arousal.

There was time. He had to go slow, to take his time. But her eager kisses, her virginal hands . . . the thin scrim of a nightgown and wrapper all that separated him from her undulating body . . .

How long could a man hold out? Or a woman newly made?

He forcibly reined himself in. It had to be *her* choice, her need, this time, and his sole function to nourish it, to feed it, and to make her still virginal soul want him beyond all rational thought and reason.

She was almost there, at the point where her body's need pitched over into that swamping mindless capitulation.

He eased her up against the wall, pressing himself against her with a lucid and restrained urgency. He felt her hands groping toward him, pulling and tearing the material that impeded her way.

And then her hands digging deeply against his skin, against the hot male essence of him with the certainty of a woman of experience.

He sagged against her as she grasped him *hard*, and held him as if she would never let him go.

And what more did he need after all? The heady taste of her, and the feel of her questing hands learning all of him he had to give. That was enough. It could be enough.

It wasn't enough.

"Francesca . . ." his lips were barely a breath above hers. "It won't hurt this time."

"Oh . . ." she whispered on a tiny wondrous sigh. This was the secret, then. This. That once a woman was initiated, she was as free to love as the air. Free as a man.

Free as Samara Teva.

"*Oh . . .*" she breathed, in clarity and comprehension. *She* had the power, just like Samara, because he wanted *her* body, *her* sex, *her* heat and what was between her legs. "*Yes . . .*" she whispered. "*Yes . . .*" because she needed to know.

Yes. That one luscious word that promised paradise.

He eased up the thin material of her nightgown and wrapper until he could feel her bare skin, and he slid his hand up her thigh and around her buttocks. She was warm, silky, willing.

He pulled her closer, shifting his body as best he could with her hands still holding him, so that he was angled against her.

"You," he whispered before he claimed her mouth again. "You—"

Her choice, her need, but he wasn't sure he could hold back much longer. Her hands were magic, fondling him in the most innocent, the most erotic way, but he wasn't made of stone, although he felt invincible, immutable, endless and potent.

And then he was *there,* not by his will or her guidance, but by that ineffable moment of insensate joining because nothing less would do.

And—"*Oh . . . !*" as he pinned her against the wall, and she felt the first full moment of possession, like nothing she'd known before. She felt trapped and invaded and so full she could never get away.

And she *needed* to get away from him in the worst way.

He calmed her, stroking her, kissing her, undulating against her gently, enticingly so that she felt the slip and slide of him within her, the wet, the heat, the coiling pleasure of his possession, gently, gently, to draw her with him, to him, into the billowing carnality of his desire.

This was the part that wasn't familiar; uncharted ground for her who had used her untouched body to such erotic effect with strange men. This was the part—this . . . the pumping explosiveness of his desire and his sole goal to release it in her.

This . . . made for this—wanted to bring him to this . . . *this*—

She felt her strength, her power, her femininity as she opened herself to him. And then the first flaring furl of pleasure radiating outward from her very center, claiming her, changing her, seducing her forever.

She sank down into the swirling heat of his possession. The sensations were almost unbearable, and utterly unknowable. They just *were,* streaming through her body like molten gold and pooling at the thrusting point between her legs.

He came at her, reaching for her, with her, for the peak, whispering to her, urging her, kissing her, goading her with words, with his hands, with his endless pumping rock hard maleness.

And then, and then . . .

. . . *and then*—

She shattered, her body convulsing as she rode him down, down, down to his own erupting tumultuous release . . . and into silence.

The culmination of everything—this . . .

She felt liquid, boneless, thick with the essence of him. They couldn't move, either of them, couldn't speak. Couldn't, couldn't, couldn't . . . couldn't put a name to the thing that had for so long defined her as the woman she wasn't.

But now she was that woman and she knew every secret, and maybe that was all she could ever have hoped to take from this adventure.

He eased away from her, the heat between them still palpable, and he pulled her down with him into his desk chair, and onto his lap.

It was, for him, the defining moment: He had poured himself into her and she was his now, for whatever it meant, better or worse, until the end of this nightmare and beyond.

And, he thought, as he cradled her against his chest, they would figure it all out together. All the pieces, until the puzzle fit together.

Silence enfolded them, and she forced herself not to think beyond the next moment. Or maybe the next, because there *had* been a reason she couldn't sleep, and she'd sought him out.

She'd spoil the moment, she thought. If she said one word, she would erase the tenuous connection between them and catapult them into the reality of their situation.

And if she didn't, the monster would live.

She was on the brink of another ineffable moment of decision, and it had to be made—by her.

She pulled away from the reassuring circle of his arms.

"I think he's here," she said, diving right into it. "He told me he seduced Phillippa. And now, he can't have the others, so he'll come back to see if he made a child with *her.*"

The child of the seed. She shuddered at the thought of an innocent child, the image of Colm in all ways.

"Jesus."

She hated to think it, but she had to say it: "Phillippa is the key."

Phillippa was feeling miserable that morning, her stomach queasy and her thoughts unkind. So the last thing she needed was Alastair at the door of the Rectory where she was taking care of some of Marcus's chores.

"News travels fast, my darling," he murmured. "I just heard that Alex is home, and the lovely is with him."

"Is she? I didn't notice." But the creature had a flat stomach and didn't look like a ghost. The creature wasn't staring into a bedpan every morning, unable to keep her breakfast down.

"Come, Phillippa. This can't be good for the child."

"Don't talk about that!" Phillippa whirled away from him. "Oh, God, I want to die. . . ."

"Never say that!" Alastair grabbed her arm. *"Never.* That's stupid, Phillippa, and negligent of your child. Look, what are you doing this morning? Marcus is busy as usual, I take it. So he wouldn't mind if I took you out and cheered you up."

"I wouldn't mind," Phillippa said. It was better than nothing, Alastair's company. At least he was amusing, and he knew about the baby, she didn't have to keep anything back or hold anything down.

"I have a surprise for you," he said, when he had settled her in his carriage, and they were on their way.

"Surprises are nice," she said, but her tone was apathetic at best.

"My dear. We're going to my house and you'll see. . . ."

That took another half hour.

What Phillippa liked best was the way the servants rushed out to help them, just as they did at Meresham. Thank God, they lived at Meresham. If they'd lived at the Vicarage, she didn't know what she would do.

"We'll have tea. You just go on straight ahead to the last door on the left, will you? I'll join you in a minute."

Phillippa wandered down the hall, admiring the family portraits. Alastair's house was a little less grand than Meresham Close, more intimate, and therefore, she thought, more comfortable.

She felt better already. She pushed open the door to see a man framed by the window, his face in shadow.

But she knew those shoulders, that body, that stance.

"Oh my God—oh . . . !" She felt faint, but he was by her side in an instant, his strong arms around her, leading her to a chair.

"My dear, dear darling . . ." he murmured, kissing her hands.

"Oh, I can't believe it, I can't. I almost died of wanting you—"

"And now I'm here." He buried his face in her lap, and she stroked his hair.

"Really here?"

"For as long as you want."

Bless Alastair, bless him—how had he known? But she didn't care: Apollo had come back for her, and that was all that mattered.

"Take me away."

"We can talk about that, my darling."

"There's a child."

"Oh God—is there?" He moved his head so that he could brush her belly with kisses. "Oh, aren't you the clever one?"

"Aren't you . . . ?" she murmured, her eyes filled with tears. She was never going back to Marcus now.

* * *

And so it was Marcus who arrived to dinner that night in a state of panic. "I haven't seen Phillippa all day," he said, wringing his hands. "She *must* be here."

"We haven't seen her either," Alex said. "Sit down, Marcus. You look as if you're going to fall apart."

"She's been acting so strangely. So strangely. And she looks so—haggard. I'm so worried about her and she won't tell me what's wrong. Alex, you have to do something. . . ."

"Sit *down,* Marcus." He poured his brother a tot of brandy. "Drink this and collect yourself, and then we'll figure it out."

"Where's that woman?"

"She's upstairs right now, getting ready for dinner."

"Who can eat?" Marcus groaned. "What if something has happened to Phillippa?"

"Well, then we'll know soon, won't we? She can't have gone far afield, and someone will know."

Marcus sipped the brandy. "But if she did—?"

"Where would she go?" Alex asked practically. And indeed that was the question. Phillippa's life was fairly circumscribed. Such friends as she had were all in the village, and every social event in which she participated was connected to the church. "I think you should join Mother in the dining room. She's wonderful at wringing her hands and making problems seem more complicated than they are. And after you're done with that, I'll go get Francesca."

Marcus shot him a resentful look. "Phillippa doesn't do things like this. She is scrupulous about being on time."

"Well, then—there's some explanation, and we will find out what it is." But Alex was afraid he knew, and it was not for him to tell his brother that Phillippa had had an affair with a madman, that she might be having his child, and that she was probably with him right now.

But where? He could be miles away or at the house next

door. Colm was clever enough to insinuate himself anywhere. He had gotten to Phillippa, hadn't he?

"Go on. Mother is waiting. You can tell her the whole thing."

Alex met Francesca halfway up the stairs. "Phillippa has gone missing. Or at least Marcus thinks so, but he may be overstating the case."

"Or maybe not," Francesca said gravely.

"It's true. We think he's here. He would want the child, if there is to be one, and someone is giving him aid. We have to smoke him out, Francesca. He must not only want the baby. He must also want you . . . us . . ."

"Dead, you mean," Francesca said bluntly.

"He wouldn't have told you about Phillippa if he'd thought you'd still be alive by now. And on top of that, we destroyed his nest, we killed the aunts, and we know too much about his plans."

"What are you thinking to do?" Francesca asked.

Alex searched her eyes, looking for either acquiescence or acceptance. Those deep, beautiful, compassionate eyes. He knew she understood.

"I think we have to tell Marcus," he said. "We can't do this alone. And then—I think Samara Teva must dance again."

I will kill them all. All.

It was the last thing he had to do, before he spirited Phillippa away. He would leave the colony—so loosely formed as yet that it didn't matter if it disintegrated now. The child was the thing. And his seed. With it, he could grow a superior nation any place he found fertile soil.

And it was all around him. It was one thing he knew.

And the only obstacle was Francesca and that whore's house of maggoty aristocrats. He'd have to kill them all, of course, but that was nothing compared to the devastation they'd wrought on him.

Oh no, it would give him great pleasure to dispense with Francesca. Stupid little gypsy, mewling and hanging on to him the way she used to. And now look at her: the darling of a peer.

He'd take care of all of that as soon as he could figure out a way to get them all here.

It was blessed Alastair who solved the problem. Alastair, with his malice and his desire to dive into the most fashionable excesses, no matter what they were. There was no loyalty there, just a supreme desire to be the first to latch on to a vogue, whether it be fashion or philosophy.

And he rather liked being the deputy director of a fiefdom.

"See here," Alastair said, during one of Phillippa's frequent naps, "he's got that creature back at Meresham. We could invite her to come dance for the crowd. I was so disappointed I didn't have her first, but God, she is something. And of course, Alex will come—and that prudy prune Marcus, if you want. And voila! The thing is done."

"See to it," he commanded. Yes, commanded. Because he was still revered as the seed, as the king. And Alastair, like all of his supporters, immediately set out to do his bidding.

The stage was set in the ballroom. Several dozen guests milled around, drinking champagne, Alastair having deliberately invited a larger crowd this time. A person could get lost in a crowd. And so could a scream, a cry, a moan. It had to be perfect. He wanted it to be perfect—for Colm.

Alastair would never admit it, but he was just a little in love with the boy. Colm was so beautiful, so perfect, it was a pleasure to do things for him and make him smile. And all the other mumbo jumbo was a side issue, just fine if it became the thing, and if not, Alastair could dispense with it as easily as he unwound his cravat.

So going to Meresham to ask if Samara would dance was an easy thing. He almost wished that Colm had demanded something more difficult—something that would prove Alastair's affection for him.

But no. All Colm wanted was the dancer and Deveney—things that seemed irresistible to Colm.

The stage was set. The musicians were to hand. Samara Teva was in the dressing area, taking off her clothes.

And Alex and Marcus were mingling with the guests.

Colm watched from the musicians' balcony, planning his assault, the knife his weapon of choice. Knives were so discreet and quiet and instantly *there*. One thrust with a knife and a man was dead. One twist, and you could gut out his heart.

And for Francesca, it would be the sweetest, cleanest death she could ever desire. And Colm would make very sure her bohemian blood didn't stain Alastair's floors.

Francesca moved to the music, thrusting her hips this way and that, the gold disks on the cincture and on the hem of her transparent skirt whirling and catching the light. Around her neck, she wore gold chains that poured down between her naked breasts, and she had made sure that her face was properly veiled.

Step, thrust, step. Don't forget the hands. Shake your shoulders, your breasts, and grind your hips into their fantasies.

The seductive power of it all was evident and there. There wasn't a part of her when she was dancing that they didn't own.

The air thickened, ripe with lust. They wanted her, and they wanted the illusion that she belonged to no one, and to each one of them.

And she, who belonged to no one, danced the landscape of *their* desires and never gave a thought to any of her own.

Colm was waiting, but where?

Cautiously, he and Marcus made their way out of the ballroom. Slowly they edged their way down the hall and up the stairs, Marcus fighting the white-hot fury that threatened to consume him that Phillippa should be there.

It will only work if you can remain calm, Alex had told Marcus, and he fought hard to remember that he had to keep his head. He wanted to kill the bastard, and save Alex the trouble. He wanted to gut him and throw him to the hounds.

There were too many dark corners in Alastair's house, and Colm could be hiding in any one of them.

But he would be where there was the least noise, the most danger, Alex thought, and the best chance to attack on the sly.

Up the stairs. And that was taking a big chance, but he didn't have the time to wait Colm out. They had to get him now, while Francesca had the others distracted.

"Shhh . . ." His back to the banister, Alex crept up the stairs, with Marcus right behind. Marcus's instructions were clear: When Colm finally confronted them, he was to leave Colm to Alex and get Phillippa clear.

Silence except for the faint sound of the music, and dim light and darkness in the upper hall.

How the hell had Alastair gotten involved with the likes of Colm?

They were almost at the landing now, step by step, cautious and discreet.

Colm jumped them then, hurling a bolt of velvet over Alex's head and launching himself on top of him so that they both fell.

Marcus froze as down, down the steps they rolled, Alex fighting to get free. Marcus watched as they tussled this way and that, as Colm's hands reached and squeezed whatever part of Alex's body he could get.

The dilemma almost killed him. Help Alex or find Phillippa—Marcus didn't know which he wanted worse. And finally he gathered his wits and ran down the upper hall and started opening doors.

He found her in the fifth bedroom, alone and wan, heard the pounding footsteps up the stairs, just as he held out his hand.

Too late, too late. Colm burst in the door and blocked the bed. "You can't have her. She doesn't want you. She carries my seed."

Marcus felt the white fury rising in his head. Colm stood there, taunting him, stroking his wife. "Go away, Marcus. You're not wanted here. Phillippa will be the mother of a nation. You paltry priest. Can you give her that?"

Marcus saw red and he lunged at Colm. He didn't care. He wanted to die in the worst way, and how fitting it would be if his wife's lover killed him. No sacrifice was too great, and Phillippa would bear the guilt and remorse forever.

Marcus had a choke hold on Colm like a vise. They bumped around the room like two raging elephants while Phillippa huddled on the bed.

"Oh my God," she moaned, "what have I done?"

But they didn't hear her, and Marcus was only listening to his own internal fury. He meant to wound the bastard before he let him take him down.

Down, down, down—he was losing consciousness as Colm grabbed him by the throat. It was over now, the pain, the humiliation—

And suddenly there was a crash, and he gulped the turgid air.

Beside him, on the floor, Colm lay moaning, and Phillippa stood over him, a broken glass pitcher in her hand.

Alex stumbled in the door. "Get her out of here."

Marcus shook his head. "But—Francesca . . ."

"Get her too. *Now.*"

Marcus looked at Phillippa, and she nodded, and he took her hand, and they left Alex standing over Colm.

I could kill him here, Alex thought, fighting to catch his breath. *I could beat the life out of him. The monster. Monsters are beautiful. They hide their evil under a veneer of civilization and they seduce the masses.* Colm was almost too beautiful to kill, but if Alex left him alive, he would plant his ideas and his seed in places unknown.

And Alex couldn't take the chance. Or that Colm wouldn't come after Francesca again.

He nudged Colm with his foot. And even Phillippa had made a choice: She hadn't wanted Marcus to die.

And now the choice was his.

Not—Colm's snake hands grabbed Alex's leg and toppled him over so he fell to the floor on his belly, and Colm immediately levered himself up to straddle Alex and contain his hands.

"Oh, the seed doesn't kill easily, my friend. If it did, new nations would never be born. But the likes of you—prick you and your blood flows like water," he whispered. "And now—" He had a knife. "I will make the cleanest, nicest cuts, my lord. You'll feel it as your lifeblood trickles away . . ." He pulled the tip of the blade across the side of Alex's neck. "I'll stay with you until the end."

Colm liked the torture too. He nicked and flicked here and there as Alex lay quiescent under him.

"I know you think you're going to win, Alex. But I promise you, you and Marcus and Francesca will die—"

Francesca tiptoed in, her bare feet making no sound on the hardwood floor. And in her hand, she carried a poker, with its curved little points on either end, and Marcus couldn't have stopped her with his worried detaining hands.

She stood poised, just on the theshold, perfectly placed to get a good shot at Colm, because he was so busy down on the floor cutting Alex's skin.

Well, that would end now: The seed would be destroyed, and it was only fitting that she, who had begun this adventure in order to protect Colm, should carry out his sentence of death.

Francesca waited. How well she had learned the value of waiting.

And then, with Colm so intent and enjoying so much what he was doing, it was time. It was perfect. He had just, for the first time, drawn blood.

And now she would make sure that Colm's blood soaked the earth.

She braced herself, she took aim, and she took one hefty swing.

The curved hook caught him right at the back of the neck. He turned, awkwardly, to see who was behind him and what was coming next.

My beautiful boy. My lying madman—the seed must die—

She swung and she swung, not giving him a moment to defend himself—at his shoulders, his back, his face, his head, calm, cool, collected, until he fell over—

. . . the seed is dead . . .

Samara Teva was dead. The most famous exotic dancer in the world—who had performed for kings and potentates all over Europe and the Mediterranean, and who had ultimately given up everything to marry the youngest son of a powerful Earl—was dead.

Her purpose had been served; the mourning was over, and Samara could finally rest in peace.

Alex watched from afar as Francesca wandered the gardens of Meresham Close. He wasn't sure she was ready for him to come near her. The wounds were too raw.

Even Marcus, with the greatest of forgiveness, felt them deeply, and had chosen to raise Phillippa's child as his own.

But Francesca was quite another matter. She'd not only destroyed the evil, she had killed her greatest love. Alex wondered, with each of them bearing such guilt, how they could live with that.

But he would never let her go. Even as he'd grappled with the paradoxes in her, he'd known that, he'd told her that, and he reined himself in.

More than ever, he wanted to explore all those contradictions in her. He'd had a taste. He wanted so much more.

Time—he just had to give her some time.

And Francesca wondered what he was waiting for. After everything they'd been through, everything they'd shared, she didn't understand why he didn't—or wouldn't—come to her.

All *she* could think about in the aftermath of the nightmare was *him*.

She couldn't wait, now that she had experienced the pounding pleasure of sex with him. She wanted more, more and more, and nothing that had happened should stand in the way.

She wanted to seduce him, to use all the powerful tricks she had learned imitating the most notorious courtesan in Europe to bring the most austere Earl in England right down on his knees. Worshiping her. Needing her. Devouring her.

She wanted to dance for him.

Everything else at the moment seemed superfluous.

It was easy enough to gain entrance to his room. And everything was exactly as it had been before. It was the room of a man who lived alone.

But not anymore.

He found her there when he finally came upstairs. "What are you doing here, Francesca?"

"I came to dance for you, my lord."

His whole body seized up and he closed his eyes in gratitude. *Yes.*

"As you wish, Francesca."

"I hope to please my lord," she murmured, sliding into the dressing room where she had everything prepared.

But she knew from watching him what it was he liked. The chains, the veils, all the submissive devices that would put him right into her hands.

She wound them around her arms and her neck. A thin one around her hips that dangled down her rounded bottom. The veil revealing her eyes, and she was ready to shimmy into the room, step by step, hip thrust by hip thrust, her breasts bobbling, she moved across the floor.

The chains glittered in the light, her body moved like silk in ancient rhythm of pure seduction that was all Francesca.

The hands . . . the hands tell a story—

She moved her hands in a serpentine motion and then drew them up her body to emphasize her nudity.

The hands . . .

His hands—

She wanted his hands . . . that was the thing she had learned, the power of a man's hands, a man's kisses. The power of that part of him that was solely at his command.

"My lord," she murmured, undulating close.

"My lady," he whispered, catching her between his knees, wrapping her in his arms, in his kisses, slow, slow kisses, easing all betrayals away. "You will be my lady, when the pain heals."

She felt the full bore essence of him pulsating against her. She felt his hands, stroking slowly, knowingly, intimately. She felt everything melting inside her, pooling at that pleasure point that only he would know.

She arched herself against him and he lifted her and carried her to the bed.

She watched as he stripped off his clothes, and she marveled at the naked male beauty of him, this time.

Just the sight of him made her want to touch him the same way he had touched her, to stroke, to know—this time.

He climbed onto the bed, over her, caging her with his arms and legs, presenting himself, and inviting her caresses.

"I don't know how—" she whispered—this time.

"You know," he murmured, still amazed at her innocence, her generosity. "I'll show you . . ."

And he eased himself within her tender body, and began the mating dance, this time, forever, long and slow.

BOOK YOUR PLACE ON OUR WEBSITE AND MAKE THE READING CONNECTION!

We've created a customized website just for our very special readers, where you can get the inside scoop on everything that's going on with Zebra, Pinnacle and Kensington books.

When you come online, you'll have the exciting opportunity to:

- View covers of upcoming books
- Read sample chapters
- Learn about our future publishing schedule (listed by publication month *and author*)
- Find out when your favorite authors will be visiting a city near you
- Search for and order backlist books from our online catalog
- Check out author bios and background information
- Send e-mail to your favorite authors
- Meet the Kensington staff online
- Join us in weekly chats with authors, readers and other guests
- Get writing guidelines
- AND MUCH MORE!

**Visit our website at
http://www.zebrabooks.com**

YOU WON'T WANT TO READ
JUST ONE—KATHERINE STONE

ROOMMATES (0-8217-5206-5, $6.99/$7.99)
No one could have prepared Carrie for the monumental changes she would face when she met her new circle of friends at Stanford University. Once their lives intertwined and became woven into the tapestry of the times, they would never be the same.

TWINS (0-8217-5207-3, $6.99/$7.99)
Brook and Melanie Chandler were so different, it was hard to believe they were sisters. One was a dark, serious, ambitious New York attorney; the other, a golden, glamourous, sophisticated supermodel. But they were more than sisters—they were twins and more alike than even they knew . . .

THE CARLTON CLUB (0-8217-5204-9, $6.99/$7.99)
It was the place to see and be seen, the only place to be. And for those who frequented the playground of the very rich, it was a way of life. Mark, Kathleen, Leslie and Janet—they worked together, played together, and loved together, all behind exclusive gates of the *Carlton Club*.

Available wherever paperbacks are sold, or order direct from the Publisher. Send cover price plus 50¢ per copy for mailing and handling to Kensington Publishing Corp., Consumer Orders, or call (toll free) 888-345-BOOK, to place your order using Mastercard or Visa. Residents of New York and Tennessee must include sales tax. DO NOT SEND CASH.